PRAISE FOR

The Eloquence of Blood

"Rock's second novel featuring Charles du Luc is every bit the equal of her impressive historical thriller debut, *The Rhetoric of Death* . . . Readers will hope this energetic and engrossing sequel will be the first of many." —*Publishers Weekly* (starred review)

"Rock's historical accuracy resonates here, transporting you to 1686 Paris. Her intriguing plot and protagonists with whom readers are becoming good friends make this a necessary read for all who enjoy historical mysteries, especially those by Ariana Franklin." —*Library Journal* (starred review)

"Thrilling . . . engaging." —*Sarasota Magazine*

"Rock provides meticulous details of everyday life across various social classes with an engaging style . . . touches of humor and insight . . . In du Luc, Rock has created a highly likeable scholar-detective. I hope that his adventures will play out for many books to come." —*Historical Novels Review*

"Rock nails everything about characters, dialogue, setting, historical research, pacing and story development . . . fascinating . . . all of this detail is woven so seamlessly into the story that the reader never falters . . . Rock has the start to an excellent historical detective series." —*Bookgasm*

continued . . .

"Not only satisfies the taste of historical mystery lovers but anyone who likes complex plots, twists, and elaborate mysteries . . . Judith Rock's research is as impeccable as her writing style . . . a great read."

—*Mystery Tribune*

"Amazing . . . Ms. Rock takes you back to fascinating and dangerous seventeenth-century Paris so well that I suspect her of being a time-traveler who's been there."

—Ariana Franklin, national bestselling author of *A Murderous Procession*

"Rich with telling detail and a deep feeling for time and place."

—Margaret Frazer, national bestselling author of *The Apostate's Tale*

"Rock skillfully builds her suspense plot, all the while incorporating splendid detail of seventeenth-century Parisian monastic and street life and the relationship between church and Crown . . . She proves herself a promising new talent by creating this powerful, absorbing, complex, and thoroughly satisfying novel."

—*Historical Novels Review* (editor's choice)

"[A] superb historical debut . . . With an experienced writer's ease, Rock incorporates details of the political issues of the day into a suspenseful story line."

—*Publishers Weekly* (starred review)

"Rock brings firsthand knowledge of dance, choreography, acting, police investigation, and teaching to what is hopefully the beginning of a mystery series . . . [A] fascinating historical mystery . . . Plenty of derring-do and boyish mischief sprinkled into the plot make this a fun read, and Charles's thought-provoking struggles as he questions his vocation lend added depth . . . sure to satisfy those eager for a great new historical mystery."

—*Booklist* (starred review)

"Rich with historical detail . . . meticulously researched. [Rock] captures a city and time that is lively, dangerous and politically charged, and makes it sing . . . [Her] fine eye for historic detail and well-drawn characters will continue to engage readers."

—*Kirkus Reviews* (starred review)

"Rock is an exciting new discovery. Her plotting holds your interest, her characters are real, and her attention to details of the time period is extraordinary. Highly recommended for fans of historical thrillers and readers who enjoy Ellis Peters, Edward Marston, and Ariana Franklin."

—*Library Journal* (starred review)

"Rock balances perfectly the differing claims of detection, romance, suspense, and historical detail. As a mystery, as a kind of coming-of-age novel, or as a docudrama on early Jesuit pedagogy, *The Rhetoric of Death* works remarkably well . . . Very entertaining."

—*Commonweal magazine*

A Plague of Lies

JUDITH ROCK

BERKLEY BOOKS, NEW YORK

THE BERKLEY PUBLISHING GROUP
Published by the Penguin Group
Penguin Group (USA) Inc.
375 Hudson Street, New York, New York 10014, USA
Penguin Group (Canada), 90 Eglinton Avenue East, Suite 700, Toronto, Ontario M4P 2Y3, Canada
(a division of Pearson Penguin Canada Inc.) • Penguin Books Ltd., 80 Strand, London WC2R 0RL,
England • Penguin Group Ireland, 25 St. Stephen's Green, Dublin 2, Ireland (a division of Penguin
Books Ltd.) • Penguin Group (Australia), 250 Camberwell Road, Camberwell, Victoria 3124, Australia
(a division of Pearson Australia Group Pty. Ltd.) • Penguin Books India Pvt. Ltd., 11 Community
Centre, Panchsheel Park, New Delhi—110 017, India • Penguin Group (NZ), 67 Apollo Drive,
Rosedale, Auckland 0632, New Zealand (a division of Pearson New Zealand Ltd.) • Penguin Books
(South Africa) (Pty.) Ltd., 24 Sturdee Avenue, Rosebank, Johannesburg 2196, South Africa

Penguin Books Ltd., Registered Offices: 80 Strand, London WC2R 0RL, England

This book is an original publication of The Berkley Publishing Group.

Copyright © 2012 by Judith Rock.
"Readers Guide" copyright © 2012 by Penguin Group (USA) Inc.
Cover art: Pink Dress copyright © by Mohamed Itani / Arcangel Images, Chapel Royal, Versailles
copyright © Art Resource. Grand Appartement De La Reine, Versailles, France, copyright © JNS/Gamma-
Rapho / Getty Images, Torremocha del Jarama, Madrid, Spain. Landscape with clouds at sunset copyright
© Carlos Muina / Getty Images.
Cover design by Danielle Abbiate.
Interior text design by Tiffany Estreicher.

PUBLISHING HISTORY
Berkley trade paperback edition / October 2012

Library of Congress Cataloging-in-Publication Data

Rock, Judith.
A plague of lies / Judith Rock.—Berkley trade paperback ed.
p.   cm.
ISBN 978-0-425-25310-6
1. Maintenon, Madame de, 1635–1719—Fiction.
2. France—History—Louis XIV, 1643–1715—Fiction.   I. Title.
PS3618.O3543P57 2012
813'.6—dc23
2012011227

PRINTED IN THE UNITED STATES OF AMERICA

10 9 8 7 6 5 4 3 2 1

For Damaris Rowland, agent extraordinaire,
whose patient and brilliant teaching and encouragement
resulted in these books.

ACKNOWLEDGMENTS

Once again, heartfelt thanks are due to my incomparable team of expert advisors: John Padberg, S.J.; Patricia Ranum; and Catherine Turocy. All three take me beyond my own research, telling me things I didn't know—and correcting what I mistakenly thought I did know! Thanks, as always, to the enthusiastic and sharp-eyed early reading team, and to all the people at Berkley who turn what I give them into a book—especially my editor, Shannon Jamieson-Vazquez, and the artists who create such beautiful covers.

A NOTE TO THE READER

In this story, I have given Louis XIV an imaginary daughter: Louise Marguerite de Bourbon, titled Mademoiselle de Rouen, nicknamed "Lulu," daughter of the king and his mistress Madame de Montespan. From 1670 to 1674, Madame de Montespan had a child every year—except in 1671. So my fictional Lulu's birthday is May 30, 1671.

All other characters related to the king in this story are real people.

Chapter 1

The storm-riding demons of the air were gathered over Paris, hurling fire and thunder at the city's cowering mortals. Every bell ringer in the city was hauling on his ropes, and his bells—baptized like good Christians for just this purpose—were wide-mouthed roaring angels fighting off the storm with their own deafening noise. The spring thunderstorm had begun north of the river, but now it raged directly over the rue St. Jacques, sending thunder echoing off walls and stabbing roofs and cobbles with spears of rain. In the Jesuit college of Louis le Grand, teachers and students were praying to aid the clanging bells. But the prayers of the senior rhetoric class dissolved into gasps and cries when lightning struck nearly into the main courtyard. The near miss made assistant rhetoric master Maître Charles du Luc's skin tingle. And startled him into wondering if the demons of the air, in whom he mostly didn't believe when the sun was shining, were bent on making this day his last on earth.

"*Messieurs*, I beg you, calm yourselves," he shouted, over the noise, to his students huddled together on the classroom benches. "All storms pass. The bells are winning, as they always do, because we baptize them to make them stronger than the demons of the air. Listen! The demons are fleeing toward the south now." By force of will and voice, he called the boys back to their unfinished praying.

When he looked up after the "amen," one of the students, Armand Beauclaire, was frowning thoughtfully at the oak-beamed ceiling. Beauclaire, a round-faced sixteen-year-old with a thick straight thatch of brown hair, put up a hand and shifted his gaze to the teacher's dais at the front of the room.

"Yes, Monsieur Beauclaire?" Charles called, over the storm's receding noise, girding his mental loins. Beauclaire's questions were always interesting and never easy to answer.

"Is it really demons, *maître*? If the demons of the air cause thunderstorms, why do the storms always end? Why don't the demons win sometimes?"

"Win? You *want* that demons win?" The outraged speaker was the elder of a pair of brothers from Poland.

"No, Monsieur Sapieha, he doesn't want them to win." Charles hoped he was responding to what Sapieha had actually said. It was often hard to tell, Latin being the language of the college, but the Sapieha brothers' Latin was heavily accented and mixed with Polish. "Monsieur Beauclaire only wants to know why they *don't* win, which is a very different question and an excellent one." But it was not a question Charles was going to discuss there and then. When not dodging lightning, he personally doubted the demon theory, though many people—including most of his fellow teachers at Louis le Grand—did not. And he had to get the class through a lot more pages of Greek before the afternoon ended.

Charles was in the scholastic phase of his long Jesuit formation, with ordination and final vows still some years away. Teaching was part of Jesuit training, and Charles was a teacher of rhetoric, the art of communication in both Latin and Greek.

He raised his eyebrows at Beauclaire. "Perhaps the demons always lose because good is stronger than evil," he said. And hoped that his belief in the second half of his sentence was enough to justify his evasion. "But now, back to our book!"

As the storm receded outside and he tried to find his place in the book open on the oak lectern in front of him, Charles wondered if he looked as unconfident as he felt. The senior rhetoric master, Père Joseph Jouvancy, was in the infirmary recovering from sickness. And the second senior master, Père Martin Pallu, had just fallen ill with the same unpleasant malady. Which left Charles in sole charge of the thirty senior rhetoric students. But, no help for it, there were still two hours of class before the afternoon ended. He smoothed the book's pages open, pushed his black skullcap down on his curling, straw-blond hair, and twitched at his cassock sleeves. The long linen shirt under the cassock showed correctly as narrow bands of white at wrists and high-collared neck, and the cassock hung sleekly on his six feet and more of wide-shouldered height. With a deep breath and a prayer to St. John Chrysostom, the only Greek saint he could think of at the moment, Charles tackled the Greek rules of rhetoric, sometimes reading from the book, sometimes explaining what he read.

But under the reading and explaining, he felt more than a little overwhelmed by his responsibilities. Behind the teacher's dais where he stood was a tapestry showing the unfortunate philosopher Socrates drinking his fatal cup of hemlock. Its graphic rendering of an unpopular academic's fate made for an uncomfortable teaching backdrop, he'd always thought.

He paused, giving the class time to write down what he'd

said, and let his eyes wander over the benches. The boys were bent over small boards braced on their laps, their feathered quills scratching across their paper, and all he could see of them were the tops of their heads above their black scholar's gowns. Louis le Grand's students ranged in age from about ten to eighteen. The youngest in this class was thirteen, a little Milanese named Michele Bertamelli, whose mass of curls was as black as his hat. Most of the bent heads were French and every shade of brown, apparently God's favorite color for hair. But there were also boys from England, Ireland, Poland, and the Netherlands—one with hair flaming like copper, some as blond as Charles himself was, thanks to his Norman mother's Viking forbears. Today, though, there were fewer boys than there should have been, because three of them were in the student infirmary with the same contagion Jouvancy and Pallu had.

Charles glanced out at the courtyard and saw that the rain had nearly stopped. The storm was south of the city now, and the bell ringers of Paris were letting their ropes go slack. Relieved at no longer having to shout over the noise, he went back to feeding his fledgling scholars Aristotle's rules for rhetoric. But even as he tried to make his dry morsels of knowledge tempting, his thoughts kept circling around all that he should have finished and hadn't.

His biggest worry was the summer ballet and tragedy performance, only two months from now, on August sixth. In Jesuit schools, both voice and body were trained for eloquence, and part of his job was directing the ballet that went with the school's grand tragedy performance every summer. This year, under Jouvancy's watchful eye, Charles was working on the ballet's *livret*—the plan of its four Parts—and would be directing the ballet itself. Happily, this year's ballet was an updated version of the 1680 college ballet, so he was only rewriting instead of coming up with something new from scratch. Full rehearsals were about to start, but because of Jouvancy's illness and this extra teaching, Charles was seriously behind. And what if Jouvancy's illness returned and worsened, as illness so often did? If that happened, Charles knew that he might end up directing the tragedy *and* the ballet.

He finished his lecture and told the class's three *decurions*—class leaders named for Roman army officers commanding ten men each—to collect the afternoon's written work and bring it to the dais. Then he set them to hear each of their "men" recite the assigned memory passage. Today it was from St. Basil's writings. Greek recitation was never popular, and when the *decurions* delivered the bad news, thirteen-year-old Bertamelli sprang from his seat and flung his arms wide.

"But, *maître,*" the Italian boy wailed, "I cannot speak Greek, it hurts my tongue!"

Snorts of laughter erupted along the benches, and Charles bit his lip to keep from laughing himself. Henri de Montmorency, the eighteen-year-old dull-witted scion of a noble house, turned on his bench and gaped at Bertamelli.

"You're mad. Words can't hurt anything!"

Charles called the class back to order, fixed Bertamelli with his eye, and schooled his face to stern disapproval. The boy's scholar's gown had slipped off one shoulder to reveal his crumpled and grayed linen shirt, and his huge black eyes were tragic with pleading. He was one of the most gifted and passionate dancers Charles had ever seen, but he was also proving nearly impossible to contain within Louis le Grand's rules—and probably its walls, though Charles preferred not to think about that. He suspected that the little Italian would not be with them long, though who would crack first, Bertamelli or the Jesuits, he wouldn't have cared to predict.

"To put Monsieur Montmorency's puzzlement more politely," Charles said, with a sideways frown at Montmorency, "how does Greek hurt your tongue, Monsieur Bertamelli?"

"That language has hard edges, sharp edges, *cruel* edges. It bites me! My tongue is a tender Italian tongue!" To be sure Charles understood, he stuck the sensitive member in question out as far as it would go.

"No need for scientific demonstration, Monsieur Bertamelli, and please pull your gown closed over your shirt. And if at all possible, compose yourself."

Bertamelli yanked his gown onto his shoulder, pulled it straight, and clasped his thin brown hands together under his chin. His eyes grew even larger. "My tongue—"

"Let your tongue rest, *monsieur*, and make your ears work. Hear three things that I am going to tell you." Charles held up his thumb. "Number one: Learning Greek will strengthen the sinews of your tender Italian tongue." His first finger joined his thumb. "Two: Every educated man must learn Greek. We speak Latin here in the college because Latin is the international language of scholarship, but what the Romans wrote in Latin is rooted in what the Greeks wrote." Charles's third digit uncurled and his eyes swept the classroom and came to rest on Montmorency. "Three: And this is for each of you. You will observe the rules of classroom behavior. If you want to speak, put up your hand—as you all know very well. Now, Monsieur Bertamelli, sit down and prepare yourself for your Greek recitation."

Bertamelli sat. Two tears spilled from his wounded black eyes and he wiped them with the edge of his gown, gazing at Charles like a martyr forgiving his tormentors. The room filled slowly with a quiet, dogged murmuring that Aristotle surely would not have recognized as his native language.

Charles left the lectern and opened one of the long windows, letting in a rush of the unseasonably cool air the storm had brought. The rain had stopped, leaving behind the music of water dripping from the blue slate roofs and splashing onto the courtyard gravel. Charles had come to the school from the south of France less than a year ago, but he'd quickly learned to love Louis le Grand's sprawl of ill-matched buildings grouped around graveled courtyards. Some buildings were five stories of weather-blackened stone, the oldest were two stories and half-timbered, and a few were bright new brick with corners and windows trimmed in stone. All the roofs bristled with chimneys and towers. Some of the courtyards had shade trees and benches, two had gardens, one had an old well, and one boasted an ancient grapevine on a sunny wall. Rounded stone arches led to passages between the courts and from the enormous main courtyard, called the Cour d'honneur, out to the rue St. Jacques.

It was in the Cour d'honneur, outside the rhetoric classroom windows, that the outdoor stage for the summer ballet and tragedy was built each year. As Charles stood at the window, he began imagining scenery to go with the final section of his ballet *livret*. This year's ballet was called *La France Victorieuse sous Louis le Grand*. The title, like the school's name, was in honor of King Louis XIV. Charles knew that one reason for the trouble he was having with the *livret* was his dislike of Louis XIV's passion for glory, which the ballet would so grandly praise. Charles especially deplored the king's indifference to his people's suffering under the draconian taxes that paid for the glory-bringing wars. And he particularly loathed the Most Christian King of France, as Louis styled himself, for outlawing and hunting France's Protestants—

called Huguenots—in God's name. Part of his own family was Protestant, and he knew their suffering all too well.

But Holy Mother Church—the Catholic Church—had nurtured Charles all his life, and he loved her. He was certain that God was Love. Demanding, relentless, even terrifying Love, but Love nonetheless. Which meant that cruelty in God's name was blasphemy. Which amounted to calling the king a blasphemer. Which was treason, pure and simple.

Even as Charles grappled with that thought, King Louis XIV himself stared blindly at him from the top of the Cour d'honneur's north wall. The recently installed bust was a copy of one shattered by a storm-felled tree the year before, and Charles had developed a teeth-gritting dislike of those sightless eyes overseeing his daily comings and goings. He turned away from Louis and watched the dripping water dig a small pool in the gravel under the window. The tiny but deepening pool comforted him a little. Small persistent forces often won in the end. He had the sudden thought that maybe he could slip something into the ballet *livret* that didn't praise Louis, some small piece of a different truth to raise disquiet in those with ears to hear . . . But even as he thought it, he knew it was impossible. Père Jouvancy would never let it pass. *Of course he wouldn't, it would be treason on the college stage,* the cool-eyed critic in him said acidly. *The king is the divinely anointed body of France. Kings preserve order. Order allows good to flourish.* Charles shook his head. *But whose good?* he thought back at it. Not waiting for its predictable answer, he turned from the window to his work.

The ending bell finally rang. The students filed out and were met by a *cubiculaire*, a Jesuit scholastic who shepherded groups of boarding students to and from classes and saw that their chambers had sheets, candles, braziers, and the like.

As the *cubiculaire* chivied the boys toward their living quarters in the student courtyard, Charles went gratefully out into the watery late-afternoon sunshine. But before he was halfway across the court, someone called his name, and he looked back to see the college rector, Père Jacques Le Picart, the head of Louis le Grand.

Bowing, Charles greeted him, noting Le Picart's muddy riding boots and spattered cloak. "You've had a wet ride, *mon père.*"

"Wet enough, *maître.* The storm caught me on the way back from Versailles."

They walked together to the rear door of the main building where their rooms were, Le Picart asking Charles about his own afternoon and nodding in sympathy at his worry over the approaching rehearsals. But the rector seemed preoccupied, and before they reached the door, he said, "Have you visited Père Jouvancy today, *maître?*"

Charles shook his head. "I've had no chance, *mon père.* But Père Montville told me as we were leaving the refectory after dinner that he's much better and able to eat now."

"Good." The rector studied Charles for a moment in silence. "Will you come with me to the infirmary? I must speak with him. The matter may concern you, as well."

"Of course, *mon père.*" Wondering uneasily what "the matter" was, Charles turned with Le Picart toward the infirmary court.

Most of the previous month had been blessedly warm after the hard winter, and the physick garden in the infirmary courtyard was already blooming. The afternoon's rain had left the blossoms somewhat bedraggled, but the air was drenched in fresh sweet scents. Charles filled his lungs eagerly. Which was a good thing, because the fathers' infirmary, below the student infirmary and beside the ground-floor room for making medicines, smelled pungently of sickness. Frère Brunet, the lay brother infirmarian, turned from a bed at the room's far end as Le Picart and Charles entered and bustled toward them, his soft shoes whispering along the rush matting between the two short rows of beds. All but two beds were empty. Before he reached them, Père Jouvancy called out, "Ah, *mon père, maître*, welcome, come in, come in!"

His bed was in the left-hand row, between two windows, and he was sitting up among his gray blankets, the fitful sunshine warming the new color in his face.

"I would ask you how he is, Frère Brunet," Le Picart said to the infirmarian, "but I see for myself that he really is better." He smiled affectionately at Jouvancy. "You've had a hard time of it, *mon père*. But if you feel as much improved as you look, you will soon be back among us."

"Oh, he will, certainly he will," Brunet said, surveying his patient with satisfaction.

"And Père Pallu?" Le Picart asked, looking toward the other bed.

Brunet shook his head. "Poor man, he seems to be in for the same hard time. Oh, he will no doubt do well enough, but for now he is suffering fever, chills, aches in his body, sore throat." Brunet glanced ruefully over his shoulder. "And he can keep nothing down."

"Sit, *mon père*, if you have the time," Jouvancy said hopefully, and Le Picart pulled the only stool nearer and sat down. As befitted a lowly scholastic, Charles remained standing at the foot of the bed.

"Visit, then," Brunet said, laying a hand on Jouvancy's forehead and nodding approvingly. "But see you don't tire him." Behind him, the sound of retching began and he hurried away to Père Pallu.

Charles swallowed hard. In several years as a soldier, he'd

helped care for bloody wounds without turning a hair. But spewing—his own or anyone else's—turned him weak-kneed.

Jouvancy beamed at Le Picart and Charles. "Thank you for coming, both of you! I only need to get my strength back now." He shook a finger at Charles. "So do not become too fond of your independence, *maître*, I will be back before you know it."

"*Mon père*," Charles said fervently, "I will give thanks on my knees when you are back! I fear I am a poor substitute."

Jouvancy eyed him shrewdly. "Greek today, was it?"

"Greek indeed."

"Yes, on Greek days, I often find myself moved to volunteer for the missions." His blue eyes grew dreamy. "Less use for Greek in the missions. And I understand they do theatrical pieces, operas, even."

Le Picart laughed. "That is as good an opening as any for what I have come to say. Because I do want you to go somewhere."

"I will, of course, go wherever you bid me, *mon père*. To Tibet, if you say so!"

"Somewhere much closer to home. As soon as you're well enough to travel, I want you to go to Versailles."

Jouvancy blinked. "And what might a lowly rhetoric professor do at court?"

"You are a connection of the d'Aubigné family, I believe."

"D'Aubigné?" Charles looked in surprise at Jouvancy. That was Madame de Maintenon's name, the king's second wife, who was born Françoise d'Aubigné. "That makes you nearly a relation of King Louis, *mon père*!"

"Yes, I suppose it does. My father's mother was a cousin of the d'Aubignés. But that makes me as distant as China from the trunk of the family tree," Jouvancy said. "For which I am thankful when I think of how worthless Madame de Maintenon's father was. He was in prison when she was born, did you know that? For conspiring against Cardinal Richelieu—which at least made a change, since he was more often jailed for debt and dueling. His daughter, though, seems to be a pattern of uprightness. I have met her only once, you know, when she came here a few summers back, to see the tragedy and ballet. And our family connection was not mentioned."

"Still, that you have met her is to the good. And what Maître du Luc has said is true. Consider, *mon père*," Le Picart said, leaning forward in his chair. "You are a distant relation of the king's wife, which, as Maître du Luc has said, makes you a relation by marriage to Louis himself, and that is going to be useful. I am just returned from Versailles, where the Comtesse de Rosaire asked me to come and talk to her about Louis le Grand. She wants to send her twin sons to us next autumn. Because she is recently widowed—and a comtesse—I went." He shrugged sheepishly. "Afterward, I knocked at Père La Chaise's door on the chance that he was there rather than at the Professed House." The Jesuit Père François La Chaise, the king's confessor, lived at the Jesuit Professed House in Paris when he was not with the king. "He was not, and as I turned from the door, I met Madame de Maintenon and her ladies in the corridor. I uncovered my head and made my *reverence*. She glared—at Père La Chaise's door and at me. She did acknowledge me with a '*mon père*,' though just audibly and between her teeth, before she and her entourage swept on."

"Oh, dear," Jouvancy said. "I thought that after Père La Chaise made no objection to her marrying the king, she would think better of us Jesuits." He looked questioningly at the rector. "I've heard that Père La Chaise was even present at the ceremony that made her Louis's wife."

"Wife, yes," Le Picart said, ignoring the curiosity about Père La Chaise's role. "But *not* queen, because she's too lowly born. And even as a wife, she is unacknowledged. Rumors even deny the marriage. She is very angry at Père La Chaise over that. He has encouraged the king to keep the marriage secret because of her rank. He and others fear the outcry there would be if the marriage were publicly proclaimed. Glory must shimmer around everything connected to the king of France, and an aging lady of besmirched minor nobility is far from glorious."

Jouvancy's eyes danced with sudden laughter. "Well, at least she didn't mention the nickname when she saw you outside Père La Chaise's door."

Le Picart grinned. "No. But I'm sure she was thinking it."

"What nickname?" Charles said.

Jouvancy looked at Charles in momentary surprise. "Oh. Of course. I doubt it ever went as far as Languedoc. Long before the king married Madame de Maintenon, she was also very angry at Père La Chaise for his refusal to force the king to part with his mistress, Madame de Montespan. La Montespan and the king did part, finally—and Père La Chaise had a hand in that—but then she came back to court, and the result was two more children. Madame de Maintenon was furious. She had been governess to their first set of children, which was how she met the king. But she refused to have anything to do with the second set of royal bastards. And she began calling our Père La Chaise *Père La Chaise de Commodité* for not stopping the liaison. As though he could have stopped it. But the nickname was the delight of the gossips, and all Versailles and Paris laughed themselves silly."

"She really called him that?" Charles was fighting laughter himself. The name *La Chaise* of course meant chair, so *Père La*

Chaise de Commodité, to put it plainly and rudely, meant Père Toi-
let. "Is she gutter-mouthed?"

"Yes, she did. And no, she isn't," Le Picart said. "She's not
low born—just not noble. And she's normally very uprightly
righteous. I don't think she'd call him that now; it would be
below her new dignity. But it's common knowledge that she
would love to see Père La Chaise replaced. With a confessor of
a severer piety like her own. And," he added dryly, "of a more
pliant nature. Unfortunately, the king does listen to her opinions, especially about the state of his soul. And anything that
threatens Père La Chaise's tenure as royal confessor threatens
the Society of Jesus, because he is our Jesuit presence there, our
conduit of knowledge about and influence on court affairs. Beyond that, I believe that Père La Chaise is a good director of the
king's conscience. He knows how to influence without demanding, since who could *demand* anything of Louis and keep his
position? It would only harm the king to lose a confessor who
knows how to work for good within that constraint. So, Père
Jouvancy, I want you to go to Versailles and sweeten your good
cousin Madame de Maintenon."

"Cousin she is not. But I will do whatever you require and
with a good will, *mon père.*" Jouvancy drew himself up higher on
his pillows and tugged his long white linen shirt straight, as
though preparing to set out immediately. "But what exactly do
you want me to do?"

"I thought we'd start with flattery and bribery."

The two priests exchanged a wryly knowing look.

"A time-honored method," Jouvancy said. "What are we
bribing her with?"

"Saint Ursula's little finger. Given to us by your family and
therefore, by extension, hers."

"If one makes a very long extension. But, yes, well thought."

The rhetoric master's face lit slowly with enthusiasm as he pondered what the rector had said. "I do remember how much she admired Saint Ursula's reliquary when she came here."

"The lapis and gold cross in the chapel?" Charles looked in surprise from one to the other. "You'd give that away?"

"Why not?" Le Picart was frowning at his interruption. "It is ours to give. Père Jouvancy's family gave it to us when he came here to teach. And all the better if Madame de Maintenon admired it when she visited the chapel during the summer performance." The rector lifted a bushy gray eyebrow. "Though I don't think she admired the ballet." He turned back to Jouvancy. "So I want you to take the reliquary to Versailles, *mon père*. The gift will mean that much more, coming from the hands of a family connection."

So this was why Le Picart had brought him on this visit, Charles thought in dismay. He was going to be left even longer in charge of the rhetoric class and the approaching rehearsals. In spite of himself, Charles said, "But why now? I mean—is this the best time?"

The two priests gazed expressionlessly at him. Le Picart said dangerously, "Have you a better plan, Maître du Luc? Since you often do have what you consider a better plan."

"No, no, *mon père*. I only wondered—I mean—" Charles rummaged through his mind for something to say that didn't reek of self-interest. "Do we have a—a pretext, if I may put it that way—for giving the relic now?"

"Since you are so selflessly concerned," the rector said, "I will tell you that in fact, we do." He turned to Jouvancy. "It is now nearly a year since Madame de Maintenon founded her beloved school for impoverished noble daughters. Saint Cyr opened last July. So we are sending her this relic of Saint Ursula as a compliment to a fellow educator. What better gift and protection for a girls' school than a relic of Saint Ursula and her ten thousand—or is it eleven thousand?—sister virgins? We must contrive the presentation to take place in the presence of Père La Chaise—"

"And in the king's presence?" Jouvancy asked eagerly.

"That may be too much to hope for. The king is only recently back from inspecting his border fortresses and may have too much business in hand. But I will ask Père La Chaise to see that as many courtiers as possible are there. The more witnesses, the better. It won't change Madame de Maintenon's mind about Jesuits, of course. But it will give the king more reason to ignore her complaints, and will give Père La Chaise a little more ammunition for countering them." He looked down the room and called softly to the infirmarian. "Frère Brunet, a moment, please?"

Brunet turned from bending over the unhappy Pallu and hurried down the line of beds. "Yes, *mon père?*"

"When can Père Jouvancy travel safely? For a short distance?"

"How short?"

"To Versailles."

Brunet eyed Jouvancy. "Riding?"

"Yes."

The infirmarian tsked disapprovingly. "Not for another two weeks, if I had my way." He eyed Le Picart. "But since I am obviously not going to have my way, I suppose he could ride by the end of this week. *If* the weather is dry and warm. And *if* someone is with him. And *if* when he arrives, he goes straight to bed and rests until the morrow. And no late nights, mind you," he said, with mock severity, to Jouvancy. "No court revels!"

"You are a terrible spoilsport, *mon frère,*" Jouvancy said, with an aggrieved sigh. "I was only going for the revels!"

Le Picart nodded. "He will not go alone, *mon frère.*" He smiled at Jouvancy. "I will go, as will our assistant rector, Père Montville." He turned to Charles. "Maître du Luc, you will go, also."

Charles's mouth opened in dismay. He saw the importance of supporting Père La Chaise, whom he'd met and liked. But the thought of playing the courtier, even briefly, to a king he detested made him feel mulish. Le Picart held up a warning hand. "You will go as Père Jouvancy's servant and caretaker and relieve him from as much effort as possible. You have some medical knowledge from your soldiering; you can help look after him, if need be." His shrewd gray eyes measured Charles. "You will do all of that for the good of the Society."

"I will welcome his assistance," Jouvancy agreed.

Charles held out his hands. "But who will teach the senior rhetoric class? And take my place assisting in the morning grammar class?" He knew it was useless, and unwise, but he kept trying. "And we begin full ballet and tragedy rehearsals so soon—"

The rector cut him off. "You will be gone only a few days. We can certainly replace you in the classes. Père Bretonneau has often taught rhetoric."

"Père Bretonneau will do very well," Jouvancy said. "And while we are gone, Maître du Luc and I can work on performance plans and finish the *livret.*" He smiled happily at Charles. "Have you ever been at court, *maître?*"

"No, *mon père.*" Nor had he ever wished to be, Charles didn't say, folding his hands. He looked up and saw Le Picart watching him and seeing—as usual—more than Charles wanted seen. Charles forced obedience across his tongue.

"I will do my best, *mon père,*" he said. "For Père Jouvancy."

"And for our king." Le Picart emphasized every word.

"With all our hearts," Jouvancy said, making the words sound like a liturgical response in the Mass.

Charles bowed his head, letting Le Picart take the gesture for agreement if he would.

Chapter 2

It was five wet, cool days before Père Jouvancy's health and the weather were finally judged fit for a ride to Versailles. They were five distractedly hectic days for Charles: trudging back and forth from the infirmary with the ballet *livret*, rewriting all that Jouvancy didn't like of what he'd written during the rhetoric master's illness, assisting in the morning grammar class, and teaching the rhetoric class. He also met with the college dancing master, Pierre Beauchamps, to decide which dances should be taught next and oversaw the older students' weekly almsgiving. As he passed and repassed the bust of the king on the courtyard wall, Charles had the absurd conviction that Louis's bland stone face grew increasingly smug and satisfied at his unwilling preparations for visiting court. Finally, all seemed done that could be done, and Père Jouvancy, Père Le Picart, Père Montville, and Charles were all ready to leave that Monday.

But on Monday morning, Père Le Picart and Père Montville found themselves embroiled in a dispute over the college water pipe and could not leave Paris.

"No help for it, Père Montville and I will have to hire a carriage early tomorrow morning. That will get us there in time for the presentation. But I want you and Père Jouvancy to go this morning, as planned," Le Picart told Charles. "A slow ride in the good air will be better for him than a lurching gallop in a carriage. And he can rest well overnight—I understand from Père La Chaise that we will be expected to make an appearance at several court events tomorrow."

So with Le Picart's blessing, Charles and Jouvancy rode away from Louis le Grand into a day that was early summer perfection. The climbing sun promised warmth and the air was sweet. As sweet as it got in Paris, anyway. The sky's soft blue looked newly washed, and courtyard trees were bright clouds of green above the stone walls. The people in the streets seemed as glad of it all as Charles was.

Père Jouvancy, expansive in the little rebirth of convalescence, was smiling on everyone and everything and letting the dappled mare Agneau, "Lamb," choose her pace. Charles held his own horse, the restive black gelding called Flamme, to the same sedate walk. The gelding, named for his fiery spirits, tossed his head and danced, trying to change Charles's mind about their speed until the crowded street forced him to give in and pick his way.

As he rode, Charles finally admitted to himself that he was more curious about this visit than he'd anticipated. His parents had met at court, after all. Not at the palace of Versailles, of course, which had not existed in their young days, but at the old Louvre palace across the Seine. And if he didn't enjoy it, well, at least the visit would be short. The Jesuits would be presenting the gift, then returning to Paris on Wednesday, or Thursday at the latest, if Jouvancy needed an extra day to rest after all his exertion. Meanwhile, Charles told himself, it was a perfect day, he was on horseback, and there was no Greek to teach.

Though the sun was not far above the Left Bank's blue-gray roof slates and thrusting spires, Paris was already hard at its selling and buying. As Charles and Jouvancy reached the rue de la Harpe, a water seller's eerie, quavering cry of *"A-a-a-a-l'eau!"* rose from a narrow lane like the wail of a damned soul. A girl ran suddenly in front of Flamme and Agneau, holding out a bunch of late jonquils, yellow as the ribbons in her black hair, to a young professor in a clerical gown. Smiling and making suggestions Charles tried not to hear, the cleric told her he had no coins and tried to take a kiss instead of the flowers. She snatched back the jonquils and held them up to Charles, who also had to confess to a lack of money.

The girl smiled at him. "You're better to look on than that other one. A kiss from you, then?" She hung for a moment on his stirrup, her red lips forming a kiss.

Jouvancy chose that moment to turn toward Charles. "Begone, girl," he shouted, flicking a hand at her as if she were an errant chicken. "Go, out of his way!"

The girl let go of the stirrup and shrieked with laughter, pointing at Charles's flaming face. Charles, grateful that the street din made it impossible for Jouvancy to say much to him, mustered what dignity he could and rode on. Street sellers shouted themselves hoarse, vying with one another like competing opera singers. "Asparagus! Leeks! New brooms!" rose above a rumbling chorus proclaiming old pots, lottery tickets, rosaries, and spring salad greens. A clutch of miaowing cats added their voices as they followed a woman balancing a two-handled pot on her head, gesturing with a ladle and singing the freshness of her milk.

"Bonjour, Maître du Luc!" a familiar deep voice called over the cacophony.

Charles reined in his horse and turned in the saddle to see Lieutenant-Général Nicolas de La Reynie, head of the Paris police and one of the king's most influential officeholders, doffing his wide-brimmed, gray-plumed hat and smiling slightly. Behind him, a burly sergeant in the plain brown coat and breeches of La Reynie's men kept his eyes stolidly on the swirling crowd.

"A very good day to you, also, *mon lieutenant-général*," Charles called back, bowing slightly in the saddle. "I am glad to see you." He'd occasionally helped La Reynie in the past, and though at first his help had been unwilling, he'd come to respect the man, and even like him.

La Reynie pushed his way past a leek seller to Charles's side and said, with a half smile and a raised eyebrow, "Do you know, I think that's the first time you've ever said that."

Lifting his hat again, he bowed to Père Jouvancy. Charles introduced them, and Jouvancy smiled absently at La Reynie, then went back to watching a loud quarrel over the right of way between a vinegar seller and an impatient Benedictine on a mule.

"Is it well with you, Monsieur La Reynie?" Charles asked.

"Well enough," the police chief returned, but his eyes were following something across the street.

Knowing that look, Charles turned his head to see who was unlucky enough to be on the receiving end of it. A pair of men, short capes rakishly draped on their shoulders and swords at their sides, turned into a shop doorway beneath a sign with a golden quill.

Charles looked down at the *lieutenant-général*. "Are you thinking of visiting that bookshop?"

"I am. And inquiring about what they're selling upstairs."

"Ah," Charles said, knowing—as anyone in Paris would

know—that La Reynie meant books from Holland. "Dutch pornography or Dutch politics?"

"There's a difference?" La Reynie said ironically, his black gaze still on the shop.

Holland was a perpetual source of pornography and of books and pamphlets attacking everything French, especially the king and his policies. Louis had made finding the illicit imports, and their sellers and buyers, part of La Reynie's job.

"A new spate of tracts has turned up," the *lieutenant-général* said, turning his attention back to Charles. "Vile things that look like pornography at first glance, but are in fact libels on the king and Madame de Maintenon."

Charles tried not to imagine what such tracts might look like. "Well, I wish you good hunting."

La Reynie grunted. "Where are you and Père Jouvancy riding to?"

"Interestingly enough, to Versailles," Charles said. "To present a gift to Madame de Maintenon."

"Well, don't mention the tracts. As far as I know, she hasn't heard about them, and God send she never does." La Reynie eyed Charles. "You don't look eager to arrive at court."

"I'm not." Charles glanced at Jouvancy to make sure he wasn't listening. But the rhetoric master was absorbed in watching a hatter shaping the brim of a shiny black beaver hat just inside the open window of his shop.

"Maître du Luc." La Reynie put a lace-cuffed hand on Charles's bridle. "Do me the favor of keeping your eyes open while you are there."

"Open for what? Don't you have *mouches* at Versailles?" La Reynie, like everyone with power, had "flies"—spies—in high places, listening and reporting.

"Swarms of them. And everyone, no doubt, can identify them on sight. Do you know who the Prince of Conti is?"

"I know he's a Prince of the Blood. Close kin to the king."

"Yes." La Reynie studied the cobbles, as though debating what to say. "Questions are being raised—again—about Conti and his intentions toward the king. I would like you to store up anything you hear. Gossip, who Conti talks to, everything. It would be a great favor to me if you would do this."

"Why do I think you're not going to tell me why you're asking this?"

"Because you'll listen more acutely if you're not trying to hear what you think I want you to hear. Send me word when you return to Paris, and I will come to the college to hear what you have to tell me."

Charles hesitated, his interest piqued and his conscience protesting. On the Friday just past, his confessor had reminded him—yet again—that he must learn to live quietly within the bounds of his lowly place in the Society. *On the other hand*, his logical self said, *isn't Père Le Picart sending you to Versailles for the good of the king?*

"Very well. If I hear anything, I will certainly tell you—though you know that I will have to tell Père Le Picart first. And I will not be free to come and go on my own at court."

La Reynie laughed. "I don't recall that that has ever stopped you, *maître*."

The shot went home, and Charles winced. "Anyway, I cannot imagine that a lowly Jesuit scholastic like myself will hear or see much of use to you."

"Oh, come, surely you know that it is in the presence of those who don't count that people are careless."

"You flatter me," Charles said, straight-faced, and they both laughed.

La Reynie's eyes went to the bookshop again, and Charles, watching him, thought about how much his opinion of the man had changed. Something he would have sworn would never happen when they were first thrown together. The early sun was strong on the *lieutenant-général's* face, and Charles saw how deep its lines were growing. Well, the man was sixty-one, more than twice Charles's own twenty-nine. Sixty-one was a full age for working day and night, as La Reynie did. He turned back to Charles, reaching to steady a radish seller who stumbled beside him. The woman glanced up at him, mumbled her thanks, and walked on a few paces. Then she stared, round-eyed, over her shoulder as she realized who had helped her. La Reynie's courtesy to the lowly street vendor made Charles respect him all the more.

"When you return," La Reynie repeated, "send for me."

"I will. Monsieur La Reynie—please—how is it with Reine?" Reine was a beggarwoman whose mysterious past was intertwined somehow with La Reynie's own, though he refused to say much about how and why.

La Reynie's chin came up and his eyes turned wary.

Having good reason to know that this man's secrets were inviolable, Charles said quickly, "It's only that I think of her sometimes and hope she's well."

The wariness softened and the older man smiled fleetingly. "She's well. Growing older. Like me. But well. She's asked about you, too."

Charles smiled, inordinately pleased by that. "She's in my prayers."

"As, I hope, am I. I wish you a good ride. And that you will go about your court business looking as lowly as possible and letting your ears flap." He looked toward Jouvancy. "I wish you both a good journey."

Charles called Jouvancy's attention, the priest signed a blessing toward La Reynie, and the two Jesuits rode on. Telling himself that whatever trouble came of what he'd just been asked to do, it would be La Reynie's trouble and not his, Charles nudged Flamme into the lead. They passed the Convent of St. Michel and the line of the old walls, and the road angled southwest, past the Prince of Condé's townhouse and toward the village of Vaugirard. Beyond Vaugirard they would join the royal Versailles road, which left Paris on the Right Bank and crossed the Seine at the village of Sevres. The ride from Paris to Versailles was a short one for a man in a hurry, but Charles had strict orders to take the journey slowly for Jouvancy's sake, stopping often, and they did not expect to arrive until the afternoon.

"How far is it to Versailles, exactly?" Jouvancy asked, craning his neck to look up at the dome of the Luxembourg palace as they passed it. "I've been there, but not for many years, and then not from Paris."

"It's five miles," Charles said, filling his lungs with the scent of flowering trees from the Luxembourg Gardens. Then he looked sharply at Jouvancy. "Are you tiring, *mon père?*"

"No, no, we've just set out, I am very well. Five French miles, I suppose you mean."

"I could give you the distance in some other country's reckoning, if that would please you better."

"Pride is a great fault in a lowly scholastic, *maître*," Jouvancy said with mock gravity. "But go on, show off your knowledge."

Twisting in his saddle, Charles answered with a grin and a small mock bow. "Know, then, *mon père*, that we have fifteen English miles to ride, or, if you prefer, twenty Russian miles. In Spanish miles, the figure is less tiring—something under four and a half miles. And the German distance is easier yet, only a *soupçon* more than three miles." He frowned and then shook his head. "I used to know Italian miles, but I've forgotten them."

"I, also. Well, then, I shall ride in German miles and arrive fresh as the world's first morning. Or at least," the rhetoric master said wryly, "still able to stand up after I dismount."

As the road bent south, the houses and convents thinned and gave way to fields and vineyards. They rode companionably, without speaking, listening to the country sounds of birdsong, cows and sheep, and field laborers calling to each other. Then there were more vineyards than fields, and the houses of the wine-growing village of Vaugirard began to line the road. They rode past the old church, with its carvings of vines and grapes, and stopped in the little arcaded marketplace to let Jouvancy rest for a time.

They tethered their horses to an iron ring in the stone arcade and Charles loosed the saddlebag with Madame de Maintenon's gift in it and tucked it under his arm. As they walked slowly across the cobbled square to drink from the fountain in its center, Charles saw several curious faces watching them from upper windows, but it wasn't a market day so the square itself was mostly empty. Jouvancy sat down on a tree-shaded bench, and Charles sat beside him. The church bells rang nine o'clock and the office of Terce, and Jouvancy took out his breviary. As a priest, he was required to say the offices, though in the solitary Jesuit manner, unlike the Benedictines. As merely a scholastic, Charles was not yet bound to say them, but he knew many of the prayers by heart and joined Jouvancy silently.

At the prayers' end, they sat quietly. Then Jouvancy put his breviary away in his pocket. Charles opened the saddlebag, brought out two winter-withered but still sweet apples, and offered Jouvancy one. They munched in companionable quiet and watched the little there was to see: maidservants with pitchers and buckets coming and going from the fountain, and a few old men walking under the arcade, their sticks tapping the stone. Pigeons drank from the puddled gravel near the fountain, the males strutting and chasing the softly cooing females.

"Spring," Jouvancy snorted, watching them. He looked sideways at Charles. "You will do well to remember that it is always 'spring' at Versailles, Maître du Luc."

Charles turned to stare at him and then began to laugh. "*That* sort of spring, you mean?" He nodded toward the pigeons.

"It is no laughing matter."

"But I've heard the court is greatly changed, *mon père*, since the king has become more sober and devout."

"The *king* may have become more sober and devout—and not before time, he's in sight of fifty—but the court is forever full of ill-disciplined young people, and even Madame de Maintenon cannot change young blood into old."

Charles considered the rhetoric master with some surprise, wondering at this irritable, moralistic fault finding. He'd never heard Jouvancy in this mood before.

"And so you are warning me, *mon père*?" he said carefully.

"Yes, and you can stop laughing up your sleeve about it. I saw that little flower seller flirting with you on the way out of the city! The court is also full of young, bored, pretty women."

Torn between laughter and offense, Charles kept quiet and watched the pigeons. After a moment, he said, "Do you really think me so vulnerable, *mon père*? So uncertain in my vows?"

"I don't doubt the sincerity of your vows, but you are young and male and well featured. As for what uncertainty there may be, time will tell."

"Well," Charles said, trying for lightness, "then it's to the good that I passed my twenty-ninth birthday on Saint Bobo's Day, and am rapidly becoming not all that young."

"Saint Bobo?" Jouvancy frowned and shook his head. "I have never heard of any Saint Bobo."

"He lived a long time ago, in Languedoc. He's much loved in the south and we call him Bobo, though his Christian name was Beuvron. He fought Saracen pirates to stop them raiding our coast. My father gave me Beuvron as my third name, since I was born on his day." Charles grinned sheepishly. "But my family likewise calls me Bobo."

Charles expected laughter, but Jouvancy only grunted and smiled faintly. Anxiously, Charles studied the priest's fine-drawn profile, thinking that if the rhetoric master was already tired enough to be so fractious, perhaps they should turn back to Paris now. The priest's light blue eyes were still shadowed and he was thin, but he had always been small. His slenderness added to his grace, which seemed bred in the bone and not something learned.

Thinking that Jouvancy might have personal reasons for cautioning him, Charles said, "Were—forgive me, *mon père*— but were you already a Jesuit when you last visited Versailles?"

"No."

"Then I can imagine that you must have attracted much attention. But I am already a Jesuit under first vows. There must be some respect for clerics at court."

Jouvancy snorted. "Have you forgotten Madame de Maintenon's nickname for Père La Chaise, who holds what many would judge the most eminent clerical position in France?"

The little priest stood up, slapping the crown of his wide-brimmed black hat farther down over his fine fair hair, and stalked back toward the horses. Hoping that his superior's current mood was not going to color their whole trip, Charles hastily closed the saddlebag and followed him. He held the older man's reins and stirrup and helped him mount, strapped the bag on the front of his own saddle, and swung himself up.

They rode in silence until they reached the southwest side of the village. There, Charles asked a boy with a flock of hissing geese if the road they were on joined the road to Versailles. Told that it did, somewhere beyond the village of Issy, they rode on, still without speaking. The warming air was thick with the smell of earth and Flamme danced and curvetted, shaking his head against the reins. Charles held him back reluctantly. The horse was not the only one who would have loved a gallop through the sloping vineyards green with new leaves, but Jouvancy could not be left to follow in Charles's dust. They both had to content themselves with drinking in the spring air as though it were the local white wine. But under Charles's pleasure in the day, he was still uneasy about Jouvancy's mood and concern for his virtue.

Charles had indeed had a sharp struggle with his vow of chastity, but that was known only to his confessor. He'd done his penance and remade his vows, choosing chastity finally and with his whole heart. Before entering the Society of Jesus, however, he'd had plenty of experience with women. During his two years as a soldier, he'd bedded several willing and pretty women, whom he remembered with affection. He hoped their memories of him were equally happy. But all that was past.

Charles and Jouvancy heard the royal road to Versailles before they saw it. Galloping hooves, rattling harness, bouncing carriages, and belligerent cries disputing the right of way made them feel they were back in Paris. When the small road they were on unwound its last curve, they reined in, gaping at the stream of fast-moving traffic in both directions. Luxurious private carriages, red and gold and black, and drawn by anything from two to eight horses, sped along the wide and level road surface. Charles caught glimpses of brocaded interiors and richly dressed men and women inside—and once, of a beady-eyed lapdog at a carriage window, its black-and-white ears streaming in the wind. A slow-moving hired coach trundled past, weighed down by fifteen or twenty laughing, singing tourists returning from Versailles to Paris. The road was also thick with agile pedestrians, women as well as men, dodging not only coaches but also riders on horseback. Young men in wind-tangled wigs under plumed hats, dark velvet-trimmed coats, and gleaming riding boots—boots that made Charles catch his breath with forbidden covetousness—rode their lathered horses as recklessly as the king's hard-bitten mail couriers, going as though their lives depended on arriving before anyone else at Versailles or Paris. Charles and Jouvancy joined the cavalcade, going slowly and steadily like the tortoise in Aesop's fable, and were quickly covered in everyone else's dust.

By late afternoon, the road had climbed gently and the Versailles-bound traffic had thickened even more. A voice behind Charles and Jouvancy bellowed, "Way! Way!" and a four-horse coach passed so closely that Charles nearly brushed knees with the postillion mounted on the right-hand lead horse. Flamme, exasperated at having been held back all day, shied madly sideways, tossing his head, and Jouvancy's mare bared her teeth and snapped, nearly catching his ear. Just as Charles got Flamme settled, another coach going like devils out of hell hurtled toward them, the postillion blowing long and loud on a brass horn. Flamme reared, pawing the air. It took all of Charles's horsemanship to get him to the side of the road. The mare, Agneau, having shaken her reins loose from Jouvancy's grip, was now ignoring everything except the grass she was pulling up. Jouvancy sat motionless in the saddle, squinting straight west into the late afternoon sun.

"There it is," he said.

At the end of the tree-lined avenue, the sun struck gleams of gold from towering, gilded iron gates on the far side of a trapezoidal plaza. Two other tree-lined avenues, one on each side of their own, converged on the plaza, where what looked like half the population of a small town walked, lounged, and loitered, careful to stay out of the way of the busy gate traffic. There were men exercising horses on lead reins, other men walking braces of leashed dogs, and off to one side, Charles thought he saw two men dueling. But it was a good quarter mile from where they sat to the open space, he realized, and he might be wrong.

"Shall we go on?" Jouvancy said. "I confess I am ready to be done with riding." His tone was light, but Charles saw with concern that there were gray shadows under his eyes and he was slumping tiredly, which he hadn't been earlier.

"By all means, *mon père*. I, too, am ready to arrive."

As the palace grew nearer, Charles felt as though a mounting wave of architecture were about to break over him. *Palace*, Charles thought, was really the only word for the place. Calling this sprawling pile of buildings a chateau was like calling Louis XIV merely a bureaucrat. As they crossed the plaza, Charles's eye was caught by what looked like a shop front in the wall to the left of the gates. One horizontal wooden shutter was propped up as a sloping rooflet, the other let down to make a counter, behind which a *concierge* was renting out swords and plumed hats, required wear for all laymen entering the palace, to men too low in rank to have their own. Vendors from the new town that had grown up around the palace were selling pastries and lottery tickets and *eau de vie*. Obvious palace officials attended by retinues of lesser officials walked slowly, deep in talk. Several ladies—by their dress and bold looks, of doubtful virtue—watched the men with practiced eyes, and one of them let her eyes linger on Charles as he passed.

At the gilded gate, the guards on duty asked their business. While Jouvancy explained, Charles stared balefully at the golden sun as big as a carriage wheel on the gate's top, feeling already scrutinized by the Sun King's personal surveillance. The guards let them pass into the wide green expanse that still lay between them and most of the palace buildings. Beyond was a second gilded gate that Charles hadn't even seen till now. He shook his head, thinking that the scale of the place was so huge that some things were simply too big to be seen.

At the second set of gates, another guard questioned them and directed them to their right, across the smaller—but still enormous—court toward the palace's south wing. Here there were no carriages, just strolling courtiers and clutches of pointing, gawking sightseers. When they finally reached the door, Charles dismounted and helped Jouvancy down from the saddle. Two grooms appeared seemingly from nowhere, one taking the horses' bridles and the other removing the saddlebags. A young royal footman in a blue serge coat with red velvet cuffs and pockets hurried through the door, spoke sharply to the man with the saddlebags, bowed to the two Jesuits, and scanned the court beyond them.

"I've been watching for you, *mes pères*," he said, in a voice that rasped like an old file and consorted oddly with his comely face and warm brown eyes. "But I was told there'd be four of you."

"Père Le Picart and Père Montville were detained in Paris," Jouvancy replied. "They will be here tomorrow morning."

"Then if you please, I will conduct you to Père La Chaise. He's waiting in his chamber."

Jouvancy gently removed himself from Charles's supporting

arm and drew himself up, wavering a little as he found his feet again after the ride. "We thank you," he said, with a relieved sigh, and they followed the footman into the palace, trailed in turn by the lower servant with the saddlebags.

The footman led his little procession along a corridor, up a flight of marble stairs to the next floor, and to the left along another corridor. This one was so crowded with people coming and going that its black-and-white-patterned marble floor was hardly visible beneath the rustling, swinging skirts and cloaks. Stopping at a door at the courtyard end of the building, the footman scratched at the door with his little finger. A tall, solidly built Jesuit in his late middle years opened it. Charles, who had met him before, recognized him as Père La Chaise and inclined his head. Jouvancy did the same.

La Chaise returned the gesture. "Welcome, Père Jouvancy. *Entrez*, I beg you. But where are the others?"

Jouvancy again explained. La Chaise nodded slightly at Charles, stood aside for them to pass into a small anteroom, and turned to the footman.

"Thank you, Bouchel, see that your man leaves the bags there." He pointed to a table standing beside a copper water reservoir.

The footman pointed imperiously in his turn and stood over the other servant as he deposited the bags.

Waving his guests through the anteroom into the larger chamber, La Chaise said to Jouvancy, "Please, sit. I know that you have been ill, *mon père*." He pulled an upholstered, fringed chair forward and turned to a small polished table that held a silver pitcher and five delicate cone-shaped, short-stemmed glasses. Jouvancy loosed his cloak, handed it to Charles, and sat, groaning audibly as his hindquarters met the chair seat.

"It is a long while since I've ridden," he said ruefully.

La Chaise laughed and handed him a glass of rich red wine. "This should help ease the pain—and build up your blood, too. Always necessary after illness, I find." Returning to the table, he said to Charles, "Put the cloaks on my bed and bring the stool from beside the hearth."

Charles folded the cloaks and laid them on the thickly blanketed and well-pillowed bed, whose red curtains were looped back and tied to its carved posts. When he had moved the small, cushioned stool nearer to Jouvancy, La Chaise held out a glass to him.

"It is a pleasure to meet you again, *mon père,*" Charles said, bowing once more before he took the wine.

La Chaise again nodded slightly in return and gestured Charles to the low stool. Charles sat obediently. La Chaise poured his own glass of wine and seated himself in the other chair. Seen close up, the king's confessor looked to be sixty or so. His fleshy face was lined, his dark eyes resigned and knowing. He had the air of someone long past being surprised by anything—only to be expected, Charles thought, from a man who had spent more than a decade as the confessor of Europe's most absolute monarch. But Charles could see in him none of the bitter cynicism such a king's confessor might have had. La Chaise's eyes were knowing, but they were also warm.

Charles drank gratefully, realizing as the wine went down how hungry he was and wondering when something might be done about it. Jouvancy was giving La Chaise an account of his illness, and Charles let his eyes wander over the room, the first palace room he'd seen. Its small size was a relief from the massive scale of the exterior. The chamber's ceiling was undecorated; its walls were plain wood paneling below and plaster above; and the two armchairs, the stool, the table, a tall cupboard beside the fireplace, a prie-dieu, and the bed were all its furnishings. The large window opposite the door had small wood-framed panes of clear, faintly bluish glass. Its interior shutters stood open and the late afternoon sun, coming and going now among gathering clouds, fell obliquely, lighting a patch of bare, dusty parquet floor.

Charles realized that he'd expected something more, something grander, even though La Chaise used this room only when events compelled his overnight presence at Versailles. Otherwise, the king's confessor lived in Paris, in the Jesuit Professed House beside the Church of St. Louis. La Chaise was not outwardly a courtier; he wore the same plain black cassock, with a rosary hanging from its belt, that every other Jesuit wore, and rode horseback or hired a carriage when the king sent for him.

As though he'd been reading Charles's mind, La Chaise said, smiling, "I see you wondering at my accommodations, *maître*. I fought hard to get the brocade taken off the walls and to keep the gaggle of palace artists from painting overfed angels on my ceiling. Which gained me a reputation with a few people for ascetic sanctity, and with a great many more for pretended sanctity and secret luxury, and for myself, one space at least in this palace where I can breathe." He nodded toward a door beyond Jouvancy. "Your chamber is just there, through that door. It, too, is plain."

Jouvancy gave him a tired smile. "We thank you." Then he sighed and said, "*Mon père*, I think I must go and rest soon, but before I do, may we know what the arrangements are for giving our gift tomorrow?"

"Of course, yes. You are certain that Père Le Picart and Père Montville will be here in good time?"

"That is their intention. They will take a coach after the first Mass."

"Good. Then that leaves only . . ." La Chaise pursed his lips and tapped a foot, staring at Charles without seeming to see him. Then he nodded, as though agreeing with himself, and stood up. "There is one last detail still to settle. Pray excuse me and I will see to it—it will be faster than sending someone. I will return as quickly as may be."

He strode from the room, leaving Charles and Jouvancy looking at each other. Jouvancy was pale and the shadows beneath his eyes had darkened.

"Perhaps you could sleep a little in your chair while he's gone," Charles said.

"Yes. Yes, perhaps I could. Forgive me, I am absurdly tired."

Jouvancy's eyes closed and the wineglass tilted in his hand. Charles saved it from falling and set it on the table. Then he went into the adjoining chamber, took a blanket from the larger bed standing there, and put it over Jouvancy's knees. The rhetoric master did not so much as stir when Charles tucked it in around him. Picking up his own wineglass, Charles went to the window and saw that it looked down into an interior courtyard, where a boy, two girls, and a small black dog were playing some game with a ball. Charles watched with pleasure as they darted after the ball and threw it, laughing and calling to one another, indifferent to the small sprinkling of rain that had started. The dark-haired boy was slower than the two girls, visibly limping as he chased the ball over low bushes bordering the court's checkerboard of flower beds. He and the older girl, whose tall headdress of red ribbons and lace had fallen off, leaving her curling fair hair to fly in every direction, were in their teens. The other girl was much younger and very small, and Charles was thinking that it was kind of the older two to play with her, when he belatedly recognized the limping boy as the young Duc du Maine, the king's eldest bastard son, who had come to the Louis le Grand pre-Lenten performance back in February. And the older girl was his sister, Mademoiselle de Rouen, who had come with him. The little girl Charles did not know.

Charles was turning away from the window when a shout from the courtyard drew him back. A man in coat and breeches of rich brown was crossing the courtyard toward the three, one hand on his belly, shaking a fist at the older girl. She stood with hands on her hips, bust thrust out, shouting back at him like a market woman. The cocked front brim of the man's black hat showed only part of his face, but something about his walk seemed familiar to Charles. The Duc du Maine hobbled toward the man, but the little girl was backing away. To Charles's astonishment, Mademoiselle de Rouen bent down, scooped up a handful of courtyard gravel, and flung it at the man's face. His howl of anger was loud enough to make Jouvancy sit up, and Charles went to see how he did, leaving the scene below to play itself out.

"It was only a noise outside, *mon père*," Charles said soothingly. "You can sleep a while longer."

Jouvancy blinked and mumbled something, and his eyes closed again. Charles went to see if there was more wine in the pitcher. Thanking St. Martin, patron of winemakers and beggars, he poured a little more into his glass and wondered how much longer it would be before he got anything to eat. He was eyeing the cupboard's closed doors when the gallery door opened and Père La Chaise hurried through the anteroom.

"All is well," he said. "I—oh. Sleeping, is he?"

But Jouvancy had heard him and struggled upright. "Only a little nap, *mon père*, and very welcome."

La Chaise settled himself again in his armchair and Charles resumed the stool.

"So. Here is how tomorrow will go," La Chaise said. "I want you both to accompany me to the king's morning Mass at ten o'clock. If the other two are here by then, well and good. If not, no matter. You will not be presented to the king before the Mass, but he will see you."

Jouvancy's eyes widened. "Do you mean that he will be at the presentation of the cross?"

"No. I have advised him not to be there. You are presenting it to the lady, not to the king, and his presence would only call attention to their—connection." Jouvancy and Charles both opened their mouths, but La Chaise's face made it clear that there would be no discussion of that interesting question. "Now," he went on, "know that Louis misses nothing that happens around him. He sees and he remembers. His public presence is even-tempered and courteous almost to a fault." La Chaise shrugged and lifted open palms. "The man raises his hat to kitchen maids. Any failure of courtesy infuriates him, and so does any breach of ceremony. No, no, *mon père*," he added quickly as Jouvancy opened his mouth to protest. "I am not in the least implying that you might be discourteous, I am only trying to give you some understanding of the king. Because unless you somewhat understand him, you will not understand our Madame de Maintenon, and it is she whose heart you must touch tomorrow."

"It's said she doesn't have one," Charles murmured, mostly to see if he could provoke a little useful indiscretion and a little more information.

Jouvancy frowned, and La Chaise eyed Charles in surprise. Less, Charles thought, because of what he'd said than because a mere scholastic had ventured to say it.

"Many things are said about those who live here," La Chaise retorted. "As you obviously know." Charles bowed his head slightly to the riposte, which La Chaise softened by saying, with laughter in his voice, "Many things are said about *me* by many people, including Madame de Maintenon. As I am also sure you know. Even though I spend less time here at court than at our Professed House in Paris." His face sobered. "Madame de Maintenon has not only a measure of wit but also an essentially kind heart, I assure you. But she gives her heart very rarely. So far as I know, she has given it only twice: to the king and to his eldest son by Madame de Montespan, our young Duc du Maine. She was governess, you know, to him and some of his brothers and sisters. She loves all those children, the more because she feels their mother has virtually ignored them. But Maine has a lame leg and is her favorite. She did everything that could be done for him, though little helped his lameness. He is her heart's darling."

Jouvancy was watching him curiously. "As I listen to you speak of her, *mon père,* I could almost believe that you do not dislike the woman."

La Chaise's eyebrows rose. "Dislike her? I don't know that I do dislike her. She is without pretense my enemy. But I often have the feeling that if we had been thrown together under different circumstances, we might have been friends."

Fascinated, Charles ventured, "Why do you think so?"

"There's much about her I respect. Her piety. Her austerity of mind. She has no use at all for self-indulgence. Or for false or easy answers. Or for impiety—under the Caesars, she would probably have ended in the arena."

Jouvancy laughed. "One might feel sorry for the lions."

"One might, indeed." La Chaise shrugged and held out his

hands. "But things are as they are, and we are not friends. She is an idealist. I am a realist. She loathes my realistic lenience with my royal penitent. But a king, especially this king, can only be guided by a loose rein. I choose to think that better than no guidance at all."

Jouvancy and Charles nodded somber agreement with that. They all sat without speaking—busy, it seemed to Charles, with thoughts loosed by what La Chaise had said. The light was fading, and Charles saw that it was raining in earnest now. Out in the gallery, the clattering noise of heels echoed on the marble floor, and Charles found himself wondering how late it would go on. Louis le Grand was a noisy enough place during the day, but quiet was the rule at night.

La Chaise sighed. "What I fear most just now is the king's lust for war. Which is coming—and not altogether at his behest this time. Now that the Turks have been beaten back in the east, the Protestant countries of the League of Augsburg—the Holy Roman Emperor and the Germanic states, Sweden, and Spain—have breathing space to think of clipping France's wings once and for all. Or at least, to try."

"How soon do you believe they will try?" Jouvancy's pinched face had grown anxious.

"The spies and rumors are saying it may not be this year. But by the next, for certain."

"Well, you may be sure," Jouvancy said triumphantly, "that in our own small way, we are doing what we can at Louis le Grand to help gird the loins of France."

La Chaise looked at him in surprise. "Oh, yes?" he said, half smiling. "And with what are you girding her loins, *mon père*?"

"With our rousing August ballet. It's called *La France Victorieuse sous Louis le Grand.* I chose it to proclaim the strength of our realm and our Most Christian King in the face of our enemies. Our students performed it several years ago, but Maître du Luc is revising it to make it more current, so that it fits with what is happening now."

Charles bit his tongue.

"*France Victorious under Louis the Great*," La Chaise said meditatively. "Yes, that's good. Perhaps I can contrive to mention that tomorrow morning." He peered at Jouvancy. "I must let you go and rest, but first, let me briefly explain what will happen tomorrow after the king's Mass. From the chapel, we will go to Madame de Maintenon's antechamber and wait there until we are called into her reception room. Some of the royal children will be there, and an assortment of courtiers. We will go over the ceremonial procedure in detail tomorrow, but the crux of it is that you, Père Jouvancy, should present the reliquary directly into Madame de Maintenon's hands—unless it is too large or heavy?"

"No, no," Jouvancy said, "it is only about the height of two spread hands."

"Good. After she takes it from you, she will thank you and the Society of Jesus, and everyone will admire the gift. Then she will give the signal for the three of us to retire. And then it will be dinnertime. What I went to confirm just now is where we will eat. I am happy to tell you that we are invited to the Duc de La Rochefoucauld's table. A very good table indeed. He is a friend of Madame de Maintenon's and pleased by your gift." La Chaise smiled at Jouvancy and stood up. "For now, let us get you settled in your own chamber for a little more rest. Besides the door from this chamber, there is also a door into the gallery. You will find a latrine in the corner of the gallery to your left."

Jouvancy began to struggle out of his chair, and Charles went quickly to help him.

"Oof! I feel as stiff as a new boot," he said, holding to Charles's arm as he slowly straightened. "Will you get our saddlebags, *maître?*"

La Chaise took his place at Jouvancy's arm, and Charles went to the anteroom for the saddlebags. As he hefted them over his shoulder, what sounded like thunder crashed and echoed out in the gallery, and women began to scream.

Chapter 3

Charles left the saddlebags and ran out into the gallery. A huddle of courtiers blocked the way, crowding around the staircase he and Jouvancy had come up. Some were trying to get closer and some were already retreating, staring at one another, hands pressed to their mouths. Two young women turned hastily and hurried in Charles's direction, the linen and ribbons of their fontange headdresses quivering as they leaned close and whispered avidly to each other.

". . . old Fleury," he heard, as they came closer.

He stopped where he was. The Comte de Fleury? Surely not. Surely not the same Comte de Fleury he'd known as a soldier.

"Well, no one will miss *him*," the other woman said, half laughing. "None of the young serving maids, anyway. Dear God, the man was a lecher!"

"Such an undignified way to die, though." The first woman's mouth puckered in a moue of distaste, quickly smoothed away as she saw Charles. "But may God receive his soul," she said loudly. Both women crossed themselves and disappeared, giggling, around the corner.

Charles pushed his way to the front of the crowd and looked down at the man sprawled at the foot of the marble stairs. It *was* the same Fleury, and from the way he lay, it was clear that he'd broken his neck in his thunderous plunge down the stairs. Charles stared down at the man's dead, empty eyes, remembering . . . It had been ten years ago, in April 1677, outside the defeated city of Cassel in the Spanish Netherlands. He'd pleaded with the Comte de Fleury for the lives of three terrified common soldiers. The oldest was eighteen. It had been their first battle, and they'd fled in terror through the broken bodies of friends and enemies. Caught and brought back to face their commanding officer, they'd cowered, weeping, beneath the hanging ropes already strung in a tree. Charles had begged the Comte de Fleury to give them a second chance, but he was a hard and arrogant commander and had hanged them then and there. He'd nearly hanged Charles, too, for interfering.

A courtier bent over Fleury, searching uselessly for signs of life, straightened, and took off his white-plumed hat. "He's gone."

The young footman Bouchel, standing white-faced at the foot of the stairs, slowly crossed himself. The men in the crowd of courtiers removed their hats with a decent show of respect. But one laughed and said, "Well, our poor dear Conti will never collect *those* gambling debts, anyway! And at least Fleury's nephew can stop shaking in his boots, now that the old man won't be after his money anymore." That got muffled laughter and knowing looks, but the courtier standing beside the body shook his head reprovingly.

"Trying to reach the latrine, I think, poor soul," he said, and Charles realized that Fleury was without coat and hat and that his brown breeches were partly undone. The smell of bowels was thickening the air, and vomit streaked the front of the dead man's linen shirt.

Bouchel swallowed and nodded. "I was up there putting a pot under a ceiling leak. I saw the old—I saw him run out of his room toward the stairs."

"Ah, yes, he lived up above," someone said, jerking his head at the ceiling, "and the latrine up there is closed. They're making it into a lodging."

Someone else groaned. "That one, too? So we'll have even more—nuisances—left in the gallery alcoves."

A hand gripped Charles's shoulder and Père La Chaise said, "Go to Père Jouvancy. He's lying down and should stay in his bed, he doesn't need to come and see this."

Charles pulled himself together and stepped back, and La Chaise took his place at the front of the crowd. As Charles started back to the chamber, someone said, with the carrying diction of an actor, "I wonder, though, why the poor old thing didn't just use his *chaise de commodité?*"

Charles spun on his heel and saw a young man in a gold-trimmed coat and a frothy wig nearly as golden as the trim smiling brightly into La Chaise's face.

"A good question," La Chaise answered evenly. "Though from the smell of him—if, of course, it's him I smell—I'd say his *chaise de commodité* might well be full."

"Oh, well said, Père—ah—La Chaise." A small man in russet satin grinned, lynx-eyed, over his shoulder at the crowd and raised a ripple of stifled laughter.

Ignoring the insults, La Chaise turned to Bouchel. "Did you see him fall?"

"No, *mon père.*" Bouchel jerked his head at the stairs. "But as I said, I saw him come out of his room, and he was groaning as if he might die. And I know there was water on the floor—from the leak, you understand. He must have slipped as he started down the stairs."

La Chaise nodded and looked again at the body. "We have to get this body out of the palace. And quickly." By tradition, a king of France could not stay in a building with a corpse.

Bouchel nodded. "Shall I go for the Guard?"

"Yes. And then for Monsieur Neuville. When the Guard has Fleury in the mortuary, the physicians will have to look at him to confirm how he died." La Chaise's dark gaze swept across the courtiers. "Did any of you see the Comte de Fleury earlier?"

"I saw him at dinner today, at the Duc de La Rochefoucauld's table," an older woman in burgundy velvet said hesitantly, flicking a lace-edged painted fan in front of her nose to disperse the smell. Her eyes were troubled and she frowned at La Chaise. "He seemed quite well then. I know he was old . . . but to be so suddenly ill . . . one could be forgiven for wondering . . ." She shivered and crossed herself.

"One could," La Chaise said grimly, and also crossed himself. "While we wait," he said firmly, "we will say the prayers for the dead."

A chastened hush descended. Charles left the Comte de Fleury's soul to La Chaise—or more likely, he thought uncharitably, to the devil—and turned back to the bedchamber and Jouvancy. He went in through La Chaise's anteroom, picked up the saddlebags, and made his way to the adjoining chamber. In spite of all the noise in the gallery, Jouvancy had fallen fast asleep on the wide, green-curtained bed, curled into himself like a snail in its shell. *Good*, Charles thought, and untied the bed curtains and closed them. He tiptoed to the second, smaller bed and pulled off his riding boots to make his moving about the room quieter. The second bed was tucked into a tiny alcove between this second chamber and its antechamber, where the door into the corridor was. Narrow and plain, obviously meant for a servant, it was still softer than any Jesuit bed he'd ever slept in. Charles opened the larger saddlebag and began taking out his and Jouvancy's fresh linen. His head came up as a sudden tramping of feet passed in the corridor. *The Guard coming for the Comte de Fleury's body*, he thought, and found himself utterly unable to pray for the man, unable to be anything but glad he was dead, hoping even that he'd suffered at least a taste of terror at the end, like the men he'd hanged. But those were sinful thoughts, because vengeance belonged to God. Though it was easy enough to see Fleury's end as appropriate divine vengeance.

As he put tomorrow's clean shirts away in a tall cupboard of polished dark wood, the door opened and closed in La Chaise's chamber. Charles went through the connecting door, expecting to see the king's confessor returned, but instead found the footman Bouchel on one knee at the hearth, beside a basket of wood. Hearing Charles, he looked up, smiling, and shook his thick brown hair back from his face.

"Making a fire, *mon père*," he said in his rasping voice. "Dark soon. And Père La Chaise will likely want to cook."

"I'm only *maître* as yet, *monsieur*." Then Charles said, startled, "Did you say 'cook'?"

"Yes, he boils up his *bouillon* most nights."

Charles's heart sank into his empty belly as the visions he'd entertained of a laden supper table disappeared. La Chaise probably felt it was unfitting for Jesuits to feast openly, or at least too often, he thought with a sigh, admonishing himself for gluttony.

The footman got to his feet as a blaze rose from the neatly built new fire. "The courtiers all do it—well, more do than don't, anyway."

"They all cook?" Jesuits supping frugally on a *bouillon* made over their own fire was one thing. But courtiers? "Why?"

Bouchel laughed and rubbed his thumb and forefinger together. "No money. Plenty of pretty clothes and mortgaged jewels, but half of them haven't got the price of a radish in their purses. Sometimes they eat in the Grand Commons refectory—that's across the street from the south wing. But that costs them, too. Sometimes they eat at the Tables of Honor, but one can't always be invited, so the courtiers get cooking pots—or their servants get them—and man or master cooks the *bouillon*. Usually they send someone like me out into the town for bread and cheese and a little pot of wine. And—*voilà*—*le souper!*"

Bouchel took a copper pot from the cupboard, carried it into La Chaise's antechamber, brought it back half filled with water, and set it on a solid iron trivet at the edge of the fire. Then he pulled the square table out from the wall and brought over a round loaf of bread, a little cloth-wrapped cheese, and a sadly small pottery pitcher of wine, which he set on the table next to the silver pitcher that was already there.

"There," he said, adding a candle in a brass holder to the table array. "Père La Chaise will take over from here when he comes back."

Bouchel made as if to go, but Charles said, "I thought I heard the Guard go by."

"You did. They took the Comte de Fleury's body away, but we've not heard the end of it, you can be sure as rain of that."

"Why do you say so?"

Bouchel's harsh, damaged laughter filled the darkening room. "This is Versailles, *maître*. Drop dead from anything, including a broken neck, and before Mass tomorrow, the whole palace will be saying it was poison." He shrugged, bowed, and became again the well-trained royal footman. "With your permission, *maître*. I wish you a good night."

"And God give you a good night, also," Charles said absently, his thoughts gone to poison. Poison was often suspected when a death came suddenly, and not just at court. But Fleury's death seemed so obvious—sickness, a rush to the privy, a wet floor, a headlong fall down marble stairs. He eyed the unpromising pot of water on the hearth. On the other hand, perhaps it was just as well to cook over one's own fire here.

The door opened again to admit La Chaise, who walked heavily to the fire, shaking his head. "A terrible thing to happen. But marble stairs are slippery at the best of times, and if the floor upstairs was wet . . . And it clearly was not the best of times for the Comte de Fleury." He shrugged as though to shrug off his thoughts. "Is Père Jouvancy resting?"

"He's asleep, *mon père*. May I help you with the supper?"

"Yes, thank you." La Chaise glanced down at the simmering water, then out the window at the densely clouded sky visible above the roofs across the courtyard. "Light the candle on the table, if you will. Rain brings the dark sooner, even in June." He took a long wooden splinter from a box beside the hearth, lit it, and handed it to Charles, who used it to light a short, stubby candle.

"Wax?" Charles said. "That's pleasant, instead of tallow."

"Yes, Bouchel saves me from the evil smell of tallow. He gathers wax candle ends from courtiers' servants and keeps them aside for when I have to stay the night. A good servant, and a pleasant one. And he knows everything about the town, he was born in the village here."

"Village? Most of the buildings I saw riding in look as new as the palace."

"They are. But yes, there was a village. Small, but it had been here time out of mind. The king demolished it when he decided to turn his father's old hunting lodge into this palace."

Charles shook his head. "And how did the villagers take that?"

"Not well. But the king employed them in the building, so they got something out of it. If I remember correctly, Bouchel said once that his father was one of the masons."

"Oh? And now Bouchel works in the palace his father helped to build. Do you know what happened to his voice?"

"No, but I do know that while the palace was being built, there was an enormous camp for the workers. During the work, the whole place, including the old village, became very wet and unhealthy because of massive digging and rerouting of water. I suppose anyone who lived here—villagers as well as incoming workmen—risked chest and throat sickness." La Chaise went to the cupboard and brought out a tall pitcher covered with a white linen cloth. Crouching down, he removed the cloth and poured the contents of the pitcher into the simmering water. "The remains of last night's *bouillon*," he said, straightening and taking a long spoon out of the cupboard. The savory smell of onions and leeks in beef broth filled the room. Charles's stomach began trying to climb up his backbone to get to the food.

"And I am going to add a little more beef and another bone, though my mother would be scandalized at my short way of making *bouillon*." La Chaise reached into the cupboard and brought out a bloody paper packet, unwrapped it, and dumped its contents into the pot. "Now we have only to wait."

Charles swallowed hard. "How long will it need to cook?"

"Not long, the meat is chopped somewhat fine." La Chaise smiled suddenly. "When I was a scholastic, I was hungry all the time. If you're hungry now, break some bread from the loaf there. And let us have a little wine while we wait for the soup to become soup and for Père Jouvancy to wake." His face fell as he looked at the pot of wine Bouchel had brought. "Oh, dear. A *little* wine is the apt word, unfortunately. Oh, well, we can water it. Or not water it and drink water with our supper. Anyway, wine now!"

Charles looked for a knife to cut the loaf, that being the polite modern custom, but La Chaise only said, "No, no, break it. If Louis can use his fingers to eat, so can we."

Gratefully, Charles broke a piece off the brown loaf and La Chaise refilled the cone-shaped glasses they'd used earlier, but only to the scant side of half full.

"To your health, *maître*," he said, handing a glass to Charles and raising his own.

Charles returned the compliment and they drank.

"Sit. No, have the chair." La Chaise gestured Charles to the thinly cushioned chair fringed with red silk where Jouvancy had sat, and settled himself in the other. "Aaah." He drank again and closed his eyes briefly. Seeming to open them again with an effort, he said, "Have you had much sickness in the college?"

"Yes, these last weeks. Our infirmarian thinks it's some unbalance of humors caused by the weather going from cold to warmer after such a bad winter. He says the change makes the stomach and bowels grip, and then the blood boils trying to get through them, which raises a fever. Though hardly anyone dies of it, he says."

La Chaise grunted. "Unless they fall downstairs trying to reach the privy. Does this illness come on suddenly?"

"Oh, yes. Père Jouvancy was well one afternoon at the beginning of the rhetoric class, and deathly ill and spewing before it ended. I could hardly get him to the infirmary."

"Have you, too, been ill?"

"No, thank Saint Roch and Saint Stephen," Charles answered fervently, naming two saints known for protecting against contagion. "If I may ask, *mon père*, are you thinking that the Comte de Fleury was ill in the same way?"

"Possibly. You may have heard the woman in the corridor say he seemed well enough at dinner today." La Chaise rose and stirred the soup, whose scent was so enticing now that Charles felt like biting at the air to see if it tasted like it smelled. To distract himself, he said, "I saw three young people playing in the court below the window soon after we arrived and recognized two of them as the king's children, who did us the honor of coming to our college performance in February, the Duc du Maine and Mademoiselle de Rouen."

"Two of our *legitimées de France*. You know, of course, that he had his children by Madame de Montespan declared legally legitimate."

"The other was a small girl. But very quick at the game they were playing."

"Very little? Bright brown hair?" When Charles nodded, La Chaise said, "That was Anne-Marie de Bourbon, Princess of the Blood, a daughter of the new Prince of Condé."

"Ah." Charles nodded. The Condés were Bourbons, as royal blooded as the king and in line for the throne. The present Prince of Condé had come into his title only in December, when his father died.

"In case you have to speak to the princess," La Chaise said, "she's styled Her Serene Highness and her title is Mademoiselle d'Enghien. She looks six, but she's eleven or twelve, I think. The new Condé's daughters are all tiny, like their grandmother Claire Clemence. People call them 'Dolls of the Blood.'" Watching the fire brighten as the light faded, La Chaise said reflectively, "Have you ever thought how oddly things are passed on in families? Take those two children of the king you saw. Maine is dark like his father. But Lulu, as Mademoiselle de Rouen is called, is nearly blond, like her mother, Madame de Montespan. And her character could not be more different from her brother's if she came from the other side of the world. Maine's a quiet boy, doesn't seem to like public life much. He'd rather be in the woods with his huntsman and the dogs, so I hear. Though his limp doesn't help his riding. I will tell you—in confidence— that he's the king's favorite child. Though they say he's not living up to his promise. He was a brilliant little boy, but now he has—well—faded, somehow. In my opinion, Madame de Maintenon has kept him too close, too tied to her, probably because of his limp. She tried very hard to cure him, you know. But limp or not, it's high time the king sent Maine to the army. The boy is seventeen. Far too old to be mooning around here at court playing children's games."

"And what of Lulu, as you called her? How old is she?"

La Chaise sighed. "Yes. Lulu. She's—let me see—almost sixteen. Her Highness's real name is Louise Marguerite. Louise after her father, of course, and Marguerite after his mother's mother, Marguerite of Austria."

"So she's nearly marriageable."

"In fact, nearly married. And furious about it. She's tried to change the king's mind. But he pays no attention and she's causing a world of trouble. I live for the day she's finally dispatched to her husband, I assure you."

"Who is he?"

"A Polish prince, the younger son of King Jan Sobieski. We need to strengthen ties with Poland, since Sobieski has too often aligned himself with France's enemies. Particularly the Hapsburgs and the Holy Roman Empire. Of course, Sobieski had no choice but to fight on the Hapsburg side against the Turks at Vienna and Buda, the Turks being such a danger to Poland. But Louis hopes to make Sobieski our ally with this marriage."

"However the girl herself feels about it?"

La Chaise looked at Charles as though he'd begun speaking

Chinese. "She's known all her life that she would be married for royal reasons. Why she's making so much trouble about it, I can't imagine." He shook his head and sipped from his glass. "Poland is an odd place. Did you know that Polish nobles elect their king? They usually choose the old king's son, but not always. It seems to me an affront to God to show so little trust in the royal lineage."

Charles was silent, wondering how different things might be in France if the French king were elected.

"With his daughter married to Sobieski's son, Louis will have more influence on the next vote, whenever that should come. So Lulu's marriage—" La Chaise stopped short and turned in his chair as the connecting door between the chambers opened.

Jouvancy stood in the doorway, blinking in the firelight and yawning. "*Bonsoir, mon père, maître,*" he said indistinctly, turning politely aside to cover another wide yawn. "I see I have slept into the evening. I thank you for letting me rest so long. I am a new man." He sniffed the air. "Supper?" he said hopefully.

"*Le bouillon, mon père.*" La Chaise got up and set his wineglass on the table. "And to start, let me pour wine for you."

The firelight made a twisting red rope of the wine as he added what was left in the small pot of wine to the silver pitcher. He filled a glass for Jouvancy, who took it with a satisfied sigh and sank into the chair Charles offered him.

"You feel better, then?" Charles said, watching Jouvancy narrowly.

"Much better, I was only tired." Jouvancy settled stiffly on the seat's thin cushion and smiled up at Charles. "Don't fuss over me—go and help our host."

La Chaise straightened from stirring the pot. "No need, we have a few minutes yet to wait. What you can do, though, is show me the gift we're giving to Madame de Maintenon tomorrow. I would like to see it."

"With pleasure, *mon père*."

Charles brought the well-wrapped reliquary from the connecting chamber and held it out to Jouvancy.

"No, please—you unwrap it, *maître*."

When the heavy canvas and the soft silk wrappings beneath were peeled away, the cross stood glowing among the supper preparations, the bread and the wine, so that for a moment, Charles saw the table as an altar.

"Very beautiful," La Chaise said, coming closer to examine the shining gold and the deep blue inlay of the stone called lapis lazuli.

"Show him the relic," Jouvancy said.

Charles picked up the cross, turned it facedown across his hand, and pressed a tiny flange in its back. The cross's back opened like a door to reveal a little compartment an inch wide and three inches long that held a thin bundle of tightly wrapped and yellowing old silk.

"Saint Ursula's finger bone," Charles said.

"Her little finger," Jouvancy added. "The silk has always seemed too fragile to unwrap."

"Very nice. A well-thought gift, indeed. And perfect for Saint Cyr, as Saint Ursula is also a patron of students." La Chaise nodded at Charles to reclose the reliquary and went to peer again into the soup pot. He laughed softly. "We must hope, though, that Madame de Maintenon does not know how uncertain Saint Ursula's legend is."

Jouvancy bridled, frowning. "What do you mean, 'uncertain'?"

An unholy glee showed briefly in La Chaise's dark eyes. "As uncertain, you might say, as Madame de Maintenon's 'leg-

,end' is in our own time—her 'uncertain' marriage to the king, I mean."

"Oh, dear Blessed Virgin!" Dismay furrowed Jouvancy's pale face. "The lady won't think—she *can't* think—but that isn't at all what we mean by it. I've never believed that Saint Ursula's story was other than truth!"

Charles bit his tongue for courtesy's sake and hoped that Madame de Maintenon was as credulous as Jouvancy. He supposed that St. Ursula and her martyrdom might be real enough. But many people—including him—found her eleven thousand martyred virgin companions a bit much to swallow.

"Of course," La Chaise said soothingly. "I'm sure nothing of the kind will occur to her. And even if it did, she wouldn't think of any connection to her marriage. Her mind doesn't work like that, especially about holy things." With a disconcerting glance at Charles, he added, "But you must admit, it's amusing, if your mind does work like that."

Charles's mind definitely worked like that. Trying and failing to keep the laughter out of his voice, he said, "There's something else we didn't think of. Or I didn't, anyway. When Ursula was martyred by the Huns, eleven thousand other virgins were martyred with her. So it's said, at least. That's a lot of virgin bones."

"This isn't just one of those other virgins, it's Ursula herself—her own finger!" Jouvancy was sitting militantly upright now. "My grandfather brought it back from Cologne when he visited the Basilica of Saint Ursula. It cost him a *fabulous* sum."

"Yes, *mon père*, I'm sure it must have," Charles murmured, not daring to look at La Chaise.

"Beyond price, surely," the king's confessor said gravely.

"And you can be sure that Madame de Maintenon will value the gift accordingly."

Jouvancy sat back in relief. La Chaise gave a final stir to the *bouillon*, pronounced it ready, and armed himself with a ladle.

"Bowls and spoons are in the cupboard," he said to Charles, who got three brown pottery bowls from a shelf and set the small table with the spoons. The king's confessor placed the fragrantly steaming bowls beside the spoons and brought a knife for the bread and cheese, and the three of them stood with folded hands and bowed heads while he said the grace. Then, tired and momentarily at peace in the darkling room, they sat and ate hungrily, comforting their bodies with bread, wine, cheese, and La Chaise's hot soup, and comforting their minds with good talk. Charles watched the candlelight gleam on St. Ursula's reliquary and thought that perhaps their souls were comforted, too, by her presence. For the good of what they had to do here, he hoped she *was* present, because whatever the reliquary's gold and lapis had cost Père Jouvancy's pious grandfather, the little cross seemed smaller and more insignificant by the moment here in the grandeur of Versailles.

Chapter 4

Before half after nine the next morning, after a late and hasty breakfast of bread and the rest of the bouillon, Charles followed Père La Chaise and Père Jouvancy along the gallery corridor toward the central, royal part of the palace. Their heels echoed sharply on marble and parquet as they passed through a seemingly endless chain of sumptuous chambers opening one into the other. In spite of his determination not to admire the king's ill-gotten grandeur, Charles caught his breath in wonder when they reached the Galerie des Glaces. Not long completed, the Hall of Mirrors was already one of the wonders of Europe. It was more than two hundred feet long, and the inner side of it was lined with "windows" whose panes were mirrors, reflecting back the sunlight from the outer windowed wall and the colors and jewels of the people moving between. Staring and blinking in the unaccustomed light, Charles realized that the benches and tables, and the enormous pots of orange trees in every window embrasure, were made of what looked like silver. He edged toward the nearest pot to see if it really was silver and walked into Jouvancy, who had stopped and was gazing upward.

"Thank the *bon Dieu* for so much beauty," the rhetoric master whispered, and Charles looked up, too.

He had to admit that the ceiling was beautiful. Until he looked closely and saw that it was war spread over his head in sky blue and blood red and every other color in the artist's palette. Louis XIV, in a billowing wig and a Roman soldier's scanty armor, ramped over the battlefields of Europe, leading charges and trampling enemies against a background of smoke from burning cities, while a sky full of cheering angels watched and bosomy classical goddesses waited to bestow laurel crowns. Charles turned his attention to trying to catch sight of Père Le Picart and Père Montville among the throng of courtiers waiting for the war god's appearance. La Chaise had set Bouchel to watch for the other two Jesuits outside and bring them to the gallery the moment they arrived.

The king's day, La Chaise had explained, rarely varied from its set schedule of private events and royal appearances, and there was little chance that this morning's appearance would be late. From being waked at half after seven and the succeeding ritual of the royal dressing, to the reverse ritual of undressing and retiring to bed at half after eleven at night, Louis was the center around whom everyone else's day revolved.

The palace clocks began to chime the quarter before ten. Beside Charles, La Chaise sighed with relief at the sight of a pair of three-cornered formal Jesuit hats called *bonnets* coming toward them, bobbing behind the footman Bouchel, who was cleaving the gathered courtiers like Moses in the Red Sea. As the footman delivered Le Picart and Montville, a hush fell and every head turned toward the door opening into the middle of the Galerie des Glaces. La Chaise drew his delegation a little forward to stand at the front of the crowd. In spite of himself, Charles felt his heart begin to speed. After all, he was about to see the king of France. He'd never seen a king, and quite apart from any personal feelings, the anointed king was the body of France itself.

Suddenly, the darkness stirred beyond the open door. France's fourteenth Louis let the doorway frame him for the length of a breath, stepped into the light arcing between the windows and the mirrors, and paced along the center of the Galerie. As Louis went, he raised his white-trimmed hat with its fashionably rolled brim to every lady. The mass of courtiers jammed between the royal pathway and the walls dipped like wheat in a wind, making their deepest bows and curtsies as he passed. Men—and a few women—darted forward and spoke quickly to him or placed small folded notes in his hand. Charles stared at the royal face as Louis drew nearer. Its expression of Olympian courtesy never varied. The man was more than merely regal, Charles thought, in unwilling admiration, he was regality's ideal, its pattern. Light flamed from his diamond shoe buckles and made his brown velvet coat shine like the pelt of a sleek beast. And then the king's dark blue-gray eyes were looking back at him. La Chaise nudged Charles, who removed his *bonnet* and deeply inclined his head, the protocol for clerics before their king, showing that they honored and served him, but bent the knee only to God.

Still looking down, Charles watched the shapely black-stockinged legs and red-heeled shoes pass along the glowing Savonnerie carpet. Then La Chaise shoved at Charles again, and he lifted his head and followed his companions into the royal train behind the king's almoner. The procession, lengthened every moment by courtiers falling in behind, made its way back through the long chain of rooms to the chapel, where most of the courtiers went down into the sumptuously gilded nave, but the king and his immediate train, including the Jesuits, took their places in the balcony. Louis knelt on his thickly cushioned

prie-dieu, set in front of a cushioned armchair, and his attendants stood in a semicircle behind him. Most had kneeling
cushions set ready for them on the floor, and out of the corner
of his eye, Charles saw that even these were pawns in the game
of grandeur. He watched as one shining square-toed shoe inched
its owner's cushion forward, closer to the king, and then a different shoe inched another cushion beyond it. Someone else
cleared his throat, and both cushions were inched back to where
they started.

The Mass began, celebrated by a Franciscan priest. The
heart-lifting musical setting was gloriously sung by a choir of
men and boys accompanied by violins and oboes, but instead of
losing himself in the liturgy as he usually did, Charles could not
stop drinking in the colors, the music, the rich fabric, and the
jewels of the crowd. Not to mention how the sunlight played
over all of it, since the chapel's windows, fittingly for a king who
likened himself to the sun, were mostly clear glass, in the new
fashion. And there in the midst of it, the Sun King—the man
who rode his charger over the dead and dying on the ceiling of
the Galerie des Glaces—was praying.

Which was more than Charles managed to do, and by the
time the Mass was ended, he was in a thoroughly bad humor
with himself. Feeling as though he'd been caught in a trap of
richness, he kept his eyes rigidly on his low-heeled, square-toed
black shoes as Louis left the chapel, and kept them there as he
waited with his fellow Jesuits for the royal attendants to sweep
through the door after the king. *Oh, for God's sake—and I do mean
that literally—can't you just enjoy the beauty?* the acid part of Charles's
mind said. *I* am *enjoying it,* Charles said even more acidly back,
that's the trouble. Oh, yes? the inner voice said. *What a very un-Jesuit
position to take. A very Jansenist position, in fact,* the voice taunted,
Jansenist Catholics being so austere that they rejected beauty

entirely, insisting that it distracted the soul from God. The voice went on needling him. *Jansenists say they love only what is ugly. Are you going to join them, then? Of course not,* Charles returned indignantly.

"And shut up!" He realized he'd said it out loud only when Jouvancy turned an outraged face on him.

Fortunately, La Chaise called their attention. "Come, we will get the reliquary, and then go to Madame de Maintenon's antechamber."

The five men hurried to La Chaise's chamber, where Charles fetched the reliquary while Le Picart and Montville washed the road's gritty dust from their faces and Jouvancy gave the reliquary's satin-smooth, carved box a last polishing. He started to hand it back to Charles to carry, stopped, told him to pull his white shirt cuffs another fraction of an inch below his cassock sleeves, barked at him to straighten his *bonnet*, put the box tenderly down on La Chaise's bed, hurried to the bowl of water still standing on a table, washed his spotless hands again, dried them, picked up the box, and finally handed it to Charles. With an amused glance at one another over Jouvancy's head, La Chaise and Le Picart and Montville got him out the door, followed by Charles with the box.

Madame de Maintenon lived on the south side of what had been Louis XIII's little royal hunting lodge. The placement of her rooms, nearer than anyone else's to the king's, made Charles wonder why there was any gossiping question at all about her status. When the Jesuits reached the guardroom that was the only access to her reception chamber, a large, impassive soldier barred their way. Charles found the Swiss Guard's ceremonial indoor uniform, in the fashion of his grandfather's time, slightly comical. Patterned in red, black, and white, it sported a starched white ruff, a padded doublet, and loose breeches gathered and fringed at the knee. But there was nothing comical about the pike in the soldier's white-gloved fist. It was a menacing weapon, taller than a tall man, with a steel ax head and a long, glittering spear point.

When the guard was satisfied that the Jesuits had reason to be there, he allowed them into Mme de Maintenon's antechamber. Bright with sun from its big south-facing window, the room was full of men and women, talking and shifting from one little group to another. Charles was startled to hear the word *poison* slipping in and out of their talk like a sibilant snake. He saw that Le Picart heard it, too, and watched him whisper a question to La Chaise.

Not everyone was gossiping, though. A few courtiers watched the door to the inner chamber like dogs watching a man with a leg of lamb, and more than a few looked merely bored, fanning themselves, fingering their jewelry, examining their lace or fingernails. Tapestries and gilt-framed religious paintings hung on the walls, and Charles could see himself in the shine of the parquet. It was as slick as a mirror, too, and when Charles sidestepped to avoid a glowering man striding out of the audience chamber, he skated into Jouvancy and nearly dropped the reliquary. Jouvancy yelped and grabbed it from him, holding the box to his chest as though it were a lady's frightened lapdog. Montville patted Jouvancy's arm, and Le Picart looked sternly at Charles.

"A man who dances as well as you do cannot keep his balance on two feet?"

"Not here, it seems, *mon père*," Charles murmured.

La Chaise drew them all to the side of the room, out of the path between the antechamber doors, and gave them a brief education in court ceremony.

"To my surprise, the king expressed a desire to be here," he began. "But early this morning he told me that he cannot leave his council meeting after all, since he returned from inspecting the fortifications at Luxembourg only on Saturday and there is much business to be done." La Chaise gave them a moment to murmur their disappointment and then took them through the steps of the ceremony, finishing with, "You, Père Jouvancy, will be flanked by Père Le Picart and Père Montville. I will stand to one side, and Maître du Luc will stand behind you with the box. When you finish your presentation speech, he will hand it to you. You will open its lid and hold it toward Madame de Maintenon, so that she can see the reliquary. When she has admired it and thanked you, someone, probably the Duc du Maine, will step forward and take the box from you. Then all of us will step back, make our *reverence* to her, turn, and leave the chamber. Not backward, remember, for the same reason that we do not remove our *bonnets* to her: she is not royalty."

The audience chamber's door opened and the crowd turned as one. A liveried footman nodded at Père La Chaise. Charles took the reliquary box from Jouvancy, who, with Le Picart and Montville, crossed the antechamber close behind La Chaise. Suddenly dry-mouthed and feeling his heart thud like any provincial's, Charles brought up the rear. With a mental shrug, he silenced the acid-tongued part of himself before it could comment and gave himself up to the experience. The footman spoke their names as they entered a large chamber that Charles registered only as a brief blur of color before La Chaise stopped halfway down the room and led them in their *révérence* to the woman who waited for them in a chair upholstered in yellow brocade. She wore a ribbon-edged, rose-embroidered black satin gown that covered her shoulders, with a filmy black scarf partly covering her abundant dark hair. Behind her, a dozen young courtiers and two brown-robed Franciscans stood in a rough semicircle, their eyes flicking from her to the Jesuits. Among them, Charles recognized the three young people he'd seen playing ball last evening in the courtyard: the king's eldest legitimized son, the Duc du Maine, his sister, Mademoiselle de Rouen, and the Condé child. Mademoiselle de Rouen's eyes swept dismissively over the Jesuits until they reached Charles. Then they widened, and she smiled and whispered something in the Duc du Maine's ear. Maine shook his head and hushed her, but she shrugged a round white shoulder at him and kept watching Charles.

Madame de Maintenon nodded to La Chaise, who stepped to the side, and Jouvancy led the other three in their approach to her. Clutching the box and walking carefully on the polished floor, Charles tried not to stare. He hadn't expected the king's secret wife to seem so youthful. She was more than fifty, but her round cheeks had natural-seeming color and her eyes were as large and dark as an Italian madonna's. They were also full of a cool, assessing intelligence as she watched the Jesuits.

The three in front halted, Charles hovering a step behind Jouvancy's right shoulder, and they all bowed their heads to her again. As he raised his eyes, Charles realized from her expression—or lack of it—that she was simply waiting for this to be over. Jouvancy made his short, perfectly composed presentation speech, claiming Madame de Maintenon as a fellow educator and praising her school for young noblewomen, flattering the king's children she'd raised, and reminding her briefly and delicately in the course of it all that they were kin (which brought, if anything, more frost into the atmosphere, Charles thought). Then Charles handed Jouvancy the box, and Jouvancy held it toward Madame de Maintenon, open like a book to show the reliquary. Her face thawed into a slight smile as she gazed at it. She nodded graciously and crossed herself, everyone else doing likewise. Then she made a brief response, praising the beauty and holiness of the gift and commending the young people present to the protection of St. Ursula. Dragging his lame leg, the Duc du Maine stepped forward and courteously took the box from Jouvancy. La Chaise added graceful thanks for the honor the lady had done them in receiving their gift. Madame de Maintenon listened politely and then, at her gesture of dismissal, the Jesuits made their exit.

"Well," Jouvancy said, with a shaky sigh, when they were through the door and back in the antechamber. "Thank the Blessed Virgin that's over!"

His words raised a ripple of laughter among the waiting courtiers as the Jesuits started toward the guardroom and the stairway. Behind them, the reception chamber's door opened and closed again and a light voice said, "I beg your pardon, *mes pères*." A young man in rich black velvet and a beautifully curled dark wig passed them hurriedly. He looked back, smiling, his smooth face unmistakably Bourbon. "Very prettily done in there, if I may say so." Sudden mockery flashed from his eyes. "But you'll need more than a virgin's little finger to touch that lady's heart."

That brought a louder and harsher ripple of laughter from the courtiers, which made Charles stand solidly on both feet, stifling an urge to trip the man as he swept from the room. The sudden harsh clash of weapons made Jouvancy startle and gasp, but La Chaise said, "It's only the Swiss; they always present arms to a Prince of the Blood. Come."

"And which Prince was that?" Jouvancy said indignantly, when they were on the stairs and out of anyone's hearing.

"His Serene Highness, the Prince of Conti," Le Picart replied noncommittally, exchanging knowing looks with La Chaise and Montville.

So, Charles thought, running an appreciative hand along the stair's yellow-veined marble balustrade, that was the man the police chief La Reynie had asked about as Charles rode out of Paris. Charles tried unsuccessfully to place this Prince of the Blood in the Bourbon family. Conti, Condé, too many branches, too many royal sprigs to keep track of.

"The Contis are a younger branch of the Condés," Jouvancy said, seeing Charles's confused frown. "And no better mannered, either, as you saw." He looked up at La Chaise, walking beside him. "Do you think we will see the king again before we leave?"

"His first *valet de chambre* told me earlier that tomorrow morning he receives the envoys from Poland, coming to negotiate Mademoiselle de Rouen's betrothal agreements. If you are still here, you can be present with the court for that."

Jouvancy looked hopefully at Le Picart, who smiled indulgently at him.

"I think we can stay for that. After all, we have schools in Poland."

Montville nodded his pleased agreement and Charles admitted grudgingly to himself that he, too, would like to see such a ceremony.

"How many *valets de chambre* does the king have?" Montville asked curiously.

"Only one sleeps in his room at night," La Chaise said. "But there are household officers without number, from dukes to little Parisian barbers who have bought some minor post." The king's confessor sighed. "I must say, I had the unhappy feeling in the audience chamber that we still rank somewhere below the barbers."

The others commiserated ruefully and Jouvancy said, "Our gift isn't going to help much, is it?"

"I think," Le Picart said judicially, "that it will weigh in our favor. The lady is reputed to be more often just than warm. Is that not so, Père La Chaise?"

"On the whole, yes."

Le Picart smiled and shrugged. "Let us trust, then, to her sense of fair play and believe that our little occasion went off well enough."

"And we did have a goodly gathering of witnesses," La Chaise said. "So let us leave it in God's hands and turn to happier things. Such as dinner at the Duc de La Rochefoucauld's Table of Honor."

His companions' faces brightened, and they followed him gladly through more of the palace corridors. When at last they reached the north wing's garden front, the opposite side of the building from La Chaise's modest chamber, they found the gallery thronged with richly dressed men and women making their way into La Rochefoucauld's rooms. Charles tried not to stare at the women. Tall headdresses, confections of ribbon, lace, and starched linen, waved above discreetly padded puffs of hair and curls like bunches of grapes, and scarves like woven air fluttered on their bare shoulders. The men's gold-embroidered waistcoats glittered beneath open black coats, their sticks tapped, and their dark velvet and wool coat skirts hung nearly to their knees. Precedence—the prescribed order of entrance by rank—was taken, given, and rearranged with narrowed eyes and coldly honeyed words.

The Jesuits' turn finally came to greet their host. Francois

VII, Duc de La Rochefoucauld and grand master of the king's wardrobe, was an urbane, tired-looking man who passed the Jesuits on to a footman, who seated them at the large horseshoe-shaped table draped in white linen. When all twenty or so guests were seated, La Rochefoucauld took his place at the table's center and invited La Chaise to return thanks, and the meal began. After a pigeon bisque so delicious that Charles wanted to find the kitchen and sing an aria to the cook, they began on roast chicken with olive sauce, served on silver plates. Charles was savoring the sauce, which reminded him of his home in the south, when his neighbor on the left said into his ear, "You saw him fall, I believe?"

"I beg your pardon, *monsieur*," Charles said in surprise. "Saw whom?"

"Fleury. Last evening." The small spare man in tobacco-brown velvet eyed Charles sardonically from under his double-peaked wig. "How many men have you seen fall downstairs since you arrived?"

"Only the one," Charles admitted with a smile. "I have not the pleasure of your acquaintance, *monsieur*."

"Forgive me, everyone here knows everyone. I did not mean to be rude. I am the Comte de Vannes. I guessed who you were, Maître du Luc, the moment I heard your name. And your Languedoc accent. My father met yours long ago, when the court was at the Louvre. My unhappy father was in love with your mother, and you look very like his description of her. I think he still mourns that your father won her away from him. She was wondrously blond, he said, with conversation that sparkled like a diamond."

"She's no longer blond," Charles said, storing up the compliment to tell his mother, "but her conversation sparkles still."

"I will tell my father. Or perhaps I won't, poor man." He

lifted an eyebrow at Charles. "So, tell me. *Did* you see old Fleury fall?"

"No, *monsieur*. I only heard him. By the time I reached him in the corridor, I saw only that his neck was broken."

"A nice diversion from the fact that someone gave him his *bouillon*."

"I—what? I don't understand. You mean he didn't make his own?"

The Comte de Vannes bayed with laughter. "Forgive me— you are from the south and perhaps you don't have this saying there. 'Giving someone his *bouillon*' is what we say to mean someone's been poisoned."

Remembering the whispers about poison in Madame de Maintenon's antechamber, Charles studied Vannes's face to see if he was serious and decided he was. "But why should people think Fleury was poisoned? He was sick, certainly. But there is a sickness in Paris now that takes people just that way. Half the staff at Louis le Grand have been struck down by it. Isn't it more likely that the man was simply ill?"

"It might have been, had the Comte de Fleury not annoyed so many people." Vannes applied himself to his chicken for a moment. "I understand that they're doing an autopsy tonight, so perhaps that will settle the question. The king, of course, wants the rumors of poison stopped." He smiled. "Or confirmed." With a courteous nod signaling the conversation's end, Vannes turned to the woman on his other side.

Charles glanced over his shoulder and gestured for something to drink from the serving men stationed along the wall, where glasses and wine waited on a sideboard. A serving man handed Charles a glass of red wine, and he drank. His eyes widened and he drank again, sighed with pleasure, and gazed into his glass as though he'd never seen wine before. As, by comparison, he hadn't, he thought wryly, at least not lately, college wine being mostly poor quality to start with and well watered. Beside him, Jouvancy put his glass down on the spotless cloth, and Charles turned to make an appreciative comment about the wine. But Jouvancy spoke first.

"Help me out of here, *maître*," he whispered, "before I disgrace myself." His face was white and sheened with sweat, and the words were barely out of his mouth before he clapped both hands to his mouth and pushed his chair back with his feet.

Chapter 5

Charles sprang up, fracturing the table conversation to silence. Before the others could voice their bewildered outrage at his discourtesy, he pulled Père Jouvancy upright and half carried him toward the outer door. Behind him, La Chaise apologized on their behalf for the disturbance, and Charles heard footsteps following him. A servant touched his arm and guided them into an alcove, pointing to the chair-like closestool standing ready near the wall. The servant hurried to open its lid and Jouvancy tottered toward it. Charles held the little priest's head while the worst happened.

"Dear Blessed Virgin, so ill again?" Le Picart said from the door, and Charles glanced up to see Montville's equally worried face peering over the rector's shoulder. "We will help you get him to his bed."

"Tell the servant to bring a wet cloth, if you will," Charles said, trying to ignore the weak-kneed feeling Jouvancy's spewing was giving him.

He pulled Jouvancy gently upright, sat him down on a chair Le Picart pushed forward, and took the cool wet cloth from the arriving servant and wiped the rhetoric master's face. Jouvancy's eyes were wide with terror.

"I heard what the Comte de Vannes said to you," he whispered. "Poison! First that old man and now me!"

"No, no," Charles said robustly, "this is just your sickness come back because you've pushed yourself too far, with the riding yesterday and today's business. We'll go to our chamber and you can sleep. You'll be better after that. And then we'll—"

"What is it?" La Chaise said, coming into the room behind them. "What's wrong with him?"

"Poison, *mon père*," Jouvancy moaned dramatically. "It must be! I felt very well before we sat down to eat, and now I'm poisoned, too. Don't eat anything else here, I beg you, or we will all—"

"Hush!" La Chaise stood over Jouvancy, his face dark with anger and something else Charles couldn't name. "You're raving, *mon père*. In God's name, be quiet!"

Charles put a hand on Jouvancy's forehead. "He's fevered. So he's most likely not poisoned, only ill again. We must get him back to our chamber."

Instead of answering, the other three Jesuits conferred for a moment.

"Can you manage alone, *maître*? In courtesy, the rest of us should stay and finish our meal. I will explain that Père Jouvancy has simply had a return of his illness," La Chaise said, ignoring Jouvancy's protests. "Go now, the less fuss, the better. Follow the corridor around to your right. We will come when dinner is over."

With last worried looks at Jouvancy, La Chaise, Le Picart, and Montville went back to the *salon* and the loud, excited buzz of talk around the table.

Swallowing hard and telling himself he was perfectly well, Charles helped Jouvancy stand, put his *bonnet* back on his head, and walked him out of La Rochefoucauld's rooms into the corridor. The passage was blessedly empty, since most everyone was at dinner.

"Walk as best you can, *mon père*," Charles said. "But if it comes to it, I can carry you." Though he hoped it wouldn't, for the sake of his own oddly weak knees, as well as to lessen the gossip about Jouvancy's sudden indisposition in case anyone saw them. Of course, as soon as he'd thought that, two men turned the corner ahead of them, walking in their direction.

"What's the trouble?" one said, taking in the two Jesuits in surprise.

The other grinned. "Too much indulgence at dinner, I see."

"He's ill," Charles snapped, adding, "It's contagious, I think," for the satisfaction of seeing them scuttle away.

Jouvancy was too short to rest an arm over Charles's shoulder, and by the time they were making their way along the north side of the wing, the rhetoric master was limp, his feet barely shuffling. With a sigh, Charles picked him up in his arms like a child. Jouvancy's head lolled against Charles's shoulder and his eyes closed.

Peering anxiously at the rhetoric master's deathly pale face and closed eyes, Charles muttered anxiously, "Don't lose consciousness, *mon père*, please!"

"I haven't," Jouvancy quavered, opening one eye, "but I would like to."

With a relieved snort of laughter, Charles turned the corner of the gallery, where their chamber door was finally in sight. He edged through it and across the anteroom and laid Jouvancy carefully on the green-curtained bed. He removed the priest's *bonnet*, untied the sash of his cassock and pulled off his shoes, and covered him with the green silk coverlet. Then he stood wondering what else to do.

"Do you want a doctor, *mon père*?"

"You're supposed to take care of me," Jouvancy said faintly.

"Yes, but my experience is with battle wounds," Charles replied. "If someone shoots you or runs you through with a sword, I can help you. But they haven't."

"Such a pity," Jouvancy returned, trying to laugh.

Charles saw that he was starting to shiver and pulled a blanket over the coverlet. "Try to sleep a little, *mon père*. I will be here beside you, if you need me."

Jouvancy sighed and turned his head into the pillow. Charles went into La Chaise's chamber for the stool. When he came back, Jouvancy was asleep. Charles watched him carefully, trying to remember what he'd looked like the day he'd fallen ill at the end of the rhetoric class. Pale, he remembered that. And weak. And spewing. But he hadn't been so fevered as he seemed now. Charles went back to La Chaise's chamber and rummaged in the cupboard for a towel. Then he emptied the old basin of water out the window into the courtyard and refilled it from the copper reservoir. Sitting on the stool with the basin in his lap, he prayed steadily as he wiped Jouvancy's flushed face every few minutes to cool him. When the others returned, the rhetoric master was still fevered.

"*Mes pères*, I think he needs a doctor," Charles said, looking up at them from the stool.

"Do you? But he isn't as ill as he was at the college," Le Picart said, looking anxiously at Jouvancy. "This was probably brought on by too much exertion, as you said earlier. I blame myself—I should have waited longer before sending him here."

"He is still very weak," Charles said. "I realized yesterday as we traveled that he was weaker than I'd thought. That's why—"

"Oh, rest will probably cure him," Montville said comfortably. "We must just let him sleep and feed him nourishing broth when he wakes. Isn't that what Frère Brunet does?"

"Plus his medicines," Le Picart said.

"Yes, medicines." Charles was trying to curb his impatience. "I think Père Jouvancy needs them. Which is why he needs a doctor."

That got him surprised looks for his flat lack of deference.

"A court doctor will bleed him," La Chaise said, and Charles realized that till now he'd said nothing. "That will make him weaker."

Montville turned shocked eyes on La Chaise. "Don't you believe in bleeding, *mon père*? It's the soul of medicine! It will rid him of whatever is making him sick."

"Or whatever has poisoned him," La Chaise said grimly. "Do you know where the Comte de Fleury ate his dinner yesterday? At the table of the Duc de La Rochefoucauld."

Le Picart frowned. "Fleury? Oh, yes, the poor man you told us about, who fell downstairs yesterday." He shook his head at La Chaise. "But what you say is absurd. Who would want to poison Père Jouvancy? He hasn't been at court since before he joined the Society."

La Chaise simply looked at his companions one by one. Charles felt himself go cold, because he saw fear in La Chaise's eyes.

"How do you feel, *mes pères*?" he said softly. "And you, Maître du Luc?"

No one spoke. Charles was sure the others were checking their bodies' feelings as carefully as he was.

"Père Le Picart, Père Montville, come with me," La Chaise said. "I will show you where you will stay tonight." He looked at Charles. "And then I will bring a doctor. Just know that gossip will spread like fire through the palace, true or not, if a doctor comes."

The three priests went out through the antechamber, and the gallery door shut heavily behind them. In the quiet they left behind, Charles breathed deeply and tried to get hold of himself. Jouvancy was still sleeping. At least, he looked as though he were sleeping . . . Charles bent over him, listened to his breathing, and straightened, reassured. But as he straightened, his stomach roiled and sweat broke out on his face. He got up and walked to the window. *Why would anyone poison* me? he thought, feeling his bowels go watery with fear. *I'm no one, I know no one, I just got here. And I'm not ill, it's just seeing Père Jouvancy like this. And the travel, the strain of being here, the*—he cast about for something for it to be. *The water,* he told himself, *water often causes stomach upset, I'm used to Paris water now.* The familiar acerbic voice in him said back, *So you're used to water straight out of the Seine, but the water here has undone you?* Charles went to the copper fountain in the anteroom, thinking that a drink would help settle his insides. But he put the glass down untasted. If someone *had* poisoned them, the poison might be in the fountain. He picked up the glass again and held it to the light beginning to stream through the west-facing window.

As he looked into the innocently clear water, his fear conjured the face of Madame de Maintenon, her deceptively madonna-like eyes gazing coolly at him. The king's wife might dislike Jesuits, but surely not to the point of poisoning them. *Oh, no?* the acid-tongued voice said. *Have you never heard of queens ridding themselves of inconvenient people? Not by their own hands, of course . . .* The door opened behind him, and he turned so quickly that he dropped the glass, which shattered and sprayed water everywhere.

"*Maître?* Forgive me, I didn't mean to scare you." The footman Bouchel stood in the doorway to the antechamber, carrying two wooden buckets and looking in bewilderment from Charles to the glass shards and water on the parquet.

"I—I was—yes, never mind." Charles looked over his shoulder and saw, to his relief, that Jouvancy still slept.

"I'll clean that up, *maître*, after I fill the fountain."

Bouchel turned back into the antechamber and Charles heard him set down the buckets and take the cover off the copper reservoir. Water gushed as both buckets were emptied into it, and then the cover clanged shut. Bouchel reappeared with a towel over his hand and went toward the bed.

Charles's body acted without his brain's cooperation and he launched himself toward the bed and stood at bay between Bouchel and Jouvancy. The footman's brown eyes opened wide, and he kept one eye on Charles as he picked up glass and put it carefully on the towel. Then Jouvancy roused, retching direly, and for the next few minutes Charles was miserably busy, grateful for the footman's bringing basins and towels, and even more grateful for his taking them away when they'd been used.

Finally, Jouvancy lay spent, breathless and whiter than the bedsheets, and Bouchel left with the last basin. "Thank you," the little priest whispered, looking up at Charles. His fingers closed around Charles's wrist with surprising strength. "It's poison—I'm sure of it!"

"Of course it's not poison," Charles said vehemently, in spite of his doubts. "It's surely only a return of your sickness. You'll be better soon, *mon père*."

Jouvancy shook his head, and his anxious eyes wandered over the room. "Where is Père La Chaise?"

"He went to find a doctor."

"Good." Jouvancy's fingers dug deeper into Charles's sleeve. "I didn't think she hated us that much."

Before Charles could decide what to say to that, La Chaise

came in, followed by a slender, grave-faced man in a long black wig and a black and scarlet coat. A short, round assistant followed, carrying the implements for bleeding a patient: a wide basin, a glittering steel lancet, and a sturdy piece of cord.

"This is Monsieur Neuville, one of the king's physicians," La Chaise said, and drew back. The doctor nodded slightly at Charles and went to the bedside. The rhetoric master let go of Charles and reached for the doctor, who drew himself back and out of reach.

"Urine, *mon père?*" he said abruptly to Jouvancy.

Jouvancy eyed him sourly. "I doubt there's anything left in me to make water with, *monsieur.*"

The doctor grunted and held out his hand to the assistant with the basin. The man handed him the cord, Charles brought a chair from La Chaise's chamber, and the doctor sat down beside the bed.

"Have you been bled this spring?" Neuville asked, tying the stout cord tightly around Jouvancy's upper arm. When the rhetoric master shook his head, the doctor said, "Then we'll hope that's your trouble." He picked up the lancet. "Though I doubt it."

"He's been very ill, *monsieur,*" Charles put in, "with the sickness we've had in Paris these last weeks. I think the effort of riding from town brought on a relapse."

Neuville ignored that, and Charles turned away as the rhetoric master's blood spurted from an incision near his elbow into the basin the servant held. Charles wondered if he had caught Jouvancy's sickness. He was usually unfazed by blood, but now his stomach was climbing toward his throat. Muttering his excuses, he fled toward the privy.

As he returned, weak but eased, the footman passed him in

the antechamber with the basin full of Jouvancy's blood. Charles held the door for him and then stopped to wipe his face with a wet towel lying on the water reservoir. Neuville and La Chaise were talking in the chamber.

"I doubt this will be enough," he heard the doctor say.

Charles threw down the towel and hurried into the chamber. "Why not, *monsieur*?"

Both men frowned at his interruption.

"Because this isn't sickness," Neuville said. He looked over his shoulder and lowered his voice. "I saw them," he hissed. "Saw *her*—deep in talk with the Duc de La Rochefoucauld. That was the day before yesterday. Yesterday Monsieur Fleury ate at La Rochefoucauld's table. And died. Today you Jesuits ate at his table. And at least two of you are ill."

"Not two," Charles said, "only Père—"

"No? You just returned from spewing in the privy."

La Chaise looked at Charles in surprise. "Did you?"

"Yes, *mon père*, but I am not ill. Only a little unsettled. And I learned from the footman Bouchel that the floor outside Fleury's room was wet from a ceiling leak. Which is probably why he fell."

"And which has nothing to do with why he was ill to begin with. You should both be bled," Neuville said grimly. "Now. Before the poison takes more hold. And the other two as well. Where are they?"

"I am not in the least ill, and neither are our other companions," La Chaise snapped. "You overreach yourself, *monsieur*."

"Then why did you come for me? You know it is poison, and you know you will be ill." Charles heard more than a little satisfaction in the doctor's tone. "And then perhaps you'll come to your senses and let me bleed you before it's too late." Neuville's scarlet embroidery rippled and glowed in the afternoon sunlight as he bowed to La Chaise. "Because she really does hate you."

Neuville withdrew, the assistant marching behind him, and left La Chaise and Charles staring in horror at each other.

"He's obsessed with poison. Like everyone else here," La Chaise said, seeming to have forgotten his own earlier fears.

"But you thought it might be poison, too, *mon père.*"

La Chaise sighed gustily. "I did. It's the normal thing to fear here. But fear clouds reason, and aside from where we ate, there's no connection at all between us and the Comte de Fleury. Why poison any of us?" But La Chaise's worried face belied his words. "I am going to pray that the man was only ill with this stomach sickness Jouvancy and so many have had, and that he met with an unfortunate—unrelated—accident." La Chaise crossed his arms and stared at Charles as though daring him to contradict. "But until we know what the truth is, we'll eat only what the footman brings and what we cook at my fire."

Moans from the curtained bed put an urgent end to their talk. The hours that followed had the evil tinge of nightmare, as the doctor's predictions that the bleeding wasn't enough began coming all too true. La Chaise sent for extra chamber pots, and for Le Picart and Montville, who helped lift and sponge Jouvancy. By the time the rhetoric master slept again, it was nearly dark. La Chaise's face had gone from pale to green-tinged, but he insisted that he and Charles could manage and sent Le Picart and Montville to supper in one of the Grand Commons refectories across the road. Almost as soon as they left, La Chaise clapped his hand over his mouth and vanished into the gallery.

By midnight, La Chaise had been sick half a dozen times, as had Charles, who was vying with him for the privy's use. Between sprints down the gallery, Charles asked if they should send for Neuville again.

"He'd probably give us the antimony cup, and our purging is already hellishly efficient. At least mine is. And he'd bleed us. Is your stomach up to watching your own blood run? Mine is most certainly not." He pushed hastily past Charles to the chamber's outer door.

"At least there would be a basin handy," Charles muttered, and tottered to the other chamber to collapse on his bed in the narrow alcove.

He woke, feeling better, what seemed like hours later. A single candle flickered somewhere in the room. Holding his breath, he listened, but there was no sound from Jouvancy or from La Chaise next door. A candle was burning on the table near Jouvancy's bed, and the bed curtains were drawn. Charles got weakly to his feet and parted the bed curtains, holding the candle so he could see the rhetoric master's face. Jouvancy was deeply asleep, pale, but no more so than he had been. With a relieved prayer of thanks, Charles let the curtains fall closed. His nose wrinkled at the stench of sickness hanging in the air and he longed to open the window, but everyone knew that night air was dangerous for the sick. Carrying the candle, he padded to the outer door and was pushing it open to let a little air in, when a light flared to his left and startled him. The corridor's only permanent light was a single sconce beside the privy, but this light was growing brighter as someone came down the stairs, too bright for a candle.

Charles saw the unsteady flame of a small wax torch, then the hand that held it and the arm, and then the Duc du Maine came quietly onto the staircase landing from the floor above, his limp making the torch jump and waver in his hand. Charles slid back out of sight but kept the door open a crack, wondering why the king's son was creeping around the palace, and apparently alone, in the dead of night. And what he'd been doing upstairs, where the dead Comte de Fleury's chamber was. As Maine passed him, Charles saw that he had something in his free hand that gleamed when the torchlight caught it. Charles stretched his neck to see what it was, tipped his candle, and grunted in pain as hot wax splashed onto his hand. The Duc du Maine spun toward him.

"Who's there?" the boy demanded harshly. But his face showed fright, not anger, in the wavering torchlight, and he put the hand holding the gleaming thing behind his back.

Charles stepped forward into the gallery. "I beg your pardon, Your Highness. I was opening the door for a little air. Forgive me for startling you."

Maine peered uncertainly at him. "Oh. It's you—you carried the reliquary today. Or yesterday, now, I suppose."

"Yes, I am Maître Charles du Luc, from the College of Louis le Grand. You did us the honor of coming to our performance back in the winter."

Maine's smile transformed his thin, tense face, but his carefully rigid stance didn't soften. "It was very good. I liked the singing and the dancing more than the Latin tragedy. But don't tell Madame de Maintenon! And your little Italian boy is an astonishing dancer. I wish we had him here and could have ballets like the king had when he was young."

"You don't have many ballets now, it seems."

The boy shook his head regretfully. "Not that I could dance in them, even if we did." He gestured shyly at his lame leg. "But I love to watch dancing. My father no longer cares so much for ballets. Nor does Madame de Maintenon. And I doubt there will be much dancing when Louis—the Dauphin, I mean—becomes king in his turn. Though he's the legitimately born son, he has nothing of our father's talent for dancing." He sighed. "It must be terrible to be old."

Charles couldn't help laughing. "I hope not, since, with God's help, we will both be old someday."

Maine laughed a little, but his face was pale and sweat stood on his forehead.

"Are you feeling ill, Your Highness?"

"Oh. No. That is—perhaps a little."

"I hope you will not take this sickness we're having."

"Oh. No. I'm never ill. Just lame."

"That is surely enough to bear." Charles smiled sympathetically. "I have heard that Madame de Maintenon tried everything to cure you when you were little."

"Oh, she did, she's the very best woman in the world! She's been more than a mother to me. To my brother and sisters, too, but especially to me. I owe her everything."

Smiling mechanically, Charles asked himself what he'd expected to hear. Of course the boy wouldn't say that his beloved governess poisoned people. He nodded toward the staircase. "Did you know the man who fell down those stairs yesterday?"

The boy's head whipped around and he looked at the stairs as though he'd never seen them before. "I—yes—of course, everyone knew Fleury."

"Had he been ill?"

"I don't know. I mean, he wasn't earlier in the day."

Charles smiled. "Ah, yes, I remember now that I did hear that. Were there signs of sickness in his room?"

"Yes, it was—" The boy froze, seeing the trap too late.

Charles nodded amiably at Maine's right arm and the hand behind his back. "Whatever you went to his room to get, I see that you found it."

The boy's slender shoulders rose and fell, but even as he sighed, his carriage remained as upright as that of the dancers he envied. "I'm a terrible liar. I told her she should send someone else."

Her? Madame de Maintenon? However bad a liar Maine was, Charles guessed that he would not name whoever had sent him to Fleury's room. "Being a bad liar is an admirable trait," Charles said mildly. *Which you yourself unfortunately do not have*, his inner voice murmured. "Forgive me if I seem curious," Charles went on. "I asked about Fleury's room because my superior has fallen ill, and I am wondering if the unfortunate Comte de Fleury might suddenly have taken the sickness we've been having in Paris. I hear it's very catching." Which was at least within sight of the truth.

Maine grimaced. "Yes, well, his room stinks of sickness. I could hardly make myself stay long enough to find this. Since you already know I was there, I should tell you why. So you won't think me a thief." He took his hand from behind his back and held out a small, elaborately chased silver box. "Finding it took time, because it was under a loose piece of the floor. It's my sister's. Lulu's, her tobacco box. She threw it at the Comte de Fleury one day when he found her smoking her little pipe in the garden. The old wretch kept it."

Which might explain what Charles had seen in the courtyard, the girl so angry at Fleury and flinging gravel in his face on the afternoon he'd died. Keeping the box certainly sounded like Fleury. In the army, no way to squeeze an extra penny out of some miserable soul and enrich himself had been too petty for the man. But—smoking? The king's daughter? The more Charles heard about Lulu, the more he understood why the king was sending her so far away.

"Well, it's good that Fleury's chamber was unlocked so you could get her box. I assume it was unlocked?"

Maine nodded, not really listening now, and looked over his shoulder. "I've been a long time about my errand, *maître*. She's waiting for me, I must go. A *bonne nuit* to you."

Charles gave Maine a respectful nod. As he watched the boy limp hurriedly toward the royal heart of the palace, he wondered why Maine could not simply have said the box was his and he'd lent it—or some such story to protect his sister—and sent a servant to fetch it in the light of day. Charles turned his gaze thoughtfully to the stairs.

When Maine's footsteps had faded beyond hearing, Charles left La Chaise's rooms and went soundlessly along the gallery and up to the top floor. Not even a wall sconce lit that corridor. He stopped at the top of the stairs and looked toward the sound of water dripping. Then he bent and held his candle near the floor. The black-and-white tiles glistened wetly. A tiny trickle of water was running from the big iron pot set to catch the ceiling drip. Stepping carefully, he went farther from the stairs and held his candle up, peering in both directions and hoping that Maine had left Fleury's door ajar. Charles turned to his right, studying the doors as he passed them until one opened nearly in his face and the physician Neuville came out.

"What are you doing here, Maître du Luc?"

"Is this your chamber?" Charles returned, rummaging through his mind for a reason to be where he was.

"No. What are you doing up here?"

"I was hoping to find the—um—*convenience* on this floor. The one below is occupied. Has someone else fallen ill?"

"No. And there isn't a convenience up here. Not any longer. So you've fallen ill, as I predicted."

"As you predicted, but I'm feeling better."

"And the others? Is Père La Chaise ill now, as well?"

"He was, but not as ill as Père Jouvancy. They're both sleeping now, and I'm sure it's just the common illness people have been having lately."

Neuville shook his head sadly. "The stubborn often die from their refusal to take medical advice. Surely you know that poison affects different people very differently."

"So does illness."

"Of course it does. The courses of illness and poisoning go according to the balance of men's humors."

Charles couldn't resist saying, "And according to the stars?" He found it impossible to believe that the stars had any interest in the state of his stomach. But Neuville didn't seem to hear his mockery.

"Of course. To some extent." The physician preened himself a little, lifting a hand to flip the long curls of his black wig over his shoulder. The candlelight showed that his hand was covered with dark stains.

Startled, Charles said, "Is that blood? Have you hurt yourself?"

Neuville glanced at his hand and held it out to Charles. "Yes, it's blood, but it's the Comte de Fleury's. I've just now come from his autopsy. I and the king's other physicians opened him together. And before you ask again, this is his room. I wanted to see if there were signs of how ill he'd been before he tried to go downstairs."

"I see," Charles said, wondering why the doctor had waited

till now to look for signs of sickness. And thinking that the Duc du Maine had been lucky to leave Fleury's room when he did. "And what did the autopsy show?"

"His liver was shriveled and dark. No question about it, the man died of poison."

Chapter 6

THE FEAST OF ST. BARNABÉ, WEDNESDAY, JUNE 11, 1687

"No, I tell you!" Père Jouvancy flailed an arm at the metal cup Monsieur Neuville was holding out to him, and the physician drew it quickly out of range. "I won't drink *antimoine*! I have *already* been poisoned. You only want my poor body to practice on for your autopsies! Oh, yes, Maître du Luc told us how you cut that poor soul to ribbons in the dead of night. What will happen to him at the resurrection of the body? *That* will be charged to you, and you'd better think on it!" He turned his fever-bright eyes on Père La Chaise. "Why are you letting this man torment me, *mon père*? You and Maître du Luc have already refused his cup yourselves!"

Seething with offense, Neuville looked accusingly from Père La Chaise to Charles, and then at Le Picart and Montville, who stood on the other side of the bed. The doctor's portly little shadow of an attendant did the same, his double chin quivering with indignation.

La Chaise, pasty-faced from his bad night, cast his eyes up. "*Mon père*," he said, his voice ragged with trying for patience, "I cannot afford to take a purge this morning. The king has commanded our Jesuit presence at the Polish envoys' arrival this morning. No, no, don't fret, he knows you are ill and holds you excused. Therefore, since we have been told that the Comte de Fleury was poisoned, and since you were the sickest of us last night, I strongly advise you to do as this good physician counsels you. The most learned doctors at the University of Paris agree that wine steeped in the antimony cup is the surest way to rid your body of unbalanced humors and—anything hurtful and alien."

Jouvancy shook his head frantically against the pillow. "But that cup is made of *antimoine*, don't you understand? The metal's very name means anti-*monk*! It works against the bodily substance of monastics and kills us; that's been known since time out of mind!"

Le Picart laid his hand on Jouvancy's shoulder. "It can't hurt you just because you're a Jesuit. *Antimoine* does not mean anti-*moine*—anti-monk—that's an old tale." Le Picart eyed the doctor. "But it's dangerous. To people of *all* conditions, so I've heard."

"Say no more." The red-faced Neuville waved a dismissive hand. "If he dies from poisoning, the consequences of your refusal will fall on you, on all of you, not on me." He handed the antimony cup to his attendant, who received it as though it were a sacred offering. "I tell you Fleury's liver was as black as a demon after eating at the Duc de La Rochefoucauld's table. Where all five of you ate yesterday. And three of you were sickened." He glared at Le Picart and Montville, who had experienced no illness at all. "Sometimes poison works very slowly."

"But none of *us* are dead," Charles said mildly.

"Not yet," Neuville said through his teeth, with, to Charles's ear, a tinge of regret.

The three priests leaned over Jouvancy, trying to soothe him. Neuville swept out of the room and the attendant waddled after him, his russet coat skirts swinging like a goose's tail feathers.

As the door shut, La Chaise looked up in relief and escaped into his own chamber.

Le Picart came to join Charles. "Are you well enough to go on seeing to Père Jouvancy?" he asked.

"Yes, *mon père*. Only a little tired."

Montville pulled the bed curtains shut. "Père Jouvancy has fallen into a doze. Nothing like a nap for putting everything right." He smiled regretfully at Le Picart. "I would advise a nice preventive nap for all of us this afternoon, if you and I were staying, *mon père*."

"You're leaving?" Charles said in surprise. "But I thought you wanted to see the Polish ambassadors."

"We did," Le Picart said. "But a messenger arrived from the college when we'd hardly risen. The argument over our water supply that delayed us now calls us back early. If we are to stop our neighbor going to court, we must start back as soon as we can find a carriage." He beckoned Charles away from the bed. "Père Jouvancy certainly cannot travel yet," he said softly, "and you must stay with him till he's better. Only a day or two, I hope. If it begins to be more than that, send me word. Otherwise, I leave him in your care. And a doctor's, if need be." He grimaced. "There are certainly other court physicians besides Neuville."

"I will do my best, *mon père*." Charles sighed inwardly. Staying at Versailles was the last thing he wanted.

The two priests took their leave and went into La Chaise's chamber. Charles heard them explaining their departure, and then heard the gallery door open and close as La Chaise took them down to the court to find a coach. Charles settled again on the stool beside Jouvancy's bed.

"Is he gone?" Jouvancy whispered, suddenly waking and opening his eyes. "That doctor?"

"He is. No more need to worry. What you need now is rest. Père Le Picart and Père Montville have gone back to town, but you and I will stay here until you're ready to travel."

"I hate to stay," Jouvancy said weakly. "We have so much to do before our tragedy and ballet rehearsals begin. But I cannot ride." His face grew even more worried. "We could hire a carriage, but the motion—though I suppose I could manage it. If I must," he added plaintively.

"No need at all. Hush now."

Half unconsciously, Charles began to hum an old Provençal song, a lullaby his mother used to sing. It soothed him as well as Jouvancy, and even after the priest was sleeping, Charles went on singing, rocking a little on his stool until he, too, closed his eyes. La Chaise's soft laughter woke him. He'd slipped sideways from the stool, his head resting on Jouvancy's covers, and he struggled to his feet, momentarily not quite certain where he was.

"Oh. Ah. I—forgive me, *mon père*, I must have—"

"No need to apologize. He still sleeps?" La Chaise moved nearer the bed and peered at Jouvancy. "Good." He sighed and looked at Charles. "I have come to remind you that we are to attend the Polish ambassadors' arrival."

"Oh." Charles's heart sank. "I had forgotten."

"It is nearly time. I will wait in my chamber."

Charles untied the towel he'd put around his waist to protect his clothes, went into the anteroom and splashed water on his face, drew his fingers through his thick curling hair, and adjusted his cassock's sash. Not daring even to look at his bed because he wanted so badly to lie down on it, he presented himself before La Chaise. The king's confessor took a small, one-handed watch, shaped like a skull, from a pocket under his cassock and peered at it. As he put it back, a shout rose in the gallery and Bouchel scratched at the door, calling hoarsely, "Time, *mon père.*"

La Chaise heaved himself to his feet. "The Introducer's carriage is in sight. We must go."

Charles put out a hand. "I don't think we should leave Père Jouvancy alone. In case these poisoning rumors are true."

"In case? If Neuville is right about what he saw in Fleury's autopsy, the rumors are all too true. Wait here a moment." La Chaise went into the gallery and returned with Bouchel.

The footman's face was drawn and bleached, as though he, too, might have been ill during the night, and Charles started to ask if he had, but La Chaise cut him off.

"Lock the door of the chamber where Père Jouvancy is," La Chaise said to Bouchel. "And keep watch in here, but near the door, in case he needs you."

Bouchel bowed without speaking, and they left him standing in the middle of the room, rubbing his forehead and staring at the floor.

As they went out into the gallery, Charles asked, "Who is this Introducer whose carriage is coming?"

La Chaise was craning his neck to see beyond the mass of courtiers pressed against the gallery windows. "He is the official who leads ambassadorial processions from Paris. These Poles made an official entry into the city yesterday. Normally, they would stay there for some days before coming to Versailles, but the king is anxious to get on with the marriage negotiations."

His height letting him see over the crowd, Charles watched a long line of gilded, red-wheeled carriages passing the first of Versailles's gates and rolling toward the palace.

"Quickly, so we can get a place." La Chaise pulled Charles away and they hurried along the route they'd traveled yesterday until they reached a small dark flight of stairs. "We'll have to find a place at the foot of the Ambassadors' Staircase," La Chaise said, starting down. "We're not grand enough to stand at the top near the throne."

"Not even you?"

La Chaise shook his head. "Not unless there's a religious statement to be made. When the king receives an envoy from a foreign prince who is not Christian, he might ask me to be there. But Poland is a Catholic country."

In the sumptuous entrance hall, where the wide marble staircase rose beneath a painted and gilded coffered ceiling, a large crowd had gathered, talking and laughing excitedly and jockeying for space. The hall bristled with the pikes of the Hundred Swiss, spear points catching and scattering light as the guards stood lined up on each side of the path to the stairs, watching the crowd and the doors. Some made a fence of their pikes to keep back tourists, others stood around the antechamber walls, and more were outside the doors, the clusters of white plumes in their cocked-brim black hats making Charles think of menacing long-legged birds.

"I've heard that Louis is the best-guarded monarch in Europe," he said, watching them. "It seems true."

"Of course it's true." La Chaise began worming his way through the crowd, and Charles did his best to stay close behind. La Chaise elbowed ruthlessly until he had them close enough to the first step and the front rank of watchers to see and be seen. Craning his neck to see around La Chaise, Charles counted twelve steps of colored marble leading to a landing where classical figures of gilded bronze reclined beside the sculpture of a fountain. Above the figures, courtiers stood immobile, leaning on balustrades covered with cloth of gold and waiting for the envoys. Charles wondered why such stillness—before the ceremony even began—and then realized with a start that they were only painted. To their right and left, the staircase branched, each side rising to the level of the royal apartments, where the king would receive the Poles in the royal bedchamber.

La Chaise sighed and righted his *bonnet*. "I hope this doesn't take long. I still feel like I could fall on my face."

"Don't," Charles said gravely, glancing significantly up the stairs. "Fall on your back—isn't that the protocol? Don't show royalty your back?"

That raised the ghost of a laugh. "A timely reminder."

Charles hesitated. "*Mon père*, do you truly believe that we were poisoned yesterday?"

"I don't know what to think. But I can easily believe it about Fleury. He was a grasping, arrogant man who liked no one." La Chaise leaned close to Charles's ear and said, under the noise of the crowd, "And he was known to be writing a *mémoire* of the court."

"Ah." Charles nodded thoughtfully. An acid-tongued *mémoire* of the court could well give someone enough reason to poison Fleury. He thought about his nighttime encounters with Neuville and the Duc du Maine. People had certainly been taking an interest in Fleury's room. How many souls in this hive of gossip and hard-won position might fear that Fleury had vented his pen on them?

A blare of trumpets sounded, and every head turned toward the doors. The Swiss soldiers stood at rigid attention, the trumpets settled to a stately march, and the head of the Polish procession appeared. First came the Introducer of ambassadors and the grand master of ceremonies, gravely resplendent in shining black-satin suits. Behind them was a small tight formation of Polish soldiers, fair haired and impressively moustached. Then came the pair of envoys sent by King Jan Sobieski to negotiate his son's marriage: a stocky elder and a taller, darker man perhaps in his thirties. The watching crowd stared eagerly at their quilted robes of heavy calf-length silk—one robe scarlet and the other blue—with rows of gold tassels across the front. Both men were sweating under small fur-trimmed hats, and their moustaches were even longer and thicker than their soldiers' luxuriant growths.

The crowd made its bows and curtsies as the men passed, watched them climb the stairs and take the left-hand branch toward the king's *apartements*, and then began murmuring and making ready to move on to somewhere else. La Chaise turned to Charles.

"There are a few things I must do, *maître*. Go back and see how Père Jouvancy does. I will return as soon as I can. Do you feel you'll be able to eat?"

"Yes, something, at least."

"Me, I am not altogether there yet." La Chaise raised an eyebrow. "I imagine that you do not wish to return to the Duc de La Rochefoucauld's table."

"On the whole, no," Charles said, somewhat shamefaced. In spite of his reluctance to believe that a poisoner was at work— even after what Monsieur Neuville had said about Fleury's blackened liver—he kept remembering the doctor's whisper that he'd seen the duke and Madame de Maintenon in close conference. "But if there is bread and cheese in your chamber, *mon père*, that will do for me. When you return, if you have no objection, may I leave Père Jouvancy with you and go out into the gardens for a little air? While I work on our ballet *livret*?"

"Very well. I will return as quickly as I can."

They parted and Charles went slowly back to his and Jouvancy's room. But before he reached the black-and-white tiled gallery, a clamor of ominously low-pitched barking pulled him up short. He looked around, expecting to see large dogs running toward him, but there were only a few courtiers in sight, and none seemed to notice the noise. Perhaps they were used to it, Charles thought, wondering why someone kept large dogs inside. The noise and crowding of Louis le Grand were beginning to seem positively pastoral by comparison with this place, and he had an overwhelming urge to bundle Jouvancy into a carriage and go home.

When he reached La Chaise's chamber, Bouchel told him that the rhetoric master hadn't stirred. Charles went to Jouvancy's bed and parted the curtains. The little priest's flushed face and hot forehead put paid to Charles's thoughts of leaving. He wrung out a cloth in cold water and sponged the priest's face, smiling reassuringly and murmuring, "Go on sleeping, all's well," when Jouvancy briefly opened his eyes. Then he closed the curtains, glad for the west-facing windows that left the room still dim and cool, and left the chamber.

Bouchel turned from staring out the courtyard window. "Do you need me anymore, *maître*?" His eyes were shadowed, and his face was pinched and gray.

"Are you well?" Charles said, peering at him in concern.

The footman tensed and darted a sideways glance at Charles. "Well enough, thank you. Are you better?" He jerked his head at the door into the other chamber. "Is he?"

"We're all better, thank you."

"I was thinking—I don't mean to step out of my place, *maître*, but whatever happened to old Fleury, I doubt you three were poisoned."

"Why not?" Charles went to the cupboard and opened it, looked for bread and cheese.

"Well, Père La Chaise set the leftover *bouillon* back in the cupboard after your breakfast yesterday." He wrinkled his nose.

"I didn't find it till this morning, and it was high and ripe. Enough that it had to be already going that way yesterday. So it could have been what made you sick."

Charles nodded slowly. The *bouillon!* Of course. An unpleasant but ordinary explanation. What could be simpler? "Thank you, I'll tell Père La Chaise. But you look as though you may be getting Père Jouvancy's sickness. You should take care of yourself."

Bouchel grunted his thanks and left. But when he was gone, the simplicity of spoiled soup began tangling itself into unwelcome subtlety. The soup had not smelled off when they'd had it for breakfast yesterday, but putting poison in *bouillon* would be easy enough . . .

Stop it, he ordered his mind. *There is no poisoner. It wasn't poison. It was spoiled soup. And I've heard our infirmarian say that too much drink can blacken a man's liver. Maybe that's why Fleury's liver was black. God knows the man drank enough in the army.* Wobbly with tiredness—and some measure of relief—Charles stood up and stretched. Impatient to get out of the palace's fog of rumor and suspicion and into plain sunshine and air, he hoped La Chaise wouldn't be long about his errands.

He wasn't, and as soon as he returned, Charles told him what Bouchel had said.

"Oh. I suppose that could explain it. I should have thrown away what was left after dinner. But, do you know, I always find that hard to do, perhaps because my mother would never let the servants throw soup away . . ." La Chaise smothered a yawn. "For now, I am not going to think about soup or poison or anything else. I am going to sit here in my chair and doze."

Glad to get out of the palace, Charles made his way down to the ground-floor corridor and started around it to the south wing's garden front. He hoped he wouldn't have to walk too far before he found a shady secluded place to sit and work on the ballet *livret* he'd retrieved from the saddlebag. But when he was finally outside, he found himself in a wide desert of hot gravel, only to discover that the greenery beyond was an inhospitably formal checkerboard of walkways, plots of grass and shrubs dotted with classical statues, spiral paths to nowhere among carefully placed and manicured trees, and stretches of high horn-beam hedges as impassable as walls. There was solitude enough, but the grass seemed the only place to sit. He walked on, toward a jet of water playing above a balustrade topped with urns, and found two sets of steps leading down to the fountain, the bottom flight shaded by a wall. Surprised at how tired he was by the walk from the palace, Charles settled himself on a lower step, turned so that he could lean against the wall, and opened the ballet *livret*. The next thing he knew, a flight of cawing crows was passing overhead and the *livret* was at the bottom of the steps, where it had tumbled from his lap. Blinking, he stretched and went to the fountain's basin to splash water on his face and wake up. He dried his face with his cassock skirt, picked up the *livret*, unstoppered his bottle of ink, and got to work.

He finished writing out directions for the comic *entrées* of Scaramouches and Harlequins in Part two of *La France Victorieuse sous Louis le Grand*, turned the page to Part three, and began to read Jouvancy's most recent editing, done in the college infirmary. Charles had known there would be changes, since this third Part was called *La France Victorieuse de ses Ennemis par les Armes*, and his own version of the French military victories had emphasized celebrations of peace. But Jouvancy had the *livret*'s French Heroes trampling their foes in a manner worthy of Versailles's painted ceilings, conquering first Spaniards, then Germans, and finally the Dutch. He stared unseeingly at the *livret* in his lap, trying not to remember his own experience of war. He'd seen too much death and, in the end, had found the death he'd seen—and caused—pointless. And this ballet's drum-beating for the illusory glory of battle left him feeling as though he were mourning for the not yet dead.

Charles let his quill rest and watched the fountain playing in front of him. The sound of the rising and falling water eased him somewhat, but his sense of calm vanished as he looked more closely at the fountain's sculptures. On a stone island in the fountain's center, the goddess Latona was turning angry peasants into frogs to protect her children Apollo and Diana from their wrath. The intended allegory hit Charles between the eyes. The matronly Latona would be Anne of Austria. Which made Apollo into Louis, and Diana, well, it wasn't hard to understand Diana as Louis's rouged and beribboned brother Philippe. And that meant the frogs were the eternal poor, always angry—usually with good cause—and perpetually baffled and defeated. *So much for "blessed are the poor,"* Charles thought sourly, closing his eyes.

Someone laughed, a hot tongue licked his hand, and his eyes flew open. A small black dog was standing in front of him, wagging its ragged plume of a tail. A young woman and a little girl stood between the dog and the fountain. Charles recognized Mademoiselle de Rouen—Lulu—the king's legitimized daughter about to be sent away to Poland, and the girl he'd seen playing ball, one of the Condé's tiny daughters, a Doll of the Blood.

The chestnut-haired little girl drew the dog away by its red ribbon collar. But Lulu came closer and bent toward him. The smell of tobacco and the sight of an impressive *décolletage* assailed him, but it was her blazing vitality that made him blink. She glittered with it and a warning instinct that he ought to get out of its path brought him to his feet.

"Were you dreaming?" Her smile widened and she looked him up and down. "Of me? You saw me yesterday, you know."

Charles put the *livret* aside on the step, made his face a social blank, went down the two steps to her level, and removed his *bonnet*.

"Your Highness," he said tonelessly, inclining his head.

Her blue-gray Bourbon eyes mocked him. "Or perhaps you weren't dreaming. Only praying. Oh, dear, did I disturb your devotions?"

"And if I said yes?"

Slowly as a stalking cat, she closed the distance between them. The green jewels hanging from her ears and her cream and sea-green satin skirts shimmered in the sunlight. "Then I would say that perhaps you could find something more entertaining to do." The music of her laughter vied with the fountain's music, and the ruche of pale pink lace that edged her *décolletage* rose and fell. The Bourbon eyes were full of challenge. And something else that he might have called desperation if he hadn't been too angry at her rude familiarity to care.

"If you will excuse me, Your Highness?" He replaced his hat. "I have work I must do." He looked beyond her for her attendants. But except for the child and the dog, she was alone, which no young woman of quality, and especially no king's daughter, should be. He looked again at the child and saw that she was watching him gravely, her small oval face oddly knowing and resigned.

"It's all right," she said. "You may go. I will stay with her. And I am not a child, I am nearly twelve, though I don't look it."

"*Mademoiselle,*" he began, but she stopped him.

"I am Anne-Marie de Bourbon. You must call me Your Serene Highness."

"I beg your pardon, Your Serene Highness."

Her dignity dissolved into a smile. "Well, I have to say that, don't I? If I don't, everyone will treat me like a child, even if I live to be a hundred years old, since I probably won't grow any more."

Charles smiled back. "Very well thought, Your Serene Highness. One must keep one's dignity at all costs. But now I certainly cannot leave, because there are two young ladies to guard."

"No," Lulu said sweetly, "you cannot. So you must stay and talk with us. Besides, I know you're not a priest, you could still decide to be—" She looked up at him through her dark eyelashes. "—a man. So why should you work so hard? You see that I know all about you, Maître du Luc. Don't you want to know how?" Her eyes sparkled invitingly.

"On the whole, no, Your Highness." Charles bent to ruffle the dog's ears.

"Oooh!" Lulu laid a small white hand on his cassock sleeve. "I think you are afraid of me!" Her nails scratched like a cat's as her fingers moved on his woolen sleeve.

"Lulu!" someone called from behind her, and the dog bounded away, barking joyously. Her Serene Highness Anne-Marie picked up her blue skirts and ran after the dog.

Lulu swore and looked over her shoulder.

"*What* are you doing hiding away with Maître du Luc?" The Prince of Conti, the young man who had mocked the Jesuits' gift in Madame de Maintenon's antechamber, strolled lazily around the fountain toward them. "Everyone's searching for you, my sweet Lulu. You'll be late for dining with your handsome Poles." He waggled his fingers at the dog, which was jumping and barking in greeting, and reached out to pull one of Anne-Marie's brown curls. She slapped hard enough at his hand that he snatched it back and muttered something under his breath.

Lulu's brightness died like a doused flame, and she looked as though she might cry. "No. I won't eat with them today. Soon enough, I'll have no one else." She whirled and picked up her skirts as if to run. "Come, let's go to a *traiteur* in town for our dinner."

Anne-Marie de Bourbon shook her head in alarm. "No, Lulu, you mustn't!" The little girl turned to Conti. "Don't let her go."

Conti ignored them both and gazed limpidly at Charles.

"So sorry to interrupt your pleasures, *maître*."

"Not pleasure, Your Serene Highness, work." Charles doffed his *bonnet* to Conti with an inward sigh and every outward appearance of respect. Conti's arrival was a chance to try to learn something for Lieutenant-Général La Reynie. Charles admitted to himself that the more he saw of Conti, the less he minded causing trouble for this arrogant young Bourbon. "I had the pleasure of seeing you yesterday in Madame de Maintenon's antechamber, *mon prince*."

"Yes. I am surprised to see you still here. But court life always does agree with Jesuits, I believe."

"Does it?" Charles showed his teeth in what the prince might possibly mistake for a smile. "And does it always agree with you, Your Serene Highness?"

Conti's eyebrows lifted, and he seemed to really see Charles for the first time. "How could it not, when I am near my kinsman the king?"

"How not, indeed? Royal kinsmen, of course, feel nothing but brotherly love for one another."

At that, Lulu burst into laughter so deep and loud that Charles thought it would have doubled her over, had her bodice not been so boned and laced. Anne-Marie only looked gravely from one speaker to the next, like someone watching a game of *jeu de paume*.

But this conversational game felt to Charles more like a skirmish on the edge of battle. "You disagree?" he asked Lulu.

Still burbling with mirth, she waved a beringed hand at Conti. "My royal father hates this dear Bourbon prince! And this dear prince is only waiting—"

"Shut *up*, Lulu." It was Conti's turn to bare his teeth in a dangerous smile. He caught her hand. "You are shocking our good cleric. No one hates anyone here."

The girl winced and pulled her hand away, and to Charles's surprise, her lip trembled. "You hate *me*," she said.

Conti shrugged at Charles. "Sometimes I think I will become a monk of some sort. To get away from women. They're utterly incomprehensible. My darling Lulu, what does hating or not hating matter? You are going to Poland. I am desolate, but what can I do about it?"

"Much, if you only would!" She gathered her skirts and fled, like some rare silvery green bird taking flight, and disappeared beyond the fountain.

Anne-Marie and the dog followed her, and Conti rolled his eyes at Charles and strolled after the three of them. Charles replaced his hat; picked up his *livret*, ink, and quill; and went quickly up the steps in the other direction, with an irrational feeling—half irritation and half fear—that more Bourbons would appear in his path, no matter what direction he chose. He turned aside along a dark green hornbeam hedge, wanting to be out of sight of the fountain, and kept walking. Turning repeatedly and at random among hedges and rosy brick walls surrounding a myriad of small gardens, he kept walking until dizziness reminded him that he was still recovering from last night's sickness. He slowed as he turned yet another corner and saw an enormous expanse of water ahead of him. It was half surrounded by piles of dirt, and two workmen were doing something at the water's near edge. As Charles's footsteps crunched along the gravel walk, one of them straightened and waved his arms.

"*Mon père!* Come quickly—he's dead, poor sod, and you're needed!"

Chapter 7

The workman met Charles halfway, squelching water from his shoes, wiping his hands dry on his stained brown-linen coat, and still talking. "Your prayers will be worth more than mine, that's sure!" He dropped his voice. "He looks like he drowned, but he didn't. You'll see what I mean. Will you stay with him, so me and my boy can go for the Guard?"

"You're sure the man is dead?" Charles was reluctant to encounter a second man, in just three days, dead practically at his own feet. "Who is he?"

"Bertin. Bertin Laville." He shook his head sadly. "My daughter's husband. He works—worked—in the kitchen garden. Over there." He gestured vaguely toward the palace.

They reached the edge of the lake, where a white-faced teenage boy knelt beside a man's prone body. The boy got up awkwardly and bowed to Charles. Charles squatted on his heels and put a hand on Bertin Laville's sodden chest, though it was plain enough that the breath had long gone from this man. Squinting in the glare of the sun off the white gravel, he ran his eye carefully over the body and then gently turned Laville's head to one side. Charles took off his *bonnet*, held it to block some of the sun's glare, and parted the man's dripping dark hair at the crown.

"So. You see," the elder workman said.

Charles winced as his fingers found the jagged-edged circle of bone and felt lightly at the sickening hollow inside the circle. Dropping his hat beside the body, he cupped the ruined skull in his hands as though he could still protect it and said a quick silent prayer. When he crossed himself and stood up, the workmen hastily crossed themselves, too.

"Shall we go for the Guard now, *mon père*?" the older one said.

"In a moment. When did you last see your son-in-law?"

"Me? Not since yesterday. Sometimes he helped in this part of the gardens, but I didn't see him today." The speaker jerked his head at the boy. "Nor did my son."

"May I know your names?" Charles said. "I am Maître Charles du Luc."

"Me, I'm Jean Prudhomme. Gardener. My boy is Jacques."

"Who might have wanted to kill your son-in-law, Monsieur Prudhomme?"

The father gave his son a warning look, and they both shrugged.

Charles opened his mouth to say he would pray for the dead man. Instead, he heard himself say, "Was there any talk about Bertin? Did he dice? Run after women?"

The boy looked up, but his father's heavy hand descended on his shoulder and he looked down again.

Prudhomme eyed Charles. "Why are you asking? He's the Guard's business now."

"Not that they'll do much," the boy muttered at the ground.

Why do I want to know? Charles asked himself wearily. The obvious answer was that he was religious and the man had a soul about which he had to care. And did care. In truth, though, he would rather not care about this unknown peasant beyond a few prayers. He wanted no more barriers in the way of his going home. Though if this turned out to be no more than a peasants' quarrel over money or women, the Guard would do less than if a man of quality had been found dead in the royal precincts.

Charles said, "Your son-in-law was a man, and he's dead. Without chance to be shriven. And with the rest of his life stolen from him. And from his wife. So if you know something . . ."

The gardener's seamed, sunburned face went still and watchful. His deep-set black eyes were as opaque as a raven's, and Charles had the feeling that this man could wait as enduringly as a tree in the garden, if he had to. Young Jacques opened his mouth, but his father's look made him shut it again. The shadows at their feet had shifted a hair's breadth or two before Prudhomme finally said, "There were women, yes."

"Other men's women?"

"Maybe." The gardener sighed. "My daughter just gave birth. You know—or maybe you don't—what men do when their wives are breeding."

"Whose woman did he poach?"

That got only another long raven's stare.

"Well, if you will go for the Guard, I will stay with the body."

Taking his son with him, Prudhomme trudged toward the palace. Charles knelt beside the body again and studied the battered skull. The wound seemed too rounded to have been made by a shovel. A large stone, perhaps, though the grounds were too manicured for stray stones large enough to be lying ready for use. He rose to his feet and scanned the nearest brick wall around one of the small formal gardens. The wall was intact, and a brick wasn't rounded enough, anyway.

Exasperated with himself for going after answers like a dog after the scent of deer, Charles turned his back determinedly on

the wall and the dead man. He was never going to know what—
or who—had killed Bertin Laville, because he and Jouvancy
were leaving. Tomorrow, please God. He watched occasional
chattering tourists cross the opening of the path he'd come
down, until he realized that he was also watching for a sea-green
gown and the king's alarming daughter. And that if he saw her,
he was going to flee in the opposite direction and leave the dead
man to take his chances. *Coward*, he told himself, and knelt
again, shut his eyes, and prayed determinedly for Bertin Laville's
violently ejected soul.

"So now you've found a drowned rat."

Charles's eyes flew open, and what the Prince of Conti saw
in them made him compose his grinning face a little.

"So sorry to interrupt your prayers. I returned our dear Lulu
to her ladies and decided to follow your admirable example and
take a healthful stroll." He smiled down at Charles. "By all
means, go on praying." He widened his eyes facetiously. "Why
not pray for a miracle? I've always wanted to see one. Especially
a resurrection. Even a peasant's would be remarkable. Oh, make
no mistake—my desire to see a miracle is not from any special
holiness of mine, I assure you. As Père La Chaise would also
assure you. But you Jesuits exist to help souls, do you not? Here
am I at your disposal, a soul greatly in need of the convincing
help of a miracle!" Conti threw his arms wide, displaying his
coat's deep braided cuffs and sparkling buttons.

Charles had picked up his hat—unpleasantly wet now from
the water around the body—had put it on, and was standing
between Conti and the dead man, instinctively blocking Conti's
view of the broken skull. He was also badly wanting to smack
the face of this Prince of the Blood for making light of death.

"Your Serene Highness, the dead man's soul is in far more

need of help than yours. And though a Jesuit, I am not a priest. Of your courtesy, will you go for a priest?"

Conti's mirth vanished. "Find a servant." He looked coldly at Charles. "Or, better yet—and perhaps suiting your quality—run your own errands."

Charles produced a smile as charming as Conti's had been and even more insincere. "Ah, how could I be so naive as to think that death takes precedence over precedence itself?" He swept off his wet hat, snapping his wrist to make sure the hat sprayed water on the fine fall of lace down the front of Conti's coat.

There was a tense silence. Then, to Charles's surprise, Conti laughed uproariously.

"Well. You *are* surprising. Touché." He eyed Charles with new and disconcerting interest.

His dark eyes wandered appreciatively over Charles's face and then shifted beyond Charles to what he could see of the dead man. "No point in hiding him from me, you know. Everyone will know everything about him by supper. A workman, by his clothes. They died like flies when the place was being built. I suppose this one took a glass too much at the tavern and fell into Louis's nice new lake?" He walked around Charles. "Oh, oh." He prodded the corpse's head with his stick. "Not drowned, then. Yes, you do need the Guard. Though that may not be all you need." His dark eyes lingered on Charles's face for a moment, and then he strolled away.

Wishing he could drown his anger—if not Conti—in Louis's nice new lake, Charles scanned the walkways from the palace, hoping to see the Guard coming to take this situation off his hands. He couldn't just leave the body. Not only would that be irreligious, but he was sure that the body had not been long in the lake and was guessing that someone had put it there temporarily. Which meant that someone might be coming back to dispose of it more permanently. Probably not in daylight, but why take chances? He turned to look out over the water, which was wide enough for the maneuverings of a ship or two, and wondered how long it had taken—and how many men—to dig this improvement on nature. Digging like this was the sort of thing soldiers were often set to do, and just the thought of that made his old shoulder wound ache. He picked up his *livret* and pen, glad that his battles were on paper now, and that Jesuit life did not involve digging lakes.

Footsteps crunched heavily on the path behind him, and he turned with relief to confront a stocky, grim-faced officer, by his blue coat one of the French Guards.

"Captain Yves Frenel, *maître.*" The officer bowed, and Charles noted with surprise that the man had called him by his correct title. "The men you sent told me what they found." Captain Frenel went to the body and bent over it. Then he straightened and faced Charles. "Dead—or nearly—when he went into the water, from the looks of his head. I believe you arrived day before yesterday?"

"We did." So the Jesuits' comings and goings were well watched. But then, Louis being the best-guarded king in Europe, everyone's movements here must be watched. "My companion and I would have been gone by now, except that he is unwell. We hope to go back to Louis le Grand tomorrow or the day after."

"No reason I can see why this should keep you." The captain shrugged. "If you were conspiring against the king, you'd hardly be doing it with a casual laborer. That's too subtle even for Jesuits." He laughed.

Charles didn't.

"No need to stay with the body," the captain said. "My men are coming to move it."

"Where will you take it?" Charles asked curiously.

"To the mortuary near the guard barracks."

Reminding the man to call a priest, Charles took his leave and started back toward the palace. He had done what he could. His task now was to get Jouvancy well enough to travel and take him back to Louis le Grand. And once there, Charles told himself, even if he had to take over directing the tragedy as well as the ballet, he would manage. He felt willing to cope with anything, as long as he didn't have to do it here at Versailles.

He went into the south wing of the palace by the nearest garden door, and as he turned the corner, he again heard deep-throated barking and wondered, as he had during the night, why on earth someone was keeping a dog that size indoors. The barking grew louder, a chamber door burst open, and Charles stopped in alarm, hoping the dog was friendlier than it sounded.

But to his surprise, it wasn't a dog, it was a man. Three men, in fact. The disheveled little man in the lead was baying, nose to the sky, and two larger men barked halfheartedly in his wake as they chased him.

"No, *mon prince*," the closer one said wearily, grabbing a fistful of the little man's dirty yellow brocade coat skirts. "The moon is not up yet, it's too soon for us to be out."

Charles realized with a shock that he'd seen *mon prince* before. This was the new Prince of Condé, son of the Great Condé, who had died in December. At the funeral Mass in the Jesuit church of St. Louis, the son had seemed ordinary enough— though Charles had heard whispers that he was more than a little peculiar. But this was beyond anything he'd imagined.

"We should go back and eat our dinner," Condé's second

attendant said, taking hold of the prince's arm. Seeing Charles, he pointed a finger at his own temple and rolled his eyes. "Come now, *mon prince*, you must eat to be fresh for roaming later."

Courteously enough, but very firmly, they turned the little man around and took him back to the door he'd come through. Anne-Marie de Bourbon stood forlornly in the doorway, cradling her little dog in her arms. As she stepped aside to let her father and his attendants past, she saw Charles watching. Her face flamed, and she withdrew into the Condé's rooms in a swirl of blue skirts. The door closed and deep-throated barking began again behind it.

Feeling deeply sorry for the child, Charles hurried through Père La Chaise's antechamber. Resisting the urge to bolt the door behind him, he took a glass from the side table, filled it from the copper reservoir's tap, and drank thirstily. With a sigh, he went into the adjoining room to tell La Chaise about the dead workman, but La Chaise was asleep in his armchair. On a wave of panic, Charles hurried past him into the adjoining room and pushed Jouvancy's bed curtains apart. He let his breath out in relief. Jouvancy was sleeping quietly and there was faint color in his face. Charles closed the curtains and turned to contemplate his own bed. But La Chaise stirred in the next room and called out to him.

"I saw you come in, *maître*. No one has gotten past me, you need not worry."

Reluctantly, Charles went back to the other room, closing the door between to keep from waking Jouvancy, and stood respectfully before the king's confessor. "I am glad to hear it, *mon père*. He looks some better."

"Yes. He ate a little bread and kept it down. Sit. We need to talk about this evening."

"This evening?" Charles's heart sank. The only evening he wanted was supper and prayers and bed.

"There is a ball this evening to honor the Polish ambassadors and Mademoiselle de Rouen. Unfortunately, I am bidden to attend. And so are you, in Père Jouvancy's place. It begins at seven, and there will be festivities after, but we need not stay for all of that."

"Why are we summoned to a ball?"

"To stand near the royal chair and remind the Poles that Louis is Europe's Most Christian King. And I suspect that the invitation is also meant as a way of thanking us for giving the reliquary to Madame de Maintenon."

Summoning resignation, Charles said, "Of course, *mon père*. Meanwhile, there is—"

"—the question of getting a little sleep before this evening. And also the question of our supper," La Chaise finished firmly, smothering a yawn. "Bouchel is bringing us a roasted chicken from the town." He started to get up from his chair.

"*Mon père*," Charles said, "please, there is something I must tell you."

La Chaise slumped into his chair again and regarded Charles without enthusiasm. "From your face, it's something I don't want to hear."

La Chaise was clearly not in a mood to listen, and Charles decided there was no real reason to mention Lulu. Or Conti— at least, not yet. Charles kept his story brief, and about only the dead body. "The back of the man's skull was crushed, it has to be murder," he finished.

"At least he wasn't poisoned. What does the Guard captain think?"

"That it was most likely a workmen's quarrel."

"Good." La Chaise rubbed his head as though it hurt. "Anything more serious than that we do not need here just now."

So a workman's murder is not serious? Charles just stopped himself from saying.

But it must have shown on his face, because La Chaise said impatiently, "I am not indifferent to the man's death. But my point is that it probably has nothing to do with the king. If there is a threat to him, it will come from much closer at hand."

"Meaning?" Charles hazarded.

"You do not seem to know your place, *maître*," La Chaise said ominously.

"Is it not the place of any Jesuit to want to know the truth?"

"Knowing when to hold your tongue is also a virtue."

"But if I know more of the truth, I will know better when—and with whom—to hold my tongue."

La Chaise studied Charles for so long, he might have been weighing him in St. Peter's scale to determine his entrance—or not—into heaven. He finally said, "Very well. For that reason, and that reason only, I will tell you. But if thereafter you do not hold your tongue when you should, it will be the worse for you when you return to Louis le Grand." He sighed. "The most likely source of a threat to the king is the circle of young men who have gathered around the heir to the throne. They began courting the Dauphin, last winter when the king was ill, clearly hoping that he would die so that his timid and malleable son would become king. The intimates of a weak king are like pigs at an endlessly full trough. And they push ruthlessly to gain a place there before the feeding starts."

On impulse, Charles said, "Is the Prince of Conti one of them?"

La Chaise's eyes narrowed. "Why do you ask?"

"He—" Charles nearly said *happened along*, then didn't, realizing that he didn't believe Conti had been there by chance. "He was there while I was waiting with the workman's body. I also saw him earlier, with Mademoiselle de Rouen."

Shaking his head, La Chaise frowned and said, more to himself than Charles, "Those two should not be together." Then he caught himself and said, "What did he say about the body?"

"He seemed indifferent to it. But—I wondered if he'd been following me."

"He well might." La Chaise's look was eloquent. "Stay away from him. For many reasons. He's just been admitted back to court after a year of exile in Chantilly, with the old Condé, and the king is still none too sure of him, or of his loyalty. The man seems to have spies everywhere."

"Here at court, you mean?"

"Yes, but not only here. Don't be seen with him and don't talk to him. Or about him."

"What did he do to get himself exiled?"

La Chaise hesitated. "For one thing, a few years ago he wrote letters making fun of Madame de Maintenon and saying the king was only a 'king of the theatre.' The letters were intercepted. And two years ago, he fought briefly on the side of the Hapsburg Holy Roman Emperor against the Turks. The king considers the emperor a much more dangerous enemy than the Turks."

Charles's mouth fell open. No wonder Lieutenant-Général La Reynie wanted to know more about Conti. It was Charles's turn now to hesitate as he remembered gossip he'd heard at Louis le Grand. "It's rumored that our Most Christian King himself encourages the Musselmen to keep the Hapsburgs too busy fighting to turn west and attack us."

"Kings weaken their enemies in any way possible." La Chaise lifted his chin as though daring Charles to say more.

Charles took the dare. "So the rumor is true. And you are saying that ends justify means?"

"Sometimes, yes."

"When the Prince of Conti fought on the Hapsburg side, was it at the king's behest? To help keep the Hapsburgs occupied—and help them lose against the Turks?"

"Aren't you forgetting that Conti was exiled from court for joining the Hapsburgs?"

"Exiled to the comforts of the Condé chateau at Chantilly. Hardly a dire punishment."

"Is not exile from the king's presence considered the worst punishment a nobleman can have?" La Chaise's face warned Charles not to answer that question. "In any case, Maître du Luc, none of this is your business. Your business relative to Conti is to avoid him at all costs. And now, if you wish any rest, leave me, go to your bed. Evening will come soon enough."

Deciding that obedience was the better part of valor at this point, Charles started toward the adjoining chamber. And turned back. "*Mon père*, I saw the new Prince of Condé just now in the corridor. He was—" Charles paused, but no euphemism came to his aid. "Barking."

La Chaise grunted unhappily. "This Condé is peculiar even for that peculiar family."

Sensing that La Chaise wanted to say more, in spite of the order to leave him alone, Charles drifted toward the adjoining chamber as slowly as he could. He was nearly in the doorway when La Chaise burst out, "That is another thing I worry about. The Bourbon lineage. Not one of the Princes of the Blood has the king's ability to command respect, let alone his self-sacrificing devotion to duty."

Charles turned and stared. "Self-sacrificing?! When has he ever—"

"Self-sacrificing, *maître*," La Chaise said coldly, across Charles's indignation. "I do not use words lightly. Something you should remember. The king works every day, most hours of the day. With his council, with his advisors, with his officers. He leaves no detail unchecked or unregarded. Not one!"

All of which seemed to Charles only what a king ought to do. "But he also sacrifices everyone and everything else to his own ends. To his blood-soaked *gloire*."

La Chaise surged out of his chair, and Charles realized too late that he'd thrust his verbal knife not only into the king but into the king's confessor, director of the royal conscience. And thereby director—at least in theory—of the royal actions. But it was too late to take back the words, even if he'd been willing to do so.

"Never," La Chaise said between his teeth, "*never* say those things again. Not here, not anywhere. If you do and the wrong people hear you, I will not lift a finger to save you from the consequences. I will also see that your own confessor hears of your opinions. King Louis is God's anointed sovereign, the king God Himself has given to govern France. King Louis is the mystical body of France. You and I and every soul in the realm are members of that body, and he is the head. Rebel against the king, and you rebel against God Himself."

"I know that," Charles said unhappily. His conscience was all too familiar with this particular moral struggle. "Of course I know he is divinely anointed, and that gives him his royal body—"

"Not only that. His birth also gives it."

"But he also has a natural body, he is also a man like you and me. After all, he sins—if he did not, he wouldn't need a confessor!"

"Of course he sins. But that natural sinning body is subsumed within the anointed mystical body of the king. The royal body can do no wrong. None." Seething with anger, La Chaise waited for Charles's agreement. When it didn't come, he strode to the window and rubbed his hands over his red face. "What is the matter with you?" He sounded almost afraid. "How did you ever become a Jesuit?"

"*Mon père*, I know that by blood and the holy chrism with which he was anointed in the cathedral at Rheims, the king is divinely sanctioned to rule." Charles flung out his arms, pleading for understanding, even though La Chaise's back was turned. "I am loyal to him—I *must* be loyal to him in order to obey God. But—but how can I not hate the suffering the king causes his people? His greed for *gloire*, for triumphs, for turning Europe into a blood-soaked battlefield, is ruining France. And didn't the prophets criticize the kings in the Bible?"

La Chaise shook his head, still looking out the window. "You are not a prophet. You are also not a stupid man, so why do you talk like an idiot? Without making himself feared across Europe, the king of France cannot rule. Our enemies would overrun us—the Holy Roman Emperor, the Protestants, the Turks, the League of Augsburg countries. Do you not know how hated France is for its power? Do you not realize what will happen if Louis dies, as he could easily have done last winter? Who would hold France together? Who would protect it? Not the king's heir, God help us. The poor Dauphin is not only terrified of his father, he cannot say boo to a goose. But he's young and strong—he'll live for years. In that time, if he were king, France could lose everything. Anything King Louis can do now to make France sovereign in Europe and feared across the world, he *must* do. And I must help him do it." The king's confessor rested his forehead against the window glass. "And I must somehow help him save his soul at the same time," he added, almost too softly for Charles to hear.

Charles was not one iota moved to agree with the king's actions, as either mystical body of France or natural man. But he understood for the first time the danger looming beyond Louis's death, whenever it came. And he understood much more of La Chaise's impossible position and his struggle, saw that it was far more perilous than his own.

"I will pray for you both, *mon père*," he said gravely.

"Do. God knows we need it."

Chapter 8

Charles thought he might faint from heat. He and Père La Chaise were standing together behind the king's chair, looking over the outsized white plume on the royal hat, waiting for the ball to begin. Around the other three sides of the large *salon*, members of the royal family and the highest-ranking courtiers were settling in what was called the Ring, whose back rows were raised on wooden forms so that everyone could see and be seen. Lower-ranking courtiers stood wherever they could find room, crowded sleeve to sleeve and bare shoulder to bare shoulder, sweating in their layers of silk and wool and brocade and satin. The women's painted fans beat the air like the bright, fragile wings of butterflies, doing about as much good toward cooling anyone. Charles smiled as he caught sight of little Anne-Marie de Bourbon, in a yellow gown with her dog in her lap, sitting in one of the Ring's raised rows of chairs and swinging her feet, which didn't reach the ground.

The Polish ambassadors sat on the king's left. On his right was his son the Dauphin, also named Louis. The Dauphin was said to be the image of his mother, the dead Queen Maria Teresa. Like her, he was blond, plump, and pink-faced. And unfortunately, none too intelligent.

"Where is the Dauphin's wife?" Charles whispered, speaking

Latin to keep his questions even more private. All educated men learned Latin, but only the scholarly kept it up. Courtiers used it little.

"Pregnant again, or so I understand. Even when she's not, the Dauphine rarely goes anywhere."

Beyond the Dauphin was a smallish man in a beautifully curled dark brown wig, moving restlessly, gesturing with slender, heavily ringed hands at the crowd. As he turned his head, Charles saw that his cheeks were brightly rouged. Beside him, a large woman in gray satin and red jewels sat immovable as a mountain.

Seeing where Charles was looking, La Chaise mouthed, "Monsieur and Madame."

Styled simply Monsieur, Philippe d'Orleans was the king's younger brother. The gray satin mountain was Philippe's second wife, the formidable German princess called Liselotte.

"Where is Madame de Maintenon?" Charles said softly in La Chaise's ear. "I thought she would be here."

La Chaise shook his head. "She makes few and brief appearances at occasions like this. Since her position is not acknowledged, you understand."

"And Madame de Montespan, Mademoiselle de Rouen's mother? Or is she no longer at court?"

"Of course she is," La Chaise murmured, keeping an eye on the white plume. He smiled without mirth. "I doubt she will give up trying to retake the king's affections while there is breath in her body. But she's too indolent to bother much about her children."

The king suddenly stood, and everyone sitting stood with him. He gave the signal for the proceedings to begin, and everyone sat down. A dozen men in the first row of the Ring rose again and bowed to a dozen women. As always, the ball would open with a *branle*. All the pairs came onto the floor, made their honors of bows and curtsies to the king and each other, and linked hands in order of rank to form a long line. Music began beyond the open double doors of an adjoining room, and the line began to wind its way around the dance floor. Each of these couples would dance a paired dance before the evening was over.

Though Charles had been a good dancer, and part of his work at the Jesuit college was creating and producing the student ballets, he couldn't, of course, dance in public now. But he loved watching people dance. He did wish, though, that someone would open a window to cool the thick air. He scrutinized the dancers performing the *branle*. The *branle* was a simple dance, an occasion to show off rank and finery, and because the occasion was in honor of the king's daughter and the Polish nobles who had come to negotiate her marriage contract with their prince, the finery was very fine indeed. At the head of the *branle* was the Prince of Conti, devastatingly handsome in a suit of what Charles at first thought was black satin. But as Conti moved, the bright candlelight struck gleams of dark red and blue from his coat and breeches, and Charles saw that the suit was of a costly weave called, appropriately enough, "Prince." The cloth reminded Charles of the man—changeable, neither one thing nor the other, beautiful. Conti moved with the grace of Apollo himself, the blue and silver plumes of his broad beaver hat waving as he danced. He was such a magnificent dancer that Charles almost forgot his dislike of the man in the pleasure of watching his entrancing skill.

His partner, of course, was the bride-to-be. Her rose satin gown, covered with a delicate web of snow-white lace, was so obviously meant for a maiden's blush that the effect was nearly comic. Her curling dark blond hair shone under an old-fashioned net of pearls, and ropes of pearls were wrapped around her bare shoulders, hugged her long neck, and swung from her ears. As the dance went on and the room grew hotter, Charles found himself wondering how much the girl's finery weighed.

When the *branle* ended, the dancers separated, men standing in one row, women in the other, and faced the king. They made their honors to him and then to each other, and the men escorted the women back to their seats. But the Prince of Conti, instead of resuming his seat, returned to the floor. He faced the king, standing gracefully in dance's fourth position, one foot advanced before the other, and bowed deeply. As he replaced his hat, the sound of a foot beating grave triple time was heard, and the traditional second dance of a ball, the noble *courante*, began.

"King Louis used to dance this himself," La Chaise murmured, nodding slightly down at the white plume waving above the high-backed royal chair.

As Charles watched Conti stepping and balancing and turning his way through the dance's sinuous floor pattern, he caught sight of the Duc du Maine sitting near the king's end of the Ring. Absorbed and wistful, the boy's shoulders twitched as he watched, his breath visibly catching in his throat as the excitement of the dance reached out to his lame body. Watching him, Charles thought sadly that but for his lameness, Maine might have shown his father's talent reborn. He clearly had the passion. Conti ended his dance and made his bow. Then he returned to Lulu and, with another fluid bow, invited her back onto the floor.

The two took their places and made their honors. As the girl rose from her curtsy, she raised her eyes to her father, and the fury in them took Charles's breath away. Then the upbeat of the *gavotte* sounded and her face became as smooth and expressionless as a mask. Her dancing burned with life; as she turned, jumped, balanced, and posed through the lively *gavotte*, her feet might almost have set fire to the floor where she stepped. Charles felt her every move in his own body and wished he could dance with her. The *gavotte* was also a proud dance, and the blue-black and rose pattern of royal order and balance she and Conti wove together coaxed sighs of pleasure from the watchers. When the pattern was complete and they made a final *reverence* to the king and to each other, Conti took his seat again in the Ring.

With another brief glance at the king that Charles thought must have struck him like lightning, Lulu advanced on the younger of the Poles. Charles felt almost sorry for the hapless ambassador as she gave him her hand—and a look colder than the Polish winter. The Pole, wearing French coat and breeches now, was competent enough at French dances, though his carnation-colored suit clashed badly with Lulu's rose silk. He was also sweating heavily, and Charles saw the girl flinch as sweat flew from his moustache during a jumped turn. When the dance ended, the Pole returned Lulu, who had steadfastly refused to look at him, to her chair. His face was as red as his carnation coat—with embarrassment as well as exertion, Charles thought—and his coat's back was dark with sweat. The man's sigh of relief was audible as he regained his seat, and a woman in a bright yellow wig, in the Ring's second row, laughed loudly. A ripple of laughter spread through the *salon*.

But near the door, the laughter turned to protest, and Charles looked to see what was happening. He stared in disbelief as one of his students from Louis le Grand, eighteen-year-old Henri de Montmorency, pushed through the standing watchers, apparently headed for the dance floor. Montmorency's pride and high nobility had not saved him from being painfully bewildered in the classroom or from being the only student Charles had ever had who was incapable of even the simplest dancing. Charles watched him narrowly. Surely Montmorency did not mean to dance here. Surely even he knew that all the dancing pairs and their dances had been chosen before the ball began. But Charles had learned that with Montmorency, it was best not to make assumptions. He began trying to edge through the crowd toward the boy, but La Chaise pulled him back.

"What are you doing?" he rumbled in Charles's ear. "No one can leave yet."

"One of my students just arrived." Charles nodded toward the boy, as wedged in now by the crowd as Charles was and obviously seething with frustration. "I need to find out what he's doing here."

La Chaise frowned. "You think he's here without permission from the college?"

"He may be," Charles said. It was as good a reason as any to get to Montmorency, and it might well be true. The closer some boys got to leaving the school, the less they cared about offending the rules they'd lived by for so long.

"No matter," La Chaise said, "you'll have to wait till the ball ends. The king brooks no interruptions to these ceremonies."

And, indeed, as though to underscore the words, King Louis slowly turned his head and looked up at the whispering Jesuits, who whipped off their *bonnets*.

"Forgive us, Sire," La Chaise murmured, and they bowed their heads.

The annoyed king turned back to the dancing, and La Chaise's grip on Charles's cassock forbade him to move so much as a toe.

To Charles's relief, Montmorency stayed where he was, even as the final dance of the evening began. Charles was interested to see that it was one of the new English *contredanses*, in which all the evening's couples danced facing each other in two lines. He'd heard of this style's recent import to France but had never seen it, and he was fascinated by the simple but lively meeting and parting of the dancers and the bright swirl of color as pairs changed places up and down the line.

When it was over, he checked to be sure Montmorency was still there. He wasn't. Which made Charles uneasy, but at least now the dancing was over and Montmorency couldn't disgrace himself—and Louis le Grand—by trying to dance.

Charles turned to La Chaise, hoping that they could go, and saw that La Chaise was leaning over the back of the king's chair, listening as Louis talked. Wondering irreverently which royal body was speaking—God's mystically anointed king or the natural man who begat children—Charles watched the white plume wave above a royal nod.

La Chaise straightened and nodded in turn to Charles. "We must go to the buffet *salon* for a time, not to our chambers yet."

They joined the crowd's slow drift toward the door and into the adjoining *salon*, where courtiers gathered around tables covered with platters of cold meat, plates of heaped pastries, and elaborately constructed pyramids of hothouse strawberries, plums, and peaches. Wine pitchers and ranks of short-stemmed glasses reflected the chandeliers' flickering light.

"They'll be pillaging the tables for a while," La Chaise said, under the pitch of the crowd's loud talk. "It does look inviting, doesn't it?"

"You must be feeling better, *mon père*. Are we allowed to pillage, as well?"

"If we do it without making an unclerical spectacle of ourselves. And you're right, I am better." After filling plates and glasses, La Chaise led the way toward a dark alcove where they could eat unobserved. But when they got closer, they saw a man's back and the rose-colored edge of a woman's skirt framed in the alcove's arch.

La Chaise muttered in exasperation and looked around for somewhere else. But Charles put his plate and glass down on a side table and strode to the alcove. The rose-colored skirt was overlaid with delicate white lace and the coat was the same black brocade as Henri Montmorency's.

"*Bonsoir*, Monsieur Montmorency," Charles said, loudly and brusquely.

Montmorency twitched a shoulder without looking to see who spoke. "Leave us. You intrude."

"Turn around, *monsieur*."

The flat order made the boy turn so fast and angrily that his sword smacked against Lulu's skirt and she exclaimed impatiently. To Charles's surprise, Montmorency seemed not at all alarmed when he saw who was talking to him. And seemed not to see La Chaise, standing a little aside, at all. Instead of giving Charles the courteous greeting and bow he owed a professor, Montmorency glowered. "What do you want?"

"To know what you are doing here." Charles glanced into the shadows where the king's daughter stood. "'Here' in all senses of the word, Monsieur Montmorency."

That produced a giggle from Lulu and a darker scowl from Montmorency.

"I am here with the rector's permission," the boy said stiffly.

"I am relieved to hear it," Charles returned. "Why are you here?"

Montmorency shifted his feet and groped for words, which never came quickly to him. "The ball. Why should I not be here?" He lifted his square chin and fell back on the central tenet of his universe. "I am a Montmorency."

"And so the king invited you? But you were rudely late."

The whites of Montmorency's eyes showed as he glanced into the shadows. "Yes! I mean, no, but—"

"Oh, have done!" Lulu surged out of the alcove, twitching her fan like an angry bird flicking its tail. "I invited him, *maître*." Her eyes traveled caressingly over Charles, who removed his *bonnet* and willed himself not to blush. She tapped him on the arm with the fan. "I sent him a note. So of course he came. Isn't he fortunate? Wouldn't you like to have a note from me?" Charles's distantly polite expression didn't alter and her voice chilled. "You, I see, only came to celebrate my being sold to Poland." Her lips trembled and she bit them to stillness.

"No, Lulu," Montmorency cried, "you know I will never let—"

"Shut up, *mon cher!*" Her false brilliant smile was back, and she kept it trained on Charles. "Your pupil has the Montmorency love of lost causes, *maître*. But who knows? Perhaps when I get to Poland, I shall at least enjoy the wolf hunting."

"You will never go there." Montmorency tried to take her hands. "I will—"

"You will nothing," she said, pulling her hands out of reach. As she moved, something clattered to the floor. Montmorency bent to retrieve it, but she was before him. Charles saw that it was a ring, old and heavy, with a deep blue stone capping an elaborate raised setting.

"A lovely jewel, Your Highness," he said.

Montmorency swelled with pride. "I gave it to her."

"A small parting gift." Lulu slipped the ring onto her right-hand middle finger.

"I put a lock of my hair in it," Montmorency said proudly. "Show him, Lulu."

She shrugged slightly at Charles and held out her hand. "It's a locket ring." She touched the side of the blue stone and the setting opened like a tiny book. A coil of fair hair nestled inside. "Monsieur Montmorency wished me to take something of him with me to Poland. He knew it would be a comfort for me."

She closed the ring and folded her other hand over it. Montmorency gazed at her with his heart in his eyes.

"I have one, too," he said, thrusting his hand at Charles. His locket ring had a red stone. He opened it to show the dark blond curl it held.

Lulu glanced at it and looked down. "I must go now," she said gravely, moving her shoulders a little, as though trying to shrug off the weight of the gleaming pearls. "My women will be looking for me."

She turned and left, and Montmorency started to follow her, but La Chaise cleared his throat and stepped into his path. "Why are you private with the king's daughter, *monsieur*? What business of yours is her going to Poland?"

Penned between the alcove's archway and the two Jesuits, Montmorency shifted uneasily. "Oh. Well, only that—that she's—well, going. And—" He flushed and stared at his shoes.

"And what?"

Charles watched the all too familiar spectacle of Montmorency making a mental effort. The results, if any, were unlikely to get the boy off whatever hook La Chaise was trying to hang him on.

"*Mon père—maître—*" Montmorency looked miserably from one to the other. "Can you not make the king change his mind?" He clasped both hands over his heart. "I shall die if she goes!"

Moved in spite of himself by the boy's unhappy devotion, Charles shook his head slightly at La Chaise, who was clearly not moved in the least.

"Monsieur Montmorency," Charles said carefully, "you must know that Mademoiselle de Rouen is not for you. Your house is ancient and great, but the king will marry his daughter only to royalty. I am sure you are aware of that, painful as it is to accept." Charles had learned the hard way that appealing to his sense of family was the only way to reason with the boy.

Montmorency bowed his head and stood with one hand on his sword—the very picture, Charles thought, of noble renunciation.

The boy drew himself up, resolution in his dog-brown eyes. "I am going to ask the king if he will let me win her right to stay in single combat. I am not so bad with a sword. Even if she could not marry me, at least she would be where I could still see her."

Charles told himself sternly not to laugh. "Single combat with whom?"

Montmorency shrugged. "I don't care. One of those ambassadors? Whomever the king chooses."

Very gently, as though each word were an egg that might break, Charles said, "Your heart does you credit, Monsieur Montmorency. But single combat is no longer done. Your request would not be granted."

La Chaise, unfortunately, found his voice. "Of course it wouldn't. You are talking like a fool. Go back to Louis le Grand and stay there. The girl is going to Poland and if you lift a finger to stop her, you will be guilty of treason. Come. I will find you a carriage."

Montmorency was a head taller than La Chaise, and as he glared at the king's confessor, his considerable bulk seemed to grow. For the first time, Charles saw a man's anger showing hard and bright behind the boy's yearning.

"I am not going back. I have leave to be here."

Charles had the feeling that if La Chaise had not been a cleric, Montmorency might have invited him out to the garden to settle the matter. But then the façade of Montmorency's new manhood wavered, and the boy showed through. "Leave me alone!" He dodged clumsily around La Chaise and made for the doors.

"Dear God," La Chaise muttered. "We have to get him out of here. Do you realize what he's flirting with?"

"I realize who."

"Don't you start playing the fool. Montmorency is the perfect dupe, and the girl will use him if she can. If he goes on talking about challenging the king's plans for her—or, God forbid, actually makes a move to challenge them—we'll be blamed nearly as much as he will, because we've educated him."

Charles snorted. "No one has educated Montmorency, believe me—" Something hit his shoulder and he turned sharply, jostling La Chaise, who spilled wine down his cassock. A thin middle-aged woman stood in the alcove's archway, frowning up at him.

-◆┨ *Chapter 9* ┠◆-

Sweeping her fan from side to side like a sword and frowning—
which made several of her star-shaped beauty patches collide
over her nose like an ominous planetary conjunction—the
woman pushed her way between Charles and La Chaise.

Openmouthed, La Chaise watched her green gown and
bright yellow wig disappear into the crowd. "Blessed Saint
Roch." He turned to stare at the alcove. "Did she come from in
there?"

"She must have," Charles said, wondering why La Chaise had
invoked a plague saint.

"So she was in there all the time, in there with the two of
them." La Chaise stood on his toes, trying to see over the mass
of talking, eating courtiers. "You're taller; can you still see her?"

Catching sight of the yellow ringlets, Charles nodded. "She
hasn't gone far, she's talking to someone. Who is she?"

"Her Royal Highness Marguerite Louise, Grand Duchess of
Tuscany. Known as Margot. She's the king's cousin, and twelve
years ago he sent her, much against her will, to Italy to marry
Cosimo de Medici. She has fought constantly against her husband and the marriage, and Louis has finally permitted her return to France. All of which makes her the very last person who
should be anywhere near Mademoiselle de Rouen just now." La

Chaise finished his wine in one gulp and put down his glass on the little table where Charles's own untasted wine and food still waited. "I will find Montmorency and make sure he goes back to Paris. You engage the Grand Duchess of Tuscany in talk. Stay with her. If you can't stay with her, watch her. And for God's sake, keep her away from Lulu. Do not let the duchess out of your sight until she is in her carriage and the carriage is turned for Paris. When you've seen her carriage pass the gates, report to me."

When Charles didn't move, La Chaise said grimly, "I know I am not your religious superior. I know you are only a scholastic. But I am asking you to help me. You say you are loyal to the king. Prove it now."

Since the only possible answer to that was agreement, Charles nodded and waded into the crowd after the bobbing yellow wig. His path crossed the duchess's near a door into the gallery. She was carrying a half-empty glass of dark red wine and swaying happily on her high heels. Some of her thickly plastered beauty patches had come unglued in the heat and landed like black shooting stars on her bare bony shoulders. She checked for a moment when she saw Charles and then greeted him loudly, spilling wine down his cassock as she tried to kiss him.

Courtiers around them egged her on. "Ah," someone sang out, "the Grand Duchess of Tuscany is a veritable Venus tonight, and who can resist her?"

Sighing inwardly, Charles fended her off. "May I be of service, *madame*? May I escort you to a seat?"

Margot laughed in his face. "Do I look so tired? Is Venus ever tired? Or are you too tired, poor celibate stick?" She regarded him, head to one side. "We might go back to that pretty little alcove and find a cure for your—limpness."

That brought delighted gasps and caws of merriment, and Charles felt himself turning as red as his tormenter's wine.

"Shall we walk out into the gallery, Your Royal Highness? It is cooler there and will stop your face from losing its celestial beauties."

The apt double entendre made the listening courtiers eye Charles with new respect. He stepped aside so that Margot could precede him through the door and followed in the wide wake of her summer-green skirts, praying fervently that Jouvancy would be well enough in the morning to ride in a carriage back to Paris and get them out of this place.

Not only was the gallery cooler, but it was nearly deserted and quieter, except for what Charles took at first for the sound of an indoor fountain, then realized was an unseen man pissing in one of the small dark gallery alcoves. A few couples sat on scattered benches or strolled, whispering together, along the black-and-white tile. Charles led Margot to a bench, and as she sat down and spread her skirts, he bent to look more closely at the bench's soft luster in the light from the wall sconces.

"Silver?" he said incredulously.

"Of course, silver. Whatever my dear cousin Louis wants, he must have."

"And you?" Charles said boldly, sitting on the bench's end. If he had to dog her steps, he might as well find out all he could about her. "It seems you've gained what you wanted in coming back to France."

She drained her glass. "Yes. And it took twelve miserable years of my life. How long do you suppose it took Louis to get this?" She slapped a hand down on the gleaming silver and hiccupped.

"Not twelve years," Charles said, knowing that was his next line in this script. "Do you dislike your husband so much, then?"

She gave him a wide, gap-toothed smile. "I loathe Cosimo de Medici. I loathed him on sight. I loathed the very thought of going to Italy and marrying him. But what did that matter to Louis?"

"A hard fate for a woman," he said, both because it was the truth and also to see how she might respond.

"You may well say so." She glanced sideways at him. "And now I must watch poor little Lulu go through it all. And Poland is much farther away and will be harder to escape than Italy was. But perhaps her little prince will be less disagreeable than Cosimo. So ugly, Cosimo, and I always dislike ugly men. I wouldn't even bother sitting here with you, if you were ugly." She tapped him on the chest with her closed fan. "You are not ugly at all, are you, *mon cher*?"

"Whatever else I am, I am a cleric, Your Highness," Charles said quietly.

"Whatever else you are, you are a silly young prude," she mocked, "and you will have to account to the *bon Dieu* for such waste." She hiccupped again and turned her head toward the sound of another man making use of an alcove. "Ah, the sweet sound of flowing water. Always it calls to my own water. And, alas, I cannot make use of an alcove. Help me up, *mon cher*."

Charles stood quickly and pulled her to her feet. Her skirts swept her empty glass from the bench, and it shattered on the floor.

"No, no, we must not be indelicate," she laughed, as Charles made to accompany her. "You cannot escort me to *la chaise de commodité*—the real one, I mean, of course. I have no desire to meet the other one any more often than I must." Giggling drunkenly, she wove her way down the gallery.

Charles hesitated, wanting no more of her company. But his orders were not to leave her. Soft footed, he followed, keeping her just in sight. The farther they went, the more deserted the gallery was. The wall sconces grew farther apart, but even in the dimming candlelight, the yellow wig led him like a beacon. And the beacon's progress was straight as an arrow. Margot's drunken wavering was gone and her heels tapped purposefully along the marble. Which made Charles follow with greater interest and think, as she turned corner after corner, that surely she must have passed a privy by now. But she never slowed. She vanished suddenly and he heard her pattering rapidly down a staircase. He ran lightly to its opening and felt his way down. At the bottom, he heard her steps fading away on his right. Knowing that if he lost the duchess he'd never find her in this maze, he put on a burst of speed. And cannoned into a massive figure who stepped suddenly into his way without seeing him.

The man swore, lumbered backward, and stood against a door, glaring at Charles.

"Did a woman in a yellow wig and a green gown pass just now?" Charles said.

The man—a footman, Charles supposed—set his back more solidly against the closed door.

"If she didn't pass you, she must have gone through that door you're guarding so well."

The footman ignored him and Charles drifted a little aside, as though giving up the effort to communicate. He hit the wood-paneled wall as hard as he could with the flat of his hand, and the footman jumped and swore again.

"So you're not deaf," Charles said pleasantly. "Which means you're probably not mute, either. "Did a woman go into the rooms you're guarding?"

"What's that to you?" the man growled.

His stare was beginning to remind Charles of an implacably belligerent dog deciding where to bite, and he stepped a little farther away. "Whose rooms are these? Come on, *mon brave*, you may as well tell me; I can easily find out from someone else."

"Then go find out."

Charles withdrew. When he reached the staircase, he stepped into the dark stairwell and settled himself against the wall, veiled in shadows, and watched the door. Unless Margot decided to stay the night, she would eventually emerge into the gallery. With luck, she would then simply find her carriage and leave. And he could go to bed. After, of course, reporting to Père La Chaise. He wondered why Margot had feigned drunkenness. Simply to be rid of the "silly young prude"? But she was royal; she had no need to be subtle when she tired of someone's company. Had she been making sure he wouldn't follow her? And what had she truly been doing in the *salon* alcove with Mademoiselle de Rouen and Montmorency? Charles shook his head. Were La Chaise's suspicions of the women—both Margot and Lulu—justified, or did they only mean that he'd been too long in this hothouse of rumor and suspicion?

Charles sighed with weariness and began to recite one of Cicero's speeches to himself to pass the time. When he was done with that and there was still no sign of Margot, he tried to pray, but closing his eyes took him to the edge of sleep. Last night's sickness, he supposed, had left him more tired than he'd realized. He tried planning the next section of the college ballet, but the ballet made him think about the king's wrongdoings and his own helplessness against them. From there, his thoughts jumped to courtiers and then to the Comte de Fleury lying dead at the foot of the gallery stairs, and then to the dead gardener beside the lake. He heard the Prince of Conti's lazy, ironic voice in his head. *So now you've found a drowned rat.* For no reason he could fully explain, Charles was still certain that Conti had followed him from the fountain. But why?

Torchlight flared from the stairs, and Charles withdrew farther into the darkness. A servant with a small wax torch came from the stairs and led a chattering group of men and women along the gallery. Returning from the ball, Charles guessed, from the glitter of their clothes in the torchlight. They passed by the footman and twinkled and glimmered into the distance. As Charles settled against the wall again, the footman moved suddenly and the door opened. The Grand Duchess of Tuscany emerged, cloaked and hooded. She walked briskly in Charles's direction, and the footman fell in behind her.

Following after her stolid watchdog, Charles breathed a prayer of thanks when she made for the forecourt where Charles and Jouvancy had dismounted on their arrival at the palace. Which seemed weeks ago now, Charles thought dismally, though this was only their third night there. From a gallery window, he watched with relief as the footman handed Margot into a waiting carriage and climbed up behind. The coachman turned the pair of horses and the carriage began to roll toward the palace gates.

But Charles would have been more relieved if Margot's drunkenness had not disappeared so abruptly when she'd left him.

Suddenly needing to breathe fresh air, Charles went outside. The evening was mild. There was a small breeze, and the stars were half veiled in rags of cloud. The courtyard wasn't busy; only a few carriages waited for nobles, and members of the Guard stood at their posts or patrolled their appointed territory. Charles wandered across the gravel toward the south wing, breathing in the breeze-blown sweetness of grass and trees, glad even for the pungence of horse smells and burning torches, glad for anything that wasn't the smell of sweated cloth, dirty wigs, and bodies less clean than their snowy linen. At least, he thought, he was spared breathing air drenched in clashing perfumes, since the king had grown to dislike them.

Dogs barked in the town and dogs in the royal kennels answered them. The swift gray flight of an owl brushed Charles's cheek. And something—the dogs, the kiss of the owl's wing—made him nearly cry out with longing for home, for the hot dry smell of Languedoc, the call of nightjars from dark trees, the spare coolness of his mother's old stone house. Grapes swelling in the vineyards, fatter in the morning than they'd been the night before, the sight of Pernelle at fifteen in the firelit doorway, all fine bones and a cloud of black hair, calling him to come in. Himself, seventeen and blind with love for her. He closed the memory gently, the way he closed old books, and prayed for her.

His prayer finished, Charles looked up at the windows of the palace's south wing, most with shutters still open on candlelit rooms. Tired, but not wanting to shut himself back inside yet, he walked slowly to the end of the wing and turned toward the garden side, thinking to go in by a back door. Sounds of the forecourt fell away as he turned the building's corner and went slowly toward the dark gardens. But when he turned along the torchlit side of the wing, he stopped short. Half a dozen chattering men in court dress came out of a door onto the gravel.

"You do me too much honor, *monsieur*," a light, ironic voice said.

Charles retreated from the torchlight. The last thing he wanted at the end of this day was another meeting with the Prince of Conti. But as he watched the men stroll toward the gardens, he recognized the largest among them as Henri de Montmorency. Whom La Chaise should have had on his way back to Paris by now. Hoping that the Lulu-besotted Montmorency had not left the king's confessor somewhere with a broken head, Charles stayed out of the light and considered what he ought to do. Montmorency was following Conti like an overgrown puppy, all but treading on his heels. That the boy would want to curry favor with a Prince of the Blood was no surprise. The surprise was that Conti was tolerating him, and it seemed politic to find out why. Not least for Montmorency's sake.

Charles set himself to follow the courtiers. Unexpectedly, Conti turned suddenly aside, through the gate of one of the walled gardens. Charles had thought the men would stroll the paths, chattering and vying for Conti's attention, and had intended to come upon them as if by chance and draw Montmorency away. But now, full of misgiving, he stepped off the gravel onto soft turf and slipped into the garden. At first, he heard nothing. Then he caught a low urgent voice away on his left, and as he moved toward it, he realized it was Conti's.

"Of course," Conti said, "Monsieur le Dauphin is the— mildest, shall we say, of men. He understands that he will need the help—"

Someone sneezed and covered Conti's words. Then Charles heard, ". . . and last winter, we all—um—feared—the time had come." There was a low rumble of exclamation and a snigger of laughter, quickly hushed.

"I wish it had!" The voice was Montmorency's, and his words created a taut silence.

Charles winced, wondering if anyone could really be as innocently stupid as Henri de Montmorency seemed.

"Well—I mean—if he'd died, Lulu wouldn't have to go to Poland!" Montmorency said lamely.

"Your heart does you credit, does it not, *messieurs*?" Conti said softly.

The others murmured agreement with the prince. Charles's hair rose on the back of his neck. Neither Conti nor the others were laughing.

The prince said, "And exactly *how* will you help her?"

Charles barely stopped himself from charging into the little coterie and dragging Montmorency out of it by main force. Conti was smoothly herding the boy to the edge of treason—treasonous talk, at least. And doing it before a gathering of avid courtiers in the palace garden.

Charles ran soundlessly out of the garden and a small way along the turf back toward the palace. Then he stepped onto the gravel, faced away from the walled garden he'd left and shouted, "Monsieur Montmorency!" That, of course, got no answer, and Charles walked innocently on, peering into the darkness, until he reached the edge of the torchlight from the palace. "Monsieur Montmorency," he called again, "are you here? Madame, your mother wishes to speak with you."

He waited until he heard heavy quick steps on the gravel behind him. Then, as though he'd heard nothing, he called again, facing along the building, "Monsieur Montmorency, are you in the garden?"

"I am here," Montmorency panted, and Charles turned to meet him with a creditable show of surprise. The boy's face loomed anxiously in the torchlight. "Where is she?"

"We must go inside." Charles led him into the first door they came to and hurried him along the corridor to the gallery leading to the south wing.

"But where is she?" Montmorency's eyes were searching the gallery in confusion. "Why is she here?"

"She's not. Though wherever she is, I'm sure she always wants to talk with her son. We're going—"

"You lied?" Montmorency stopped short and scowled at Charles. "I don't have to go—"

"I didn't lie. Not technically. We are going to Père La Chaise. Unless you did away with him when he tried to send you back to school."

"He has no right to give me orders."

"You are still a student and under the college's protection, and therefore the protection of Jesuits. And I am your professor and *do* have a right to give you orders. Come."

"I do not need your protection."

"Oh, but you do, *monsieur*," Charles said grimly.

Montmorency was tall and broad, but he still had to look up a little at Charles, and what he saw in Charles's face closed his mouth. Charles gripped the boy's arm, and they made the rest of the long walk to La Chaise's door without speaking.

They found La Chaise dozing in his chair by the light of a single candle, to the accompaniment of Jouvancy snoring lightly in the next room. The king's confessor opened his eyes and re-garded them owlishly for a moment. Then he swore and leaped to his feet.

"What in the name of all hell's devils are you doing back here?" He scowled at Charles. "And you—is the lady gone?"

"Yes." Charles pushed Montmorency farther into the room. "And Monsieur Montmorency has come to tell you what he's doing here, *mon père.*"

"I haven't come to tell you anything." Montmorency gripped the hilt of the light, slender court sword hanging at his side.

"Unless you are thinking of relieving your feelings by draw-ing on me," La Chaise said, "remember the manners our college has taught you and leave your sword alone."

"Oh." The boy dropped his hands to his side as though his sword had caught fire. He blinked at La Chaise and bowed slightly. "I wouldn't. Draw on you, I mean." And then he added, "You're not armed."

Charles and La Chaise exchanged a look, and Charles had to turn his face away to hide his incredulous grin.

"When did you ever see an armed Jesuit, Monsieur Mont-morency?" La Chaise raised a hand as Montmorency opened his mouth. "Never mind. Maître du Luc, perhaps you could jog this noble pupil's memory about what he's come to tell me."

"I came on him in the garden, in company with the Prince of Conti and his friends."

Montmorency's gasped. "You didn't—"

"I did. I saw you leave the palace and I heard you talking. Monsieur Montmorency told the prince that he wished the king had died last winter. And said again that he intends to prevent Mademoiselle de Rouen's going to Poland."

"You young idiot!" La Chaise was white with anger. And fear, Charles suspected. "Are you too stupid to see that you spoke treason in the hearing of a Prince of the Blood? If the Prince of Conti chooses to use that against you, you will most likely find yourself the object of a royal *lettre de cachet* and locked up in the Bastille."

To Charles's astonishment, Montmorency blazed back at La Chaise. "That kind of letter comes from the king only if you disgrace your family, and I will never disgrace the name of Montmorency. I only said what I feel. The king is breaking Lulu's heart, and I won't let her go to Poland! And she is not my only reason for hating the king. He beheaded my kinsman—I don't forget that, even if everyone else does!"

La Chaise and Charles looked blankly at each other.

"What kinsman?" Charles said. "When?"

"The one I'm named after. Henri de Montmorency."

La Chaise rolled his eyes. "Who was beheaded more than fifty years ago by Louis the Thirteenth, the present king's father. For joining the present king's uncle in rebellion. Do you learn no history at Louis le Grand? Louis the Fourteenth did not behead your kinsman. Louis the Fourteenth was not even *born* when your hapless ancestor died."

Stubbornly, Montmorency plowed on. "Anyway, King Louis is banishing Lulu. And I will say what I like to the Prince of Conti. *He* is my kinsman, too. And that makes the other Henri de Montmorency *his* kinsman. Don't priests say that the crimes of the fathers fall on the sons?"

"Not precisely," Charles murmured absently, trying to work out Montmorency's relation to Conti. He looked at La Chaise. "How are the Montmorencys kin to the Contis?"

"Henri the Second of Montmorency's sister married the Prince of Condé," La Chaise said impatiently. "The prince who was the Great Condé's father. And Conti is the Great Condé's nephew."

Charles gave up trying to untangle the twisted family tree. "Is everyone here related?"

"More or less."

Montmorency, slightly openmouthed, had been straining to follow the talk. Seeming to find himself on solid ground again, he wrapped a meaty hand around his sword hilt as though taking an oath. "So it is my sacred duty—"

"Hold your tongue," La Chaise said dangerously. "It is your duty to return to Louis le Grand. And to stay there, *monsieur*, until your schooling ends in August. No." He held up a hand. "Say nothing." La Chaise sat down at the small table that served as his desk, found paper, inked a pen, and wrote. Then he turned to Charles. "Keep him here." Folding the note, he went swiftly out into the gallery.

Montmorency started after him, but Charles stepped into his path. "If you defy Père La Chaise any more tonight, who knows what might happen? You wouldn't want to find yourself as beheaded as your kinsman, *monsieur.* Then you could truly do nothing to help Mademoiselle de Rouen."

"No one's going to behead me." Montmorency's eyes shifted uneasily.

"Beheading is very bloody," Charles went on conversationally. "Very painful, I imagine, unless you have an experienced headsman. And there are fewer beheadings these days, so"—he shrugged—"you can imagine the lack of practice."

Montmorency stared, wide-eyed.

Fortunately, La Chaise swept back through the anteroom and into the chamber, the footman Bouchel at his heels.

"This time you will arrive at Louis le Grand, *monsieur,* because our good Bouchel is going with you. He will get you a carriage in the courtyard, and he will not leave you until you are inside the college. He will also deliver the note I have written to Père Le Picart, telling him why you have been sent back. And that you are to be kept there. Unless you want heavier penance than you ever imagined possible, you will make no trouble over this or anything else. And you will keep your tongue behind your teeth concerning the king or his daughter Mademoiselle de Rouen. Whom you will not, under any circumstances, see again. Go."

Though he was a head shorter and built altogether on a smaller scale, Bouchel had Montmorency out of the room before he could splutter out a protest. Charles and La Chaise listened to their steps receding along the gallery, and then La Chaise flung himself back into his chair.

"Dear God, the boy is a menace! At the worst possible age for fancying himself a hero and even stupider than the other Henri de Montmorency. If he eludes Père Le Picart's surveillance and comes back here before Lulu's gone, there's going to be hell to pay."

Charles was suddenly too tired to care much about hell, or anything else but sleep. "If I may excuse myself, *mon père*, I will wish you a *bonne nuit* and a blessed rest."

"You may not." The king's confessor was looking at him as though he were something on a buffet table that might or might not be worth trying. "I saw the way the girl looked at you tonight."

"What girl?"

"Lulu. Mademoiselle de Rouen. Who else are we talking about? You could make yourself very useful while we wait for Père Jouvancy to improve. I want you to talk to her. Counsel her. Amuse her; keep her away from Margot and Conti."

Charles couldn't believe his ears. "I cannot play the attentive courtier to the king's sixteen-year-old daughter! I'm a Jesuit!"

"Precisely. You are a Jesuit. And I am the king's Jesuit confessor, and I need your help." He eyed Charles. "I presume you anticipate ordination at some time in the future."

Startled, Charles nodded.

"Well, let me tell you, when—if—you become a priest, you will face situations that require you to counsel women. So what if they flirt with you? Lulu flirts with every handsome man of quality she sees—and some neither handsome nor of quality. No one will pay any attention. Tell her that you want to help her find some peace in accepting this marriage. For the good of her soul. Spend some time with her, gain her confidence, counsel her to be dutiful."

"Why not set one of her women to watch her? I think Père Jouvancy may be well enough tomorrow to take a carriage back to Paris. And I will take both horses back."

"Even if he should be well enough to travel tomorrow, he will no doubt be willing to extend his recovery a little while you do what is in the king's best interest."

With a sudden pang of sympathy for the flailing Lulu, Charles folded his hands and stared down at his hard clasped knuckles.

La Chaise said softly, "Are you afraid of your own response if she flirts with you?"

Charles's head came up. "No! But I do feel sorry for her, because of all the ways people are manipulating her. Now you are telling me to manipulate her. For your own ends."

"For the Society's ends. And how is that different from what you did just now to Henri Montmorency?"

"I did not—"

"Oh, but you did. You are young Montmorency's superior, his professor. You used your knowledge of him and your authority over him to make him behave appropriately and do what was necessary. What I am asking of you is even more necessary."

Stinging from the lash of unwelcome truth, Charles stared at the darkness beyond the window. He felt pushed into a spinning whirlpool. The coolly ruthless part of himself he so disliked suddenly spoke. *You might at least be honest,* it said. *You're noble. Now you're a Jesuit. Your kind is always near the heart of power. And when you're a priest, you'll be even nearer.*

─❧╂ *Chapter 10* ╂❧─

Charles woke to a dark day and a darker mood. The only bright thing was that he felt much better, and Père Jouvancy seemed better, too. When Charles had him sitting up and hungrily eating the fresh bread and rich broth Bouchel had brought from the town, he left him in the footman's care and took himself to the chapel. Père La Chaise was already out and about his own business, and Charles was relieved to avoid more talk about last night. Facing his assignment for today was enough.

The chapel was empty of people and full of early morning quiet. Charles knelt at the Virgin's side altar. He prayed for Jouvancy's quick recovery and then gazed disconsolately at the large gilt-framed painting of the Madonna and Child hanging above the altar. She and the baby in her arms had none of the homely peace of the little painting in Charles's bedchamber at the college. This Virgin's robes billowed around her, as though a strong wind blew from the world into her frame. The stern-faced baby looked as though he were already judging that world as irredeemable. Charles bowed his head onto his clasped hands. It was so easy to believe that this world of Versailles had fallen further from grace than the rest of the world he knew. Maybe he himself was the one judging too harshly. Maybe doing as Père La Chaise had asked, helping Lulu reconcile herself to her duty and go peacefully to Poland, might be a means of grace to her. Except that the king's sending her there had nothing to do with wanting good for her. Just as La Chaise's concern was for the king, for France, not for the girl herself. Unless, of course, you granted that doing one's duty helped one's soul. Which Charles usually did at least *try* to grant. Except . . .

Heels echoed on the chapel floor, and Charles turned from his unsuccessful praying to see who had come in. It was the Prince of Conti, and Charles watched him go briskly to a side altar where, instead of kneeling, Conti went up the two small steps and bent over the altar. Something about the man's intent stillness brought Charles to his feet. Most courtiers were said to be up to their ears in gambling debts, and a wild suspicion that Conti was stealing the gold and jeweled candlesticks went through his mind. Telling himself that he was growing as insane as the rest of Versailles, Charles went quietly across the chapel. But Conti's hearing was as good as his own.

"*Bonjour, maître.*" The young man turned and came quickly down the altar steps. "You see how our good Madame de Maintenon has honored your gift." He gestured gracefully at the altar, and Charles saw that Jouvancy's gold-and-lapis reliquary stood between the candlesticks.

"She wants it to be seen here before she takes it to Saint Cyr," Conti said, smiling.

Chiding himself for labeling everything the man said as mockery, Charles said, "I am glad to see it here, Your Serene Highness. Our college is indeed honored. Have you come to pray to Saint Ursula?"

"Of course! I assure you, I have a great devotion to Saint Ursula and her companions, the eleven thousand pious virgins." Conti grinned at Charles.

"Commendable," Charles replied, who couldn't help but think that the handsome young prince might indeed be devoted to virgins, but probably not in the way presently under discussion.

"I was perhaps not listening closely at the presentation—but I do remember the priest saying that the bone inside the cross is a finger."

Charles nodded.

"So one might pray here for—direction, shall we say? That the holy saint will point the way? To the speeding of one's purposes?"

"Depending on the purposes you wish to speed, Your Serene Highness."

"But of course." Conti laughed and put a hand on Charles's sleeve. "Are you always so righteous?" He squeezed Charles's arm. "What a shame," Conti sighed. "You might be very— ah—entertaining if you were a little more—unrighteous, shall we say?" He sauntered away, giving Charles a regretful glance over his shoulder as he went through the chapel door.

Charles's hands twitched, and he had an unholy urge to throttle the man.

"Point him toward something he'll trip over, Holy Virgin," he suggested to St. Ursula, and went in search of Lulu.

He didn't find her until the late-morning Mass, when he saw her in the train of courtiers gathering in the Hall of Mirrors to follow the king to the chapel. The gray day had taken the magic out of the Hall of Mirrors' light, but the crowd had brought its own glitter in its bright, shimmering clothes and gold-set jewels.

Lulu, dressed in gray silk and straw-yellow lace, seeming as quenched as the day's light, stood beside a silver-potted orange tree, twisting one leaf after another from its branches. The king came from his counsel room, accompanied by the Polish ambassadors, and paced toward the chapel, everyone making a deep *reverence* to the royal presence and moving slowly after him. Louis glanced at Charles as he passed and gave him a slight nod of acknowledgment. Dismayed at being singled out, Charles belatedly whipped off his formal *bonnet* and bowed his head. And remained staring at the carpet. Had the king's look meant that he knew of the plan to quiet Lulu, and approved? Among the many things Charles did not want, the attention of Louis XIV was high on the list.

He looked up just in time to step into the flood of courtiers behind Lulu and her women. When the king and his retinue, including La Chaise, turned aside to go up into the royal gallery facing the altar, Charles crowded into the nave with the rest and found an unobtrusive place to stand near a wall. The Mass began, but he was too taken up with deciding how to approach Lulu to do any better with his devotions than he had earlier. When the service ended, he jockeyed for position in the moving crowd, trying to keep the king's daughter in sight. As he passed through the chapel door, fortune—or perhaps St. Ursula—smiled on him and Lulu dropped her prayer book, which slid on the shining marble floor and came to rest at his feet. Charles swooped on it, pretending not to notice that one of her women had bent to retrieve it, and straightened with it in his hand.

"Your Highness?" He stepped around the affronted attendant and bowed, holding out the prayer book. "Allow me to restore this to you."

The girl's pale, somber face lightened. "Oh, it's you." She

nodded at the listening woman, who took the book from Charles. "Thank you, *maître*." She hesitated and then said, "Will you walk with me?"

Surprised by the invitation, and even more surprised that it was given without coquetry, Charles nodded. As she gestured her women to make room for him to walk at her side, Charles saw that Anne-Marie, the Condé child, was among them, cuddling her little black dog. He smiled at her, somehow reassured by her presence, and fell into step with Lulu.

"Are you going to your dinner, Your Highness?" he asked.

"Not yet." She sighed. "Shall we walk outside? The rain has stopped."

"As you please."

She led him to a door opening onto the gravel that led to the gardens. As he opened the door for her, she dismissed her women with a wave of her hand. The one carrying the prayer book started to object, but Lulu talked over her.

"Surely you can trust me with a cleric! Leave us. Not you, Anne-Marie, you may come."

Gathering her gray skirts, Lulu swept through the door, and little Anne-Marie ran to keep up with her. Charles bowed gravely to the startled attendants, did his best to shut the door without seeming to close it in their faces, and followed. Lulu's subdued quiet had vanished and she strode across the puddled gravel, indifferent to the little girl's anxious warning of wet shoes and splattered hems. The vitality that made her seem twice as alive as other people swirled around her like a whirlwind. Feeling a little like a foolish chicken chasing a hungry fox, Charles caught up and kept pace with her. She flashed him a look, and in the harsher outdoor light he saw the shadows under her eyes and how pale she was.

"Aren't you also going to tell me it's too wet, that I should go in?"

"No."

"Are you so eager to be alone with me, then? You weren't yesterday."

"We're not alone. And no, I'm not eager to be alone with you."

She spun to face him in a spray of water. "That is an insult!"

"I imagine you don't often receive truthful answers."

For a moment he thought she might slap him. Instead, she burst into tears and Anne-Marie looked reproachfully at him. Charles, certain that the tears were a ploy, said nothing. Lulu drew a small transparent handkerchief from the little bag hanging at her waist, wiped her eyes, burst into fresh sobs, and stumbled away from him along a garden path. Maybe not a ploy, Charles decided, and went after her, smiling reassuringly at Anne-Marie, who was at Lulu's heels with a fresh handkerchief. Lulu stumbled again, and he caught her arm to keep her from falling. She mopped her face with the little girl's handkerchief and stood catching her breath and staring down at the path. Charles thought she looked like a beautiful but bedraggled young bird, flown from the nest too soon and lost, and his heart suddenly went out to her.

"I would suggest we sit somewhere," he said, "but it's too wet."

"You can go back," she said drearily. "Anne-Marie and I will come to no harm here. You can tell my women where I am, if it makes you feel better. The old one will be hanging by the door still. She never wants me to have a moment away from her. Ever since this betrothal, I can hardly ever get away from my guards." Her eyes slewed sideways to Charles. "But sometimes I used to."

"Would you care to walk more, then? Instead of going back to your guards? It's not quite the same as being alone, but you could pretend I'm a tree." He grinned at the little girl. "Anne-Marie could be a bush."

Anne-Marie eyed him. "And what would he be?" she said, holding up her dog.

"Um—still a dog, I think. Dogs are often better company than people. So you are alone, Your Highness, except for a tree, a bush, and a dog."

Lulu was laughing in spite of herself. "You are nearly as tall as a tree."

The three of them followed the path quietly, the dog running ahead. The sky was beginning to clear, and the day was promising the thick heat that followed summer rain. But the air was clean and sweet, and Charles was glad to be outdoors. They wandered for some minutes without speaking, Charles letting Lulu choose their direction. She turned aside beneath a rose arbor, and when they were all under it, she reached up and pulled at a tangle of branches, showering them with glistening raindrops. Anne-Marie shrieked and covered her little blue lace and ribbon fontange, but Lulu threw her head back and laughed, suddenly shining with life again.

"There! Now you're all as wet as I am!"

Charles took off his *bonnet* and shook the water from it. "You seem to feel better. Crying often does that, I find."

Both girls looked at him curiously. Anne-Marie, walking now on Charles's other side, said, "Do you cry, too?"

"Everyone does."

"My father doesn't." Lulu's tone was suddenly venomous and the words spilled out. "He's *never* miserable, he only makes other people so. Especially women." She stopped in front of Charles and faced him. "Do you know what he said when his first daughter was born? His only legitimate one. It was—oh, thirty years ago, and she soon died, but of course, he didn't know she would and he had all the bells rung in Paris and bonfires lit. And when they asked him why he did that for a girl, he said that a daughter was something to celebrate because she would make a valuable marriage connection with some other prince. That's all a daughter means to him." She spat impressively into the gravel.

"It may be true that some fathers care less for daughters, but God doesn't make that distinction."

"Oh, no? Priests talk enough about Eve's daughters and all the evil we've brought into the world."

"The story doesn't say Eve shoved the apple down Adam's throat. I imagine he gobbled it down and asked for another."

"And then blamed Eve when his belly hurt!" Lulu laughed, in spite of herself.

"Of course he did!" Charles said, laughing, too.

Anne-Marie, digging a thinly shod toe in the wet gravel, was watching them so somberly that Charles wondered if the little princess ever let go of her dignity long enough to behave like a child.

"Margot's husband was just like that," Lulu said disgustedly, taking Charles's arm and beginning to walk again. "The Duchess of Tuscany, I mean. You probably don't know her. Anyway, her husband blamed her for his bellyache when he didn't like the marriage he and my father forced her into!"

Charles let her hold on to him, not wanting to disturb the growing confidence between them. "The Duchess of Tuscany was with you in the little alcove last evening, wasn't she?"

"How did you know that?"

"She came out after you and Monsieur Montmorency left."

"Oh."

Charles decided to seize the moment and hoped she wouldn't

take offense. "Your Highness, I beg you not to encourage Monsieur Montmorency. He is very much in love with you. But you must not—" He searched for words, but there was no other way to say it. "You must not use him."

Lulu made a dismissive noise. "At least he doesn't want me to go to Poland! Is it my fault he throws himself at my feet whenever he can get away from your school and come here? Which is hardly ever. Anyway, you needn't worry, I'll probably never see him again." A fleeting smile brightened her face. "Last night Margot kissed him, and you should have seen him blush! I wish Margot were here all the time. She's the only one who really knows how I feel. Her marriage was so terrible—her husband tried to poison her, did you know that?"

Charles shook his head.

"Of course, he said she tried to poison him first."

"Did she?"

"Of course she didn't. It's always the Italians who poison people."

Not always, Charles thought, remembering suddenly that in the Paris poison scandal that had rocked France a few years back, it was Lulu's mother, Madame de Montespan, who had been accused of trying to poison the king. Though nothing had come of the accusation. But since he was thinking about poison . . .

"Is the Grand Duchess of Tuscany acquainted with your mother?"

"Of course. Though they don't like each other much. They don't have much in common."

Except poison, Charles thought, *if rumor was to be believed*. Which it usually wasn't.

Lulu leaned closer, her eyes suddenly sparkling with glee. "Do you know what Margot did in the convent where my father makes her live in Montmartre? No? Well, the mother superior was trying to keep her from going out so much—Margot comes here often to gamble. And Margot got her pistol—"

"*Pistol?*"

"Perhaps ladies have them in Tuscany, I don't know. Anyway, she got her pistol and grabbed a hatchet from somewhere and chased the mother superior through the convent until the poor woman relented! Now Margot leaves when she pleases!"

"I can imagine she does," Charles murmured, hoping that hatchets and pistols would not be much in evidence at the Polish court, since Lulu seemed so charmed by Margot's example.

Lulu dropped his arm and sighed. "But I'll never come back from Poland."

"Your Highness, why does this marriage seem so terrible to you?"

"Because the Polish prince is nothing but a child! And he—he can't—" Fresh tears ran down her face, and she wiped angrily at them with her hand.

"A child? What do you mean?"

"He's ten years old. Oh, there's an older brother, but the Polish king has other plans for him. What good is a little boy to me?"

"Not much," Charles said injudiciously, appalled at this piece of news. For the ten-year-old husband, as much as for the sixteen-year-old bride. "Or not much good yet," he made himself add. "Children do grow up."

"I'll be old before then! When he's my age, I'll be almost twenty-two!"

"Hardly old." Charles made a face at her and said confidingly, "Though I myself am so old, perhaps my opinion hardly matters."

"You? You don't look old. What age are you?"

"Twenty-nine, Your Highness. One foot in the grave, I fear."

She laughed a little. "I never knew Jesuits were so amusing. First you are a tree and now you are pretending to have one ancient foot in the grave." She sighed, gazing at him. "I wish you were Jan Sobieski's second son!"

"Not a drop of Polish blood in my veins, I fear," Charles said lightly, and widened the space between them. The dog turned from nosing through the wet grass and jumped up on him with muddy paws.

"No, Louis!" Anne-Marie tried to pull the dog away as Charles leaned down to fondle its long black ears.

"No matter, the mud's the same color as the cassock."

Lulu suddenly scooped up the dog, cradling him as though he were a baby, and buried her face in his fur. For a moment, she was so still she seemed not to breathe. Then she put him down, picked up her gray skirts, and ran down the arbor path like a small fierce storm.

Anne-Marie glared at Charles. "You shouldn't make her run. She's been feeling ill."

"She doesn't seem ill. Although she does look pale."

"Yes."

Charles and Anne-Marie found Lulu beside a fishpond with a small dolphin spouting water in its center. Standing at its rim, she was taking crumbs from a pocket under her skirts and throwing them to the fish. With a sense of girding his loins, Charles decided that it was time to do what he'd agreed. Though he was even less sure now whether doing it was a good or a bad thing.

"Your Highness, there is something I would like to say to you."

"What?" she said, without turning.

Charles went to the pond's edge. "I would like to see you

find a measure of peace in this marriage the king is demanding of you. So that some good can perhaps come from it, though you dread it now. You were never meant to be a darkling, angry soul!"

Behind him, he heard Anne-Marie catch her breath. He looked over his shoulder and she nodded eagerly at him. But Lulu's stare was cold.

"So that's why you're willing to walk with me? Not for the pleasure of my company, but to 'help' me stop being in-convenient?"

"Your company is more pleasure than I expected. I would like to help you for you yourself. No one else."

She shrugged, but a wary hope showed in her eyes. "Every-one else only wants me out of the way. Because I smoke and flirt and swear and—" She bit her lip and grabbed a handful of her skirts and shook the soaked hem's straw-yellow lace trimming at him. "I ruin my gowns, I run away from my tedious women . . . such very grave sins."

Charles said nothing, and the three of them walked on. The path opened suddenly into a long vista down the newly dug lake. Unlike the bank where the gardener's body had lain, this bank was already covered in thin grass and the piles of dirt had been removed.

Wondering again at the lake's vast size, Charles said, "Where does all the water come from?"

"The Machine brings it," Anne-Marie said. "Haven't you ever seen it?"

"No, Your Serene Highness. What machine is that?"

"The Machine de Marly. It's by the river at the king's cha-teau of Marly. It's immense!" The white lace ruffles fluttered at her elbows as she stretched her short arms as wide as they would go. "And it makes a terrible noise. No one can sleep near it. It pumps water up the hill to Marly's fountains and then here to Versailles."

"Yes, even the water has to obey my father," Lulu said bitterly. She went to a small stone bench at the lake's edge, but turned back. "It's wet."

"I'll dry it for us." Charles pulled a large handkerchief from his sleeve and wiped the bench with it.

The girls sat close together and Charles remained standing, but Lulu reached up and pulled him down beside her.

He let a few moments go by and then said carefully, "Is no one trying to help you through this time, Your Highness? Not your mother? Nor Madame de Maintenon?"

"My mother doesn't want me to go, but what can she do? The king cares nothing for what she wants, not anymore. And Madame de Maintenon only really cares about my brother; he was always her favorite." Lulu twitched a dismissive shoulder. "Though she did put her new relic temporarily in the chapel, so I can go there every day and pray to Saint Ursula for help in doing my duty."

Charles winced at the chill of that. But the Duc du Maine had said that Mme de Maintenon did not care much for the troublesome Lulu. "So you have no one to help you." *Or love you,* he thought sadly.

"Except Saint Ursula," Anne-Marie whispered. "And me." But Lulu didn't seem to hear her.

Charles did, but he paid no attention. He was remembering himself at sixteen, remembering how the love of God and the saints and everyone else had paled beside the love he'd really wanted then, from Pernelle.

Forcing himself to go on, he said, "Your Highness, may I—"

She laughed bitterly and waved him quiet. "If you're going to suggest a convent, I think I'd rather go to Poland."

"It's good that you can think of something worse than Poland. But no, I can't imagine you in a convent. I was going to say that what helps is giving over your own wants to God. I know from experience that it's very hard to do that. But if you manage it, then God will give you more than you can possibly imagine."

He expected anger, but she turned on the bench and studied him. A small frown gathered between her eyes. "You believe that, don't you?"

"Yes."

Suddenly the wary hope in her died, and she hugged herself as though something hurt. "No. I can't. You don't understand, you're a man—" White-faced, she jumped up from the bench. "I must go. Come, Anne-Marie."

She pulled the little girl up by the hand and walked away, stumbling on her petticoats in her haste. Dragged in her wake, Anne-Marie gave Charles a look so formidably displeased that he glimpsed her grandfather, the legendary Great Condé, in the tiny, twelve-year-old princess. The dog, Louis, followed them, barking and wagging. Charles watched the trio out of sight and then went on sitting, gazing at the dark, dead waters that obeyed the king and knowing he'd failed utterly.

Chapter 11

That evening, Charles stood in the doorway of one of the large *salons*, watching the famed Versailles gambling. This *salon* was for cards, and in the one beyond, a lottery was in progress. Candles in tall lampstands were set along the tables, bathing the piles of coins in gold and silver aureoles. As the gamblers' stakes changed hands, shouts of triumph and disappointment rose to the ceiling, which was painted, appropriately enough, with scenes of Fortune and her wheel. The king himself was there, strolling sedately through the room, his gentlemen following at a distance as he spoke amiably to the gamblers. La Chaise had said that the gambling tables were the only place where anyone and everyone could sit in the presence of the king, and indeed, as Louis passed through the room, no one rose. Some of the players barely noticed him, avid as they were for their games. Besides the usual lotteries, there were card games: *lansquenet*, *reversis*, and *bassette*. There was even a *hoca* board at a corner table, though the notorious game had been banned from Paris years ago, after it ruined too many citizens.

"Have you come to pray for us, *maître?*" The young Duc du Maine paused beside Charles in the wide doorway. "I could use your prayers against the Prince de Conti."

Maine nodded toward a table farther down the room, and

Charles saw Conti lounging in a chair, gazing expressionlessly at the cards in his hands. The Grand Duchess of Tuscany sat on his left, her yellow wig clashing with her crimson bodice and slipping a little sideways as she tried shamelessly to see what he held. Across the table from them, rings flashed on the fingers of three men hunched over their cards, murmuring to each other and glancing unhappily at Conti from time to time.

"How the Prince of Conti plays so well I can never understand." Maine smiled ruefully. "I keep thinking that I've watched him and learned, but I always lose. It makes Madame de Maintenon furious, but she never comes to the gambling, so I'm safe till someone tells her. Or till I have to borrow money from her to pay him back!"

Fascinated by this glimpse of royal life, Charles couldn't help asking, "Does she lend it?"

"Usually. But with very high interest—I have to listen to long and severe lectures on my morals and my duty as a prince." The boy's smile was irresistibly sweet. "But if you pray for me tonight . . . is there a patron saint of gambling, I wonder?"

"I've never thought to wonder that," Charles said, laughing. Then, wickedly, "Shall we ask Père La Chaise?" He inclined his head toward the adjoining *salon*. "He's just there in the buffet room."

Maine grinned. "Yes, let's!" But then he looked suddenly down the room. "The king is coming this way," he said urgently, and his hand went to his hat.

Louis was making straight for them—or for the door, Charles hoped. Charles stepped aside and snatched off his *bonnet*. Maine made his bow and Louis paused, his eyes resting warmly on his son. Then the king turned his gaze, so like Maine's, on Charles, who clutched his *bonnet* as though it were a lifeline and hoped he didn't look as hunted as he felt. There was a deep, watching quiet about Louis that Charles found oddly disconcerting. This was not a man easily fooled.

"Père La Chaise informs me that you are persuading Our unhappy daughter to a more seemly acceptance of her duty," the king said. "You have Our thanks." He added, "She is at the lottery table in the next room. There is no other door from that *salon* except the one you see from here."

Louis walked serenely on. Charles let his held breath go and looked down at his half-crushed *bonnet*. He felt as though Louis had hung Lulu around his neck.

"I esteem him above all men on earth," Maine said, his eyes following the royal back. "But—" He sighed.

"But it is not easy being his son," Charles hazarded.

The boy nodded feelingly. "You can have no idea. He is kindness itself to me. But still, how can one ever please a—a— well, a god, almost? A hero, at the least!"

Charles thought of all the Jesuit college ballets he'd seen in which the king was depicted as Hercules. Or Apollo or Jupiter. No, it couldn't be easy to be Louis's son. Or daughter. It was difficult enough being one of Louis's anonymous subjects— and it seemed to Charles now that he was no longer anonymous.

Maine drew closer. "But do you know who I feel most sorry for? His real son, Louis. The Dauphin, I mean—he's the one who matters, because he is legitimate and will rule after him. And our father is so constantly disappointed in him, because the poor Dauphin isn't—well—very quick. And that disappointment has made the Dauphin terrified of most everything."

"That's very unfortunate," Charles said thoughtfully, remembering what he'd heard from Conti and his coterie in the garden. A terrified king would be a gold mine of opportunity to that little coven.

"Well, I must go now and lose my pretty shirt," Maine said,

shrugging off the realm's future. "Unless you can discover which saint to pray to!" He smiled at Charles and went eagerly to where the Prince of Conti sat, raking a pile of gold coins called *louis* toward him.

Charles moved a little aside from the door, beyond a potted orange tree, and stood against the wall's dark silk brocade. From there he could look for Lulu, and also watch Conti and Margot, without being much noticed. A gambling evening was not a usual place for a Jesuit, however, and he felt distinctly uncomfortable. Not because he'd never gambled. Far from it—soldiers endured long hours of boredom when not marching or fighting, and dice and cards helped to pass the time. But that was a long time ago. And the stakes he'd played for then were nothing compared to the fortunes spread out on these tables. As the candlelight from the tables lit the gamblers and their money, it threw dancing shadows into the *salon*'s corners, where Charles could easily believe that the patient specter of ruin waited for its prey.

His attention sharpened as he saw Lulu, changed now into a gown of tawny gold satin, come slowly from the lottery room and stop at Conti's table. Her gown shone like the sun, but her face was pinched and shadowed. She leaned down to speak to Maine, her brother, who was sitting on Margot's left. Then she sat in the empty chair on Conti's right. Margot was frowning blackly at her cards and ignored the newcomer. Conti glanced sideways and gave Lulu an absent smile, but his real attention was all for the game. One of Lulu's hands disappeared under the table. After a moment, Conti's eyebrows lifted and his free hand disappeared likewise. *Well*, Charles thought, *that doesn't look to me like resignation to Conti's indifference.* Or perhaps Conti was only giving her a little brotherly comfort? But Charles had sisters, and a girl's face didn't look like that for a brother. He wondered if the girl was trying again to persuade Conti to help her stay in France. A forlorn hope, from everything he'd seen of the man.

The play at Conti's table went on. The prince's hand emerged from under the table and he threw his cards down, laughing uproariously as he raked in everyone else's coins.

"You devil!" one of the men across the table said wryly. "How do you do it, Your Highness?"

The Duc du Maine was frowning sadly at his cards, as though Madame de Maintenon's lecture already sounded in his ears. Lulu looked quickly around the room and then flung her arms around Conti and kissed him on the cheek.

"Well done!" she cried. "What a useful stake you are gathering! With my help, of course."

That got her a quick—and, Charles thought, hunted—look from Conti.

"My thanks, Your Highness, your beauty always brings me luck," he said loudly and formally, for the table of players more than for her, Charles thought, and turned back to the next game.

Lulu looked as though she'd been slapped. "But you give me nothing in return."

She stood up, knocking her chair backward onto the polished floor, and Charles glimpsed the fury he'd seen in her eyes when she looked at her father during the ball. She hovered over Conti for a moment, clearly hoping to be drawn down beside him again, but he made no move and she turned blindly away from the table. Charles moved closer to the doorway.

"*Bonsoir*, Your Highness," he said quietly, steadying her as she nearly walked into him. She pulled her arm out of his grasp and wiped her tear-blinded eyes with the cream-colored lace of her sleeve, then brushed past him into the adjoining *salon*, where the buffet tables were set up.

He watched her go, remembering the way she'd walked away from him earlier and hating his uselessness. He hoped she would stay in the *salon* so he wouldn't have to follow and hound her. About God or anything else.

He looked into the buffet *salon*. Most of the courtiers were still hard at their gambling, so there were only a few people around the tables. Lulu stood beside a towering pyramid of summer fruit. La Chaise, standing with the king at the other end of the room, caught Charles's eye and nodded almost imperceptibly toward her. A wave of revulsion hit Charles, revulsion toward himself and his failure, this place, the king, the careful plans of power. He wanted to walk out of his cassock, out of his own skin, out of Versailles, and back home to Languedoc.

But Lulu was disappearing through the *salon* doors. Gritting his teeth, Charles hurried after her. Each of these *salons* opened into the next, a long chain of them. He was starting to feel like he'd spent half his life trudging across the palace galleries' black-and-white stone floors. He'd even dreamed of their checkerboard pattern the night before, and had seen himself running desperately after something or someone, disappearing always farther into the dark in front of him.

And Lulu was disappearing now, though the *salons* in this royal center of the palace were all brightly lit. She turned suddenly through a small side door. A pair of women were coming toward Charles, and since he didn't want to be seen going after Lulu, he stopped in pretended admiration of a painting of Diana and her nymphs, waiting for the women to pass. But they stopped, too.

"Very pretty," one of them said. Her ivory silk skirts rustled like dead leaves as she pressed close to Charles under the pretense of looking at the painting. "How do you like Versailles, *maître*? You are not yet a priest, we understand."

"Not yet, *madame*." He edged away and bowed slightly, as though to let them go on their way, but they stayed where they were.

The other woman kept her distance, but looked him up and down as though considering buying him. "How long will you stay at court?"

"Not much longer, *madame*."

"Such a change for you from your college."

"Yes. And now I must take myself to my quarters, *mesdames*. The hours of the court are too much for a simple Jesuit."

They shrieked with merriment. "*Simple* Jesuit? What a wit you are!"

Desperate to be rid of them and afraid he'd already lost Lulu's trail, he walked firmly away in the direction they'd come from. To his relief, they went on toward the gambling rooms, chattering and laughing. When he glanced back, they were far enough away for him to sprint back to the half-open door Lulu had gone through. The small room beyond, lit by a pair of candles on a table in its center, was empty. A place to leave food and drink till it was needed to replenish the buffet, he guessed from the platters of cheese and pastries on the tables, and the cupboards that lined the walls. At first, he thought Lulu had vanished into the air, but then he saw yet another door in the right-hand wall.

He went softly around the table and eased the small door open. The candles behind him lit the mouth of a narrow flight of stairs leading upward. He listened, heard nothing, and ventured onto the stairs. It was only a half flight and brought him to a dark corridor, so low-ceilinged he couldn't stand upright. Deserted, it was lit by a single candle in a sconce at the stairhead and lined with closed doors whose lintels were perhaps five feet from the floor. Peering at the little doors, he lifted his head and unwarily collided with the ceiling. Glad for the cushioning of the stiff *bonnet*, he rubbed his head. These could only be servants' rooms, a sort of mezzanine inserted between two ordinary floors. Well, he told himself, many people had less and worse. But why did they have to have so little here at the heart of luxury, where the courtiers sat on silver benches? He pulled himself back to more immediate problems.

Lulu was hardly likely to be in a servant's room. Bent uncomfortably to one side, he started toward the far end of the passage to see if there were stairs there, thinking that perhaps she'd come this way as a shortcut to somewhere else. He was halfway along the corridor when something grabbed his cassock skirt. He yelped in surprise and jumped away from whatever it was, but a small voice commanded,

"Shhh! In here!"

Anne-Marie de Bourbon pulled him through one of the little doors and shut it. Charles found himself in nearly complete darkness, with something panting and jumping against his legs.

The dog, Louis, he realized, and squatted down to where he thought the child was.

"What are you doing here, Your Serene Highness? Why—"

"Hush!" She clutched his arm, an agony of fear in her voice. "He'll hear you!"

"Who? What game are you playing?"

"It isn't a game! Louis got away and I chased him up here. We had to hide because I heard someone coming and I'm not supposed to come here." He felt her shiver. "So I came in here. At least it's empty. The servants don't go to bed till after we do. Then I looked out and—"

"There's no one out there now, so you and Louis can——"

"No, listen! I opened the door a little crack to see who was coming and it was Lulu. She went into the room across the passage. It's the footman Bouchel's and he's still in there!"

Charles was glad the darkness hid his astonishment. "With Lulu?"

"No, she left. She was crying and very angry. They were shouting at each other."

"How do you know?"

"I heard them. Some of it, anyway. At first, I could just hear voices, but not what they said. Then she got louder and started crying and told him he had to help her. He tried to hush her, but she wouldn't be quiet. He was talking louder, too. He said he'd tried to protect her and what else could he do? He sounded like he was almost crying. Then something crashed against the wall and she ran out into the passage. *Maître*, she told him that if he didn't help her get away, she would kill herself!" Anne-Marie's small hand was shaking. "I'm so worried! I know she's unhappy about the marriage—but to go to a servant for help? And to say she'll commit a mortal sin if she has to go to Poland? Please, she likes you, please talk to her and make her see she cannot do that, even if——"

He heard her catch her breath. "Even if what?"

"Just keep her from doing anything terrible!"

"Your Serene Highness, you saw this morning that I can't make her do anything."

But Charles thought suddenly of the lake, and his own fears rose. "Do you have any idea where she's gone? Are there stairs at the far end of the passage?"

"Yes, she went that way."

The chapel lay in that direction. Charles hoped against hope that Lulu had taken her lonely misery to St. Ursula, that other beleaguered virgin. Or had at least taken refuge there until she had herself in hand again.

"Maybe she's gone to the chapel," he said.

"She might go there. I'm coming with you."

As Charles pulled the door open, the dog darted into the passage, and the door across the way began to open. Charles ducked out of the room, pulled the door shut behind him, and was leaning against it when Bouchel ducked through his own doorway into the passage.

"Ah, *bonsoir*, Bouchel," Charles said, wiping his forehead as though he'd been running.

"What—what are you doing here?"

"Chasing Mademoiselle d'Enghien's little dog," Charles said, with a tolerant smile. "And now I'll have to chase him farther, he's gone that way." He nodded toward the far end of the corridor.

"Oh. Yes. He'll have gone down the stairs there." Bouchel wiped his hands over his face and through his hair.

He looked, Charles thought, like a man who'd just taken a heavy blow. "I thought earlier that you seemed unwell. You look as though you're feeling worse."

"Oh. No. No, not at all!" The whites of Bouchel's dark brown eyes flared in the dim light. "I just came up to—to see to something. They'll be after me, I must go back now."

As Bouchel ran unceremoniously down the near stairs, Charles stood staring after him and wondering why in God's name Lulu had gone to the footman.

Behind him, Anne-Marie pushed her way into the passage. "See? I told you. We have to find her!"

Together they returned to the ground floor and found Louis happily wolfing down cake someone had dropped. Anne-Marie picked him up and started toward the chapel. The *salons* here were nearly deserted, since most everyone made a point of being seen at the gambling. *He is a man I never see* was the worst thing King Louis could say of anyone entitled to be at court.

When they reached the Salon of Abundance at the east end of the chain, out of which the chapel opened, Charles stopped in the doorway. "Wait," he said softly to Anne-Marie.

At this hour the chapel was lit only by the *salon's* few candles shining behind them and by the small lamp on the high altar. He heard clothing rustle and gripped Anne-Marie's shoulder to keep her from rushing into the dark. Then he heard a metallic sound and what sounded like the whispering of skirts.

"Stay here." He walked toward the sound.

He could just make out Lulu crouching at the foot of the side altar where the reliquary was. "Your Highness?"

She straightened. "There was no need to come hunting me." Her voice was chilly and remote.

"Anne—I mean Mademoiselle d'Enghien—was worried about you. She heard you in Bouchel's room."

"In—? No, she is lying."

Flying feet came down the chapel aisle and Anne-Marie flung herself at Lulu, holding to her skirts. "I am *not* lying; you were there, you shouted at him, you said you would kill yourself. I was so frightened!"

Lulu sighed but made no move to comfort her. "Very well. Since you spied on me, yes, I did ask Bouchel's help. He has always seemed—very kind." She shrugged disdainfully. "And he's a peasant. That kind of person always wants money, and I thought I might be able to bribe him to help me run away. He won't. There. Now you know. And I know what I must do. And there's an end of it."

"But you said you would kill yourself! Lulu, you mustn't even think that, you can't—"

"Don't be silly." She put Anne-Marie gently but firmly aside. "Children are so tiresomely fanciful," she said to Charles, and swept out of the chapel.

He put out a hand to stop Anne-Marie from following her. "Let her be. She doesn't want either of us just now."

"I *know* that." The little girl twisted out of his grasp and faced him. He half expected tears, but she said fiercely, "You see? There's only you and me to care about her. *Someone* has to help her, but no one will, because they're afraid of the king. So what are you going to do?"

Charles looked warily at her. This one could probably lead armies. "I don't know," he said frankly. "I'm leaving very soon. I can tell Père La Chaise I'm worried about her."

She sighed impatiently. "That won't help. Lulu doesn't like him; she won't listen to him." Her hazel-gold hawk's eyes caught light from the altar lamp as she looked up at him. "I see that I must tell you. Listen. After the Comte de Fleury—"

Louis began to bark in the aisle as heavy footsteps pounded into the chapel.

"Your Serene Highness! Come here. At once!"

"Hell's lecherous devils!" Anne-Marie said startlingly, looking over her shoulder. "I am busy, *madame*."

"Come this moment. Your father is having a fit, asking where you are!"

"My father is always having a fit." Anne-Marie turned back to Charles. "It's my nurse. She never pays any attention to me unless my father asks where I am. Please, we must talk. Tomorrow?"

Before Charles could answer, the stout, dark-gowned woman, visible only in outline against the candlelight beyond the chapel, reached the side altar and gasped when she realized he was there.

"Who are you? What do you mean, being here alone with

this child?" She took the little girl by the hand and pulled her away as though Charles had the plague. Scolding her without pause, she walked Anne-Marie out of the chapel.

Torn between fears for Lulu, worry over what Anne-Marie wanted to tell him, and his own fervent desire to be gone at first light and leave them both to others, Charles went slowly back to the evening's festivities.

He found the buffet *salon* in an uproar. It was crowded with exclaiming, pushing courtiers, and someone had apparently been shoved into a table, because a bright flood of fruit was being crushed underfoot. Charles kicked a plum aside and tried to get nearer the confusion's center to see what had happened. A woman's wail rose above the noise.

"Dear Blessed Virgin, it's just like the Comte de Fleury! Oh, Saint Benoit, protect him!"

St. Benedict? Benedict was the patron invoked against poison. Charles elbowed his way ruthlessly through a swath of outraged courtiers. Then someone shouted a command and the crowd parted to make way for the physician Neuville and Père La Chaise, supporting the king between them. Louis was hatless, his face white and sheened with sweat, and he walked slightly bent over, one hand pressed tightly to his stomach. He looked as though it was taking all his will to hold his mouth clamped shut. On the other side of La Chaise, the tearful Dauphin clutched his father's black-and-white hat to his chest, and the Prince of Conti leaned at the Dauphin's ear, murmuring solicitously. The covey of noblemen who attended the king came crowding behind them.

"Make way, for the love of God!" the doctor shouted again, and Charles leaped to clear a knot of stupefied courtiers out of the royally urgent path to the door.

As he passed, La Chaise said to Charles, "Go back to my chamber and wait."

"Yes, *mon père*." But instead of leaving immediately, Charles turned to the woman standing beside him. "What happened? I only just arrived."

Two men drew near to listen to her answer. Her diamond earrings danced in the candlelight as she shook her head. "I hardly know. I was playing *reversis* and the king was standing beside our table. He suddenly turned away and—well—doubled over—and was sick." She put a hand to her heavily powdered throat and stared at Charles in bewilderment, as though she'd just seen the sun rise in the west. "No one has ever seen him sick in public. We know he is ill from time to time. But he never lets us see it. Even when he had his operation in the winter, he was giving audiences and orders from his bed later that same day! One knew he had to be in pain, but he gave no sign at all. But this—he could not control himself at all, and—dear Blessed Virgin, what if he dies?"

"*Madame*," Charles said, "I think you are jumping too far ahead. Who can control himself when the urge to spew comes on him?"

"I know. But—" Her small black eyes were full of fear. "—he's not like us. He is the king!"

And Jupiter never vomits, Charles thought, mentally casting his eyes up. He turned away with a small nod, but the older of the two listening men, perhaps fifty or so, put out a hand to detain him. Charles knew he should know who the man was but couldn't name him. The man glanced in the direction the king had gone and then back to Charles.

"Like the Comte de Fleury," the man said quietly.

"Only, thank God, there were no stairs here," his companion

put in. He was the lynx-eyed man who'd baited La Chaise in the gallery after Fleury fell.

"You mistake me," the older man replied impatiently. He looked at Charles. "Perhaps I should have said, *exactly* like Fleury. Because, may God help us, it looks to me as though someone has poisoned the king." His words had the heavy finality of a tolling bell.

"Oh, dear. Then all we can do now is pray," the other said, but his words were light as air. He excused himself and went quickly toward the doors.

"Poisoned how?" Charles said brusquely. "Where?"

The older man gestured gracefully toward the tables.

"That can't be!" Charles said. "Unless you think it was random and any victim would have done? Anyone and everyone might have been poisoned, if it was in something on the tables."

"Don't be absurd, of course I don't mean that."

"Then what do you mean?"

The man inclined his head very slightly in the direction the younger man had gone.

Charles shook his head. "I don't understand you."

The nameless man looked casually over both shoulders and scanned the knot of gesticulating, hysterically whispering courtiers beyond Charles. "Come." Without seeming to be going anywhere in particular, he drew Charles after him into a corner. They stood sideways against the wall, watching over each other's shoulders and speaking so that their words would not carry out into the room. The man murmured, "It would not be so hard to do. The king loves sweets. And the best of the sweets are always offered first to him. Do you think he serves himself at the buffet? Of course he doesn't. He points and nods and someone fills a plate for him. And until he has eaten from the buffet, no one else can take anything."

Charles thought about that. He'd seen the king standing with La Chaise near the tables early in the evening. Neither had been eating then, but they might have eaten from the buffet before he saw them.

As though reading his thoughts, his companion said, "The king always goes immediately to the tables and has something, so that we aren't kept from refreshing ourselves." He raised an eyebrow. "I believe that tonight it was your Père La Chaise who served him."

Charles gaped at the man. "Are you accusing Père La Chaise? That's absurd!" Giving up the effort to identify the man and preserve the courtesies, he said bluntly, "Who are you?"

His companion seemed equally uninterested in the courtesies. "I am not accusing him at all. I am simply saying it would have been possible. Someone else may well have brought the king more to eat a little later. I was only briefly in this room before I went to the gambling." He smiled slightly at Charles. "I am the Duc de La Rochefoucauld. And you are Maître Charles du Luc. You and Père Jouvancy and your companions ate at my table the day Père Jouvancy became so ill. You may just as well say that I poisoned *him*. Though I didn't." He made Charles a small ironic bow. "Nor did I poison the Comte de Fleury, who ate at my table the day he died. Though I am well aware of what is being said."

"I am glad to hear it." Charles folded his hands at his waist. "Forgive me, *monsieur*, but it seems to me that everyone at court is obsessed with poison. We have had a very bad stomach sickness and fever going the rounds in Paris. Père Jouvancy had been ill with it before we came, and I feel sure he has only had a relapse. So why not assume that the illness has reached Versailles? And that the Comte de Fleury had it, and now so has the king."

"Logical, I grant you. And if some kind, innocuous man had

broken his neck on the way to the privy, I might think as you do. But the Comte de Fleury was not innocuous, as I think you know. I was there in the gallery when he fell. I saw you recognize him. Oh, yes, it showed."

"I was a soldier under his command."

"Ah. Then you do know how well hated he was. Half the court would trade its palace lodgings for a look at Fleury's reputed journal, to be sure they are not included. But the thing seems to have disappeared."

"So I've heard. I grant you that more than a few might have willingly killed Fleury. Are you saying that the king is also well hated?"

"What king is not?" La Rochefoucauld replied.

"Then the question becomes, who hates him most?" Charles stared at the rapidly shifting groups of men and women telling each other that the king had been poisoned, that the king could not possibly have been poisoned, that their aunt had had that same sickness last week in Paris, that they knew for certain who had poisoned the king, that no one would ever know who had poisoned the king.

"And who would your choice be for that position?"

"The Prince of Conti."

La Rochefoucauld's eyebrows rose, and he half bowed. "The Society of Jesus' reputation for quickness of observation continues to be well deserved."

"Does that mean you agree with me?"

"I am not naive enough to answer that, Maître du Luc. But I have long observed the Prince of Conti gathering a devoted coterie of men around him."

"Around him or around the Dauphin?"

"Conti pretends that they have gathered around the Dauphin. The king would give a great deal to be rid of Conti, but it is not easy to be rid of a Prince of the Blood."

"Louis the Thirteenth rid himself of his brother Gaston."

"After extreme provocation. Conti is, so far, too wise to offer provocation quite so extreme."

"Poisoning would seem about as extreme as provocation gets."

"You can be sure that if the king was poisoned tonight, it was not by Conti's own hand, whatever his mind had to do with it. If the king were to die, the Dauphin would be king. And Conti would be safe, because I doubt the poor Dauphin has the guts to rid himself of a mouse in his chamber. So where's the risk?"

"Assuming the king dies."

"Assuming that. *Bonne nuit, maître.*"

Chapter 12

THE FEAST OF ST. ANTOINE, FRIDAY, JUNE 13, 1687

The sun was barely up and, though Jouvancy had announced that he was well enough to travel, the day was already not going well. La Chaise had returned from the night's vigil by the king's bed. He was hardly through the door before he asked Charles where Lulu had gone from the gambling the night before. On hearing she'd gone to Bouchel's room, he'd poured himself watered wine in a grim silence.

When his glass was empty, he said, "Well, it could be worse. Thank God she chose Bouchel. He's good-hearted and absolutely trustworthy. He would never do anything to anger the king, no matter how much the girl offered him. But now that we know she's done that, she must be watched every moment so that she doesn't try it again—with him or anyone else. You will have to stay, Maître du Luc, and finish what you've begun."

And that had landed La Chaise in a furiously polite argument with Père Jouvancy. Charles, the prize in the argument, stood at the window eating bread and cheese, and praying hard that the battle would not make Jouvancy relapse again, at least not before he won.

"I cannot return without him, *mon père*." Jouvancy's words were courteous, but his face was red with anger. "If you need a Jesuit to help you, you must send to the Professed House."

La Chaise, whose eyes were hollow with exhaustion after a night at the king's bedside, looked as though he'd like to make Jouvancy walk on his knees to Jerusalem. "But *mon père*, Maître du Luc knows the situation, and he has won the girl's trust." Ignoring Charles's protest at that, he went on: "What's more, she seems to like him. Could you not leave him here until Sunday afternoon?"

"I strongly object. You need an older man for this. You told me yourself how this girl behaves. And Maître du Luc is not only young and well favored, he is a mere scholastic. He should not be tangled in these matters."

Charles chewed his bread and tried to look as mere as possible.

"He's helped me all the while you've been ill," La Chaise said, obviously clinging to his patience, "and has come to no harm. On the contrary, I imagine he has learned quite a bit that will one day be useful to him. I need him, I tell you. It is essential to prevent the girl doing anything to upset the Polish ambassadors and the marriage negotiations. The fear that the king has been poisoned already has them talking of withdrawing. I can see in their faces that they're wondering if Poland wants a princess from a court that would poison its own king! Louis needs the marriage agreement to be quickly concluded and the marriage made."

Jouvancy softened a little. "Is he very ill?"

"Very ill, during the night. He is a little better this morning."

"And his doctors truly think he's been poisoned?"

"Yes." La Chaise leaned both hands on the table, which

brought him eye to eye with the little priest. "Everyone who was anywhere near the buffet last evening has spent the night being interrogated. Even I was questioned, because I served him from the buffet table before anyone else ate. I tell you again, we simply cannot afford more scandal here."

"*You* were questioned?" Jouvancy's smooth forehead creased with worry, and he glanced at Charles. "I did not realize—then perhaps—"

"But, *mon père*—" Ignoring his better judgment's warnings, Charles swallowed the last mouthful of bread and waded into the fray. "If one so much as turns pale here, everyone cries poison. Last night the king looked precisely as you did weeks ago when you were taken ill in the rhetoric classroom, and his symptoms were exactly like yours. You know that no one poisoned you at Louis le Grand. Why should we not think that Louis was merely ill with this contagion so many have had?"

Jouvancy and La Chaise, suddenly a united front in the face of this insubordinate outburst, hushed him.

"And I think that Mademoiselle de Rouen may be growing more reconciled to the marriage," Charles said anyway.

The two priests glared at him, and La Chaise refilled his wineglass and sat turning it in his hands. "She was at the king's bedside last night," he said thoughtfully. "Until Madame de Maintenon sent her to get some rest. That she was there speaks well for her, I admit."

"And she's been praying in front of our reliquary, which Madame de Maintenon has put on a side altar in the chapel for her benefit," Charles put in doggedly.

To Charles's surprise, no one hushed him a second time. Père Jouvancy looked pleased at the news of the reliquary, and La Chaise looked thoughtful.

"That seems a good sign," the king's confessor said consideringly, "that she's praying. A young girl asking the help of a holy
virgin is very appropriate. Last night, she joined me in praying
for the king." He rubbed a hand over his face. "Very well. You
two can return to Paris. I will arrange for one of the Franciscans who cares for the chapel to keep a watch on the girl there.
And Bouchel can—" He looked at Charles. "No, perhaps not
Bouchel, after what you told me. Not that the boy would step
out of his place. But Lulu has obviously stepped out of hers in
asking him for help, and I'll give her no more chances to take
that further. The oldest of her ladies can be persuaded to extra
vigilance." He sighed. "I will take it on myself to help keep Lulu
away from the Duchess of Tuscany at the evening entertain-
ments tonight and tomorrow."

Charles's heart lifted, and he took an involuntary step toward the door.

But La Chaise shook his head. "I only ask one thing," he said
to Jouvancy. "That you, *mon père*, take your ease for the remain-
der of the morning. You have never yet seen the gardens, and I
propose that you and I spend the morning there. While you,
Maître du Luc, pay a farewell visit to Mademoiselle de Rouen
and perhaps have a last consoling talk with her. After you see
her, we three will dine together. And after that, Bouchel will find
you a carriage, *mon père*. You say you can manage both horses,
Maître du Luc?"

"I can."

"Then go and find Mademoiselle de Rouen. She is likely with
her mother, Madame de Montespan, this morning."

Telling himself that a morning was not long, and that there
would be a leisurely and solitary ride at the end of it, Charles
went to Madame de Montespan's door. He'd learned that one

never knocked on a palace door, but instead scratched lightly at the glossy white paint with a fingernail. The composure of the manservant who opened the door was almost as glossy as the paint, but when Charles said that Père La Chaise had sent him, the man's eyes widened.

"The king?" he whispered. "Is he—"

"A little better, I'm told."

The servant admitted Charles inside and went to announce him. Left alone in the anteroom, Charles turned in a slow circle, frankly gaping. Between classical pillars, the thickly carved paneling was a riot of fat, naked baby angels hovering like butterflies among botanically impossible leaves and flowers. The walls' flat spaces gleamed with polished marble and on the ceiling, a mostly naked Venus lay on a rosy cloud. Swans paddled in the air around the goddess, and doves fluttered as well, though Venus had eyes only for the hulking Adonis with Louis's face.

When Charles was ushered into the next room, he found Madame de Montespan, Lulu, and Margot sitting together. *So much for keeping Mademoiselle de Rouen away from the Duchess of Tuscany,* Charles thought. Lulu's mother was dressed in loose blue silk and sitting decorously on a sturdy chair, a cloud being unlikely now to support her weight. In spite of her size and her aging, she was beautiful. The lines of silver in her curling blond hair only made it shine more, and her fat lent a spurious smoothness to her dazzling skin. Her eyes were the bluest Charles had ever seen . . .

"Were you looking for me, Maître du Luc?" Lulu's voice was small and sad, and Charles saw that she was bent over a lacy pile of sewing in her lap.

"Forgive me, *mesdames.*" Charles inclined his head to Madame de Montespan, hoping she hadn't noticed his staring. "I've come to say that the king, God be thanked, is better."

Margot laughed. "Good for my cousin. And even better to have the news from such a handsome courier."

Charles willed himself not to blush. "I am surprised to see you here so early in the day," he said to her.

"Oh, I stayed last night. One could not leave when the king was so ill. One feared—many things."

"Thank you for coming to tell us he's better," Lulu said softly. "I was very anxious for him."

She kept her head down, curled in on herself like a small animal protecting its soft parts, and Charles wondered unhappily if his talks with her had created this subdued sadness. Had his effort at "counsel" only quenched the life in her?

"Besides my errand here," he said, "I *was* also looking for you."

She smiled a little and started to say something, but male laughter came suddenly from behind her. The Duc du Maine put his head around her chair. "*Bonjour, maître.* I was reading to them. But since I am *not* handsome, they don't want to see me, only to hear. Or perhaps it is that I am *too* handsome and will distract them from their sewing, only they don't like to say so." His sister laughed suddenly and reached down, trying to pinch him. Maine ducked aside and pulled his cushion out so he could sit beside her.

Madame de Montespan put her own sewing aside on a low stool and said to Charles, "Did the king send you to me?"

"No, *madame.* It was feared you would be worrying, if you'd had no recent word."

"Oh. I no longer worry. He has others to worry over him now." She blinked slowly, waiting to see what Charles would do with that.

The Duc du Maine said quickly, "Shall I read again, *madame*? Or perhaps Maître du Luc would read to us. Or—"

"Of course he doesn't want to read, Louis, don't be a child." Margot twitched an apricot taffeta shoulder at Maine and patted her yellow wig. "Let him tell us exactly how the king is faring."

"Sleeping, I think," Charles said carefully. "The last I heard, he was no longer spewing."

"So now all that is left is to find the poisoner." Madame de Montespan's eyes were still fixed on Charles. "Is that the real reason they sent you here? To charm me into admitting I poisoned him?"

Charles's jaw dropped. "Did you?" he blurted, before he could stop himself.

The other two women and Maine recoiled as though he'd dropped a dead rat on the blue-and-rose carpet, but Mme de Montespan only smiled.

"I ask your pardon, *madame*," Charles stammered, wanting to kick himself.

"Oh, you are delicious." Margot's caw of delight drowned his apology. "Of course she didn't poison him. But no doubt there are those saying she's at it again."

"No doubt, Margot," Madame de Montespan returned, in a voice like fermenting honey. "And no doubt they are saying it of you, as well. After all, Italy is the land of poisoners, and you lived there for years. Everyone says you tried to poison your husband."

"The *bon Dieu* knows I wanted to! But only because Cosimo was trying to poison *me*. And I've no reason at all to harm dear Louis now that he's let me come back to France."

With sudden energy, Lulu stabbed her needle through the white silk in her lap. "If he *was* poisoned. Everyone cries poison here if you eat a green apple and spend the day on your *chaise de commodité*. I'm sure he's just ill. Like old Fleury was." She glanced up at Charles. "Like you and the other Jesuits were, too—and why would anyone poison you?"

The older women exchanged looks. "Why anyone would poison you in particular, *mon cher*, I cannot imagine," Margot said to Charles. "Or that little priest your companion. But your Père La Chaise is altogether another question. We all know who might poison Père La Chaise."

"She wouldn't!" Maine cried, clambering awkwardly to his feet. "You know she wouldn't, Madame de Maintenon is the best, kindest woman in the world!"

His mother's slow blue gaze found him and he bit his lip.

"Besides you, I mean, *madame*, you know you are always first!"

His mother said nothing. With a miserable glance at Lulu, he limped to a side table and fingered the hothouse apricots heaped there in a gleaming silver bowl.

"Why might she poison Père La Chaise, Your Highness?" Charles said to Margot.

"Because they hate each other," Lulu said wearily. "Everyone knows that. But she *wouldn't* poison him because the king wouldn't like it. No one has poisoned anyone! Unless God poisoned the Comte de Fleury—it's easy to imagine God seeing that the Comte de Fleury was poisoned for his sins. At least, that is what everyone is saying!" Lulu shifted a little in her chair and looked up at Charles through her long, pale lashes. "You said you were looking for me, *maître*." Her small hand went to her throat, fingering a gold cross that hung from the tight circle of pearls around her neck.

"To see how you were faring, Your Highness. After the talk we had yesterday. And also to take my leave. We are going back to Paris today."

"Oh, no, you mustn't leave!" Margot trilled.

"Lulu has told us about your talk," Maine said, gravely regarding the crystal vase of rosy peonies beside the fruit bowl. "I should be glad that you've helped her to accept her duty as a king's daughter." He took a peony from the vase and came back to his sister's chair. "But I will miss her sorely when she goes to Poland." He tucked the flower into her hair.

Lulu let go of the little cross and reached up a hand to him. As he brought it to his lips, she said, "I will miss you, too, Louis." She drew her hand away. "As you see, *maître*, you did help me." Changing expressions flitted across her face like cloud shadows. "What could be more resigned than sewing bridal linen?"

Margot picked up the sheer ivory linen in her lap and shook it out, revealing a lace-trimmed *chemise* so finely woven that it rippled like silk. She dangled it enticingly, making it jump as though it were alive, her eyes sparkling maliciously as she watched Charles.

A wave of anger swept through him at the woman's taunting, but he said lightly, "I have sisters, Your Highness. I have seen a *chemise* before." He forced a smile and started to invite Lulu to the chapel for one last conversation. But Madame de Montespan forestalled him.

"It is nearly dinnertime, *maître*, and I am sure you don't wish to be late at the table you are gracing." She held out a smooth white hand.

Lulu looked daggers at her mother, but Charles accepted the dismissal. When he only bowed over her hand—without kissing it—she shrugged slightly and then gave him what seemed like a real, though brief, smile.

"Thank you for receiving me, Madame," he said. "I am glad to have met you." He bowed slightly to Margot. "Your Royal Highness." To Lulu, whose mouth was trembling with disappointment, he said, "I am glad you are turning your attention to being a bride. I—" He stopped as she bent her head and a shower of tears broke through her control and fell on her sewing. He looked helplessly at the pale slender neck and the white ribbons trailing on either side of it from her headdress. "God can bring good out of what seems like the blackest misery," he said softly, as though no one else were in the room.

She dried the tears with a handful of lace from her lap and looked up. Her face was so set and bleak that Charles caught his breath in pain, as though her sore heart beat suddenly in his own chest.

"Lulu—" He stopped, realizing he'd used the nickname he had no right to use, but no one chided him. "Obedience can begin bitterly. As yours begins. But, with time, it can grow sweet. I know this for myself, and it is hard learning. But it can happen."

Margot snorted loudly, but Charles ignored her. In Lulu's case, obedience growing sweet seemed more than unlikely, but *unlikely* was not the same as *impossible*.

She nodded slightly, and her hand went to the cross again. But her miserable expression didn't change.

"God go with you." Charles turned toward the door, but she called him back.

"Maître." It might have been the king looking at him. Her illusionless Bourbon eyes were as dry as though she'd never in her life wept. "I am my father's daughter. I can do what I must as ruthlessly as he does."

Charles found no answer to that. But as he crossed the antechamber dedicated to love, he looked back at the *salon*. Margot looked at Mme de Montespan, and the two resumed their sewing. Lulu took up her scissors and cut her needle free of the white cloud of lace. Charles suddenly saw the women as the ancient world's three Fates, those daughters of the gods who spun the thread of a man's life, fixed its length, and cut it off. He went out into the passage, trying to remember the ancients' other name for the Fates. It came to him as he climbed the stairs in the south wing. They'd been called Daughters of the Just Heavens.

Chapter 13

When Charles reached Père La Chaise's chambers, no one was there. Hoping he wouldn't have to search the entire gardens, he went to look for Jouvancy and La Chaise but, to his relief, found them walking slowly toward him across the gravel, deep in talk, as he emerged from the palace.

Charles reported the results of his morning's visit.

"I'm not surprised that Maine was there," La Chaise said. "He's taking his sister's leaving very much to heart and will no doubt be her shadow until she goes. Which is to the good, since we don't want her left alone. Ah," he said, as bells began to ring, "that means dinner. Come. We'll go to the Grand Commons."

They went into the palace and started along the ground-floor gallery, but La Chaise suddenly pulled them to a stop. A fast-stepping procession led by a gentleman with a baton of office was bearing down on them. All along the gallery, courtiers were drawing aside, sweeping off hats, bowing and curtsying nearly to the ground. A ripple of murmuring accompanied the courtiers' *reverences* as the procession passed.

"Uncover and bow," La Chaise hissed, whipping off his own *bonnet*.

Charles and Jouvancy did the same, and when the procession

had nearly reached them, Charles heard what the courtiers were murmuring as they bowed.

"The king's dinner," La Chaise and Jouvancy said in their turn, as the line of gentlemen carrying covered silver dishes passed, leaving a savory smell behind. La Chaise elbowed Charles. "Say it!"

Speechless, Charles turned to La Chaise.

"Didn't you hear me?" La Chaise hissed, as the three of them replaced their *bonnets*.

"Yes, *mon père.* But—why were we bowing to the king's dinner?"

"*Because* it is the king's dinner," Jouvancy said, scandalized. "It is soon to be part of the king."

Biting his tongue to keep from asking if they must bow to Louis's chamber pot as well, Charles followed the others to the Grand Commons across the street.

The Grand Commons was enormous and new. La Chaise told them that it contained a plethora of kitchens and a nicely graded series of refectories, where courtiers, guards, and flocks of servants ate. The kitchens also prepared much of the food for private chambers and rushed it across the road and through the galleries to its destination. Which made Charles think of the abortive dinner at La Rochefoucauld's table. The food had been delicious, but nothing he'd eaten had been more than faintly warm.

After a surprisingly good dinner of roasted cod in a butter sauce with cloves and capers, and a side dish of spinach with raisins, they went back to La Chaise's chamber. Charles gathered his and Jouvancy's belongings, and the three Jesuits made their farewells.

"And I beg you to remember," La Chaise said, "it is imperative to keep a close eye on Henri de Montmorency. Especially you, *maître*. He must not leave Louis le Grand until Lulu is gone. Not for any reason."

"But"—Jouvancy looked in confusion from one to the other—"if his mother demands it—"

"Forgive me, *mon père*," La Chaise said. "I forgot that you have not been part of all this. Your Henri de Montmorency fancies himself in love with Mademoiselle de Rouen and talks foolishly of stopping her going to Poland."

Jouvancy's eyes rounded in horror. "That beggars belief. How could even Montmorency be so stupid! Of course we must keep him inside the college. For his own sake!"

"And for ours," La Chaise said dryly.

Charles picked up the saddlebags and the three of them went out into the gallery.

"Are you sure you can manage both horses, *maître*?" Jouvancy said anxiously.

"Assuredly, *mon père*. But first, I will get you a carriage."

La Chaise shook his head. "You go ahead, *maître*. I will see Père Jouvancy into a carriage and on his way."

Charles bowed to the two of them, shouldered the saddlebags, and went decorously to the stairs. When he was out of sight, he bolted down the stairs two at a time, feeling like a boy let out of school and caring nothing for the looks he got from people climbing past him. Outside, the air was warm and fresh, and the afternoon promised settled riding weather to accompany two of his favorite earthly pleasures: riding and solitude. A whole afternoon of privacy rarely came his way.

But first, he had to make the long trudge from the palace to the stable. When he finally arrived there, he found himself facing a stone façade worthy of this palace for horses. The large cobbled forecourt was mostly empty, but inside the stables, he found a small army of grooms, ostlers, and saddlers currying horses as glossy as polished parquet, putting fresh straw down in stalls far larger than his bedchamber at Louis le Grand, polishing saddles and harness until the leather gleamed like the king's mirrors. Somewhere a blacksmith was making the air ring with the blows of hammer on anvil, like bells clanging above a busy city. Wishing he could have spent his days at Versailles here instead of in the palace for courtiers, Charles wandered happily between the stalls, stroking velvet noses and admiring the elegant, long-legged English hunters the king favored for the chase.

"Need something, *mon père?*" A sandy-haired groom with freckles across his nose came out of a stall.

"Yes, thank you. I have two horses here. They've been in your keeping since I arrived on Monday." With a shock, he realized he'd spent only four nights at Versailles. It seemed like a month.

"What are they called?"

"Flamme and Agneau. From the college of Louis le Grand."

"Follow me."

Before they reached Flamme's stall near the end of the aisle, the gelding put his head over the door and whickered, scenting Charles. Agneau, in the last stall, looked up from her hay rack, saw the saddlebags Charles was carrying, and redoubled her efforts to eat while she could.

The boy went into Agneau's stall. "Shall I saddle her for you?"

"My thanks—what's your name?"

"I'm Laurent."

Charles smiled at the boy and went to saddle Flamme. But first he stroked the horse's shining neck and laid his cheek against the warm muzzle, contentedly breathing in the welcome smell of clean horse. As he pulled the saddle and its blanket from their long thick wall peg, Flamme butted him in the back, clearly pleased to be going somewhere.

"Be sure you check the mare's girth," Charles called to the boy. "She'll blow up like a bladder to keep it loose."

The boy laughed. "I know that trick, I always check."

They worked in silence for a moment and then the boy said, "*Mon père?*"

"*Maître*," Charles said absently, letting the stirrups down to fit him.

"Oh. *maître*, then. I heard—Jacques Prudhomme said that a young Jesuit prayed over poor Bertin. Was that you?"

"Bertin?" Charles took the bridle from its peg, trying to think who Jacques Prudhomme and Bertin were. Guilt assailed him as he remembered the dead man beside the lake. "Yes," he said hastily, "I did. Did you know him?"

"Jean Prudhomme is my uncle. Bertin Laville was married to his daughter."

Charles pushed the bridle between Flamme's teeth, gave him a pat, and went into the stall where the boy was. "So you knew Bertin, then. Do you have any thought about who killed him?" he asked quietly.

Laurent shook his head and gave Charles a wary sideways look. "I only wanted to thank you for looking after him." He stepped away from Agneau and turned his back on her. The mare sighed out a great breath and the boy spun around, grabbed the end of the girth strap, and pulled hard. "Ha-ha!" He grinned at Charles, who was laughing, too.

"Well done!" Charles patted the displeased mare's round rump and waited to see if the boy would say more about the dead man.

Laurent took down Agneau's bridle from its peg but made

no move to put it on her. "My cousin—Bertin's wife—has just had another child." He sighed. "She cries all the time. At least she found money he'd hidden in the house. So she has something till she can find another husband."

Charles's ears pricked. Money and murder were so often locked in a deadly embrace. "Gardeners are paid well, then?"

The boy's sneer was too adult for his years. "Who's ever paid well? And Bertin couldn't hold on to money any more than he could close his fist on water. No, I think it was gambling money. He diced. Mostly he lost, but every man wins sometime. Maybe he called someone a cheat and was killed for the insult."

"That could be," Charles said. Men were often enough killed when gambling quarrels flared. "Do you have any other thoughts about what might have happened?"

The boy's face flamed and he turned away to bridle the mare, dealing expertly with her efforts to resist the bit.

"Your uncle thought Bertin might have been killed over a woman," Charles said mildly.

Laurent nodded, still with his back to Charles. "He had a—a woman in the town. And others. I suppose one of them might have killed him."

"Could a woman have hit him hard enough?" Charles asked skeptically.

Laurent turned, with a look that plainly said Charles must be a simpleton. "My mother can butcher a hog. Swinging a shovel is nothing."

Charles nodded, thinking that his own mother could probably butcher a hog, too. Though she'd probably talk the poor animal to death instead of using a knife.

"Anyway, *maître*, thank you for praying over him. He needed it."

"I'll go on praying for him." *I imagine he still needs it*, Charles thought. He looked into the stable aisle to be sure they weren't being overheard. "Is the Guard still trying to find his killer?"

"I don't know. Maybe. But probably not. He was—well—only Bertin." Laurent turned Agneau and led her out of the stall.

That was true and nothing Charles could change. He followed Laurent into the aisle, put both saddlebags on Agneau, and secured them to the saddle. "Can you lend me a leading rein?"

Laurent ran to the end of the aisle, vanished into an adjoining room, and came back with a long sturdy rein that he buckled to the mare's bridle.

"My thanks. I'll send it back. If you'll take her out to the forecourt, I'll follow with the gelding and we'll be gone."

Charles led Flamme after the mare, mounted, and took the leading rein from the boy. "Thank you, *mon brave*." He realized that Laurent was waiting for a coin, and at the same moment realized that Jouvancy had the small purse the rector had given them. "My apologies. My companion has gone on in a carriage with our small store of coins."

The boy's face fell, but he shrugged philosophically. "Oh, well, you can pay me with prayers for Bertin. A good ride to you." He lifted a hand and loped back to his work.

Charles rode under the sculptured arch and turned the horses toward Paris. Before he'd gone more than a few yards, a gleaming, red-wheeled carriage hurtled toward him and he drew rein. But Agneau, on her leading rein, plodded into Flamme from behind and the gelding curvetted into the middle of the road. The coachman swerved, shouting angrily at Charles, who was too busy fighting Flamme to a standstill to heed him. Charles quickly got the gelding under control and started to call an apology to the driver, but the carriage's occupant put his head out a side window, and the sight of him struck Charles mute.

He hadn't seen Michel Louvois, the king's minister of war, for nearly a year. And had hoped never to see him again. Louvois, perhaps the second most powerful man in the realm after the king, was not a man to cross. Let alone threaten. And last summer, Charles had threatened him, because he'd seen no other way to try for at least a measure of justice. For months, he'd lived looking over his shoulder, waiting for Louvois's retaliation, but it hadn't come. Charles had decided he was too small an enemy to merit the attention of a man with so many enemies. Now, though the malice on Louvois's heavy-jowled face sent fear rippling through him, he made himself hold the war minister's gaze until Louvois drew his head back inside the coach and left Charles choking in its dust. Charles pressed Flamme into a trot and put a quick mile between himself and Louvois. And between himself and the palace, and La Chaise, and Lulu, and all the rest. He could hardly remember wanting so much to be gone from a place, wanting so much to be home. As he rode, though, he prayed for Lulu and that good would come to her. He also prayed for the grave and lonely little Condé princess, Anne-Marie de Bourbon.

As he left Versailles behind, his body let go its watchfulness, and he began to look around him at the June day. The cold spring had made the birds' nesting late, but now harried parent birds flew from tree to grass to bush, searching for insects and worms. When lulls came in the road's carriage traffic, he could hear the small shrill cries of nestlings demanding to be fed. But thinking about nestlings made him think of the boy Laurent and his cousin's new baby, and soon his mind was once more circling around the problem of the dead workman Bertin.

Charles didn't believe in the theory of a furious, shovel-wielding woman. What the boy had said about Bertin's hidden money seemed a much more likely piece of the puzzle. Laurent hadn't thought much of Bertin's gambling skill. But as he'd said, every man won sometime. But if it hadn't been won, could it have anything to do with Bertin's murder? Perhaps he'd sold something. But what would he have to sell? Charles greeted a walking group of men and women, singing and passing around a leather bottle. Small craftsmen on holiday, he guessed from their dress and manner, as they shouted greetings back at him, on their way to marvel at Versailles from their lowly place on the social ladder. Bertin's status had been still lower. Perhaps someone had owed him money. Or a relative might have died and left him a little something. Though that was unlikely, since Laurent was kin and would probably have known about it. Or perhaps Bertin had stolen the money. That could end in murder, if the theft was discovered.

Charles stretched himself in the saddle and reached to stroke his horse's neck. "Flamme, *mon brave*, let's move! And you, *ma chère* Agneau, will have to put up with it." He nudged the gelding to a canter and tugged on the leading rein. Alternately cantering, walking, and trotting, they reached the village of Vaugirard and Charles turned off the royal road to take the smaller road to the Left Bank gate. He was thirsty, and in his haste to be gone from Versailles he hadn't filled his leather water bottle, so he made for the village fountain and watering trough. He drank and watered the horses, then sat down on the bench where he and Jouvancy had rested on Monday, thinking how much longer this week had seemed than other weeks. Women and a few serving men came and went from the fountain, exchanging news as they filled pitchers and buckets. Customers went in and out of the few shops around the square, and Charles's thoughts floated and drifted like lazy fish in a stream. A pair of beggars approached him, one missing an arm and the other half a leg. Old soldiers, they said, and Charles thought it was likely true. But he had only his blessing to give them, which they let him know was worth little.

Feeling guilty, he set himself to prayers. Name by name, he prayed for those he carried in his heart and those he felt a responsibility to remember. As he prayed, he settled into quiet. Until he came to the last name on his list, the dead Comte de Fleury, and his teeth set and his mind refused to pray. But hating the man didn't excuse him from praying for his soul, and Charles plowed through prayers for the dead until he sidetracked himself with wondering whether prayers he had no desire to pray were worth anything. But if they weren't, then feelings were more important than intention, which couldn't be true. The whole self should be given to God, including the feelings, so feelings mattered, but surely not more than will. As much, though? He got up and shook himself, drank again, and untethered the horses. If what he knew of theology was any measure, he'd grow a beard and die, right there on the bench, before his questions were settled.

But the Comte de Fleury went with him. Charles told himself he'd probably never know the truth of Fleury's death any more than he'd know the truth of Bertin's. Had Fleury been simply ill, not poisoned? Had he and Jouvancy and La Chaise fallen sick merely from spoiled soup? Was the king only ill with the contagion so many had had? The court was insane when it came to gossip about poison. When his mind ran out of explanations, Charles was left with the thought that he'd been trying since last night to bury. The thought that surely, no matter how much the Prince de Conti wanted a new, weak king, he wouldn't dare to lift his hand against King Louis. Would he?

By the time the stone spires and blue-roofed towers of Paris rose against the limpid sky, and Charles reached the paved

length of road that led in past the wall where the old St. Michel
gate had stood, his mind was a whirl of argument and suspicion. He rode along the line of the wall and turned down the
rue St. Jacques past the Dominican monastery.

What met his eyes as he approached Louis le Grand did
nothing to calm him. Henri de Montmorency stood in the
street outside the postern door, surrounded by talking, gesticulating courtyard proctors. The college corrector, the layman
who applied the disciplinary stick on the rare occasions Père Le
Picart allowed its use (members of the Society being forbidden
to use corporal punishment on the students), was also there.
Not wanting any part of whatever new crisis had befallen
Montmorency, Charles turned quickly up the small street by
the church of St. Étienne des Grès toward the lane behind the
college. But his effort to escape unnoticed failed.

Marie-Ange LeClerc, the baker's daughter from the shop
beside the college chapel, came pelting up St. Jacques toward
him, skirts flying. Going on ten years old now and as in love
with horses as Charles was, she skidded to a halt just around the
corner, where Charles had stopped when he caught sight of her.
He reached down for her hand and swung her up to sit in front
of him.

"*Merci, maître!* Did you have a good ride? Did you see the
king? And his horses? I'm sure they're not as pretty as Flamme.
Oh, I wish Flamme were mine, but bakers can't have horses, can
they, they can't afford them. And my father wouldn't let me keep
him in the back room. Did you see what's happening at the
postern?"

"*Bonjour*, Marie-Ange," Charles said gravely. "I trust you are
well?"

"Oh. Yes, and you? But did you see poor Montmorency?
They're going to beat him and he tried to run away!"

Charles's heart sank. "Beat him? Why?"

"I don't know, but they caught him just outside our shop, I saw them! He's very handsome, I think."

Charles looked down at the girl's dark, curly head with its faded green ribbons, thinking that she was fast getting too old for her years. "Stick to horses, Marie-Ange. They're much more intelligent than Montmorency."

"How can I stick to horses if I can't have one? But I can have a husband someday. *Maman* says girls have to marry."

"Well, don't marry Montmorency."

Marie-Ange giggled. "I can't. I don't want to, he gets in too much trouble. Anyway, he's head over heels in love with someone else."

Charles frowned. "How do you know that?"

"*Maman* says your postern porter told her Montmorency's in love with some girl at court, but she's going to marry someone else and go and be a queen. I'd rather be a queen than marry anyone."

She went on chattering happily, and Charles let her ride with him till they were near the back gate that led to the stable.

"Time to dismount, Your Majesty, so neither of us gets into trouble."

"Oh, I won't get in trouble." She grinned at him over her shoulder. "*Maman* won't miss me; she's too busy scolding my father and his brother for going to the tavern every night. I like it when Uncle Paul comes—he's the one who's a baker at Gonesse—because *maman* shouts at them so much about the tavern, she doesn't notice what I do! This time, though, she's been shouting more than usual. Because she's going to have a baby. My uncle told me that makes women shout at men more. But at least she's not sick anymore."

"I see," Charles said, straight-faced. "Well, I'll pray that she and the baby will be safe. But you must get down now, we're nearly at the back gate."

With a sigh, she swung a leg over Flamme's neck and slid to the ground. She reached up to pull her small white coif straight and dimpled at him. But it was the horse she thanked. *"Merci, Flamme!"* She put her arms as far as she could around the gelding's neck and kissed him soundly, then gave Agneau a smacking kiss on the nose. "So she won't feel slighted," she confided to Charles. "I hope you go riding again soon, *maître!*"

"So do I," Charles said, with more feeling than she could know.

Marie-Ange backed toward the street, waving and throwing kisses to the horses. Charles smiled and raised a hand in farewell, wondering with sudden sadness if Lulu or Anne-Marie had ever been as blithely happy as the baker's daughter. He rode into the stable courtyard, feeling as though Versailles had followed him home.

☙❧ Chapter 14 ❧☙

The lay brother working in the stable took charge of the horses and Charles went to report his return to the college rector. But when he reached Père Le Picart's office, on the main building's ground floor, the door was open and the college corrector, a large placid blacksmith, was just going in. Charles halted and turned away. But Le Picart caught sight of him and called out, "Maître du Luc, come in." Reluctantly, Charles followed the corrector.

"Shut the door." Le Picart was seated behind his desk. The head proctor, Henri Montmorency, and Montmorency's tutor stood in front of him. Montmorency had a very black eye. "I believe you can throw some light on our difficulties, *maître*," the rector said to Charles. "Let me state them as they stand. In the scant time since Monsieur Montmorency was sent back from Versailles on Wednesday night, he has twice breached our rules. At three o'clock this morning, he was discovered trying to get back into the college after leaving without permission. He says—" Le Picart gave Montmorency a scathing look. "He *says* that Père Vionnet"—the tutor got an even more scathing look—"gave him permission to go to the chapel to pray after supper. Monsieur Montmorency tells us he left by the street door while the doorkeeper there was showing our chapel to visitors who came in from the street. He expects us to believe that he merely walked alone around the *quartier*. For eight hours." The sarcasm in the rector's voice was harsh enough to take the paint off the plaster walls.

"I confined him to his chamber, except for Mass. And this morning after Mass, he attacked Monsieur Michel Sapieha in the Cour d'honneur. It took three proctors to separate the combatants, and Monsieur Sapieha is in the infirmary with a broken nose. In addition to his black eye, Monsieur Montmorency has a broken tooth. They tell me they fought about the coming marriage of the king's daughter and the Polish prince."

Reprehensible though the attack—and its reason—were, Charles couldn't help looking at Montmorency with new respect for his fighting ability. A broken nose was worse damage than a broken tooth, and Michel Sapieha, the older of the two Polish students, was a young giant who looked capable of besting a squadron of Turks.

"After this second flouting of our rules," Le Picart said, "I called in Monsieur Genet, our college corrector."

The blacksmith shuffled his feet in embarrassment and tried to hide the cane behind his gray-stockinged leg.

"He went to Monsieur Montmorency's chamber—where Monsieur Montmorency's tutor, Père Vionnet, should have been but inexplicably was not—and Monsieur Montmorency declined to take his caning and instead broke the latch on the postern door in the course of his attempt to leave. He still refuses to explain any of this. Including Père La Chaise's note to me on Wednesday night, when Monsieur Montmorency was sent back from Versailles. Now I am faced with dismissing him from the college. Before deciding that, I would like to know just what is going on. So what more can you tell us, *maître*?"

Charles had a sudden coughing fit to give himself a moment

to think. There were far too many people here for him to speak freely. His eyes met Le Picart's and he tilted his head slightly toward the group around Montmorency. "Père La Chaise did not take me into his confidence concerning his note to you, *mon père.*"

Le Picart looked hard at him. "I see." He transferred his look to Montmorency's tutor. Vionnet should have looked contrite over his failures, but he only looked bored. All tutors were ecclesiastics, but not all were Jesuits. Charles had heard that Vionnet was a superfluous priest from one of the Montmorency estates.

"Père Vionnet," the rector said, "I ask you once more, why did you not report your pupil's absence last night? And why were you not in his chamber when the corrector came?"

Charles thought that if Vionnet had been a Jesuit, the rector's tone would have made him pray for the sky to fall and hide him.

But Vionnet only looked up from examining a fingernail and shrugged. "Even tutors must sleep, *mon père*. And answer calls of nature."

"Your duties, Père Vionnet, include knowing where your pupil is at all times and having him under your eye most of the time."

Vionnet smiled and shrugged. "He finds it distasteful to have a nursemaid. I find it distasteful to play nursemaid to a man of eighteen."

"Then perhaps other employment would be more to your taste," the rector snapped. His voice would have frozen hell's flames.

Vionnet regarded him with the half-closed eyes of a disdainful cat. "Oh, Madame de Montmorency has already found me new employment, which I'll begin when this summer term ends."

"Unless you want to go earlier, you will fulfill your duties here according to my orders. Or both you and your pupil will leave the college in well-publicized disgrace. Is that how you want to return to Madame de Montmorency? And you, Monsieur Montmorency, is that how you want to return to your mother?"

Montmorency seemed to deflate and shook his head.

Vionnet returned to examining his fingernail. "Your word is law here, of course, *mon père*. I only hope nothing happens to make you lose the gift Madame de Montmorency plans to make to the college when Monsieur Montmorency leaves in good order at the end of the term."

"Plans may change for many reasons." Le Picart's voice was as dangerously smooth as an uncoiling snake. "But I sincerely advise you to hope you have nothing to do with any change there may be."

Vionnet's head jerked up and his eyes widened. "Yes, *mon père*."

Charles looked down to hide his smile. The words seemed pulled out of Vionnet without his volition, and from the startled look Montmorency gave him, his pupil thought so, too.

"Monsieur Montmorency." Le Picart rose. "Unless you wish to return in disgrace to your mother *today*, you will return to your chamber and take your strokes of the *férule* from our corrector. The choice is yours."

"Come, *monsieur*," the blacksmith rumbled at Montmorency. "It won't be so bad, you'll see. I'm sure your father has given you worse many a time."

Montmorency, whose mother had always seemed to Charles

far more alarming than any father, bowed slightly and stiffly to the rector and turned to face the blacksmith. The boy's eyes were hot with misery and his mouth was trembling. Not at the threat of the cane, Charles realized, but at being so shamed before witnesses.

"At your pleasure, *messieurs*." With more dignity than Charles would have thought he could muster, Montmorency stalked out of the office.

The silent proctor followed on his heels, and the blacksmith made an awkward and rueful bow to the rector and followed. The tutor went, too, but without taking any leave of Le Picart. Wishing he could follow them, Charles waited.

"Now," Le Picart said. "Say what you would not before the others."

Charles folded his hands and composed himself to be clear and brief. "Our errand went very well—"

"I already know all that. Père Jouvancy arrived before you and made his report. I sent him to rest. I want to know exactly why Montmorency was sent back here. Père La Chaise's note said only to keep the boy here in the college and otherwise explained nothing, no doubt because he feared that the wrong person might read it. I assume that whatever happened at Versailles explains why Montmorency has been so unmanageable since he returned. God knows he is not bright, but he has never till now been a rule breaker. The *bon Dieu* permitting, he will soon finish his time with us. And if he can be prevailed upon to conduct himself acceptably in the meanwhile, I would prefer—for practical reasons—to let him finish."

"Well you know, of course, about the Polish marriage that is being negotiated for the king's daughter. And clearly you are also aware of Montmorency's strong feelings about it, given his fight with Sapieha."

"Yes. What of it?"

"Montmorency fancies himself in love with the girl."

Le Picart brought a hand down hard on his desk. *"What?"*

"He swears that he will prevent Mademoiselle de Rouen from going to Poland. He asked me if I thought the king would let him win her right to stay in single combat."

The rector stared at Charles, slowly shaking his head. "Dear Blessed Mary."

"Montmorency is also doing his best to become one of the Prince of Conti's followers. And Conti encourages him, though I cannot see why, unless for the Montmorency name."

"Père La Chaise has spoken to me of his doubts concerning Conti's loyalty," Le Picart said grimly.

"I should tell you that Père La Chaise thinks there may have been a spy in Monsieur Louvois's entourage during the recent inspection of the eastern fortifications. He thinks it was Conti's spy. I suspect that Lieutenant-Général La Reynie thinks so, too. I saw him in the street the morning we left Paris, and he asked me to report anything I heard about Conti. But he refused to say why."

"But what possible use can Conti have for Montmorency? Who would trust the poor boy with anything of importance?"

"No one, I would think. But Père La Chaise sent Montmorency home after I heard the boy telling Conti and his *coterie* that Mademoiselle de Rouen would not go to Poland if he could prevent it." Charles hesitated and then decided to say the worst and have it over. "He also said he wished the king had died last winter, because then Mademoiselle de Rouen would not have to leave France."

The quill Le Picart was toying with bent double in his hand.

"I have always known that our Monsieur Montmorency is stupid. But the fool is flirting with treason."

"I think," Charles said, "that he means treason only in his feelings. I'm sure he would be appalled to see the king lying dead at his feet. Unfortunately, he does not have enough imagination to realize what he could bring on himself. He also harped on seeking vengeance for Louis the Thirteenth's beheading of the Duc de Montmorency fifty years ago."

"That Montmorency was nearly as stupid as this one." Le Picart made a disgusted sound and slapped in irritation at a fly, which fell from the air and landed at his feet. "For half a *liard*, I would pack this one off home and let his mother be as furious with me as she pleases!"

Charles had often thought he would pay a good deal more than that small-change coin to be rid of Montmorency. But he realized that the rector's mentioning money was not an accident.

"How much has she promised us when he finishes his education honorably, *mon père*?"

Le Picart's lean shoulders rose and fell, and he looked sideways at Charles. "More than I can afford to throw away by dismissing him now. I, the man, would turn my back on the money gladly. However I, the college rector, cannot."

The college had been short of funds since last autumn. War was in the offing and people were keeping a tight hold on their money, and a looked-for bequest to the college had gone elsewhere during the winter. In February, Madame de Montmorency had "asked" that her son be given a good part in the February theatre performance, and her satisfaction with the school's obedience to her veiled order had resulted in a welcome gift of gold. Now a second and larger gift was in the offing. So long as she was satisfied.

"I take it that you are not going to dismiss Montmorency?"

Le Picart's face worked as though he were swallowing something as bitter as antimony. "No. I am not. I will do what I can to let him leave honorably at the end of August—and what I can to keep him away from court. So we will do what Père La Chaise asks and set a watch on him. You will be responsible for him in the rhetoric class and the rehearsals. When do those begin?"

"On Monday. I hope Père Jouvancy will completely recover now."

"I think he will. I have ordered him to rest until then. Very well. Montmorency's tutor can watch him from supper through the rest of the evening." Le Picart's nostrils flared. "And I will set one of the proctors to watch the tutor. A *cubiculaire* can take the morning watch."

Charles took his leave, gave Jouvancy's saddlebag to a lay brother to deliver, and went upstairs to prepare for supper. When he reached the third floor and opened the door to his bedchamber and tiny study, a burst of gratitude sang through him. After the opulence of Versailles, the plain plastered walls and beamed ceiling, the sun pouring through the west window onto the dusty board floor, the narrow, gray-blanketed bed and scanty furniture, all seemed like a modest heaven. Heaven not least because he could close the door and have the two small chambers to himself.

Charles dropped his saddlebag on the floor, hung his cloak over the old-fashioned rail attached to the wall and his outdoor hat on the hook beside it, and pulled off his riding boots and put them in the wall cupboard. Then he shoved his feet into his square-toed, high-tongued black shoes and went to the small table to clean his hands and face. A folded piece of paper with his name scrawled on it lay beside the water pitcher. He opened it and saw that it was a note from Père Thomas Damiot, his best friend in the college, who lived across the passage. Damiot was also the priest in charge of the bourgeois men's confraternity, a religious and social group called the Congregation of the Holy Virgin, which met at Louis le Grand. Charles was his assistant. The note told Charles that an elderly member of the Congregation had died, and that Damiot wanted Charles to help him at the Monday morning funeral Mass at Holy Innocents cemetery across the river. Charles was pleased, because he rarely got to serve at a Mass. Finding his water pitcher empty and dry after nearly a week unused, he instead scrubbed the road dust from his face and hands with a linen towel. He combed his hair and, having a little while till the supper bell, opened his window and looked out.

The din of the rue St. Jacques, the Latin Quarter's main street, rose to meet him. Warm in the late-afternoon sun, the square-cobbled street was full of people walking, riders on horseback and muleback, street vendors trying to sell the last of their wares, slow loaded carts, and carriages with red-and-gold wheels, whose cursing drivers tried to find a way through it all. Across St. Jacques, the dome of the Sorbonne church shone in the sun, and Charles crossed himself as a chanting procession of clerics and laypeople passed beneath his window, carrying a statue of St. Antoine, whose feast it was. Day students just released from Louis le Grand, Montaigu, St. Barbe, and the *quartier*'s other colleges raced down the hill toward the river, shouting and shoving and taunting each other for sheer exuberance at being done with classrooms for the day. Older students in the short black gowns of the University of Paris, along with still older and more dignified students of law, theology, and medicine, thronged bookshop displays on tables set up in the street, indifferent to the traffic. Clerics of all kinds came and went in longer gowns of black, brown, gray, and white. Pairs of nuns and other women walked together, and coiffed maidservants looking for late-day bargains crowded around the illegal makeshift market stalls blocking traffic where side streets joined St. Jacques. A juggler on stilts had stopped at the corner of the little rue des Poirées just across the street and was surrounded by an applauding crowd. As a cart driver came level with him, the juggler tossed one of his six spinning balls wild, and the driver caught it and threw it back with a friendly insult.

At the river end of the street, the spire of St. Severin's church reached from its ancient gray stone and swallows soared and dove around it. The trees showing above courtyard walls along the street seemed to have twice as many leaves as they'd had on Monday, when Charles and Jouvancy rode out of the city. Summer had really come. With a sigh of contentment, Charles leaned on the windowsill, soaking up the light and warmth. During the winter, the golden afternoon light—on the rare occasions when the sun had shone—had seemed like a cruel trick, promising warmth and giving none. Just thinking about the snow-swept, frigid winter, which had lingered far into April, still made him shiver. He sent up a prayer to St. Medard and whatever other saints saw to weather that the summer would be long, and hot enough to drive even the memory of snow from his Mediterranean bones. When the supper bell rang, he left his window open and went to the refectory, happier than he remembered being in a long time.

But when he was back in his room, replete with mutton stew and the greetings of students and fellow Jesuits after his few days away, his eyes kept straying to the still unpacked saddlebag on the floor. The ballet *livret* inside was nagging at him about its unfinished scenes. First, though, he turned his back on the saddlebag and went to his prie-dieu. He'd prayed little so far that day, and it was nearly time for Compline. Scholastics weren't obliged to pray the canonical hours, but they were required to spend an hour a day in prayer, starting with the Hours of Our

Lady and going on to other prayers. They were also required to make two examinations of conscience each day, and Charles would have to tell his confessor that he had not come anywhere near that at Versailles. As he collected himself to begin the Hours of Our Lady, Compline bells began ringing from churches and monasteries across the city. Their urgent, discordant clanging suddenly made Charles think that prayers must sound like that to God: urgent, clashing, drowning each other out, some sweet, some harsh as crow calls, all wanting notice.

He finished his own pleas and opened his eyes in time to see a level ray of evening sun strike the little painting of Mary and the Holy Child on the wall in front of the prie-dieu. Mother and baby glowed in its light, and their smiles seemed to welcome him home. One of those sudden updrafts of the spirit took him beyond pleading or wanting or worrying, and he laughed aloud. He was home indeed, and here was his family.

Mocking himself a little for his overflowing feeling, he got to his feet, picked up the saddlebag from the floor, and tossed it onto his bed. He untied the flap, reached in, and pulled out the *livret*. And stared in bewilderment at what he held, because it wasn't the *livret*. It was a book of sorts, roughly stitched like the *livret*, but he'd never seen it before. Fending off the panicked thought that he'd left the *livret* at Versailles, he upended the saddlebag. And went weak with relief when he pulled the *livret* from the tangle of his dirty shirt and drawers.

Puzzled, he picked up the other book again, carried it to the window, and opened it. On its first page, in elaborate script, was written: "Armand Francois de la Motte, Comte de Fleury."

Chapter 15

FRIDAY NIGHT INTO THE FEAST OF ST. ELISÉE,
SATURDAY, JUNE 14, 1687

THE FEAST OF ST. VITUS, SUNDAY, JUNE 15, 1687

Dumbfounded, Charles turned the roughly stitched pages. Except for the flourished name, the script was cramped and hard to decipher. Charles stood at the window trying to read it until the light failed. He lit his candle and kept on reading until the wick was consumed and the flame guttered out. Then he lay awake, wondering who had put the *mémoire* in his bag. His first guess was the Duc du Maine. Maine had taken Lulu's silver tobacco box from Fleury's room and could easily have taken the journal. The journal might even have been the true object of Maine's search on Lulu's behalf, the night Charles had talked to him in the gallery corridor. But the boy seemed to Charles like someone who would mostly shut his eyes to trouble. So if Maine had not gone to La Chaise's rooms while the Jesuits were out and put Fleury's book in the saddlebag, who had?

The first part of the *mémoire* was a conventional, self-aggrandizing account of the Comte's public and military life, and the name-dropping included only other men, most far better known than Fleury. But the second part was another matter. It began innocuously enough, with comments on court happenings. But it soon degenerated into Fleury's highly colored and self-congratulatory record of lecherous escapades with maidservants. There was also an account of his violent pursuit of a female courtier whom he called simply Venus, including a tale of buying a magical powder guaranteed to make Venus throw herself into his arms. Then came page after malicious page recounting his fellow courtiers' alleged peccadillos, none of which the said courtiers would want known—or even suggested.

Lulu and her misdeeds figured largely in it. Fleury wrote salaciously of catching her wading bare-legged, skirts to her knees, in the Latona fountain, of seeing her in the arms of the Prince of Conti in a gallery arcade, of watching her climb onto the roof of the palace and sit singing at the top of her voice, until the king sent two of his gentlemen out onto the roof to bring her in. He wrote indignantly that she'd cursed and thrown her silver tobacco box at him when he scolded her for smoking her little clay pipe. He gloated over keeping the box. To punish her, he said, but from a few entries about expenses and furious envy of a rich nephew, Charles suspected that Fleury had meant to sell the little box.

But the worst was that one day late in April, so Fleury claimed, he'd been walking in the gardens, near the Grotto of Persephone, an imitation classical temple with an underground chamber pretending to be the door to the spring goddess's underworld. He'd stopped to talk to a gardener trimming a yew hedge. They'd both seen the handsome young footman Bouchel come out of the little temple, but Bouchel hadn't seen them. Then Fleury and the gardener were "rewarded," as Fleury put it, by "the sight of lovely Persephone herself, Mademoiselle de Rouen, coming languidly from the temple, rosy and smiling."

When Charles finally shut the book and went to bed, he lay sleepless, going over and over what he'd read. The night was warm, and he threw back his blanket and pushed up the sleeves of his long linen shirt. Considering the source of the story, it might not even be true. But if it were true, and if the unnamed gardener had been Bertin Laville, it could explain the gardener's death and the money his wife had found in the house after he died. If the gardener had seen Bouchel and Lulu come out of the grotto, he might have tried to blackmail the footman. Charles found it hard to think of Bouchel as a killer, but he could imagine him killing to protect Lulu.

Charles turned over and punched his pillow into a better shape. But if Bertin Laville saw Bouchel and Lulu come out of the grotto in April, why wait till June to blackmail Bouchel?

The college clock chimed midnight. Charles went over what the little Condé girl had told him about the argument overheard between Bouchel and Lulu. Anne-Marie had said that Lulu told the footman that he had to help her. And that Bouchel had pleaded—near tears, the child had said—that he'd already done what he could and that he had no money. And that Lulu had run weeping into the corridor, threatening to kill herself. With a sinking heart, Charles stared up into the darkness, seeing Lulu's pale face and darkly shadowed eyes, and thinking about her frenetic and changeable moods. He sat up in bed. Women shout more at men when they're expecting babies, Marie-Ange had confided just hours ago, when she told him her mother was pregnant. And Anne-Marie had told him not to make Lulu run, because Lulu had been feeling ill. Charles got out of bed and went to the open window.

Two and half months since Lulu and Bouchel were seen leaving the grotto. And Bertin Laville would know the signs of pregnancy, Charles realized suddenly. The stable boy at Versailles had said that Laville's wife had just had a child. A gardener might easily see a girl hiding in the garden to be sick without witnesses. Seeing unmistakable signs of a princess's secret pregnancy was a blackmailer's dream. And if Lulu were pregnant, she had every reason to feel desperate over going to Poland. She could not possibly attribute a baby to a ten-year-old husband.

Charles's mind stopped short and backed up. If this was all true, then what about Fleury's death? Bouchel had been there when the old man fell downstairs. Had Bouchel pushed him, then, in the hope of being rid of the other witness at the grotto? Bouchel had said that Fleury slipped in water, and Charles had seen the wet patch on the floor when he went up to find Fleury's room. And Lulu hadn't had Fleury's journal till later that night. So when the Comte fell, Bouchel might not even have known that he and Lulu had been seen leaving the grotto back in April.

Marching feet echoed along the rue St. Jacques and Charles saw that the night watch was returning from the river, a formidable phalanx of striding men, their swinging lantern striking flares of silver and gold from the stars and *fleur de lys* on the shoulder straps that held their swords. They passed by and went on up the hill, leaving the city drowned again in quiet and nearly invisible in the dark. In summer, the street lanterns stayed unlit, but even if they'd been lit, their candles would be nearly burned out by now. A breeze came up from the Seine and cooled Charles's face. He looked up at the sky and its thickly burning stars. Was Lulu really desperate enough to kill herself? The thought made Charles half sick. If he did nothing with what he suspected, and if she committed suicide, part of the guilt would be his. For her death and the child's. If there was a child.

He could tell the rector what he'd read and Le Picart could send word to La Chaise. Or he could tell La Reynie. But would they agree with his deductions? If they did, how long would it take them to move from talking to acting? It took only a moment to die. Charles suddenly wanted to ride to Versailles and take Lulu somewhere safe, out of the king's reach. Someplace where she would have a chance to simply live. He lost himself in a moment's fantasy of taking her to Languedoc, to his mother, where she could be just a girl and wade in the Gard River as she'd waded in the palace fountain, and harvest olives. A girl with a new name. And perhaps a baby. But free . . .

A pretty fable, the coldly logical part of him said. *It rivals the fables of Monsieur de La Fontaine. Lulu harvesting olives? She would cling to her royal living like a leech.* Shrugging off the probable truth of that, Charles said back, *I'm afraid for her life. And you're heartless; shut up.* The voice didn't. *Besides*, it said, *who is free?*

Charles leaned on the windowsill. "What am I to do?" he whispered.

The stars shifted a little, the breeze from the Seine died, and the darkness wrapped itself around him like black velvet. The air itself seemed to tense and quiver. He waited, every sense quivering. Slowly, breath by breath, the quiet deepened into the Silence that sometimes visited him. He didn't dare to name it. But it spoke to him from the deepest place in his love of God. *Charles*, it said, and it was the first time it had called him by name. *Who are you?* And that was all.

Charles finally slept, but when he woke, the Silence's question still echoed in him like soft thunder. After the early morning Mass, he went looking for Père Le Picart, only to learn that the rector had gone to the Jesuit house at Gentilly, along with the rectors of the Novice House and the Professed House, to meet with the Paris Provincial, the Society's chief official in the Île de France, and would not return until Monday morning. Père Montville, the college's second in command, had gone with him, leaving only Père Donat, the third-ranking administrator. Donat disliked and distrusted Charles and was unlikely to listen to anything he had to say, let alone act on it. He would probably order him to do nothing, which would make whatever Charles ended up doing worse disobedience than it was already likely to be.

All Saturday morning as he assisted in his assigned grammar class and then helped oversee dinner in the senior student refectory, he tried to make up his mind. He was hoping to ask advice from his friend Père Damiot, but Damiot wasn't at dinner. The meal ended, Charles made sure that Henri de Montmorency's tutor took his charge back to their chamber, and then he went to Damiot's room, across the passage from his own. But Damiot wasn't there, either. Charles went down to the postern to ask the porter if Damiot had gone out. Frère Martin, an elderly lay brother settled comfortably on a stool beside the door, nodded portentously.

"He did, *maître*. His father's ill again and Madame Damiot sent for him early this morning. To the Pont Notre Dame, that's where they live. No knowing when he'll be back."

"Is it this sickness everyone's been having?"

"No, and better if it were, poor man. Pains in the heart, Père Damiot said." Martin clapped a meaty hand over his own chest and held up his rosary. "So I'm saying my beads and calling on the Sacred Heart for him."

Charles sighed. "I will pray for Monsieur Damiot, too."

The sense of urgency snapping at his heels drove him to the alcove in the grand *salon*, where paper, ink, and quills were kept. No scholastic was authorized to send notes on his own, but Charles wrote to La Chaise at the Professed House and went in search of a lay brother to carry what he'd written. If trouble came of it, he would make sure it fell only on himself. He gave the note to a brother who was too new to question him and saw him off, praying that La Chaise was in fact back at the Professed House. He wouldn't be, if the king was still ill, but sending a lay brother all the way to Versailles was out of the question.

Feeling that he'd at least done something, Charles went back to his rooms to finish the ballet *livret*, writing with half his mind and one ear cocked toward the door. When the knock came, the brother who'd taken the message told him that La Chaise was still at Versailles. But the Professed House rector, Père Pinette, had agreed to send the note on the next time he sent something to Versailles. Charles thanked the brother, shut the door, and felt his sense of urgency becoming panic. It took so little time to let the life out of a body. He'd been a soldier, a scout, a spy in enemy camps, he knew exactly how little. One moment a man was breathing. The next moment he was not.

He went to his desk and wrote a note to Lieutenant-Général La Reynie at the Châtelet. He still needed to make his report to La Reynie about the little he'd learned of the Prince of Conti, though that did not make sending the note any more permissible. He gave it to the brother who'd taken the other note, then doggedly returned to work on the *livret*. This time, when the knock came on his door, the brother told him that La Reynie, too, was in Versailles. No one knew when he would be back. They'd kept the note, though, to give him as soon as he returned.

Charles tried to feel relieved that La Reynie was at Versailles. But La Reynie was probably there because of the Prince of Conti. He had no reason to pay attention to Lulu. *But what else can I do?* Charles asked the air. He couldn't walk out of the college and go to Versailles himself. Even Père Le Picart would not save him if he did that. It would be the end of him as a Jesuit. But suicide would be damnation for Lulu.

Charles put on his boots. And discovered, when he got to the stables, what he should have realized—the college had only two horses now, Flamme and Agneau, and the rector and Mont-ville had taken them both to Gentilly. Agreeing completely with the part of himself shouting in his head that he was being an idiot, that he was ruining his life, he walked purposefully out of the stable gate. He had nearly reached the end of the lane and the street that came up from the rue St. Jacques when he came face to face with Père Donat.

Donat, walking with another Jesuit Charles didn't know, folded his big hands across his paunch like a man contemplating a long-awaited dinner. "Where are you going, Maître du Luc?"

The other man, small and wiry and bright-eyed, was gazing at Charles's feet.

"Forgive me, *mon père.*" Charles held Donat's gaze and prayed to St. Homobonus, the patron of tailors, to miraculously lengthen his cassock and hide his boots. Or at least to keep the other Jesuit from mentioning them. "I was restless and came to walk in the lane," Charles said. Which was true, as far as it went.

Donat's smile widened. "In boots, for such a short walk?"

"Yes, *mon père.*"

"Go back to your chamber."

"Yes, *mon père.*"

Charles went back through the gate, feeling their eyes on him and hearing their hissing whispers behind him. In his room, he flung himself down at his prie-dieu. He prayed for Lulu's safety and the grace to know what he should do—or not do. When he ran out of words and pleas and bargains, he stayed there, his face in his hands, as the evening light filled his room and drained away.

The next morning, after Sunday's High Mass, Charles sat under a lime tree in the Cour d'honneur, where a group of older boys was gathering for a walk to Montmartre, to the chapel where St. Ignatius and his friends had vowed their service to God and companionship to one another. While the group waited for its accompanying professors, two of Charles's rhetoric students were telling him about a game of *jeu de paume* they'd played. Walter Connor had been one of the tennis players, and Armand Beauclaire, just out of the infirmary, had watched and kept score. As Charles listened, he watched a falcon fly from its perch on the pointed roof of a tower and wished he could come and go as easily and as unseen. *No wonder your little talks with Lulu about acceptance of her marriage had so little effect*, his ruthless inner voice commented. *You still can't accept your vow of obedience after—what is it now, eight years since you entered the Society?*

Charles dredged up a smile for the two boys, who had reached the high point of their tennis story.

"Excellent, I'm glad to hear it! Where did you play?"

"In a court near the Pré aux Clercs," Connor said. Jesuit students were sometimes taken for recreation to the Scholars' Meadow, west of Louis le Grand, on the riverbank, where Latin Quarter students had held games for time out of mind.

"Saint Ignatius went there for recreation when he studied in Paris," Charles said.

Connor laughed. "Can you imagine Saint Ignatius with his scholar's gown off, wrestling in the grass? Or running after a football?"

"No!" Beauclaire looked scandalized. "Saints don't—" He fell silent, looking toward the passage through the main building to the postern door.

Charles looked, too, and jumped to his feet with a cry of relief. Lieutenant-Général La Reynie was striding into the court.

"Join your fellows, now," Charles told the boys. "I have some business to attend to."

With sideways looks at La Reynie, Beauclaire and Connor withdrew.

"*Maître.*" La Reynie bowed slightly, his long dark wig swinging a little forward on his shoulders. His face was tired and harassed, his midnight-blue coat and breeches were dusty, and the lace frothing at neck and cuffs had lost its starch. "I asked to see the rector for permission to talk with you, but the porter said he's not here." A smile twitched at La Reynie's mouth. "He said I could see Père Donat, but I had the feeling he wasn't recommending it."

With a glance at the main building, where Donat's office was, Charles shook his head. "No, Frère Martin wouldn't recommend anyone seeing Père Donat. Who would probably refuse anyone's request to see me. Let's—"

"Why? What have you done now?"

"He doesn't like me. And if he sees you he'll turn you out. Come, we can—"

The main building's back door flew open and Père Donat emerged, making narrow-eyed for Charles, like a gundog after a shot bird.

"Hell's shit!" Charles muttered, and got a shocked look from La Reynie. "It's Donat. Use your rank. He likes rank."

"Fat little flies like honey better," the *lieutenant-général* murmured. He bowed to Donat, who gave him a curt nod and pointed a triumphant finger at Charles.

"No visitors without permission, Maître du Luc."

Charles stretched his mouth in what looked like a smile. "This is Lieutenant-Général Nicolas de La Reynie, *mon père.*"

"And I know that you are Père Donat," La Reynie said fulsomely. "I was on the point of seeking your permission for a brief talk with your scholastic. Concerning something he happened to see at Versailles. If there is somewhere private I may speak with him? I won't keep him long, but be assured his help will reflect well on the Society of Jesus. The king will certainly hear of it."

"Ah. Well." Donat eyed La Reynie. "I see. Then make him tell whatever he knows." He looked down his short nose at Charles. "See that you cooperate, *maître*. Come to me when he finishes with you."

"If I may beg your indulgence, *mon père*," La Reynie said smoothly, "my orders are that he may not speak with anyone about our conversation. It will be better if he does not come to you. So he won't be tempted."

Donat took a moment to rearrange that to his advantage. "True, he is known to be vulnerable to temptation. Return to your chamber, *maître*, when you have told Monsieur La Reynie what he wishes to know. Speak of it to no one else, as he has ordered you."

"Yes, *mon père*," Charles said gravely. "Shall I take him to the library garden? That is likely to be private."

"Very well." Donat inclined his head regally to La Reynie and bustled back to his office. "Dear God," La Reynie murmured, following Charles toward the archway to the neighboring courtyard. "When does Père Le Picart return?"

"Not soon enough." They passed under the arch, and to keep himself from asking about Lulu before they reached the garden, Charles said, "Did you see the king? Is he better?"

"Much better. Though still a little weak. His doctors say now that it was the illness everyone's been having, but a mild case of it. I came because I got your message, but I would have come anyway, knowing you had returned. I hope you sent for me to pass on what you learned at Versailles of the Prince of Conti."

"I doubt I learned much you don't already know." As they walked, Charles quickly recounted what he'd seen and heard about Conti, ending with what La Chaise had said about the man.

"So he, too, thinks Conti is working against the king," La Reynie said. "Well, that's something."

They crossed a stretch of turf toward a little garden, walled on two sides and looking toward the new library. When they reached it, they sat down on a stone bench beside the college's struggling grapevine. Charles turned to face La Reynie.

"Before I tell you the real reason I sent for you, will you tell me why you were at Versailles?"

Le Reynie looked at him in surprise. "I was called there because of a death."

"A death?" Charles could barely force his voice through his throat.

"One of my spies found the body. But you haven't said—"

"Oh, no. Blessed Virgin. How did she do it?" Charles pressed his clasped hands to his mouth and steeled himself to hear the answer.

"She?" La Reynie took Charles's wrist in a grip like a wrestler's. His dark eyes were cold with anger. "What do you know about this? You know who killed him? Was it a woman?"

"Him?" Charles felt some of the tension go out of his body. "I was afraid it was Mademoiselle de Rouen who was dead. The king's daughter."

"*Why*, in God's name?"

"Because she's—I think she's in great trouble. I've been afraid she might try to kill herself."

"Again—why?"

"I'll tell you. But first tell me who the dead man is."

"A palace footman called Bouchel. He was poisoned. They found him dead in his room in the palace."

Charles felt as though he'd been kicked in the belly. *"Bouchel?"* Bouchel poisoning old Fleury, or pushing him down the stairs—that he could imagine, indeed, had already imagined. But who would poison Bouchel? "But Monsieur La Reynie, he may have been simply ill. People at court have had the same sickness we've had here."

La Reynie shrugged. "There was an autopsy. The doctors think he was given inheritance powder, judging from how sick he'd been. You know what that is?"

"Arsenic?"

"Mixed with aconite, belladonna, and opium. They think the Comte de Fleury, who died when you were there, had been given the same thing."

"I know. But Bouchel—it doesn't make sense!" Unless, Charles thought suddenly, one of Bertin Laville's relatives suspected that Bouchel had killed Bertin. But poison seemed an unlikely, and expensive, weapon for a gardener's family. Charles tried to ignore the taunts from his acid inner voice—*trying not to think of the most obvious person, aren't you? Lulu could afford a little poison.*

"Another man died while we there," Charles said slowly. "As you no doubt know. A gardener, Bertin Laville."

"And?"

"I think Bouchel may have killed him. To protect Mademoiselle de Rouen. Bertin Laville's family might try for vengeance."

La Reynie looked at Charles as though he'd gone mad. "Why would a footman kill a gardener to protect Mademoiselle de Rouen?"

"It's a long story."

"Make it a short one. I have little time."

Charles told him what had happened at court, what he'd read in Fleury's *mémoire*, and what he'd made of it. "So if the Comte de Fleury was telling the truth about seeing Bouchel and

Lulu come out of the grotto, and if the gardener who also saw them was Bertin Laville, then Bouchel had plenty of reason to kill Laville."

"And Fleury."

"I thought of that. But Bouchel might not have known then that Fleury had also seen them. And it's possible Fleury's fall was an accident. There really was water running over the floor from a ceiling leak. I looked."

"That's not conclusive."

"No. But even if Bouchel killed both Fleury and Laville, he's dead now himself. *His* killer is not."

La Reynie looked as though he might not mind if someone poisoned Charles. "So you are telling me that the king's daughter is probably illicitly pregnant." His voice was dangerously level and full of reason. "By a footman. A footman at whom she was presumably very angry, and who has since been poisoned. Which means, if you are right in your ungodly number of assumptions, that the king's daughter has quite likely committed murder."

"Possibly. Though I still think she's more likely to kill herself. What are you going to do?"

La Reynie hurled his silver-headed stick at the ground and turned the color of a ripe strawberry. "Nothing! Are you mad? Bouchel was probably a murderer. The girl is the king's daughter. And she is on the point of leaving for Poland. Where she will be the Polish court's problem. The marriage negotiations are finished and there is a grand ball celebrating their completion tomorrow night at the palace of Marly. Do you know it? Very near Versailles, but smaller. The king likes to celebrate family occasions there. On Tuesday morning, she marries her prince there by proxy—the senior ambassador is the stand-in— and sets out for Poland. Thank God and every saint there is."

"But if she's with child," Charles said doggedly, "what will happen to her? And the child? The Poles might quietly kill her for dishonoring them."

"That's ridiculous. The Polish queen is French!"

"The Polish king is Polish. Who knows what their customs are? If Lulu murdered Bouchel and dies unconfessed and unabsolved—whenever she dies—she's damned. And if she takes her life before she goes, she's doubly damned. If we do nothing, her death will be on your head as well as mine. Do you want that?"

La Reynie glared balefully at Charles. "So now you're my confessor? I cannot go to the king with this tale about his daughter and a footman. We don't even know if it's true."

"Someone was worried enough about it to put the *mémoire* in my bag. And someone killed Bouchel."

La Reynie looked as though he might weep. "Where would the king's daughter get poison? I heard she's been watched every minute at Versailles ever since her betrothal."

"Well, the court seems to assume that everyone has poison at their fingertips. I also know that when you had the great poison affair here in Paris some years back, you discovered that Lulu's mother, La Montespan, had poison to hand."

La Reynie looked away. "I thought you liked Mademoiselle de Rouen."

"I do like her," Charles said sadly.

❦❧ Chapter 16 ❦❧

On Monday morning, Charles and Père Damiot were walking toward Holy Innocents for the funeral of their confraternity member. "Is your father better, *mon père?*" Charles thought Damiot looked as though he hadn't slept much.

"We think so. But I'm worried about him. The physician is being grave. But they always are, aren't they? Since the more they do, they more they're paid."

"True. Well, I hope this one will earn little from your father. Who has my prayers, such as they are."

"My thanks." Damiot smiled a little and stifled a yawn.

"And my thanks to you," Charles said, "for interceding with Père Donat." Extracting permission from the acting rector for Charles to go to Holy Innocents had been a near thing. "He makes me feel that he'd like to see me sent in chains to Rome and thrown into the arena," he added, as they turned off the rue St. Denis.

"I don't think there's an arena anymore. And you did bring it on yourself." He glanced at Charles. "Never wear boots if you're going on foot to somewhere you're not supposed to go. No one just goes for a stroll wearing boots."

"Do I hear the voice of experience?"

Damiot smiled complacently.

"I see. Well. I am indeed fortunate, *mon père*, to have such a pious example before me. You also handled Père Donat as though you'd done it before."

Damiot rolled his eyes. "There's very little that doesn't offend His Holiness. I imagine he's offended every morning that the sun doesn't ask his leave before rising."

"His Holiness?" Charles wasn't feeling in much mood to laugh, but he laughed at that. Only the pope was called His Holiness.

"Some of us call him that. But only behind very thick locked doors."

The narrow cobbled street, sun-soaked in strong morning light and bordered by high stone walls that held the heat, almost made Charles feel that he was walking on a street in Nîmes, the town near his family's vineyards. Here the street ran between the beginnings of Les Halles market on the left and Holy Innocents cemetery on the right. Though Charles was basking in the warmth like a lizard as he walked, he was still nearly as worried as he'd been yesterday. La Reynie had agreed to send a message ordering one of his female court spies to watch Lulu, but Charles was uncomforted. His heart was sore over Bouchel's death, and over Lulu's possible guilt. And over what she and Anne-Marie and the Duc du Maine must be feeling on this last day before the proxy marriage. And beyond his worry over all of them, too much was unexplained. Or perhaps he himself was only unconvinced. He felt like someone crouching in the dark after thunder, waiting for lightning. Whenever he closed his eyes, he saw Versailles's new lake. Saw the gardener's body lying beside it, soaked and pathetic. And saw Bouchel in his imagination, saw him dying miserable and terrified and alone in his dark little room. Charles told himself sternly to stop dramatizing his sorrow and fear. But still, just beyond the edge of hearing—some hearing of his spirit or mind—there was thunder.

"I'm sweating!" Père Damiot wiped a sleeve across his forehead and squinted at the sky. "This much sun is unnatural."

"Unnatural?! So you think Eden was gray and cold and wet, like Paris usually is?"

"I have no information on the weather in Eden. Let's hope there's shade to stand in during this burial."

Charles looked up at the stone wall on his right. "I don't see any trees, at least none tall enough to show."

"There aren't any trees. Every morsel of space is used for bodies. I meant shade in the charnel house arcade. Monsieur Delarme's family has done well in trade and has a tomb in an arcade. It's the baser people who—"

Something flew over the wall above their heads, bounced, and rolled to a stop nearly at Damiot's feet, where a pair of thin dogs fell on it, barking happily.

A passing rider guffawed. "Looks like someone wants your prayers, *mes pères*," the rider called. "Maybe it's even hotter than this where he's ended up!"

Damiot kicked halfheartedly at the dogs and picked up the human skull. "Really!" he exclaimed. "This happens nearly every time I walk along here. You'd think the diggers would learn. I'd swear they do it on purpose. I've seen skulls land among parties of women, and the shrieks are enough to open all the graves in the city."

"Ah, you've got her!" A lined brown face under a dirt-colored, bag-shaped cap was looking over the wall. "Would you mind throwing the lady back, *mon père*? They're heavy as lead when I put 'em in, and light as feathers when I pull 'em out. Just a little flick of my old spade sends them flying. Trying for heaven, no doubt, only a little late!"

Laughing in spite of himself, Damiot lobbed the skull back into the cemetery, and the digger grinned his thanks, let go of the wall, and dropped out of sight.

They walked on, Charles keeping a wary eye on the top of the wall. "Before the—um—lady—dropped into our midst, you were saying something, *mon père?*"

"Oh. Yes, it's the baser sort—little merchants and unsuccessful notaries and so on—who are buried in Holy Innocents ground. The poor get mass graves. It's said of Holy Innocents dirt that it cleans bones faster than any other dirt on earth. So the trenches aren't as crowded as the Hôtel Dieu's trenches for the destitute out at Clamart. At Holy Innocents, it's magistrates and lawyers, and wealthy bourgeois like the Delarmes—and my family—who have tombs in the arcades along the charnel houses."

They turned right at the rue aux Fers and when they came to a gate in the wall, just short of the church, Damiot said, "We've a little time still. I'll show you the cemetery so you're not gawking during the burial."

Meekly, Charles followed him through the gate. And stopped short, staring at the scene spread in front of him, at first glance more like a fair than a burial ground. A group of strolling men had stopped to listen to a lute player and female singer. An old woman with a tray of small cakes hung on a strap around her neck strolled toward the men and the musicians. Dogs slept on the shady side of several spirelike monuments topped with crosses, or lolled in the sun, scratching and gnawing—Charles realized he didn't want to know on what. Half a dozen beggars lay in the sun like the dogs. Another beggar, nearly naked, stood in an open grave, gesticulating and haranguing passersby like a preacher, and Charles wondered if the others were waiting their turn, in a cooperative effort to gather coins. A swath of color caught his eye and he watched two heavily painted women, their dirty red and yellow satin skirts trailing on the ground, stop beside the group listening to the lute player. All but one of the men quickly abandoned the music, and what looked like bargaining began.

Damiot pointed to the low buildings around three sides of the churchyard, whose wide cloisterlike arches had been filled in with wood. "Those are the charnel houses. The one with the Delarme tomb is there on the east side."

Charles saw a few small doors in the closed-in arches and wondered what it smelled like beyond the doors. He'd heard that the cemetery itself, with its full and shallow graves, sometimes smelled like death itself. It didn't today, but it smelled like the memory of death, which was somehow worse.

Damiot turned toward the church. "I have to robe for the Mass," he said. "And we have to find you a server's surplice."

The nave of Holy Innocents Church was a pool of deep, cool shadow. They walked up a pillared side aisle toward the altar, which was draped in black for the funeral, and Charles thought how much he liked churches like this, churches in the old style. Not that he disliked the new style's streaming light and open space, and he loved the airy elegance of the nearby Jesuit church of St. Louis. In St. Louis, light was the symbol of faith; people could see the altar and the Mass and feel themselves part of what the priest did. But Holy Innocents was very old and full of soaring, echoing darkness, full of mystery, and something in Charles answered back that yes, God was like that.

They went into the tiny, low-vaulted sacristy, and found the Holy Innocents priest already robing.

"Père Lambert, this is Maître Charles du Luc, one of our

scholastics, who helps me with the Congregation of the Holy Virgin. He will serve with us today and needs a surplice."

Charles greeted the bent, elderly priest, who paused in pulling a wide, flowing chasuble, black for the funeral Mass, over his head and nodded toward a wall cupboard. "In there. I hope there's one long enough to cover you," he said, smiling as his eyes measured Charles's considerable length. "And I've laid out your vestments on the table there, *mon père.*"

Damiot and Charles laid aside their hats, and Damiot went to the table. In the cupboard, Charles found a white, smocklike linen surplice that more or less reached his knees, drew it on over his cassock, and shook the wide sleeves to hang freely. Damiot was putting on a black silk-and-wool chasuble, the usual outer garment worn to celebrate Mass, that matched the other priest's.

"I'll wait in the nave, *mes pères.*" Charles said. He went out and stood at the foot of the altar steps. As the quiet closed around him, he felt the unquiet he was carrying inside himself. And would go on carrying until—when? He looked up at what he could see of the delicately arched stone ceiling, as though the answer were up there somewhere, under the prayer-soaked roof. Until Lulu was safe in Poland? Until it was clear there was no baby? Until Montmorency was gone from Louis le Grand? Until the Prince of Conti tripped up and was exposed? Until Louis XIV was dead and the burden of his search for *gloire* was lifted from France and his ineffectual son ruled in his stead? Until sin was unwound and humankind was back in Eden, whatever the weather there might be?

Charles told himself sternly that, for the next hour, all that mattered was the Mass, which he would be more intimately part of than he usually had the chance to be. Serving at Mass was part of a scholastic's learning, toward the time when he would be ordained priest. But Louis le Grand had many scholastics, and the chance didn't often come Charles's way. He closed his eyes where he stood, began a prayer for his serving, felt its self-importance, and let it go. Finally he just stood there letting the quiet hold him.

The sacristy door opened, the two priests came out, and Damiot handed Charles a smoking censer, whose bittersweet scent floated around them as they went to the street doors. When they had the door standing wide, they saw the funeral procession coming down the rue St. Denis, taking up nearly its whole width. The black-draped coffin was carried on the shoulders of Monsieur Delarme's fellow members of the Congregation of the Holy Virgin. Behind the coffin came the men of the bourgeois Congregation of the Holy Virgin, friends, and family. Behind them a mass of hired mourners shuffled, beggars who'd been given coins and black hooded robes and candles to follow the coffin. People in the street made way for the procession, men doffed hats, and everyone crossed themselves as it passed. One day, they would each want the same courtesy.

The priests led the procession into the church, Charles swinging his censer in the lead. As the familiar and majestic Latin floated through the nave with the clouds of smoke as Mass began, Charles carried the Gospel book and the Mass book from one side of the chancel to the other, and brought water and a towel for Damiot's ritual hand washing. When Damiot spoke the words of consecration that made the bread and the wine into Christ's sacrifice for lost humanity, each word sank into Charles's flesh. When he rang the little silver bell as his friend's long sinewy fingers held up the Host like a small rising sun, Charles knew with almost physical pain that he wanted more than anything on earth to do what Damiot was doing, knew it in spite of his struggles with obedience, in spite of his arguments with God.

Then the Mass was over and the procession carried Monsieur Delarme out to his tomb, Charles stumbling and blinking in the light like Lazarus, still swinging his censer. Only the priests and the close family went with the coffin into the small stone room under the arcade where the tomb was. Charles stood just outside the door, slowly coming back to the ordinary world as he waited with the hired mourners and the confraternity members. He turned slightly so that he could see part of the cemetery. The bedraggled women and the group of men were gone, and the musicians were leaning against the shady side of what looked like an outdoor pulpit, sharing a loaf of bread and a leather bottle of something. A neatly coiffed woman came in through the rue aux Fers door with several young children, who broke from her shepherding and raced, shrieking with delight, across the cemetery, the two little boys leaping joyously across the empty open grave. The door in the wall opened again and an older boy, wiry and slight, wearing a big plumed hat, came a few steps inside and gazed at the burial ground and the church. Then he backed out of the doorway, but his grace and sureness told Charles his name. What was thirteen-year-old Michele Bertamelli, Charles's student and wildly talented dancer, doing out of the college alone and at Holy Innocents?

Charles pulled his surplice unceremoniously over his head and thrust it at the startled man beside him. "*Monsieur*, give this to Père Damiot, I beg you," he said in the man's ear. "Tell him, please, to wait for me. I will return."

Charles ran toward the street door. Behind him, the man hissed, "For the *bon Dieu's* sake, just use the wall, *maître*—it's no great matter!"

Bertamelli was gone, of course, before Charles reached the door and the rue aux Fers. But he saw the hat's white plume bobbing as Bertamelli turned left at the corner and started up St. Denis. Loping after him, Charles opened his mouth to call out to the boy, then shut it. He wanted to know where Bertamelli was going. But Bertamelli, nearly as agile with words as with dance, was unlikely to tell him straight out. Following him would yield better results. Keeping the boy in sight, Charles walked seemingly at ease among the crowd, pulling his cassock skirts aside from the street dirt, shaking his head at beggars and vendors, having nothing to give or spend, and nearly falling flat when a dog chased a cat almost under his feet. Bertamelli kept straight on until the rue du Mauconseil, where he turned left again, past a low stone building with scallop shells carved on its gateway. In spite of his hurry, Charles stopped, staring at the sculptures of the apostles across the building's front and realizing that this was the Hospital of St. Jacques, a shelter for the poor where St. Ignatius himself had lived as a penniless student. Telling himself he'd come back, Charles put on a burst of speed.

He quickly had Bertamelli in sight again. Mauconseil was almost tranquil after the din of the rue St. Denis, and Charles had to follow slowly, keeping the sparse traffic and scattered vendors' stalls between him and the little Italian. The street curved briefly to the south, and as it straightened, Bertamelli stopped at a corner where crumbling walls enclosed an overgrown garden. In the midst of the tangle of greenery, an old, half-ruined tower rose, looking bereft, as though it had once been part of something more. Charles hung back, thinking that Bertamelli was waiting for a pair of horsemen to turn out of the side street before he crossed. But the boy suddenly disappeared into the garden.

Charles hurried to the breach in the wall, but Bertamelli was gone from sight. The tower, with its empty arched windows and battlemented top, was just the sort of place a thirteen-year-old would want to explore. But surely the boy hadn't slipped out of the college only for that. How would he even know the tower was here? Charles stepped back out of sight and waited for Bertamelli to come out when he'd satisfied his curiosity and go on to wherever he was really going.

But he didn't come out, though from somewhere a clock struck the half hour. Charles began to worry. Suppose he'd fallen down the no doubt half-ruined stairs? Charles waded into the rank grass, grunting in exasperation as he stumbled over hidden stones and pulled his cassock out of the grasp of wickedly thorned roses long gone wild. He started to call out, then again bit off the sound before it shattered the quiet. He still wanted to know where Bertamelli was really going.

Halfway around the tower with still no sign of a door, he looked up at the dark blank window arches and saw that the structure was at least five stories high. Wondering who had built it, and why it stood forlorn in this tiny rank wilderness, he kept on until he was nearly where he'd started. And saw the low arched doorway, visible only from the place he'd reached because dense bushes blocked it from every other angle.

Cautiously, stepping over and around stones and the remains of crumbled steps, he went to the threshold. Just inside, stone stairs twisted upward into cobwebbed shadow, but there was enough light from the broken roof to show him lichened walls enclosing the deeply worn steps like a shell. Steps it would be all too easy to slip on. If Bertamelli lay hurt higher up, wherever he'd been going was a moot question.

"Bertamelli!" Charles's voice echoed off the stones like a drum roll. "Are you—"

There was a blur of movement at the curve of the stairs and something hurtled toward him and glanced hard off his left shoulder. His knees gave way and he fell on his side on the stone threshold. Then a lumbering body was on him and he was flattened facedown into the stones. The bushes outside the door crackled and rustled, and Charles got his head up in time to see a broad, brown-coated back disappearing through them. With a vague feeling that there was something familiar about that back, he struggled to his feet, gripping his injured shoulder, and plunged into the bushes. He half ran to the wall and looked both ways on the street. His attacker was not there. Charles hesitated, wanting to go after the man. But Bertamelli was still in the tower.

Thinking morosely that whatever had been thrown down the stairs at him *would*, of course, hit the shoulder with the old war wound, he made his way back to the tower door. The ruined garden's quiet seemed ominous now, and the flat bright faces of the old roses looked back at him like red staring eyes. With a snort of disgust at his overwilling imagination, he charged up the tower steps.

"Bertamelli!" he yelled furiously, holding his throbbing shoulder. "Come down here!"

There was no answer.

"Bertamelli!"

Something knocked him off his feet again and down the few steps he'd climbed. But this time the missile was chest high and spouting desperate Italian. Bertamelli fell to his knees beside Charles, wringing his small brown hands and weeping bitterly.

"Latin, Bertamelli. Speak Latin. I can't understand you." Wearily, Charles sat up against the tower wall.

"*Maître, maître*, I accuse myself, I hate myself, I will cut off my hand!"

This time, there was enough Latin mixed with the Italian that Charles got the drift. "Did your hand throw the stone that hit me?"

"No, no, no hand threw it, the wall dropped itself, *maître*, it is so old, like my grandfather, he falls down because his knees have died and gone to heaven—or maybe hell—before him. I was only looking down the stairs to see who was there and—and—holding on to the wall and—and the stone let go of the other stones and I did not know it was you!"

"Then you've gone deaf. Didn't you hear me yelling for you? Who was up there with you, Monsieur Bertamelli?"

Bertamelli seemed to shrink, his face so white that his huge eyes were black as a moonless night.

"Who?" Charles demanded.

The boy chewed at his lip. "I—I don't know. I heard him. I was afraid—"

Charles had developed a good ear for boys' lies. Bertamelli was definitely not telling the truth. "And did you see him?"

"No!" Bertamelli shook his head and went on shaking it, as though that would make his story true.

Charles sighed. "Why did you come to this garden? Why are you out of the college?"

The boy clasped his hands on the breast of his black wool coat. "I didn't come to the garden. I came to see the Comédie Italienne. It is just there, you know." He pointed in the direction of the cross street. "Across the street. My cousin is there. I knew the rector would not let me go, so I just went."

"You could have asked the rector to send for your cousin."

"But I wanted to go and see him."

"And his show?"

"Yes!" Bertamelli looked up from picking industriously at a patch of orange lichen. "The Italian comedians are the best, you know!"

"Why did you turn aside into this garden?"

"Oh. Here?" Bertamelli blinked, and he bent over the patch of lichen again. "I only wanted—to see the tower. We have many towers like it in Italy. My family used to have one in Milan, but I have never seen one here before. So I went in."

"I see. And why did you look into Holy Innocents cemetery?"

"Oh. Were you in there? Is that how you saw me? I just wanted to see what was on the other side of the door." He shivered. "But I didn't go very far in. I don't like dead people."

"That's unfortunate, because we're going back there. Help me up."

Wordlessly, Bertamelli helped him up and they made their way to the street. Charles noticed that the boy didn't so much as glance at the Comédie Italienne's theatre. He walked silently beside Charles, his shoulders hunched as though he were trying to hide inside himself. They turned down the rue St. Denis toward the cemetery in silence, Charles keeping a wary eye on him and trying various ways of putting together the pieces of the morning to make them show what the boy wasn't telling.

Chapter 17

They found Père Damiot with the Holy Innocents priest, just inside the church doors on a bench built out from the wall and deep in talk about doves. Charles had encountered Damiot's dove obsession before and wondered how long it would take to get his attention.

". . . and she had the prettiest little curl of feathers on her head," Damiot was saying rapturously. "Like a lady's fontange. Have you ever seen one like that?"

"No. But I think my brother—he's the seigneur of Pont-Rouge—has talked of one like that."

Charles coughed. Damiot looked around and frowned, as though trying to remember who Charles might be. His frown deepened when he saw Bertamelli.

"Well." Damiot sighed and got to his feet. "I thank you for your company, *mon père*," he said to Père Lambert. "But we must go back to the college."

Lambert stood up slowly, wincing and putting a gnarled hand on his knee. "When the *bon Dieu* made knees, he did not remember how much priests have to kneel." He smiled at Charles. "Remember that." His faded blue eyes studied Charles's face. "I watched you serving the Mass."

A tremor went through Charles. "Yes, *mon père?*"

"Don't forget what you feel. It is easy to forget."

Charles was too startled to speak. Damiot, bent over Bertamelli, had seemed not to hear. Damiot said their good-byes and
they went out into the street, Bertamelli between them. Over
the boy's head, Damiot looked questioningly at Charles, who
was rubbing his shoulder and thinking about what the priest
had said.

"Where did you go? What's the boy doing here?"

"Forgive me, *mon père*," Charles said. "I know I should not
have left. But when I saw Monsieur Bertamelli in the cemetery,
I thought I should discover how he came to be there."

"Well thought," Damiot said dryly. "And how *did* you come
to be there, Monsieur Bertamelli?"

"I was only looking, *mon père*," the boy mumbled uneasily,
his eyes on the cobblestones. "At the burial ground." Something
of his usual insouciance returned, and he clasped his hands
under his chin and gazed soulfully up at Damiot. "You tell us to
remember we are all going there. To the burial ground. I was
remembering!"

Damiot's mouth twitched. "And when you had remembered?
Then what did you do?"

Bertamelli's head drooped like a dying flower. "I sinned, *mon
père*," he sighed mournfully. And glanced up from under his long
lashes to gauge the response. When none came, he said, "I was
going to the Italian Comedy. For the honor of my family. My
cousin is one of the players and I felt I must go and pay my
respects. That is all."

"Not quite all." Charles looked at Bertamelli, but spoke to
Damiot. "Monsieur Bertamelli went into a little wasteland
across the street from the theatre. With an ancient tower in its
center. When I started up its steps to find him, someone heaved
a stone down the steps and ran past me while I was flat on the

floor. Monsieur Bertamelli says no one threw the stone, it only came loose from the wall when he leaned on it."

"I am so sorry for that, *maître!*" Bertamelli struck his thin chest. "I abhor myself, I abase myself before you, before my mother, before all Milan!" He made to fall to his knees, but Charles caught him and hauled him up again.

"None of that will help my shoulder. Nor will it help your case. What will help—"

The boy's sudden strangled cry silenced Charles, who looked anxiously around for its reason. Bertamelli's feet stuttered to a halt and he clutched Charles's cassock, staring ahead. They were walking toward the Pont au Change, on the covered, cobbled way that divided the Châtelet's criminal court from its prison, and Charles saw nothing more threatening than hurrying robed lawyers with their clerks and pages. There was also a massive Châtelet guard walking toward them, his brimmed pot helmet pulled low on his forehead. But he was smiling and humming to himself, making the pike on his shoulder bob in time to his rumbling music. Bertamelli let out another terrified squeak, which broke off when the man shoved his helmet back as he passed, showing more of his wide, placid face. Charles felt the boy sag against him with relief. Puzzled, Charles turned to look again at the guard. His broad back, like the broad back of the man who'd run from the tower, struck a chord of memory in Charles. He tipped Bertamelli's face up to the light.

"What frightened you so?"

The boy twisted out of Charles's grasp and turned away, shaking his head.

"What?" Charles demanded, increasingly worried about whatever it was Bertamelli wasn't saying.

Bertamelli stayed mute. And that worried Charles even more, much more than any words would have. And Damiot, too, from the look on his face. Charles had never seen the boy this forlorn, never seen him speechless, rarely even seen him quiet outside the imposed silence of a classroom. The little Italian's frightened silence also reminded Charles of Anne-Marie, Lulu, the Duc du Maine, even of Montmorency, and by the time they were passing the Ste-Chapelle, he felt as though he had a clutch of frightened, endangered young hanging to his skirts.

Damiot suddenly pointed to the Ste-Chapelle's spire. "Look up, Monsieur Bertamelli," he said kindly, "and see the angel."

Bertamelli cast a dull but obedient look upward at the lead-cast angel on the Ste-Chapelle's roof slowly revolving to show the cross it held to all points of the compass. But the angel clearly failed to comfort him.

"What do we do with him when we get back?" Charles asked Damiot in French, so Bertamelli would not understand. The boy's French was rudimentary. "I need to find out from him what he was doing."

Damiot eyed him. "Why?"

"I can't tell you," Charles said. "But I'll tell the rector," he added quickly, seeing Damiot's disapproval.

"We'll certainly have to take him to the rector. He and Père Montville should be back—they were supposed to return this morning."

"But if they aren't back? Must we go to Père Donat?" Donat would probably dismiss Bertamelli from the college forthwith. Charles had thought for some time that the boy would leave them early because of his talent as a dancer, and Pierre Beauchamps, the college dancing master, had even said that he wanted to take Bertamelli's further training in hand. But being dismissed by Donat wasn't how Charles wanted Bertamelli's leaving to be. "I don't want him thrown out and sent home!"

"Neither do I. Though he deserves to be dismissed and sent

home!" Damiot said in Latin, for Bertamelli's benefit. Then he went back to French. "Here's a thought, if the rector isn't back. You say there's something our friend here can tell you and that the rector understands you need to know it. So I will use that as an excuse not to go immediately to Donat. The boy is in your rehearsal this afternoon, yes?" When Charles nodded, he said, "Then you can be responsible for him during the afternoon. Oh, but I'm forgetting. What about his tutor? Surely he went to Père Donat when he found the boy gone."

"Monsieur Bertamelli," Charles said, switching back to Latin, "how did you get out of the college? Where was your tutor?"

Bertamelli hunched his shoulders still farther. "I am poor and share a *dortoir* with five others. One of us was taken ill last night, and so was our tutor. They're both in the infirmary." He glanced up, and Charles saw a glint of satisfaction in his eyes. "Getting out was easy. I won't tell you how," he added stubbornly.

"Blessed Saint Benedict!" Damiot was shaking his head, but not over Bertamelli's stubbornness. "This illness is spreading like plague."

"Plague?" Bertamelli looked up, wide-eyed with fear.

"No, no, it isn't plague, people don't die of it. They just feel like they might. All right," Damiot said to Charles, "if the rector still isn't back when your rehearsal is over, I'll collect this miscreant and take him to whoever's been given charge of his *dortoir*."

The three of them crossed the Pont St. Michel and turned along the river to the rue St. Jacques. As they climbed the hill to the college, Bertamelli was visibly drooping and Charles was gritting his teeth against the pain in his shoulder. Damiot had begun discoursing educationally on doves, but neither of them was listening.

When they reached the college postern, Charles tugged at

the bellrope and a small thin lay brother nearly hidden under his canvas apron opened it.

"*Bonjour, mon frère*," Damiot said. "Do you know if our rector has come back?"

The brother shook his head sadly as he shut the door behind them. "Alas no, and won't for now. Nor Père Montville, either. They're ill, both of them. We had word from Gentilly. The sickness is there, too." He lowered his voice. "So we're left tiptoeing around His Holiness till they're well."

Charles and Damiot traded a look, and the college clock began to ring the dinner hour.

"It will have to be the second plan, then," Damiot said, and he and Bertamelli and Charles started through the arched stone passage toward the Cour d'honneur. Behind them, someone pulled hard at the postern bell and Charles heard his name called.

"You in there!" Mme LeClerc's voice was even more urgent and impatient than usual. "Maître du Luc, wait, I beg you, I need one very little word with you!"

Mme LeClerc was Marie-Ange's mother, wife to the baker who had the shop beyond the chapel's street door. She and Charles shared a warm liking, but she talked like the Seine in flood, and listening took more effort than Charles wanted to make at the moment. And he didn't want to miss dinner. Suppressing a sigh, he waved Damiot and Bertamelli on and turned back. The brother had the postern open again and was trying to tell Madame LeClerc that Charles was in the refectory.

"He is not, he is behind you. *Maître*, please—"

"I'll be just a moment," Charles said to the brother.

"A moment only? Then that will be a miracle," the brother murmured with a grin, and stepped aside.

Mme LeClerc was already launched on her news. "—so

don't let them burn, I told Marie-Ange when I saw you from the shop just now and ran out. We are still baking, the fire went out this morning. If it's not one thing, it's one hundred! But I'm taking a moment to tell you, *maître*, but don't think he goes there all the time—a man must have his pleasures, all of them, and who knows *that* better than a wife?" Her round brown eyes dropped meaningfully to her middle.

Charles rubbed his shoulder and tried to wait patiently for the point. Mme LeClerc looked up and rolled her eyes in exasperation.

"Tch! Do you need a little story about storks? Of course you don't, you are a man, we know that." She thumped her belly impatiently. "A baby! On top of everything else, my Roger has given me a baby and then what does he do, he goes off to the tavern every night with that brother who thinks he's God's own baker and refuses to believe that our good Seine water is better than the Gonesse water he's always talking about, and you can take it from me it is not water those two drink at the tavern! Well, I suppose it is in a way, they call it *eau de vie*, but it makes me doubt even more whether he saw what he says he saw, though the truth of that the *bon Dieu* only knows."

Charles caught at what sounded like a point. "What did Monsieur LeClerc see?"

"Hmmmph. The cobblestones in front of his nose, that's the pig's share of what he saw, because he fell down in the street on his way up from the river, and getting Paris mud off breeches, do you know what that takes? I am sick enough every morning without the smell of that!" She stepped closer to Charles and dropped her voice to a whisper. "He saw your Henri de Montmorency riding onto the Petit Pont and it was after ten o'clock and black dark, the tavern was closing, and what was your student doing out at such an hour?"

She had Charles's full attention now. "What night?" he said brusquely.

"Thursday night, *maître*. And then, as you know, on Friday morning he tried to run away again and nearly ran inside my shop, but they caught him just here on the pavement. I was in the back room and we were all shouting, Roger and his brother and me, but we still heard the noise outside, the dead in their tombs in St. Étienne up the street must have heard the noise, and we went to look and saw it was this Montmorency. But my turnip-brained Roger never told me till today he'd also seen the boy on Thursday night."

"He's sure it was Montmorency?" Charles said dubiously.

"He says he is. This morning I told him I was going to the apothecary on the Petit Pont to get his specific against this sickness that's all over Paris and—"

"Has your household been ill?"

"No, not yet, thanks to the apothecary's medicine, don't ask me what it is, it looks like mud. So when I told him I was going to get it, Roger said oh, I never told you I saw that young devil of a Montmorency riding onto the Petit Pont late Thursday night. I said of course you didn't, you were too drunk and what would he be doing on horseback that time of night? But Paul—that's Roger's brother—said Roger wasn't all that drunk and only tripped over a cobblestone when he fell on his face and there *was* a young man riding and Roger had told him it was Montmorency."

"May I speak to Monsieur LeClerc and his brother?"

"Certainly, *maître*, but not today. Roger's gone with Paul back to Gonesse, or more likely to every tavern between here and Gonesse, and left me and the apprentice and Marie-Ange to do all the work." She crossed her arms on the little mound of her belly and looked at Charles with what he thought was probably the look Eve had given Adam when he swore that eating the apple had been all her fault.

"Please tell him as soon as he returns that I need to speak with him, *madame*. My thanks for telling me what Monsieur LeClerc saw." Charles was skeptical, though, about whether the brothers had seen Montmorency. He glanced down at Mme LeClerc's belly and smiled. "I will pray daily for you and your new little one."

That brought a sharp, anxious nod. "I thank you. There have been others, besides Marie-Ange, I mean. But—" Her voice softened. "They died. Always, there are too many little bodies in the churchyards." She cradled her belly. Then she dimpled, looking exactly like Marie-Ange. "Roger is hoping for a son. So am I. But Marie-Ange wants it to be a little horse."

Her laughter mingled with Charles's and followed him back through the postern. Wondering over her story, he made his belated way to the senior student refectory, where he helped to oversee meals. As he went into the enormous high-ceilinged hall, he saw Bertamelli sitting with his dormitory mates at one of the long tables and that a harried-looking *cubiculaire* had taken the tutor's place. Charles went up onto the dais, where old Père Dainville, his confessor, was presiding at the professors' table.

"I was assisting Père Damiot at a confraternity member's funeral Mass, *mon père*. Please forgive my coming late."

Casting an ironic glance down the table at Damiot, already in his place, Dainville nodded mildly enough at Charles, who slipped into his own place at the table's end.

Damiot interrupted his talk with the Jesuit on his other side long enough to raise a questioning eyebrow at Charles.

Charles shrugged and shook his head. "It was nothing. She only wanted to talk about seeing Montmorency apprehended outside the bakery on Friday afternoon," he said, knowing that the rector wanted to keep Montmorency's sins as quiet as possible. He nodded toward the table where Bertamelli sat. "Did you tell the *cubiculaire* to keep our Italian friend under his eye until he delivers him to the rhetoric class?"

"I did. The poor *cubiculaire* is feeling very unsure of himself, so I'll come for Bertamelli when your class is over." Damiot raised his eyes to the faded gold stars painted on the refectory ceiling. "I pray to all the saints," he said under his breath, "that keeping so much from His—from Père Donat doesn't get us dismissed along with Bertamelli."

He went back to his talk with his other neighbor. Charles scanned the room for Henri Montmorency and was relieved to see him where he should be, sitting with his tutor. Charles ate in silence, hardly tasting the thick mutton soup with its lump of bread soaking at the bottom of the bowl, hardly hearing the buzz of voices that made the refectory sound like a giant beehive. He finished the soup and drank the last of his watered wine, looking up at the faded stars painted on the ceiling long ago. He loved the sense they gave him of sitting under God's sky. He'd been told the stars had been there since the refectory was part of the Hôtel de Langres, the private townhouse the Jesuits had bought more than a hundred years ago, and he kept hoping the college would repaint them, but there was never enough money.

But even the stars couldn't stop his thoughts circling each other. His thoughts about what the Holy Innocents priest had said to him. The unlikely puzzle of Montmorency on horseback on the Petit Pont at ten o'clock at night. The oddly familiar look of the man who had barreled down the tower stairs, pushed him down on his face, and disappeared through the tangled garden. Identifying him would tell something about what Bertamelli had been doing there, but Charles could not call to mind anyone who seemed to fit.

His shoulder's ache hadn't much lessened after dinner, and he asked Père Dainville's permission to go to the infirmary for some of Frère Brunet's ointment, saying he'd slipped and fallen on his shoulder. Brunet was not in the fathers' infirmary on the ground floor, so Charles went upstairs to the student infirmary and came almost nose to nose with the infirmarian at the door. Brunet was standing motionless, staring straight ahead and frowning.

"What is it, *mon frère?*" Charles said in surprise.

"Hmm? Oh. I've forgotten where I was going! It happens more and more often. And Saint Anthony refuses to do a single thing about it, though I pray daily. Tch! Oh, well. Do you need something? Come in." He turned and went back inside.

Leaving Charles openmouthed with revelation as the short, broad-backed lay brother plodded ahead of him between the rows of beds. From the back, Brunet looked exactly like the Grand Duchess of Tuscany's short, stocky servant. It was Margot's servant who had attacked him at the tower. But why?

─❦❧ *Chapter 18* ❦❧─

Trying to make sense out of his revelation, Charles went to his chamber for the ballet *livret* and then made his way through the last of the after-dinner hour's quiet recreation in the Cour d'honneur to the rhetoric classroom. He went to the professor's dais at the front of the long, white-walled room and put the *livret* on the seat of a high-backed oak chair. Experimentally moving his shoulder, which hurt less after Frère Brunet's salve and rubbing, he walked between the rows of benches, straightening the ones pushed out of line and casting an eye along them to be sure the morning class had left nothing behind. When the college clock began to chime, he went to the classroom door, where a line of boys, watched by tutors and *cubiculaires*, was forming. Henri de Montmorency's tutor was there, Montmorency was safely in the line, and Bertamelli was last, just behind him. *So far, so good,* Charles thought, and then saw that Montmorency was looking over his shoulder as Bertamelli whispered urgently to him. Charles and the little Italian's *cubiculaire* hushed them—Montmorency's tutor looking indolently on—and as the students came into the classroom, Bertamelli walked to his place as though tiptoeing over meringue. Jouvancy, arriving hard on Bertamelli's heels, walked to the dais with Charles.

'Welcome back to the classroom, *mon père*," Charles said warmly. "You look very well."

"Yes, thank you, I am. And you continue to escape our plague?"

"So far, thank all the saints. But Frère Brunet has told me that poor Charles Lennox is in the infirmary now."

"Terrible timing to lose him now from rehearsals! But better now than later, I suppose. If our students keep dropping like flies, how can we rehearse? We must pray none of the rest get it." Shaking his head, the rhetoric master took his place at the lectern, Charles standing behind and a little to one side. Jouvancy swept the class with his eyes. "Rise, *messieurs*."

Everyone stood and took off their hats, and Jouvancy prayed. He gave thanks for the life of St. Aurelian, whose day it was; commended the class's speaking, acting, and dancing to God; gave thanks for the king's recovery and his own; prayed for the recovery of the ill, especially their classmate Charles Lennox; and nodded at everyone to sit.

"Today we begin working harder on our August sixth tragedy and ballet performance." Jouvancy ducked his chin, swept the room with a wholly spurious glare from under his eyebrows, and gave the class his usual dire warning about the shortness of time. "I beg you to remember that the sixth of August is less than two months away. You will have to work like Trojans to be ready! Like soldiers building fortifications! Beginning on July the seventh, all three hours of our afternoon session will be given to rehearsing. Until then, we have only the second two hours, and this first hour for classroom work. Let us begin now with whatever you have prepared for the class hour." He turned questioningly to Charles.

"Cicero, *mon père*. Recitations." Which should hardly have

needed saying, Charles thought with a mental sigh. It was nearly always Cicero.

"Excellent." Jouvancy smiled happily at them. "We will see now how you do."

The faces looking back at him registered every feeling from complacence to panic. Jouvancy divided the class in half, and he and Charles took fifteen boys each. Charles settled his group on the back benches, sat down facing them, and steeled himself to listen to them recite in turn the thirty-two parts of Cicero's speech in defense of the poet Aulus Licinius Archias. In fact, the recitations, from memory, were not bad, Charles only correcting pronunciation here and there or supplying forgotten words. Each boy spoke twice, and then the first two spoke again, to make up the thirty-two parts. The only trouble was that Montmorency, already scarlet with embarrassment at needing Charles to supply nearly all his words, was one of those who had to speak a third time. But as he stood up, the hour bell rang and a very quiet sigh of relief whispered through the rest of the group like a breeze. With his own inner sigh of thankfulness, Charles told the students to move the benches to the side of the room and get the old costume hats they used for rehearsal. Then he went to consult with Jouvancy, who stood on the dais while his own group moved benches.

Shining with the excitement he always brought to the beginning of rehearsals, despite his dire prognostications of chaos and disaster, Jouvancy took the tragedy script from the lectern. "I will take the *Erixane* cast at this end of the room, and you and Maître Beauchamps will form your usual ballet 'stage' at that end. What do you hope to accomplish today?"

"I'll complete the casting," Charles said, taking the ballet *livret* from the chair where he'd left it. "And see what Monsieur Beauchamps has done while we were—"

Charles broke off as heels rapped over the floor and Maître Pierre Beauchamps swept into the room as though onto a stage. His morose skinny servant slouched behind him, carrying the wooden case that held Beauchamps's violin. Jouvancy and Charles went to greet Beauchamps, who made them a perfect bow.

Since Jesuits created the ballets but didn't teach the dances, every Jesuit college hired a dancing master from outside to prepare students for performances. Beauchamps, though, was more than a dancing master. He was probably the best dancing master in Europe and certainly the best dancing master in France, director of the Royal Academy of Dancing, dance director of the Royal Academy of Music, and Creator of the King's Ballets. At Louis le Grand, he not only taught each ballet's dances but often wrote and directed the ballet music. Having him as the college dancing master was like having St. Peter for the parish *curé*.

"Welcome back," the dancing master said. "I rejoice to see you in better health, Père Jouvancy."

"I thank you," Jouvancy said austerely. "I trust you are well, also."

"Always, always." Smiling broadly, Beauchamps turned to Charles. "I trust you enjoyed Versailles, *maître*?"

Knowing that Beauchamps had spent years at court as both the king's dancing master and fellow performer, Charles chose his words carefully. "It was certainly another world."

Beauchamps's mouth quirked at one corner. "What a very politic summing up." He stepped to the center of the room.

"Bonjour, messieurs." The dancing master bowed to the students.

"Bonjour, Maître Beauchamps," the class said in unison, and bowed in return. Then, at a nod from Jouvancy, the boys took off their scholar's gowns and hung them on the hooks provided, since rehearsing in only their jackets, shirts, and breeches

made it easier to move and easier for directors to see and correct mistakes.

As the ballet cast marked the edges of their "stage" with old costume hats, Jouvancy reclaimed Beauchamps's attention. "Maître du Luc will observe what you have done in our absence and approve it." He paused fractionally. "Or not."

Beauchamps breathed in slowly through his nose and twitched at the ivory lace cascading from his blue coat cuffs. Jouvancy was making it more than clear that he had not forgiven Beauchamps for going to Italy in January and absenting himself from preparations for the February show that had ushered in Lent.

"I'm sure all will go well," Charles said quickly, restraining himself from stepping physically between the two. "Shall we begin, *mon père?*" With a brilliant smile at Jouvancy and without waiting for an answer, he ushered Beauchamps toward the other end of the room.

"What a diplomat you have become," Beauchamps murmured. "Do we owe this to your experience as a courtier?"

"I hope not."

Charles called the ballet cast to order and told the boys who had already been assigned roles and were learning their dances to go over their steps in silence. Those not yet cast, he called together at the side of the dancing space, and he and Beauchamps looked them over. Or rather, Charles looked them over. Beauchamps looked only at Bertamelli. The little Italian, guilt apparently forgotten, stood at the front of the group quivering with hope for good roles. Which he would certainly have, being the best student dancer. Like most of the others, Bertamelli would have several parts, since *La France Victorieuse* had no single star role but many small *entrées* in each Part. Unless, Charles thought wryly, the rector took Bertamelli's roles all away when he found out about Bertamelli's trip to the tower. No reason, though, to tell Beauchamps that, not yet.

Seeing that Beauchamps would be no help until Bertamelli was dealt with, Charles said, "What roles do you want to give him, *maître*?"

"Hmm? A pity this ballet has no star part. Though he's too small yet to play heroes. And may always be. But, blessed Terpsichore, the talent in that small body is blinding. I've worked with him a great deal while you've been gone." The dancing master's eyes glowed, all his usual irony vanished. "I've rarely seen such a gift." His face sobered and he sighed. "You'll have to let him go, you know. He can't waste himself here."

"I know. God made him for the stage. We've talked about it." Charles had once been a very good dancer himself, and he knew what he was seeing when he watched the little Italian. "I only want him to stay with us until he's a little older and better able to manage himself in the world."

Beauchamps grunted. "A little while. But not long." He held out his hand for the ballet *livret*. "I had thought to give him Deceit in the first Part, Mercury and one of the Harlequins in the second, Eole, master of the winds, in the third, and one of the Furies in the fourth."

"No larger role in the fourth Part?" Charles said in surprise.

"He must also learn to be one of an ensemble. And the Furies' jumping and turning will suit his abilities." Beauchamps handed back the *livret*. "Shall I take him aside and tell him?"

"Yes, do."

With something uncomfortably near wistfulness, Charles watched Beauchamps call Bertamelli from the waiting group and walk him to the other side of the makeshift stage. One hand rested protectively on the boy's shoulder, and Bertamelli looked up at him with worship in his huge black eyes. Well,

Charles thought, he himself had had some dancing. And in a way, he still had it. But there'd been a time when he'd wanted what Bertamelli was going to have.

Putting the past back where it belonged, Charles went to work, paging quickly through the *livret* and casting the rest of the students. Finally, only the younger Polish boy and Montmorency were left. Alexandre Sapieha was the brother of Michel with the broken nose, who was still in the infirmary. Fifteen to Michel's seventeen, Alexandre was already as big as his brother. As he stood waiting in front of Charles, he cast dark looks at Montmorency. Montmorency glared back with his good eye, his other being still swollen shut from his fight with Michel. So, Charles thought, Montmorency and the two Sapiehas had better be in different troops of soldiers in the ballet's third Part, *France Victorious over Her Enemies by Arms*. Charles hoped that solution wouldn't lend too much spirit to the fighting between the troops.

"Very well. Monsieur Sapieha," he said, "in the ballet's third Part, you will be in the first troop of French Heroes. Then you will be a German soldier and then a Dutch one." He made quick notes in the *livret* and when he looked up again, Sapieha was scowling at Montmorency. "Monsieur Sapieha?"

The boy turned stolidly. "I wait, *maître*."

"You are looking at Monsieur Montmorency as though you want a broken nose to match your brother's."

Sapieha's white-blond brows drew together as he tried to unravel that. Latin was the required language for speaking in the college, and students were supposed to know some Latin before they came to Louis le Grand. But the Sapiehas' Latin was shaky and, to French ears, practically indistinguishable from Polish.

"*I* would not have the broken nose, *maître*."

"If you keep fighting, you and your brother will be sent home to Poland in disgrace. Is that what you want?"

Sapieha chewed his lip and then grinned. "My father will kill us."

"No doubt. And is this quarrel worth such a fate?"

"Is matter of Polish honor," the boy said grimly.

"I see." Charles wondered if he'd been this obsessed with honor at fifteen.

"Montmorency insulted our Prince Alexandre! He called him a mewling child. He said he hoped Alexandre would die! Alexandre does not want your old French princess, he is desolate about this marriage. It is she who should die!"

"No one should die, Monsieur Sapieha, and you are not to wish it or say it. The French princess is only a year older than you, and she is very beautiful. She does not want the marriage any more than your Prince Alexandre does," Charles said, more hotly than he meant to.

"No?"

"No. Think about that. Monsieur Montmorency is only feeling for the French princess what you feel for your prince," Charles said, wishing that were true. "Back to our business now. In the fourth Part of the ballet, you will be a gardener. And a Fury. Furies are very angry, and you can put some of your wish to fight into your role."

Sapieha brightened. "I hit Montmorency while I dance?"

"No," Charles said very slowly, articulating with his whole mouth. "No fighting. None."

"Oh. But I will still like being Fury. Being furious. I thank you. It is—" Sapieha frowned, biting his lip. "—beautiful!" he finished triumphantly.

"We shall hope so, *monsieur*," Charles said wearily. "Go and wait with the others."

Sapieha joined the group on the makeshift stage, where Charles had set Walter Connor to sort the dancers into their *entrées* for Part one. Charles gestured Montmorency to come, ignoring the rainbow spectacle of the boy's bruised face.

"In Part two's *entrée* of the sculptors and the statue, Monsieur Montmorency, I want you to be the statue, the statue of the king. Then, in the—"

"No."

Charles breathed slowly in and out. "I beg your pardon?"

"I cannot be the king. I am no longer the king's man."

"Do not repeat that. I will do us both the favor of pretending I didn't hear it."

Montmorency repeated it.

Feeling a twinge of near hysteria, Charles said, "You only have to pretend to be a statue. Pretend. It doesn't matter how you feel about whom the statue represents."

Montmorency peered owlishly out of his good eye. "No."

Charles's patience evaporated along with his scruples. "Have you forgotten our interesting conversation about unpracticed headsmen, Monsieur Montmorency?"

"They won't behead me for refusing to be a statue!"

"They beheaded your illustrious ancestor for refusing to be loyal to the king."

The boy drew himself up to his full six feet. His brown eyes were bleak with misery. "I cannot—"

"Think of it as suffering for chivalry's vows." Charles said desperately. And added coaxingly, though he knew he shouldn't, "After all, knights used to go through terrible trials. Think of Tristan and all he suffered for the love of Iseult." He waited, hardly daring to breathe, while Montmorency laboriously thought about Tristan and Iseult.

"Oh. Yes. Then I will be the statue."

"Good. Now in the third Part," Charles rushed on, before

the boy could reconsider, "you will be in the *second* troop of French Heroes. The second, remember that. And in the ballet's fourth Part, a sea god. The chief sea god, who stands on a shell." Whenever he could, he stood Montmorency on something and kept him still, since he was incapable of all but the simplest dance steps. He sent Montmorency to join the others. *Whatever it takes*, he told himself. *Whatever it takes to get him quietly finished with school and gone. Then it will be up to his mother to keep him from catastrophe.*

For a little while, the rehearsal went forward with reasonable progress and no crises. Beauchamps finished teaching the steps for the Harlequins' dance, which included nearly the whole cast, and went to get his violin. Charles, who had been helping him place the dancers, took the chance to sketch the placement in the *livret*.

Most dancing masters carried their little *violon du poche*, the small instrument used for teaching, in a long pocket on the inner side of their coat skirts. But Beauchamps disliked anything that deranged the fit of his suits, and he had his instrument carried in the box by his servant. The man flipped his greasy gray pigtail out of the way and handed Beauchamps the violin. Beauchamps went back to the silently waiting dancers and positioned the violin under his chin. Then he glanced up and erupted into fury. He tossed the violin at the servant, who leaped to catch it, and stalked through the frozen scatter of boys.

"So you became a choreographer in the last three minutes, Monsieur Bertamelli, and have changed my dance?" He glared down at the little Italian, who had left his place in the front and was standing beside Montmorency in the stage left back corner of the ensemble where Beauchamps had tried to hide his gracelessness. "This is not where I placed you."

"He forgot his steps, *maître*," Bertamelli whispered piercingly to Beauchamps. "I saw him trying to remember and didn't want him to be yelled at so soon." He patted the scowling Montmorency on the arm.

"Do not presume on your talent, Monsieur Bertamelli. You are neither a choreographer nor a dancing master. Go back to your place."

With a warning glance at Montmorency, Bertamelli scurried to the front of the ensemble, leaving Charles wondering what was going on between the two. Whatever Bertamelli might do elsewhere, Charles had never known him to come even close to disobeying during a rehearsal. Unless—surely this new piece of unlikely behavior had nothing to do with Bertamelli's visit to the tower? But Montmorency knew Margot, and Bertamelli *had* gone to meet Margot's servant . . .

Charles dragged his attention back to the rehearsal. The cast made its first stumbling attempt at the Harlequins' dance and then moved on to the soldiers' dances. With the help of Beauchamps's servant, Charles brought the chest full of wooden swords from the top of the stairway down to the *cave* where scenery and props were kept. Eyeing Montmorency and Sapieha, he issued a stern warning about using them for anything but rehearsing the dances, and then handed them out. He took one for himself and gave one to Beauchamps, and they began teaching the two troops of French Heroes how to use them while they danced.

Charles hated war, but he liked sword dances—the sweep and swing of the arm, the majestic thrusting and turning of the dancer/swordsman. Most of the students had been taught to use real swords, and Charles saw with surprise that even Montmorency wasn't doing badly. In fact, it looked as though the boy might be quite a decent swordsman. They were all sweating and happy when Jouvancy called the first break, a few minutes for rest and water between the first and second rehearsal hours.

The cast obediently put their swords down on the stage and went to the side table where pitchers and pottery cups stood. Charles had water, too, and then watched Jouvancy talking earnestly to Beauchamps, his earlier resentment apparently forgotten. Since his return from Versailles, Charles had been nursing an idea for an addition to the ballet *livret*. Now, when the rhetoric master was pleased at being well and back to work, seemed a good time to suggest it. It was a daring idea. But if he presented it as he'd planned, there was a chance that Jouvancy and Beauchamps would see only its surface, leaving the deeper meaning for the audience to see. With a sense of girding his loins, Charles walked down the room.

"This Queen of Acre," Jouvancy was saying. "I am still not altogether happy about female roles. But the story calls for them, so what can I do?"

Beauchamps pursed his lips. "Was there a real Queen of Acre called Erixane? I've never seen a Jesuit play about crusaders."

"Nor have I. I don't know of any others. I suppose playing female roles is good practice for the boys. Knowing how to play a woman does make a court actor or dancer more versatile. And Queen Erixane hardly appears. Her daughter, though, has a large role—she even dresses up like a boy and fights for her mother's honor."

"Well," Beauchamps said, laughing, "she *is* a boy. Here, anyway."

Charles, who had been standing quietly, listening, laughed with him.

"True," Jouvancy said reluctantly. "And I suppose they have to learn about girls sometime."

"Some of them have already learned," Charles said dryly, thinking of Montmorency.

"Oh, do you think so?" Jouvancy's blue eyes rounded with worry.

Beauchamps snorted with laughter, and Charles intervened before Jouvancy could retaliate. "*Mon père, maître,* may I offer a thought for a small addition to our ballet's *livret*?"

"What is it?" Jouvancy looked wary.

But Beauchamps looked interested, and Charles plunged ahead. "The ballet's third Part concerns war and the hope for triumph in war. But being mortals, we cannot know what will happen. Which makes the courage of our soldiers all the more admirable." He smiled guilelessly. "I propose that, during the third Part's musical prologue, we show the three Fates seated on a cloud above the stage where the soldiers will fight. As the prologue is played, we see the Fates spinning the thread of man's life, measuring the length of the thread that determines the length of his life, and cutting the thread at his death. Seeing that would remind our audience of our classical roots. But more, it would remind them that humanity never knows its future. And that we are always dependent on God. Whom, of course, we cannot show onstage."

The rhetoric master and the ballet master looked at each other, brows raised consideringly. Jouvancy looked up, as though looking into the overstage where the cloud would be hung. Or possibly to consult heaven.

"That might be an admirable addition," he said judiciously. "How large would the cloud be? And in what colors would we paint it? Grays might be suitable."

"Yes," Beauchamps said. "And the somber grays could be carried through in the Fates' costumes. That would be interesting." He frowned at the floor. "And they should be masked, I think. The Fates. Not grotesquely, but very simply and serenely. The impassive face of Fortune, as it were."

Charles hardly knew whether to laugh or cry at this easy reception of his wickedly subversive comment on the king's wars. Before he could respond at all, pandemonium broke out at the far end of the room.

Chapter 19

Charles reached the shouting ballet cast first. Alexandre Sapieha was swiping at Montmorency with a wooden sword and roaring in Polish so furious that its meaning was clear. Montmorency stood like a rock, staring at the Pole and seeming not to feel the blows. Bertamelli leaped forward and hung on Sapieha's sword arm, but Sapieha shook him off. The other boys backed away, a few cheering for one hero or the other.

"Stop it! Both of you! Now!" Charles was bellowing the way he had on the battlefield, but he might as well have been talking to the wall as far as the two principals were concerned. Jouvancy and Beauchamps were also shouting outraged orders, and Montmorency finally moved. He swung his long arm back and scythed Sapieha down at the knees with his wooden sword. Bone cracked, the sword broke, and Sapieha fell, yelling in pain. Montmorency dropped what was left of his weapon and made for the door. Charles got in front of him.

"Stop, Monsieur Montmorency. You have felled your enemy. Stop."

The boy seemed to look through him and kept coming. Knowing that he was breaking the college rules, knowing how sore his shoulder already was, knowing he probably didn't remember enough to do this right, Charles tackled him. His shoulder screamed louder than Sapieha had been, but he got Montmorency facedown on the floor. The boy lay still as a corpse, and except for Sapieha's moaning, the watchers fell silent.

"Get the proctors," Charles said through his teeth, from where he lay across Montmorency's back.

"I'll go," Jouvancy said. He nodded toward Sapieha. "I'll bring lay brothers to take him to the infirmary."

As Jouvancy left, Charles said to the students, "Carry Monsieur Sapieha outside. No need for more people than necessary to come in."

Murmuring comfort, four boys gathered up the crying Pole and carried him out of the room, to the building's courtyard door. Beauchamps drew to one side, his hand on Bertamelli's shoulder. Charles sat up cautiously, keeping a hand on Montmorency's neck.

"No more, *monsieur*," Charles said. "Do you hear me?"

Montmorency nodded and Charles removed his hand, poised to move quickly if he had to, but thinking he wouldn't. Montmorency sat up.

"What began this, *monsieur*?"

Montmorency looked at him blankly and shook his head. He was rubbing one hand over the other, and Charles saw that he was caressing the ring with Lulu's hair in it.

"The fight was about this marriage?"

Montmorency cradled the hand with the ring against his chest, his brown eyes pools of misery. His broad, smooth face showed several of the inflamed pustules young people often had. And something about that—the ugly spots, his misery, his awkwardly budding manhood—made Charles's heart contract.

Suddenly and to his shame, he knew why this furious grieving boy irritated him so, why he mostly just wanted him gone from Louis le Grand. It was himself Charles saw looking out of Montmorency's eyes, himself at Montmorency's age, himself when he'd known beyond hope that his beloved Pernelle would be married to someone else. His raw grief had opened hell itself. Literally opened hell, in fact, because it was what had sent him fleeing into the army.

"*Monsieur*—" Charles reached impulsively for the boy's hand and searched for words, something to keep Montmorency from making a hell of his grief. But before he found anything to say, Jouvancy came in with three large proctors.

Charles got to his feet. "No need for force," he told them. "He'll go with you to his chamber. Do we have your word that you will do that, Monsieur Montmorency?"

"Yes."

Without taking his eyes from the boy, Charles spoke quietly in Jouvancy's ear. "Even if his tutor is there, I think it would be wise for a proctor to stay outside the chamber door. If you'll allow it, *mon père*."

Jouvancy nodded and gave the order to the proctors. Montmorency got to his feet like a shambling bear and the proctors closed in on him, one on each side and one behind. Jouvancy saw them out. He came back to Charles, shaking his head, and Charles braced himself for admonishment for physically tackling a student.

But Jouvancy said fervently, "Thank you. The boy seems— almost possessed. At least out of his wits." Louder, to Beauchamps and the students, he said, "We will all pray privately for Monsieur Sapieha and Monsieur Montmorency. That they will both amend. And that Monsieur Sapieha will mend. But for now, this rehearsal will continue."

The rhetoric master kept them at it until the clock chimed four, then oversaw the replacement of the benches, gathered them for an extra prayer for the two miscreants, and dismissed them. Bertamelli lingered as long as he could, looking pleadingly at Charles. But when Charles started across the room to speak with him, Jouvancy called him back sharply to the argument over how to alter the ballet with two fewer dancers. Sapieha would be unable to walk for a while, and Montmorency would not be allowed back. He would probably be dismissed from the college.

"Well," Beauchamps said finally, "I only hope no one else decides to air their differences during rehearsals. I don't have enough professionals free to replace them. And you couldn't afford them, even if I did."

He and Jouvancy gave each other the slightest of bows, and Beauchamps stalked from the room. His long-faced servant shouldered the violin box as though it were a small coffin and trailed after him.

Jouvancy made a wry face and lifted his hands helplessly. "Now I must go to Père Donat and tell him what has happened. I'd best get it over. Will you clean up in here?"

He left, muttering disconsolately to himself, and Charles sighed and picked up the broken sword to see if it could be mended. He saw that it couldn't, put it aside, and put the rest of the swords back in the chest. Then he checked to be sure all the old hats were back on their hooks and picked up the ballet *livret*. In the time before supper, he wanted to find out from Alexandre Sapieha what he'd said to Montmorency. And he wanted to find Bertamelli. He thought the little Italian might tell him now what he'd been doing at the tower. He reached to close an open window and stopped, listening to a dove cooing mournfully in the mellowing light. Tomorrow morning, Charles thought, Mademoiselle de Rouen would go to Poland, in spite of whatever secrets she carried with her. With a sigh, he latched the window and started across the Cour d'honneur to the student court.

But his steps dragged and his shoulder hurt, and he sat down on a bench beside the courtyard wall. Montmorency's door was guarded by a proctor, and Bertamelli was in the charge of the anxiously watchful *cubiculaire*. A few minutes' rest would not hurt. Charles leaned back against the warm stones. The mid-June sun was still above the city roofs, and he was glad for the shade of the lime tree that grew beside the bench. Birds came and went in the branches, and he thought he glimpsed a nest high above his head. His eyes followed a songbird's flight and came to rest on the king's profile, above him on top of the wall. The sculptor had caught the long, slightly curved Bourbon nose perfectly, and it seemed to test the outer air as Louis le Grand gazed over the college that bore his name. Charles's brief encounters with the king went through his mind. Louis majestic at the head of the daily procession to Mass; a distant glimpse of Louis walking in the gardens with his gentlemen; the plume of Louis's hat waving above his massive armchair at the ball; Louis's assessing blue-gray gaze as he silently acknowledged Charles's attention to Lulu. Louis had seemed always quiet, always merely passing, or in the distance, or seen from behind. He'd spoken to Charles only once, in few words and hardly pausing. But his presence beat down on Versailles like the sun on the earth. Except that, for those at court, the sun never set and there was little shade.

The door to the main building banged shut, startling Charles from his reverie. Lieutenant-Général La Reynie was coming toward him across the courtyard, followed by a red-faced Père Donat. Jouvancy hurried behind them.

"Maître du Luc, stay where you are," Donat called imperiously, as though Charles were about to run.

Wondering what had happened now, Charles stood up and the trio halted in front of him.

In a hissing whisper, as though the whole college were trying to listen, Donat said, "Monsieur La Reynie has asked to speak with you. I have given my permission. The matter concerns Monsieur Montmorency."

Charles looked questioningly at La Reynie, who slightly shook his head.

Clearly trying to keep a rein on his temper, La Reynie smiled at the acting rector. "I thank you for your help, *mon père*. I will speak privately with Maître du Luc, and then he will go with me to Monsieur Montmorency." He bowed. "I will not trespass further on your time."

Donat bridled. "But you may not speak privately. Maître du Luc is merely a scholastic, and I am in charge here while our rector is away. It is my duty and my right to know all that goes on concerning Monsieur Montmorency, because Père Le Picart expressly charged me with watching him closely and seeing he keeps to the rules." He looked down his snub nose at Charles and Jouvancy. "Which he has not, because others failed to watch him closely enough this afternoon."

"Then it will be well for you," La Reynie said curtly, "that Maître du Luc and I go quickly to speak with him. Before worse happens. Maître du Luc knows the background to my matter. I need him with me—and only him—while I talk with Monsieur Montmorency."

"No." Donat glared and drew in his chin, tripling the rolls of fat above his Jesuit collar.

"This matter concerns the king, *mon père*," La Reynie said, steel in his voice. "The college cannot invoke the old liberties and their immunity. I can and will overrule you if you force me to it." Most of the city's liberties, places whose ancient authority could exclude the law, were long gone.

Donat began to sputter, but Jouvancy put a hand on his arm.

"*Mon père*, we all know that you only want to serve our rector and our king." Jouvancy's actor's voice was warm with spurious understanding. "But there are times when the better tool must be laid aside so that the lesser—and more disposable—may be used. Père Le Picart will be very grateful to you. As will the king himself. *Very* grateful . . ."

La Reynie nodded. "He will, indeed."

"Oh. Yes." Donat preened visibly as the unctuous words flowed over him. "Yes, go with him, Maître du Luc. Do exactly as he tells you. Exactly, do you hear me? And then report to me."

"Go!" Jouvancy mouthed behind Donat, and made urgent little shooing gestures.

La Reynie's glance flickered from Jouvancy to Donat. "As I said yesterday, Père Donat, Maître du Luc will not be able to speak about this matter. But I will see you before I leave."

He bowed briefly and followed Charles, who was already moving toward the archway between the courtyards.

"Blessed Virgin," La Reynie said, when they were safely in the student court. "Your Père Jouvancy deserves a thousand fewer years in Purgatory for that."

"He's a fine actor. Especially offstage." Charles stopped under a lime tree in front of an old stone house and pointed across the court. "Montmorency lives in the brick building there. Tell me quickly why you're here."

La Reynie halted reluctantly. "I've had two of my men watching the Saint Pierre convent in Montmartre. Where the Grand Duchess of Tuscany lives. I think she's passing letters to Conti from his spy on the eastern border. I haven't known how she was getting them. But on Thursday night, nearly midnight, two of my men were watching the convent. And your Montmorency rode up and passed in a letter. And the duchess came to the grille to speak to him."

"So that's where he went. I knew he'd left the school Thursday night, but he refused to say where he'd been. How did your men recognize Montmorency?"

"They saw his face by the portress's lantern when the duchess opened the grille, but they didn't know him. One of them followed the boy back here to see where he lived. But he—my officer—had been feeling ill, and by the time he reached Louis le Grand, he was fevered and could hardly keep upright. He went home, thinking to tell me the next morning, but by morning he was too fevered to talk sense. It wasn't until this afternoon that his wife sent a message telling me he'd tracked the letter bearer to the college. That, along with the description, told me it was Montmorency."

"If he's passing letters from the spy, he may not realize it. He's not bright."

"Bright or not, he'll have to prove he didn't know what he was doing. Or someone will have to prove it. Otherwise, he's guilty of treason."

"We need to talk to Michele Bertamelli." Charles jerked his head at the stone house behind them. "He lives there. I'm certain he knows something about Montmorency's letters. Your presence may scare the truth out of him, and you'll have more to work with when you confront Montmorency."

"Bertamelli?" La Reynie said in surprise. "The astonishing little dancer?" The *lieutenant-général* had seen the school's February performance. "What makes you think he's involved?"

"I think he's been carrying letters for Montmorency."

"But Montmorency took his own letter to the convent."

"But now he can't. He's been guarded since Friday morning and can't get out of the college. And his guard is heavier after his fight during this afternoon's rehearsal. He nearly crippled one of the Polish boys over this marriage. And I'm not just guessing about Bertamelli." Charles told La Reynie about following Bertamelli into the tower. "Someone—not Bertamelli—threw a piece of masonry down the tower stairs at me, shoved me flat, and got away. But I saw his back, and I'm nearly certain it was a servant of the duchess's—a squat, barrel-like man I saw with her at Versailles. Then, in the rehearsal today, before the fight, Bertamelli kept trying to talk to Montmorency. He never breaks rules during a rehearsal. But today I think he was trying to tell Montmorency that he'd been followed to the tower."

"But you didn't see Bertamelli give anything to this servant?"

"No. But your men saw Montmorency at the Montmartre convent. And even Montmorency would know he couldn't rely on getting out of the college and going there again. I think he and the duchess arranged for him to send his letters to the tower." Charles laughed a little in spite of himself. "If any student can get out of our college without being discovered, it's Bertamelli. And if it was Margot's—the duchess's—servant he met at the tower, well, it's hard to draw any other conclusion."

La Reynie grunted. "Let's find out."

They went into the stone house and up three flights of stairs to Bertamelli's *dortoir*. The harassed *cubiculaire* Charles had seen at dinner answered his knock.

"Monsieur La Reynie, this is Maître Guerand," Charles said, hoping he had the thin, sandy-haired scholastic's name right. "May we speak with Monsieur Bertamelli?"

"I suppose so." Guerand sighed in exasperation. "He's in the study. Sitting there looking like a dying martyr. Italians! No wonder Italian opera is what it is."

He took them through the tiny anteroom, into a small study where Bertamelli and five other boys, all in their scholar's gowns, sat almost cheek by jowl at scarred tables under the low-beamed ceiling. The single window was open and birdsong from the court was louder than the scratch of quills and the shuffle of pages. Bertamelli was the only one neither writing nor reading. He was staring tragically out the window, his brown hands clasped so tightly under his chin that the knuckles showed white. Charles's skeptical first thought was that the boy was planning how to get through the window. Bertamelli turned around, and his eyes lit when he saw Charles. He stood up eagerly, but Charles quickly held up a hand.

"Softly, Monsieur Bertamelli. Wait." He gestured Maître Guerand back into the anteroom. "*Maître*, will you do us the great favor of taking the other boys down to the courtyard? It's not long till the supper bell, and I know that Monsieur La Reynie wants to speak very privately with Monsieur Bertamelli."

"Yes, all right. Blessed Saint Roch, I hope their tutor recovers quickly. This day is endless." Shaking his head, Guerand gathered his charges and herded them downstairs.

Charles went back to the study, where La Reynie and Bertamelli were warily taking each other's measure. "Lieutenant-Général La Reynie, this is Monsieur Michele Bertamelli. Monsieur La Reynie is the head of our Paris police, Monsieur Bertamelli. He wants to know why you went to the tower this morning and what happened there."

The whites of Bertamelli's eyes showed. "Will he put me in his prison?" he whispered.

La Reynie looked at him consideringly. "Only if you lie to me."

Bertamelli flung himself to his knees in front of Charles, and his long-lashed black eyes filled with tears. "Forgive me, *maître*,

I wasn't going to the Comédie Italienne. I did lie to you, may my heart be torn out with guilt! But I didn't mean for you to be hurt!"

"What *did* you mean?" Charles said sternly.

"Only—only—" The boy sniffed like a small pig. "Only to have a little money."

"Ah," La Reynie said, going nearer and looking down at Bertamelli. "The eternal motive. So. You not only break the rules, you get paid to break them?"

Bertamelli dissolved in sobs.

"Look up, *mon brave*," Charles sighed. "Who paid you?"

The boy turned his wet face up to Charles. "Monsieur Montmorency. But he couldn't help it, *maître*. He is in love, and a man cannot help himself when his heart drives him!"

La Reynie took a large white handkerchief from his coat pocket and thrust it at Bertamelli. "Use this. And tell me how you earned Monsieur Montmorency's money."

Bertamelli mopped his face and clutched the wet handkerchief in both hands. "I took his love letter to a man who said he would send it to Versailles."

"And who was the man?"

"I don't know, *monsieur*, I swear it!" The boy shrank into himself and shivered. "I was only told where to go and that a man would be there."

"The man threatened you," Charles said flatly, remembering the boy's sudden fear of the short stocky Châtelet guard as they walked back to the college.

Bertamelli looked wide-eyed at Charles. "He said he would kill me if I told what I'd done or that I'd seen him." His face was a tragedy mask. "And then he tried to kill you, *maître*, but I didn't know he was going to do it, truly I didn't!" He buried his face in Charles's cassock skirt.

Charles bent over him. "He wasn't trying to kill me, only to get out of the tower unseen. And I'm not dead, *mon brave*. Only bruised. Get up, now, and tell us if you could identify the man if you saw him again."

Bertamelli got to his feet, wiping his face on his sleeve, and stood as stiffly as a soldier. "Yes. If he knows, he will kill me, but for you I will die!"

"Can we put an end to this?" La Reynie said abruptly. "I have little time."

But Charles had thought of another question, and he hoped he was wrong about what the answer would be. "Tell me quickly," he said to Bertamelli. "How did the fight start today between Monsieur Sapieha and Monsieur Montmorency?"

"Oh. They insulted each other about the Polish prince and your French princess."

"What did Monsieur Sapieha say?"

"I cannot always understand him. But he talked about— I am not sure—something called Marly? I don't know what that is. He said the princess is marrying there tomorrow. Then he—"

"How did he know that?" Charles demanded.

"He said that a Polish man came yesterday from the court to visit Monsieur Sapieha and his brother. Some relation, I think. The man talked of the wedding. Monsieur Sapieha laughed at Monsieur Montmorency for being in love with the bride. And Monsieur Montmorency hit him."

Charles's heart sank. He wasn't wrong. "My thanks," he said to Bertamelli, turning toward La Reynie, but the *lieutenant-général* was already out the door. "Come!" Charles chivied Bertamelli out and down the stairs into the student court, where the boy's *dortoir* mates lay talking in the grass under a tree while the *cubiculaire* watched them like an anxious sheepdog. "Join them, *mon brave*. Don't worry and don't talk about our conversation. And don't leave the college on your own again!" He leaned close and spoke in the boy's ear. "Because the next time you do, you will be sent straight home. Instead of going to dance for Maître Beauchamps when the time comes. Don't spoil that."

Bertamelli's eyes widened until they were half his face. "Oh!" he breathed. "Then you know I am going to him, *maître!*" He grabbed Charles's hand and kissed it fervently.

La Reynie was calling impatiently from across the court, and Charles reclaimed his hand and ran to join him. They climbed to the brick building's second floor, but at the top of the stairs, Charles stopped in dismay. There was no proctor guarding Montmorency's door. They barged into Montmorency's anteroom.

"Monsieur Montmorency? Père Vionnet?" Charles called, and rushed into the chamber beyond the anteroom. The proctor was sitting on the thick carpet, rubbing his head and groaning.

"Hell's devils! What is this?" La Reynie pushed Charles aside and stood over the proctor. "What happened to you?"

The proctor, a young, well-set scholastic, shook his head. "I—I hardly know. Père Vionnet called me in. And they rushed me. Both of them. Montmorency drove his ham fist into my jaw, and I went down." He cast a glance at the fireplace behind him. "I must have hit the hearthstones, because I only just came to myself. They're gone, aren't they?"

"I am not," a voice said weakly. Père Vionnet was standing unsteadily in the study doorway.

"Where is Monsieur Montmorency?" Charles and La Reynie demanded in concert.

"How do I know?" Vionnet went waveringly to the bed and sank onto it, holding his head. A bruise was purpling on his cheek. "How could he do this to me? I ought not to have been left alone with him!" he said indignantly, glaring at Charles and the proctor.

"Speak plainly," Charles said back. "And quickly. What happened?"

"The boy grew more and more upset. Beside himself over that girl. I called for the proctor to come and help me with him, but Monsieur Montmorency attacked him the moment he came in. I tried to pull him off, but—well, you see I failed. Then the cursed boy—"

"You came at me, too," the proctor said angrily. "You helped the boy!"

"I did not! You only saw me behind him. I was trying to pull him away from you! After he hit you, he chased me into the study and threw me against the wall with such violence that I knew nothing else, nothing at all, until just now." Vionnet put a shaking hand to his head. "Please, I need Frère Brunet!"

Charles and La Reynie exchanged a look, and Charles turned a speculative gaze on the tutor. "You say that Monsieur Montmorency was upset about the girl. Did he go after her?"

Vionnet's shoulders nearly hid his ears as he shrugged. "Perhaps. Wherever she is. If he even knows."

"He knows." La Reynie helped the proctor to his feet. "How was he dressed?"

"Cloaked," the proctor said, wincing as he talked. "And hatted." He looked helplessly at Charles. "I'm sorry, *maître.*"

"It wasn't your fault. I'll tell them it wasn't. Go to Frère Brunet." He turned to Vionnet. "You. Come with us to Père Donat."

"No! I am worse hurt than—"

La Reynie took his arm, turned him around, and parted his hair to look at the back of his head. With a glance at Charles, he said, "Not as hurt as you might be, *mon père.* Come."

He marched Vionnet down the stairs, across the student court, and toward the main building.

"Through there," Charles said, when they reached the *grand salon*. He pointed to a door in the alcove where writing materials were kept.

Donat was sitting behind the desk in his small dark office, apparently doing nothing. Behind his head, Charles could just see the painted head of St. Laurent, eyes meekly raised to heaven as he roasted on his gridiron.

"Monsieur Montmorency is gone from the college, *mon père*," Charles said bluntly.

"Gone? But how?" Donat's face blanched. "He can't be gone!"

"I don't know how. We found the proctor guarding his door knocked witless. And Père Vionnet says Montmorency also attacked him before he fled."

"I *was* attacked," Vionnet said shrilly. "I am injured and in pain and this man"—he pointed at La Reynie—"would not let me seek help!"

"Tell Père Donat what Monsieur Montmorency said to you," Charles said. "Before he attacked you, of course."

"Said? Only that he was desolate about this daughter of the king. The one marrying the Polish prince. The stupid boy thinks he is in love with her. Women drive men insane. You cannot hold him responsible; he is out of his mind over the little witch. And so I shall tell his noble mother and urge her to forgive him," Vionnet finished righteously, looking as unconvincingly meek as St. Laurent in the painting behind Donat.

La Reynie advanced on Donat, who was still sitting behind his desk. "You said you were charged with keeping Henri de Montmorency in the college. You have signally failed. He's almost certainly gone to Marly, where the king—and the girl—

are tonight. I am going after Montmorency, and I want Maître du Luc with me. He handles the boy well, and he knows the situation. Knowing what I know of Père Le Picart, I would not advise you to stand in the way of saving whatever can be saved of this situation. Which you have helped to create by your lax supervision. My carriage is in the street," he said to Charles, and was gone.

Vionnet slipped out behind him, paying no attention to Donat's sputtering command to stay.

Charles stayed where he was in front of Donat. *"Mon père?"*

Donat's color deepened, and he shook his head like someone with a palsy.

"I beg you," Charles said quietly, "give me leave to go. For yourself. For the college. And for Montmorency. I may be able to help pull him—and us—out of the worst of this tangle."

"He brought it on himself," Donat spat at Charles. "Let him take his punishment."

Charles wanted to follow La Reynie without wasting more words on Donat. But he told himself that Donat was his superior and held himself where he was. *"Mon père,* the ancients wrote of three Fates, not just one. Do you really think anyone comes to his fate without the doing of others? We were all charged with keeping Montmorency here and safe. We all failed. Do you want to tell the rector that, after that failure, you made no effort to find him? That you did nothing to prevent the damage he may do? Nothing to help his soul, when helping souls is our reason for existing?"

Donat swelled like something gone bad at the market. But he finally got out a single, strangled word. "Go."

Chapter 20

La Reynie's carriage was rolling before Charles could pull the door shut.

"I almost left you," La Reynie snapped.

"I had to make Père Donat tell me to go with you. If he hadn't, I'd be in nearly as much trouble as Montmorency is."

"What did you threaten him with?"

"Me, threaten? Only with failing Saint Ignatius. How long will it take to get to the king's chateau at Marly? Have you sent a message to Père La Chaise about Montmorency?"

"While I waited for you, I sent one of my officers, on horseback. It will take the carriage two hours to get there, perhaps less. It's very close to Versailles, but the terrain is more hilly near the chateau. Going uphill, the horses will have to walk. Assuming Montmorency is mounted, he will be there long before us. God send that, he—and the girl—will still be there when we arrive."

"There are half a dozen places near the college to hire a horse," Charles said over the noise from the street and the rolling of the carriage wheels.

"Let's hope all of them were out of horses this afternoon."

They were silent as the coach made its way through the crowded summer evening streets, until Charles said, "I don't understand why the Grand Duchess of Tuscany would endanger her position by passing letters to Conti, now that the king has let her return from Italy. She'd have to be a fool! And she didn't strike me as one."

La Reynie's mouth quirked. "The duchess is a lady of many sides. And one side is always in debt. I assume she's doing it for money, just like your Bertamelli."

"Well, it would explain why Père La Chaise and I found her and Montmorency and Mademoiselle de Rouen together in an alcove at Versailles after the ball for the Polish ambassadors."

The carriage stopped suddenly and the driver began to shout at someone. La Reynie swore and put his head out the window. "What is it?"

"Accident, *mon lieutenant-général*. Someone's cast a wheel and the way's blocked."

Charles looked out from his side and saw that they'd reached the square beyond the Sorbonne church and that the narrow way into the rue de la Harpe was full of bellowing men, neighing horses, and a gilded carriage on its side, one of its high back wheels spinning slowly in the air. He craned his neck and looked over his shoulder. Behind La Reynie's carriage was a solid line of carriages and carts, all the drivers standing on their driving boxes and demanding to be let through.

"I suppose we could walk to Marly," Charles said, without enthusiasm. "People walk to Versailles."

"Montmorency could be halfway to the coast with the girl by then." La Reynie pushed open the door, jumped from the carriage, and strode into the traffic jam, holding his silver-headed stick like a weapon.

Perhaps it would have taken longer without his furious orders, but it still took long enough before they were on their way again. They made good time along the rue des Cordeliers after that, and La Reynie was visibly relaxing into his seat when the driver pulled the horses to a bone-jolting stop.

"Now what?" La Reynie shouted.

"They're taking down a piece of the old wall, *monsieur*," the driver shouted back. "Some of it fell on the street."

Charles looked out and saw the end of a stretch of city wall straight ahead, beyond a little street that curved to join the rue des Cordeliers. Traffic on the little street was stopped, too, and pedestrians and drivers were gathered where the streets met.

"The stones of the wall are enormous," La Reynie said, opening the carriage door. "We'll never shift the damned things."

He banged his way out of the coach and Charles climbed out after him. A clutch of workmen, stoutly declaiming that it wasn't their fault, stood leaning on massive hammers as a steady stream of pedestrians picked their way across the huge stones. But the carriages and carts were blocked.

"Turn," La Reynie told his driver, who had come to stand beside him. "Somehow." He looked at Charles. "Get in. I'm going to help the driver."

The driver climbed onto the box, Charles got into the carriage, and La Reynie began working miracles. Standing in the middle of the road, wig flying, he scythed the air with his stick, bellowed directions like a war drum, ran and lunged and turned, and had the traffic reversed and his carriage turned within minutes. Sweating, he flung himself back into the carriage and they were off again.

"We'll have to take rue de l'Enfer past the walls and turn west again when we can," he said. "Dear God, I wish I had a drink."

"Rue de l'Enfer? Why do they call it Hell Street?"

"Because of the traffic," La Reynie growled. "Why else?"

Once outside the line of the walls and heading more or less west again, the driver whipped up the horses and the carriage leaped forward.

"Making up time," La Reynie said. "Whatever other treachery is afoot, pray we get there in time to at least stop Montmorency running off with the girl. If that happens, hell will be nothing to the consequences." He swore as the carriage rounded a curve and he slid across the seat into Charles. "My apologies, *maître*." He pulled his coat straight. "There's been no time to tell the relatively good news I have for you. Your Lulu did not poison Bouchel. One of my court spies learned that Bouchel was helping the Prince of Conti get the reports about our border fortifications. I've thought for some time—and so has Père La Chaise—that Conti has a spy in Louvois's entourage inspecting French fortifications along the eastern border. Though Louvois has returned, the inspections continue. And the spy is still with the inspectors. No, I won't tell you who he is. We're giving him a long rope so he can hang himself more thoroughly."

Charles frowned. "I got to know Bouchel a little at Versailles. You know he looked after Père La Chaise. I never saw sign of any hostility toward the king."

"He would have made sure you didn't. And maybe he had none, I don't know; maybe he was only helping Conti for the money. But I do know that Bouchel's father was a mason at Versailles when the place was first being built. His father fell from a wall and the overseer forced him back to work, though his leg was badly hurt. The leg made him unsteady and he fell again. That time he broke his neck. Not long after, the king came to inspect the building, and the mason's mother— Bouchel's grandmother—spit in Louis's face and called him a murderer. The king had her flogged. I've been told that Bouchel grew up hearing the story."

"Blessed Mary." Charles winced. "I would surely hate the king for that."

"It seems that when Conti heard the story, he saw that he could make use of Bouchel. Bouchel in turn recruited one of the king's couriers, a young man his own age, whose family is from the village and who knew the story of Bouchel's father and grandmother. This courier is the one who carries the spy's letters from the border to Troyes, where he disappears into the old town and passes the letters to someone else. Then someone else brings them to Paris. To the Grand Duchess of Tuscany, it seems. Possibly through your Montmorency."

"Or his tutor," Charles said suddenly. "Montmorency could not leave the college or receive anything unexamined. But the tutor could."

"Yes. While I waited for you, I sent two men to arrest Père Vionnet for questioning. So. The chief of my court spies thinks that Bouchel was killed because Conti is about to change the letters' route. And that the footman not only knew too much, he was growing greedy for more pay. For his work and for his continued silence."

"Which is now assured," Charles said sadly. He was thinking that if Bouchel had demanded more money, it might have been for Lulu. "Well, that's very good news about Lulu, anyway. That she didn't kill poor Bouchel."

The coach leaned precariously as they rounded a corner, and La Reynie clutched at the straps hanging from the carriage roof. Charles braced himself on the seat, wishing more every moment that he were on horseback, though the miles seemed to pass like single footsteps as they hurtled through the bright June evening. He'd never traveled much by carriage and never so fast. Trees, fields, houses, people whirled by so fast, they made his head spin. To his relief, the carriage slowed as the driver pulled the horses to a trot and then to a resting walk.

"What would happen between France and Poland if Lulu did run off with Montmorency?" Charles said. "Would King Louis lose the Polish king's goodwill?"

La Reynie shrugged. "I don't know. Jan Sobieski is nobody's fool. He might be able to see past the antics of two idiot children. In which case, he'd shrug and look for another bride for his son."

"They're not idiots. Not even Montmorency. I've always found him dull-witted, but he truly cares for the girl. And she is certainly bright enough. But no creature thinks clearly when it's struggling in a trap."

"So your sympathies are with those two, are they?" La Reynie said sourly.

"Far more than they are with the king's greed for glory and power."

"You'd better hope I didn't hear that. The king is the head of France's body. He is responsible for France's wealth and glory and power."

"And he's selling his people, including his daughter, to get it."

The horses began to trot again, and La Reynie bounced nearly to the roof of the carriage as the wheels hit what felt like a boulder.

"Even if the boy's not intentionally passing letters," he growled, "he commits treason if he rides off with the girl. And if he does, for two *sous*, I'd leave them to get on with it and take the consequences."

"There's always the possibility that Montmorency may not come near Marly. God send he doesn't."

La Reynie slapped his wig straight after another bounce. "Maybe he's gone home to his terrifying mother. Or to Siam. Someplace where I have no jurisdiction."

"If he does try to take the girl, and is caught, what will happen to him?"

"If he's only being used with regard to the spy's letters, he might only be exiled. If he's working with Conti—he could lose his head." The *lieutenant-général* lurched against the side of the carriage. "At the moment, damn him, I wish he'd already lost it!"

"Falling in love isn't a crime," Charles said sadly, trying to shield his injured shoulder from another collision with the gold brocade carriage wall.

"For the *bon Dieu*'s sake! You sound like every idiotic young man since Adam. I thought you were past that sort of thing."

"Montmorency's *actions* are wrong, yes. What he feels for the girl is not. How could it be? He isn't married. He—"

"She is. Almost."

"Against her will! She doesn't want the marriage and she's damnably trapped!"

"Her father has the right to impose his will. Every father does."

"And if his will is destroying his child?"

"Oh, it's like that, is it? No authority, no order, only womanish feeling. Pah! You sound exactly like my son!"

La Reynie put out a hand to fend off the front carriage wall. For a long moment there was only the thud of trotting hooves and the rattle of the much-tried carriage.

"Gabriel?" Charles said carefully. He knew La Reynie had a son, but it was the first time the *lieutenant-général* had spoken of him voluntarily.

La Reynie's big shoulders rounded suddenly, as though something hurt inside him. "I am too harsh, he says. He wants none of my rules. None of my—my life. He says he will go to Rome. And not return."

"I'm sorry," Charles said inadequately.

La Reynie crossed his arms over his chest and frowned at his rumpled brown coat sleeves. "So what will you say when you're a priest? And some fool like Montmorency or Gabriel comes to you? Will you say, oh certainly, by all means, flout the commandment, no need to honor your father?"

"Scripture also says that the sins of the fathers will be visited on the children."

"And so will yours be visited on them when you're Père du Luc and guide them wrong!"

Suddenly they were glaring at each other from opposite corners of the coach. Charles turned his head away and closed his eyes, leaning back against the thick brocade upholstery. The horses' trot on a smoother stretch of road was making the carriage rock pleasantly now . . . The carriage lurched and he sat up in alarm.

"We're nearly there," La Reynie said, glancing at him. "You've slept."

The carriage rolled to a stop and Charles put down the window glass and peered out. They were stopped at a tall, tree-shadowed, heavily guarded gate. La Reynie lowered the glass on his side and spoke to a pike-carrying guard.

"Has a young horseman passed through the gates recently? Henri de Montmorency?"

"No, *mon lieutenant-général*," Charles heard the guard say. "No horseman has come in since noon."

"You're sure?"

"Yes, *mon lieutenant-général.*"

"If Montmorency does come, say nothing about my being here or asking about him. Let him pass but send me word."

The guard nodded smartly, the gates opened, and the carriage crossed an arcaded circular court. Then Charles nearly fell forward as they began to go steeply downhill.

"The chateau is at the bottom of this slope," La Reynie said. He turned on the seat to face Charles. "You heard what the guard said? Montmorency is not here."

"Yes, but I can hardly believe it. Are there other ways in?"

"I suppose he could go through the forest. There are paths. But then he'd have to climb the garden wall. Without being seen and taken by a guard. The guards are nearly as thick here as at Versailles. Otherwise, though, Marly is different. It is private, not open for public gawking. Officials, like me, can get in on emergency business. Otherwise, entrance is strictly at the king's invitation." La Reynie braced an arm on the front wall against the incline. "I know of at least one visit Montmorency has made here. So he may know a way through the forest. But if he breaks in over the wall, that will not endear him to the king."

Charles looked out his window again and saw that they were near the bottom of the steep *allée*. The chateau was directly ahead. The last of the long evening's sun lay across its front and Charles exclaimed in surprise. "The red pillars—they're Languedoc marble, from my home region. What an incredible front the place has!"

Beside him, La Reynie merely snorted.

The sunlight gleamed on the chateau's gold balustrade, its gold sculpted figures and vases, its golden pediments and window panels, all picked out against brilliant royal blue walls. The carriage stopped at a second, smaller gate and was passed through. Charles, still gaping out his window like a tourist, gasped in astonishment.

"It's all paint! There are no pillars, it's just a flat wall, there's nothing there but paint!"

"Yes. Illusion." La Reynie bent his head and stepped down from the carriage as a lackey held the door open.

Charles clambered from the carriage and stood gazing at the chateau's *trompe l'oeil* front. "Do you suppose they intend the irony? That it's all only an illusion?"

"Illusions can be very durable." La Reynie led the way into the royal chateau of Marly.

---+|- *Chapter 21* -|+---

L a Reynie stated his business to the footman who'd let them in.

"I'll take you to the king's apartments, *monsieur*," the footman said. "We have a grand ball this evening, but His Majesty is still in his private rooms."

La Reynie nodded at the glazed doors on the vestibule's other side. "You can wait in the *salon, maître*. That's where the ball will be. I shouldn't be long." And as the footman turned away, he added under his breath, "Keep your eyes open."

Charles went through the glazed doors into the *salon*. For a moment he simply stared. The enormous room was octagonal, with identical glass-paned doors at the four points of the compass, and identical cavernous fireplaces topped with mirrors on the angled sides. Corinthian pilasters studded the ground floor walls and caryatids looked down from the next level. Between the caryatids were tall windows with balconies, but the windows were dark and seemed to open from an inner corridor. The only natural light came from roundel windows near the top of the walls. Now that the sun was behind the hills, servants were lighting the wall sconce candles, and the mirror-polished parquet floor was doubling and giving back the little flames.

Otherwise, the *salon* was deserted. But muted voices and what Charles recognized as the click of billiard balls came from the south vestibule, and he went to see who was there. As he opened the glazed doors and looked in, the men engrossed in the billiard game ignored him. Several had shed their coats, and they were all watching hawk-eyed as the Duc du Maine sighted intently along his cue and struck a ball. When it went wide, the watchers shouted in triumph. Maine shrugged and smiled. As he moved aside for the next player, he caught sight of Charles.

"Maître du Luc! Have you come for the ball and the wedding?"

Charles, still wearing his outdoor hat, removed it and inclined his head. "A grand occasion, Your Highness," he said, smiling, hoping Maine wouldn't notice his failure to answer the question. "How is it with your sister?"

Maine abandoned the billiard game and went to the side table where he'd left his coat. "I don't quite know," he said, slipping it on as they walked together into the *salon*. "Not happy. But she's—excited, somehow, I think. Which I suppose is better than just being sad." He looked a little wistfully at Charles. "I think going to Poland would be a great adventure!"

"Going to Poland might."

"But marrying a stranger wouldn't, you mean." He sighed. "I hope I will have more choice when my time comes. But I don't suppose I'll have much."

Giving up on finding a subtle way to ask if Montmorency was there, Charles said, "I suppose all her friends will be here. The little Condé girl and Monsieur Montmorency and the Prince of Conti?"

"Anne-Marie and Conti will certainly be here. I don't think Montmorency was invited." He looked puzzled. "But you should know that better than I, since he's at Louis le Grand."

"Sometimes the young nobles are given leave to go to court," Charles said vaguely. "At what time does this ball begin?"

"At nine. And it must be nearly eight, I should go and dress." He smiled and withdrew.

La Reynie was still not back, and Charles crossed the *salon* to its north vestibule and went outside. Below the steps, there was a stretch of gravel and then the wide spread of gardens. Jets of water played among what seemed acres of *parterres*, all planted with flowers and low shrubs, and crossed with formal paths. Beyond, the ground fell away toward the Seine. Charles turned slowly, taking in the stretch of the gardens, the buildings around the chateau itself, and the steep wooded hills rising on the other three sides of it all. If Montmorency was here in hiding, it would take a concerted search and sheer luck to find him. A searching, fitful wind had risen and the western sky was already piled with soft rosy clouds. In another hour or so, it would be dark.

"So you've finally come back," a high clear voice said disapprovingly behind him.

Anne-Marie de Bourbon stood just outside the doors, shimmering in silver satin covered with silvery blue embroidery. Blue gems winked in her silver-ribboned brown curls, and both arms were wrapped around her little black dog, who was happily licking her chin.

Charles removed his hat again and made his clerical *révérence*. "I have, Your Serene Highness. But how did you know?"

"The Duc du Maine just told me." She flicked an impatient hand toward the *salon* and gently pushed the little dog's head away. Then she looked carefully around the deserted terrace, grabbed his hand, and pulled him farther from the doors. In a half-whispered rush, she said, "Did you finally read the old man's book? Why did it take you so long to come? What are you going to do?"

"So it *was* you who put the Comte de Fleury's *mémoire* in my saddlebag."

She nodded impatiently. "I was keeping it for Lulu. Her women go through her things, but no one bothers about me. But you haven't answered me. What are you going to *do*?" Her voice was as worried as her pale thin face, and the little dog wiggled and anxiously licked her again.

"*Ma petite*," Charles said softly, speaking as he might have spoken to Marie-Ange, the baker's daughter. "You want me to rescue your friend. And I think I understand why now." He leaned over as though adjusting his shoe. "A child?" he murmured.

Anne-Marie nodded. "She's been so sick. I know the signs."

"I am sorry with all my heart. But I cannot stop her going to Poland. She herself has chosen not to tell the king her secret. What can anyone say to him?" He reached out to pet one of the dog's long ears. "No, don't shout at me, we don't want to be noticed. Listen. They are not barbarians in Poland. Their queen is French. It will not be as bad for Lulu as you think." He prayed that what he said was true. Though the child would be taken from her. Princes could flaunt their bastards. Princesses could not.

Anne-Marie's mouth was trembling. But she drew herself up to her diminutive height and her eyes flashed. "What you mean is that you are a coward. Well, I am not!"

In an angry whirl of skirts, she swept back into the vestibule. Grimacing at her accusation, Charles gazed after her and then picked up a leaf that had fluttered from her shoulder and turned it over in his hand. It was as fresh as the child herself, and Charles shook his head. When childhood's illusions shattered, they usually shattered painfully. Then his ruefulness shifted abruptly to suspicion. Was the girl planning something? But what could a twelve-year-old do? He put the leaf absently into his pocket and started back inside.

The door opened nearly in his face as La Reynie came out of the vestibule. He looked, if anything, more unhappy than he had in the carriage.

"What did the king say?" Charles asked him.

"Nothing I wanted to hear." La Reynie went to the edge of the terrace and looked out over the gardens. "Which is only fair, I suppose, because I also told him nothing he wanted to hear. The war minister Louvois has been at him repeatedly about Conti, and the king has tried to fend him off. Now that I've told him there's every reason to think that Louvois is right, he's furious."

Louvois. Even the man's name sent a small chill through Charles, and he thought of Louvois in his carriage, approaching Versailles on the day he and Jouvancy had left. "Is he here?"

La Reynie nodded unhappily. Charles had reason to know that La Reynie liked the ruthlessly competent war minister as little as most people did. "I haven't seen him yet. But I did manage to talk with Père La Chaise after I saw the king. Père La Chaise is livid about Montmorency, though he says that as far as he knows, the boy hasn't been here. He'll help you watch for Montmorency during the ball. The king has ordered me to keep a close watch on Conti and the duchess tonight—yes, Margot is here, too—but unless I see a letter passed, I'm not to question them until tomorrow. Nothing is to disturb the court until Père La Chaise pronounces the royal daughter a royal wife tomorrow morning and she's on her way to Poland."

"What do you want me to do if Montmorency comes?"

"Grab him and hand him over to a guard. Two guards, given

what we know of his prowess at fighting. I said nothing to the king of Montmorency's feelings for the girl—only that I want to question him about Conti's letters." La Reynie studied the horizon.

Surprised, Charles said, "Why did you keep his secret?"

The *lieutenant-général* shot Charles a warning look. "Not because I'm converted to your nonsense about thwarting parental authority and order." He glared at the tired lace covering his wrists. "Montmorency isn't here yet. Or if he is, we don't know it. If he's not here, he may never arrive. If he arrives, he may lose his nerve—or come to his senses—and never show his face. So unless he does burst in like some idiot knight out of *The Song of Roland*, let his little romance die its death. He's in enough trouble as it is, just being suspected of helping Conti with the letters."

More than enough trouble, Charles thought. He gave silent thanks for La Reynie's reserve with the king. The *lieutenant-général's* compassion might be reluctant and even furious, but it was still compassion. At least the boy might escape exposure of his silliness over Lulu.

"What do we do now, *mon lieutenant-général*?"

"They're bringing us a little something to eat in the *salon*. I'm told the ball begins at nine."

La Reynie led the way back into the *salon*, where footmen had let down the huge central chandelier on its chain and were replacing and lighting its candles. Others were setting up chairs in what Charles recognized as the Ring, seating for those who would dance during the ball. Another footman stood near a fireplace where a small table had been set with plates and cups. When he saw them, he lifted a hand and brought two chairs from their places against the wall. Charles and La Reynie ate quickly but well, cold chicken and salad and comfortingly good wine. As they ate, servants continued to set up chairs and music stands on the west wall's balcony, and the musicians gathered and began tuning their violins. The chandelier, now blazing with candles, was hauled back to its place level with the balconies, its hanging crystals sparkling in its light.

Charles suddenly felt a draft and turned to see who had come in from outside.

"What is it?" La Reynie said.

"Someone came in from outside, didn't you feel the wind?"

"Oh, the wind. The smallest breeze from outside gets into this *salon* without anyone opening a door. They say it's something to do with the glazing, but no one seems able to fix it. In the winter, you can't sit in here unless you're wearing furs." He glanced at a servant shifting from foot to foot by the wall. "I think they're wanting to move our table."

As they rose, Charles said, "I forgot to tell you that I saw the Condé child just now on the terrace. She admitted that she put Fleury's *mémoire* in my saddlebag. And she wanted to know what had taken me so long to return and save Lulu. When I told her there was nothing I could do, she called me a coward. And gave me to understand that she, on the other hand, is not. What do you make of that?"

"Twelve-year-old bravado. Come, let's go up to a balcony; it's a good place for watching the vestibules."

A sweet-chimed clock struck nine as they reached the top of a staircase to the second-floor corridor around the octagon. La Reynie led the way to a floor-to-ceiling window. As they stepped through it onto the south balcony, they heard the musicians begin to play.

"Remember," he said, "the vestibule to your right is the east entrance from the main court. The other vestibules, including the one straight under us, open onto the gardens and walks. If

Montmorency is here, he's likely to come in through one of those, not by the main court."

Below them, the *salon* filled quickly, a storm of talk and laughter above a rustling sea of satin, damask, brocade, silk, and lace, most of it in brilliant colors, much of it covered with embroidery and sparkling with gems. Wigs hung in swags of curls, fontanges bloomed with ribbons, and perfumed fans added to the breeze wandering through the room. The music broke off, and then the musicians played a brief fanfare and the inner doors of the east vestibule were thrown open. The king appeared and everyone sank into deep curtsies and bows as he walked to the regal armchair set for him in front of the east doors. To Charles's surprise, Madame de Maintenon was with him, sober in brown velvet, black lace preserving her modesty from bodice edge to neck and veiling her hair. The Dauphin, the king's brother Philippe and sister-in-law Liselotte, and the older Polish ambassador, who wore a long coat of deep blue silk over breeches to the ankle, all seated themselves on either side of the king. La Chaise came in and placed himself behind the king's chair. He raised his eyes briefly to the balcony where Charles and La Reynie were, and then let his gaze roam over the crowd.

Charles said in La Reynie's ear, "The girl's mother has not come?"

"One comes to Marly only by invitation. I imagine it's too small to hold La Montespan and Madame de Maintenon together."

They watched those chosen to dance take their places in the Ring's first row, while others entitled to sit found places in the seats behind them. Charles was glad to see that Anne-Marie de Bourbon was among the dancers, a thick cushion set in front of her chair to keep her feet from dangling. Then Lulu came in, escorted by the younger Polish ambassador, and sat in the center of the Ring's first row, facing the king. Her pink-gold skirts spread around her like a sunset cloud and it seemed to Charles that she moved with a new dignity, her face smooth and serene beneath its powder and rouge. La Reynie was watching her, too.

"Her gown is a pretty color," he said. "It's called *aurore*."

Charles gaped at him.

"My wife told me," he said sheepishly, seeing Charles's look. "I think *dawn* is a good name for it—the sky does look like that in the morning."

"It's lovely," Charles said, grinning. "And so is she."

"And wearing a very nice little fortune, too," La Reynie said. "If Montmorency shows up and rides away with her, they can live for a long time on it."

Charles looked again and saw that in addition to the heavy ropes of pearls he'd seen Lulu wear at Versailles, the front of her bodice was set with flashing diamonds. More diamonds circled her wrists and sparkled among other gems on her fingers. She was indeed wearing a portable small fortune. But it seemed more and more likely that Poland was the only place it was going.

The ball began with the customary *branle*, and then the Prince of Conti, wearing dark green wool and satin, danced a grave *loure* with a beautiful young woman Charles didn't recognize.

"His widowed sister-in-law," La Reynie said. "Another source of rumors about our prince."

Instead of resuming their places in the Ring when the dance ended, Conti and the pretty widow acknowledged the king and went out by the south door, followed by the Duc du Maine and several others.

"Where are they going?" Charles said in alarm, as they passed beneath the balcony and disappeared from view.

"It's all right, I was told they'd leave." He smiled slightly at Charles. "They'll be back."

The dancing went on, and when everyone in the Ring had danced except Anne-Marie and Lulu, the doors of the *salon* burst open and the courtiers who had left returned, masked and costumed as a gaggle of Italian comedy characters: Harlequin, Scaramouche, Flavio, the Doctor, Isabella, Brighella, and a comically limping, wide-eyed peasant. A fast-moving love story unfolded—more decorously than the real Italian comedians would have played it—and the love of Isabella and Flavio won the day and was duly blessed. The Poles shone with satisfaction, laughing and nodding as they watched. But Lulu watched gravely, when she watched at all. She mostly looked down at her lap and twisted her half dozen rings. Finally, all the characters danced a *gigue*, bowed low to the king, and withdrew to the edges of the *salon* to watch the rest of the ball. When they were gone, Anne-Marie took the floor with a handsome little boy, whose deep blue coat and breeches matched well with her blue-silver.

"Who is he?" Charles said, as the pair began their *sarabande*.

"Lulu's brother, Louis Alexandre, the Comte de Toulouse," La Reynie murmured. "The king's youngest son by La Montespan. He's nine or ten, I think."

"He and Anne-Marie do well together." Charles laughed. "But I'm surprised she's left her other Louis behind."

"Her dog? Yes, I had the same thought." Suddenly, La Reynie laughed, too. "Look, even in her finery, she's clearly been outside chasing the dog. A leaf just fell out of her hair. And there's another!"

Which made three leaves fallen from Anne-Marie's hair. A tiny *frisson* of unease flickered through Charles. He told himself not to be absurd. Anne-Marie chased her dog everywhere, and Marly was even more dense with leaves than Versailles. But to-night, anything out of the ordinary put him on the alert.

Seemingly unaware of the dropping greenery, Anne-Marie eyed her younger partner as a governess might, to be sure he did her credit. But whenever the dance took her past the chair where Lulu sat, all her anxious attention went to the princess. The *sarabande* ended; the children made their honors to the king and returned to their seats. Then it was Lulu's turn, the moment for which all the rest had been prologue.

"Ah," La Reynie said quietly, looking straight down over the balcony's rail. "There's the duchess. Late as usual. And with Conti."

Charles looked, too. As Margot jockeyed for a better view of the dancers, her servant followed her and Charles took a long moment to study the man's back. "That's him," he said in La Reynie's ear. "The man who met Bertamelli at the tower and threw the stone at me."

"You'd swear to it?" La Reynie followed the square-built ser-vant with his eyes.

"With pleasure." Charles went back to watching Lulu.

The younger Polish ambassador, wearing a long-coated Pol-ish suit of tawny silk, led Lulu onto the dance floor. As they made their honors to the king, Lulu smiled. Briefly and sadly, but it was still a smile and given to her father. Then she and the Pole made their honors to each other and she had a faint grave smile for him, too.

Well, Charles thought, his hopes rising, maybe all really was going to be well. Or at least well enough. The pair danced a lively *bourrée*, a miracle of fleet precision and ease, and Charles suspected that the ambassador had spent more time practicing than negotiating. As his feet and Lulu's wove the dance's balanced symmetry, the pink ribbons and gold lace on her headdress fluttered, and the ambassador smiled happily as his tawny silk coat rippled and swirled around his legs. The Duc du Maine had taken off his mask and was biting his lip as he watched his sister. Charles looked at the king, wondering what he felt as he watched his daughter dance for the last time. As though Louis felt Charles's eyes on him, the royal gaze lifted to the balcony and rested on Charles for the briefest of moments. With a nod so small Charles couldn't be sure he'd seen it, the king turned his attention back to the dancers, leaving Charles wondering if he'd just been thanked for his small part in Lulu's acceptance of her fate.

When the *bourrée* ended and Lulu and the Pole had bowed and curtsied to the king, all the dancers rose and formed two facing lines for the buoyant *contredanse* that signaled the ball's end. As the lines advanced and retreated and the couples whirled and wound their way up and down, Charles felt himself relax a little. The ball was over. Nothing had happened.

"They'll set up a buffet now," La Reynie said, when the *contredanse* had ended and the half dozen other people who'd been watching from the balcony were filing out into the gallery. "The musicians will play and the *salon* will be thronged with people milling and eating. I think you should go down, *maître*, and continue watching from there. I'll stay up here and we'll have each other in sight."

Charles agreed and made his way from the balcony toward the stairs. And came face to face with Michel Louvois, the king's minister of war. Louvois's round black bulk seemed to radiate anger as he stared at Charles, then shouldered him aside and went toward the balcony where La Reynie was. Charles forced himself to walk sedately to the stairs, berating himself for how much he wanted to run, for how much he feared the war minister.

The stairs took him down to the north vestibule. A steady wind swept across the floor, and as he went into the *salon*, it seemed to get stronger. It was oddly disturbing, this wind blowing his cassock against his knees in a closed, crowded room, as though a storm must be raging outside, though at sunset the sky had been limpidly clear. Watching for any sign of Montmorency—and for Lulu, Conti, and Margot—he pushed politely through the crowd, feeling a growing need to keep Anne-Marie under his eye as well. As he passed near Mme de Maintenon, who was complaining indignantly about the wind, he caught sight of Lulu.

She was standing with her father near the royal armchair, hands folded demurely at her waist, eyes downcast, listening to him. La Chaise, still standing behind the chair, was watching her. The king's brother and sister-in-law and the Dauphin watched and listened avidly. The ambassadors had drawn a little aside and were talking quietly to each other. As Charles made his way along the north wall, he saw Lulu lift her eyes, smile, and say something that brought an answering smile and nod from the king. She curtsied and went to a table in the corner where a crystal pitcher and a single gold cup stood waiting. As she started to pour a stream of wine dark as blackberries, a wandering, chattering pair of elderly women blocked Charles's view. He sidestepped them and saw that Lulu stood now with bowed head, hands clasped at her bosom. He took advantage of a gap in the crowd to get nearer, and saw that she was fingering the blue-stoned ring Montmorency had given her, the one with a lock of his hair in it. Charles wondered suddenly if she cared more for Montmorency than he'd imagined. Had she hoped, in spite of everything, that he'd come for her? The ring's blue stone opened and a deep sigh shuddered through her as she bent lower over the cup. Then she turned, and Charles saw the searing hatred in her eyes as she looked at her father, the same hatred he'd seen at the ball at Versailles. It was gone almost instantly, leaving her face a mask of submission as she carried the cup to the king.

"Lulu! Lulu, no!" But Charles's voice was lost in the swelling chatter and music. He fought through the oblivious crowd to reach her. She lifted the cup briefly to her lips. Then she offered it to her father, who took it, smiling at her.

"*Sire!* Don't drink it!" Charles leaped like an attacking wolf, slapped the goblet from the king's hand, lost his footing, and fell at Louis's feet.

Chapter 22

Chaos broke out and the music stopped. Cries of outrage filled the *salon. Lèse-majesté!* He assaulted the king's majesty! Take him, hold him! It's a Jesuit plot, a Huguenot plot, it's the English! It's the poisoner, I saw the cup! I saw a knife in his hand! Take him!

Charles lay utterly still, not daring even to speak lest the sword points pressing through his cassock and drawing warm trickles of blood under his shirt should press even harder. He had fallen with his head turned toward Lulu, and he looked through the forest of shoes and stockings for her pink-gold skirts. Then rough hands pulled him to his feet.

Guards from the vestibules held him and a hedge of sword points surrounded him, reflected candlelight running like fire along the blades. Pike-wielding guards and horrified gentlemen with drawn swords flanked the king, who was staring at the fallen cup and the wine splashed like blood across the floor. La Chaise was bent over the spilled wine, watching a fluffy white dog with red ribbons on its ears lapping eagerly at the puddle. Slowly, Louis turned his head to look at Charles.

"Regicide!" Michel Louvois, the war minister, raised his court sword from the hedging circle to Charles's throat. "Now we know you for what you are!" His chins quivered with satisfaction. "You see, Sire! I was right about him. A Huguenot sympathizer, spreading his damnable creed at Louis le Grand, plotting—"

A deep, furious voice growled, "Don't be a fool," and a lace-cuffed hand shoved Louvois's sword point away from Charles's throat. La Reynie pushed past the war minister to the king. With a quick glance at La Chaise, he went down on one knee. "Sire, there was an attempt on your life, but not by Maître du Luc. Without him, you would be dying now. Look."

He pointed, and a gasp went up from the royal family and others close enough to see. The fluffy white dog stood with its head down, heaving miserably. Suddenly it crumpled onto its side, shuddered, and lay still. A woman began to wail, but the others who had seen fell abruptly silent, and the frozen horror of their silence spread through the *salon*.

"Sweet wine, Sire," La Reynie said softly. "Everyone close to you knows you like it. Sweet wine to cover a bitter taste."

Only the king's eyes moved as he looked from the dog to La Reynie to Charles. "Let the Jesuit go." The guards took their hands away and stood at attention as Charles got slowly to his feet.

Louvois, protesting, made to secure him again, but Charles wrenched himself away.

"Sire," Louvois pleaded, "you are not yourself; you have had a terrible shock! You cannot let this man go—everyone knows La Reynie protects him, and you might do well to discover why!"

"Not myself? I am entirely myself, Monsieur Louvois. But *you* forget yourself." The royal words were full of warning. Louvois blanched and bowed.

"Find her," the king said to La Reynie. "My men are at your service." He raked the gathered courtiers with his eyes and left the *salon*, taking the speechless Polish ambassadors and the rest of his shocked entourage with him. When he was gone and everyone rose from their bows and curtsies, the courtiers edged toward the doors in their turn, chattering and staring at La Reynie and Charles as they went. La Chaise came to La Reynie. His face was the color of spoiled dough.

"What do you want me to do?" he said.

"Set whomever you can trust to watch the doors. If Montmorency shows himself, they must take him and hold him until I return."

Nodding, La Chaise looked at Charles. "We are deeply indebted to you, Maître du Luc."

Charles shook his head. "I was nearly too late. I failed her, I didn't see her clearly enough. I wish——" He shrugged, out of words.

"My failure is greater than yours. At least you saw her desperation."

He turned abruptly and went out the way the king had gone.

As he moved, Charles saw that Anne-Marie de Bourbon was standing near the wall, watching and listening. Before he could go to her, La Reynie said in his ear, "Stay near me," and called the guard captain, who had been waiting with his men for orders.

La Reynie swiftly assigned half of them to search the chateau and its surrounding buildings for Lulu, and the other half to quarter the grounds. "I was in the balcony," he told them. "I saw her leave by the north door. She can't have gone far, on foot and dressed as she is. When you find her, bring her to me."

Anne-Marie whirled and ran for the north door. Ignoring La Reynie's order to stay close, Charles went after her. He caught her arm as she started down the terrace stairs, toward the streaming torches that marked where guards were already searching.

Charles shook the child slightly. "Where is Lulu, Your Serene Highness? We both know she left by this door." He held out the leaf he'd picked up on the terrace earlier. "This dropped from your hair, I think, when we were talking before. I think it came from the place you found for Lulu to hide in. Did you know she planned to poison the king?"

In the light of the torch mounted on the chateau wall, Anne-Marie's face was as white and pinched as the king's had been. "No." She made no effort to free herself from his grip.

"But you helped her escape."

"Yes." The rising wind blew her ribbons around her face as she stared unflinchingly back at him, and he realized once more that she was as determined as her grandfather, the Great Condé, had been. But unlike the Condé, she would keep her word, once given, no matter what. And she would scorn a lie.

La Reynie burst through the door. "Maître, I told you to stay near me; what are you—" He broke off, staring at the leaf on Charles's palm. "What's that?"

Charles nodded toward Anne-Marie, cautiously letting go of her. La Reynie bowed hastily.

"This leaf fell earlier from Her Serene Highness's hair," Charles said. "Like the ones we saw when she was dancing. She admits that she helped Lulu escape. I think the leaves came from the hiding place she prepared for Lulu."

Frowning, La Reynie took the leaf from Charles and held it up to the light. "It's hornbeam. Have you hidden her in the *berceau*, Your Serene Highness?" But he sounded more puzzled than triumphant. "What good will that do her?"

"She is not there," Anne-Marie said disdainfully.

"The *berceau*?" Charles said in confusion. "Cradle? How could she hide in a cradle?"

"The *berceau de charmille*," La Reynie said impatiently. "It's a hornbeam arbor—more like a tunnel—that follows the Marly wall. She couldn't hide there, not for long. But we'll have to go and—"

"Wait," Charles said. "Your Serene Highness, you say that Lulu isn't in the *berceau de charmille*. But you went there. Someone is or was there. Who?"

She stared back at him like a statue. Until a dog began to bark in the distance and she turned toward the sound, her small face creasing with anxiety.

"That's your Louis barking, isn't it?" Charles listened for a moment, to be sure of his direction. "Monsieur La Reynie, does the hornbeam hedge circle the whole property?" He pointed northeast, toward the barking. "There, too?"

Catching Charles's thought, La Reynie said, "It does."

Charles ran down the steps. La Reynie, shouting for guards to follow them, was on his heels.

The wind drove thin clouds across the sky, but a half moon gave fitful light. The two men pounded across gravel, along paths, and straight across the planted *parterres* when there weren't paths. The barking stopped, then grew louder, and Charles nearly fell over Anne-Marie's little black dog. The dog ran around him and La Reynie in joyous circles and then back the way it had come, ears streaming in the wind. Charles raced after it, a trio of guards close behind, leaving La Reynie bent over and catching his breath. A flood of hurrying clouds quenched the moon, and Charles nearly ran facefirst into the hornbeam hedge. One of the guards held up his torch to show a manicured archway cut in the hedge a little way to their right. The guard cautiously stuck the torch through, low to the ground.

"Can't see anyone," he said. "But I hear the dog in there. I can't take my torch in, the whole tunnel might burn."

Charles went in. He could hear the dog off to his left, but

he could see nothing beyond the reach of the torchlight at the entrance. Then, as the dog came running out of the green-smelling darkness, the torch flared a little in the wind and something small and bright caught Charles's eye down where the dog had been. He went toward it, brushing his hand along the hornbeam at the level where he'd seen the thing.

Behind him, the shrubbery rustled and La Reynie caught up with him, struggling for breath. "It's like God's pocket in here."

Charles suddenly felt broken branches and then empty space. "We've found it; she got out here, the hedge is broken. Is the wall beyond?"

"Yes."

Charles's fingers closed suddenly on what felt like a ribbon. From the brief torchlight glimpse he'd had of it, it was the pink-gold color of Lulu's gown. "I'm sure she went out here. Her ribbon's caught on the edge of the hole."

"Anne-Marie couldn't have made a hole this size," La Reynie said. "I doubt even both girls could have done it together—they'd scratch themselves too badly to go unnoticed." He told the guard who'd come in behind him to have men comb the outside of that part of the wall and quarter the ground beyond. The man ran back through the hornbeam tunnel, and Charles and La Reynie squeezed through the broken place. Gritting his teeth against the ache in his shoulder as he pulled himself up, Charles gained the top of the six-foot wall and helped La Reynie up.

Grunting and swearing, the *lieutenant-général* jumped heavily down into dew-wet grass on the other side. "I want to think she couldn't get over this by herself, not in skirts. Even at her age. But that may be only my damaged dignity speaking."

"No." Trying to ignore what hauling La Reynie up the wall had done to his own aching shoulder, Charles was looking intently across the fields and forest sloping away before them. "She didn't. Montmorency is here, I'm sure of it."

Shouts made them look back along the wall. Guards with torches were running toward them.

"A horse," the nearest one called breathlessly. "A horse was tethered a little way along there." He jerked a thumb behind him. "Left its droppings."

Charles and La Reynie looked at each other.

"Can you tell which way it went?" La Reynie called back.

"Toward the river, looks like." The guard arrived, panting, his fellows at his back. "Started that way, at least."

The guards' faces showed avid in the torchlight, and Charles thought that this was likely more excitement than any of them had ever seen. Not only an attempt on the king, but an attempt by a royal daughter, a *legitimée* of France.

"Get horses," La Reynie said curtly. "Go both ways around the Machine, down to the water."

"Are there boats?" Charles said. "Could they find a boat there?"

"They could," another guard said. "There's a boat or two for inspecting the Machine. They couldn't go downstream, there's a dam, but they could get across to the other bank."

"The machine that brings water from the river?" Charles said.

"That's right. Huge thing," the guard said, "fourteen paddle wheels pushing water up the Louveciennes hill to the aqueduct. For the fountains here at Marly, and at Versailles, too, it's so close."

Charles was running before the man finished talking. The moon came and went, usually going just as he needed it. The ground began to slope downhill as he entered a belt of trees and velvet darkness. He smelled the horse before he saw it and swerved at the last minute, frightening both of them.

"Lulu? Montmorency?" There was no sound but the horse's blowing and snorting. Charles bent close and saw that it stood with its off foreleg lifted. He tried to lead it a few steps, and it nearly fell. Lamed and abandoned. Which meant that the fugitives were on foot now, too. He started running again, trying to stay upright as he slithered down an even steeper slope. Away on his right, he heard hooves and saw torches, as the mounted guards approached the river.

Charles could hear rushing water now and ran toward the sound, caroming from tree to tree in renewed moonlight, using the trunks as handholds to keep himself from plunging headlong. A great roar smote his ears as he came abruptly out of the trees and saw gleaming water ahead of him. The noise was heart-stopping. The Machine, he realized, and started downhill beside a long wooden construction higher than his head. The horsemen and torches were at the bottom of the slope on a wider pathway beside the water.

Someone reined in his horse and pointed, shouting, "There, look, there they go!"

Holding their torches high, the guards looked out at the dark mass of platforms and throbbing machinery that thrust itself like a square peninsula into the water. Charles reached the bottom of the hill and pelted across the riverside path, past the dismounting guards, who were tethering their horses and looking for a way onto the vast, multileveled Machine.

He plunged through a small door and came out on wooden planking. From its live throbbing, he guessed that it was built over churning gears and wheels. To his left, what sounded like the groaning rumble of all the mill wheels in France smote his ears. Other feet were pounding behind him now and he re-doubled his speed, feeling as though his heart were about to burst out of his chest. Below him, on his right, was a long, lower level of flooring and at its end, the river, racing westward under the moon like a fat silver snake. He could see them clearly now. Montmorency jumped down to the lower wooden level, held up his arms, and caught Lulu as she jumped. They ran hand in hand along the boards toward the river end of the Machine.

"Lulu! Montmorency! Stop!" Charles's feet pounded over the planking, which narrowed suddenly to nothing in front of him. The first of the guards was closing on him and he turned furiously. "No," he roared, "stay back! Let me bring them in."

It was his old battlefield voice, and it worked. The last-come guards skidded into their fellows, and they all stopped where they were. Knowing he had only moments before they followed him, Charles gathered his cassock and jumped to the lower level. Ahead of him, Lulu and Montmorency clambered over a low wooden barrier and ran to a rail where the Machine thrust far-thest into the river. They stopped beside an opening that led lower still and looked over the rail. Lulu shook her head at Montmorency and darted to her right and out of Charles's sight.

"Wait!" Charles bellowed, leaping the barrier.

Montmorency was still leaning over the rail, looking up and down the river and wailing, "There's no boat, Lulu, you said there was a boat!" He turned, saw Charles nearly on him, and flung himself to the right, blocking the way Lulu had gone. His sword was out and leveled at Charles. "Stay back," he shouted over the Machine's roar. "Let us go."

"Not into the river, you fool!"

"We'll find another boat, stay back!" The boy's face was grim and hard. Not a boy's face any longer.

The guards were at Charles's back now, their torches blotting out the moonlight. Someone tried to push him out of the way and he whirled and shoved back savagely, sending the man to the floor and only then realizing it was La Reynie.

"If they try to swim for it, they'll drown in the currents," Charles shouted at the *lieutenant-général* and the rest. "Let me talk to them."

The guards started past him, but La Reynie yelled, "Hold where you are, give him a chance!"

Montmorency had disappeared now, too, and Charles, hands open and visible, went to the right, the way Lulu had gone, and found the pair standing together on a small piece of decking at the side of the Machine.

"Come back with me," he pleaded over the noise. "The king will be merciful. Please, come back with me."

"Merciful?" Lulu's laughter was as silvery as the moonlight on the heavy ropes of pearls around her shoulders.

Montmorency had an arm around her, his sword still pointed at Charles. "We'll marry, we'll go somewhere else. England. Italy. Somewhere. Let us be."

"Think! You have no boat, no horse. The king's guards are here behind me. You cannot go anywhere from here. Come back with me and retrieve what you can for yourselves." Charles was remembering Louis's gray stunned face. He'd seen shock and disbelief and anger there, but not the rage that drives revenge. There'd been too much pain for that. The rage might come later, but it was a chance worth taking. "I think you won't get worse than exile. Even you, Lulu. In exile, you'd still be alive."

Lulu looked out over the racing water and shook her head.

"Lulu," Charles said, "I know your secret. I'll help you. I'll—"

She looked over her shoulder. Her slight smile was piercingly sweet. "I've lived in my father's prisons long enough. And you don't know all my secrets."

She stood on tiptoe, one hand resting on Montmorency's shoulder, and kissed him. Charles took advantage of the moment to step closer. As Montmorency bristled and warned him off with his sword, Lulu pushed herself up onto the rail. Before Charles could cry out, she seemed to spread satin wings in the moonlit air, and the Machine's roar swallowed the splash of her fall.

"Lulu!" Montmorency flung a leg over the barrier, fumbling to throw off his cloak.

Charles lunged, got both arms around him, and pulled him backward. "No! She's gone. There's nothing you can do!"

Montmorency struggled fiercely. "Then I'll die with her, that's all I want, let me go!"

They shouted the same words at each other, like responses in a hellish liturgy, until Montmorency finally stopped struggling and they wept together, huddled in the roar of the water wheels.

"Charles." A hand gripped Charles's shoulder. "Charles. Get up now. Come, I'll help you."

Blinded by tears and wondering dimly at La Reynie's calling him by his Christian name, Charles let the *lieutenant-général* help him to his feet. The two of them lifted Montmorency and steadied him, one on either side.

Numbly, Charles wiped his face on his cassock skirt and, half carrying Montmorency, they made their way back to the path along the river, the guards following. Down on the bank, a huddle of men were shaking their heads and gesticulating, and looking out at the place where Lulu had gone into the water.

La Reynie saw Charles looking and said, "Those are the

men who run the Machine. Can you manage Montmorency? I'll go and see what they're saying."

Charles walked Montmorency slowly to the riverside path and spoke to one of the torch-carrying guards, who went for horses. La Reynie came back from talking to the Machine operators. He shook his head.

"They say the currents where she went in are too treacherous for any hope of finding her. And too strong. She's probably been carried downriver, but she went in so close to the Machine that she could be—" He swallowed and sighed. "Come, let's get Montmorency back to the chateau."

The guard had brought horses for all of them. They helped Montmorency mount, but he slumped dangerously in the saddle.

"You'll have to get up behind and steady him," La Reynie said to Charles. "I don't think he can ride alone."

The guard, also mounted, led them up the slope. Charles rode with an arm around Montmorency's waist, listening to the fading noise of the water wheels moving the river from where God had put it to where the king wanted it. The wind had died and the clouds had passed by. Charles let his head fall back and looked up at the moonlit sky powdered with faint stars, but for once, the stars failed to comfort him. His mind circled around and around a single question: Where had she gotten the poison?

When they reached Marly's entrance court and dismounted, Montmorency was better able to walk. The three of them, followed by the guard, made their slow way in without speaking.

As an elderly footman hovered, the guard took charge of Montmorency, and La Reynie said quietly to Charles, "I will tell the king what happened. But he will want to question you, too. And him." He jerked his head grimly at Montmorency, who was staring indifferently at the vestibule floor.

Charles nodded in silence.

La Reynie looked at him worriedly. "Are you—can you see him now? Do you need something to drink?"

"I'm all right."

The footman conducted them to the anteroom of the king's apartments, where the Duc du Maine and Anne-Marie de Bourbon, both with pale faces and reddened eyes, stood close together against the red damask wall. They watched solemnly as the dirty, sweat-soaked men came in behind the footman, who stopped short when he saw them.

"Your Highness, shouldn't the child at least go to her bed?"

Maine lifted his chin. "Madame de Maintenon gave us permission to stay. To find out what has happened to my sister."

"As you wish, Your Highness." The footman bowed to Maine. He went to the inner door, spoke to the footman who answered, and withdrew.

Anne-Marie launched herself at Charles and fastened both fists in his cassock. "Where is Lulu?"

Charles looked helplessly down at her and shook his head. "I'm sorry."

Maine burst into tears. Anne-Marie's lips quivered and she bit them hard. "She's dead?"

He nodded, and she let her hands fall and drew in a shuddering breath. She went to Montmorency, who still stood blankly in the middle of the room, and took his hand.

"I am sorry, *monsieur*," she whispered, looking up at him with full eyes. "You were her true knight."

Montmorency seemed not to hear her. He sank onto a footstool and put his head in his hands.

Another footman came with wine. Charles drank deeply. When some of his wits had returned, he said to Anne-Marie, "I know you loved her."

"You tried to stop her going! You tried to bring her back," Anne-Marie lashed out at him, still standing beside Montmorency. "Why couldn't you just let them go?"

"Lulu tried to kill the king."

The little girl's dark eyes flashed. "The king drove her to it. She pleaded and begged for weeks, for months, and he cared nothing for her suffering, nothing!" She glanced at the door that led deeper into the royal apartments. "And I don't care if he hears me. I hate him, I hate fathers!" She began to sob. The horrified Duc du Maine led her to a chair by the wall, patting her back and trying to hush her.

The *lieutenant-général* drained his wineglass and sat down gratefully. "Your Highness," he said to Maine, when the little girl had quieted, "some questions, if you please. And forgive my not getting up, if you will. I am three times your age and very tired."

"Of course, *monsieur*," Maine said, becoming his usual politely anxious self. "Don't trouble."

"Was it you who took the Comte de Fleury's *mémoire* from his rooms?"

"Yes. My sister—Lulu—" he swallowed hard. "She wanted to know what was in it about her. And I took her silver box. But Fleury's book is gone."

"Yes, we know where the book is. Don't worry about that."

At the mention of the box, Anne-Marie had raised her tear-drenched face and was looking warily at La Reynie.

Charles watched her thoughtfully. "What I am wondering," he said, to no one in particular, "is where Lulu got the poison. Which I assume she'd had for several days, at least. Because I also assume she used it on the footman Bouchel. For refusing to help her out of the trouble that was partly his doing."

Anne-Marie and Maine froze, but La Reynie's head snapped around. Charles said nothing and waited.

"The poison was in her silver box when I brought it back from Fleury's room," Maine said dully.

"But she thought it was only a love philtre, I swear it! We all did, *maître*." Anne-Marie got up from her chair and came across the room to Charles. "Everyone knew that old Fleury used love charms. He even wrote about it in his *mémoire*." Sudden color came and went in her face. "He said he had a love philtre to make some court woman give in to him. We thought that was what the little packet in the box was—his love philtre. Lulu wanted to keep it, but she was afraid someone would find it in her room. So she put it—" She looked quickly at Charles and away. "Where she could get it when she wanted it."

Suddenly, Charles understood. "And then she started praying in front of Madame de Maintenon's reliquary," he said softly.

Anne-Marie said nothing. Charles was silent, too, remembering the night Lulu had quarreled with Bouchel and run to the dark chapel. He'd stood in the chapel doorway and heard a small metallic sound. He'd found Lulu bent over the altar where the reliquary stood, and she'd shown him a supposedly dropped earring to explain the sound he hadn't asked about. The sound that must have been the reliquary chamber in the cross snapping shut.

"What do you mean?" La Reynie said brusquely.

"I think she hid the little packet there," Charles said. "In the reliquary. And when Bouchel said he'd done all he could to help her, she went to get her 'love philtre.'"

Anne-Marie nodded. Her hazel-gold eyes were wide and pleading. "She thought it would make Bouchel do more to help her." Her voice dropped to a whisper. "She cared about him. She never meant to kill him."

The Duc de Maine sighed. "When she realized what she'd done, something changed in her." He bit his lip, trying to find the words he wanted. "I think she felt already damned because Bouchel died—so it didn't matter anymore what she did."

La Reynie's face was noncommittal as he watched Maine. "Why would Fleury have put poison in the silver box?"

"Lulu and I read some of the *mémoire* together. Fleury hated his rich nephew. He thought the nephew's money should by right have come to him. He wrote that the omens told him it would very soon be his. And poison is called *inheritance powder*, isn't it? Fleury was always horribly in debt."

"So when Bouchel died," La Reynie said, "she knew what she had and decided to use it on her father."

And I thought I was helping her, Charles thought bitterly, *helping her accept her marriage. I encouraged her so earnestly to trust that God would not abandon her, even if her father had. She saw the use of the role I offered and played it, seeming to be what I wanted her to be. And I was eager to be deceived.*

The door to the king's reception room opened and La Reynie was summoned.

"He'll want to see you in a moment," La Reynie said hurriedly to Charles. "Say as little as you can. Answer his questions. Nothing more."

He disappeared into the inner apartment, leaving Charles with the grieving children. Anne-Marie sat down on the floor beside Montmorency, and the Duc du Maine kept a wary eye on them both. The guard, who had tried to keep the little girl away from his captive, caught Charles's eye and shrugged. Coping with Anne-Marie de Bourbon, Charles thought, was going to be beyond most men.

Seeing that there was an untasted glass of wine beside Montmorency, Charles got up and put it into his hand. "Drink, *monsieur.*"

The young man obediently swallowed the wine. "If you hadn't come after us, she wouldn't have died."

"Others also came after you. You had no hope of getting away." Charles pulled Anne-Marie to her feet. "Your Serene Highness," he said gently, "please leave us for a little." She studied him for a moment and went to sit on a footstool beside Maine. Charles turned his gaze on the guard. "If you will be so good as to stand in the doorway?"

The guard hesitated and then withdrew to the passage door. Charles knelt on the blue-and-gold carpet beside Montmorency. "Listen," he said softly and urgently. "There's not much time. The king is going to call us in, and before I have to face him, I must know whether you've been helping the Prince of Conti get letters from the eastern border."

"Letters?" Montmorency looked at him blankly. "I wrote letters to Lulu. The Duchess of Tuscany gave them to her."

"No other letters passed through your hands?"

"No. Why should there be other letters?"

"Did you know that Lulu had the poison?"

"What poison?"

Charles realized with a shock that Montmorency had not been in the *salon.* "Haven't you heard what we've been saying here?"

Montmorency shook his head, staring again at the floor.

Charles shook him by the arm. "Listen to me. Lulu tried to poison the king before she ran tonight. That's why you were followed so quickly. Did you know she was going to do that?"

Horror washed the grief from Montmorency's eyes. "Poisoned the king?"

"Tried to. She failed."

"No! I didn't—I would never—no, she wouldn't! He's her father." He looked at Charles incredulously. "He's the king!"

Charles sighed with relief. This poor dull knight seemed to have forgotten his own loud denunciations of Louis. His only treason had been to fall in love with the king's daughter and try to rescue her from the king's will. Stupid. Beyond stupid. But Charles hoped the king would not require Montmorency's death for it.

"When you speak with the king," Charles said, "answer his questions truthfully. Don't defend yourself. Don't accuse him of anything. Do you understand?"

"I didn't know about the poison." Montmorency's eyes filled again with tears. "I loved her."

"I know you did."

The door to the royal reception room opened. "Maître du Luc."

Charles's heart missed a beat. He stood up and followed the expressionless footman into the king's reception room, whose damask walls and hangings were of an even deeper red than the anteroom's. In the candles' dim glow, they made Charles think uncomfortably of blood. The king sat behind a small desk. La Chaise stood beside him and La Reynie stood in front of him. Charles stopped short of the desk and bowed. La Reynie stepped slightly aside and nodded at Charles to take his place.

The king's eyes were hooded, as though what he wanted to say were written on the ebony inlaid surface of his desk. "I am told that my daughter took her own life."

Unsure of what to say, Charles was slow to respond. Louis looked up, and Charles saw that the blue-gray Bourbon eyes were looking into deep darkness, the darkness of his daughter's hatred and self-murder and damnation.

"She jumped into the river, Sire, but she may have meant to swim; she may not have known how strong the current was."

"She knew. She saw the Machine built. She knew how the current ran."

Charles bowed his head. There was nothing to say to that.

"Did she speak to you before she jumped?"

"Yes, Sire."

"Tell me what she said."

Charles felt as though he, too, were about to jump fatally. "She said that she did not want to live in—in a prison."

The king frowned. "Prison? She thought I would imprison her?"

Charles hesitated. "Yes, Sire."

"What else? You are not telling me everything. Speak!"

The last word was so loud in the lushly padded room that Charles jumped. Drawing himself up, he returned the king's hard stare. "She said that she had lived in her father's prisons long enough."

Not a muscle moved in Louis's face. But someone unseen moved in the room's shadows behind Charles, and La Chaise's eyes flicked toward the sound.

"I thank you," the king said through stiff lips. "Leave us now."

Charles inclined his head, started to turn away, and then stopped, unsure whether he was allowed to turn his back to Louis.

The king suddenly lifted a hand and gestured him back to the desk. "I am remiss," he said. "You saved my life, and I thank you. But I command you never to speak of anything that happened tonight, except to your religious superior. The Society of Jesus will receive a suitable gift. That it is given because of your action will not be said." He nodded another dismissal, but Charles didn't go. Both La Chaise and La Reynie looked meaningly at the door, but Charles ignored them.

"Sire, if I may speak?"

The king nodded.

"Henri de Montmorency, who is waiting in your anteroom, has been my student, and I know him. I think that his only crime was to love your daughter too well. I also know that there is— concern about the Prince de Conti. I would stake my life that Monsieur Montmorency has nothing to do with that concern."

"Very well. I shall see."

Louis's aging face seemed grayer and more fallen by the moment with fatigue and sorrow, a sorrow Charles was sure he would never admit and for which he would never ask comfort.

Without warning, and even though he believed Louis had brought much of his sorrow on himself, Charles felt a terrible rush of pity for him. Not for the king, but for the man.

"I will pray for you both, Sire, you and Lulu," he said. *And for your unborn grandchild*, he added silently. "God is better at forgiving than—than men are."

A sigh came from somewhere in the shadows, and Charles got himself out the door. In the anteroom, the Duc du Maine and Anne-Marie were both asleep on their footstools, Anne-Marie with her head in Maine's lap, looking for once like the child she was. The footman called Montmorency's name, but the boy didn't move, and the guard had to nudge him to his feet and through the door. Charles, shaking now from his royal encounter, sank onto a footstool. And shot to his feet as Mme de Maintenon emerged from the reception room.

She woke Maine and the sleeping Anne-Marie. "Go to your beds now. Yes, go," she said, when the little girl started to resist. "Your Louis will be whimpering for you." She walked them to the door. "Say your prayers for Lulu and then leave her to God." She stood for a moment, watching after them, and then returned to Charles. "What you said to His Majesty was bold, Maître du Luc."

Charles swallowed. "I meant no harm, *madame*."

"I know you did not. You spoke to the sorrowing man, not to the king. I came to thank you for it."

She nodded her black-veiled head very slightly and returned to her husband. Swaying on his feet with exhaustion and drained of feeling, Charles sat down again, his legs refusing to hold him any longer. He leaned against the wall and felt himself falling toward sleep. The Silence briefly held him back. *You begin to know who you are*, It said. Then It let him sleep.

Charles opened his eyes to see La Reynie bending over him.

At first, he wasn't sure where he was. Then a bright yellow wig appeared over La Reynie's shoulder.

"I knew you were going to be bad luck," Margot hissed at Charles. "People who can't enjoy themselves always are." Her eyes were frightened, and her lined face had shed most of its powder. "Stick to your prayers and stay out of what doesn't concern you!" She rustled away out of the anteroom.

Charles struggled to sit up and rubbed his face. "What happened in there? Did she confess to helping Conti?"

"No. Conti's still there. The king called the two of them in while you slept." La Reynie sat down heavily beside Charles. "They're going to get away with it. She swears, and her servant swears, that she was only helping Montmorency keep his love letters secret, and that his love letters were the only letters she sent on to Versailles. All out of the goodness of her heart, of course. Conti professes to be bewildered by the whole thing. He's had no letters from anyone. And, of course, we won't find any, because he's far too careful to keep even a scrap of paper. So Conti and Margot will both walk carefully for a while, and it will take us longer to get them. If, in the end, there's anything tangible enough to get. Dear God, I wish I were home in bed." The *lieutenant-général* yawned cavernously.

Charles frowned suddenly as a memory came back to him. "I think I saw Lulu pass Conti a letter," he said.

"What? Where?"

"At a gambling night at Versailles. She sat down next to him, and I thought they were holding hands under the table. But she could have been putting something small into his hand. Which he could have put in his coat pocket without anyone seeing."

"Ah." La Reynie's eyes closed again. "I wondered about that while I listened in there. Margot helps the lovelorn young man, puts the spy's letters inside the love letters, sends or takes them to Lulu, and Lulu gives the spy's letter to Conti. With whom she was half in love, so I hear, so who would suspect anything she gave him to be more than a *billet-doux*? Because what besides a love note could a closely watched sixteen-year-old girl possibly give him?"

"And now you'll never prove it."

"No. But if it was done that way, Lulu knew what she was doing. It would have been one more way to ingratiate herself with Conti and also get back at her father. You know, I think one reason the king disliked the girl was because they were too much alike."

"I think so, too." Charles sighed heavily. "From all I've heard about his youth—and his dancing—she clearly had his physical grace. And the vitality he's said to have had when he was young. If she'd lived—" Charles closed his eyes, trying not to see the desperate satin bird falling into darkness.

"Well, she certainly had his ruthlessness. And his ability to scheme for what she wanted and keep her own counsel," La Reynie said. "I agree with you now that she killed Bouchel, though I do think it was an accident. The one thing Conti said that I believed was that he knows nothing about the footman's death. My spy overreached himself there."

"What happened when the king questioned Montmorency?"

"Louis exiled him."

Charles said in dismay, "From France?"

"No. He's banished permanently from the court and from Paris. But no worse than that. He sleeps here tonight, under guard, and leaves tomorrow for his mother's house."

For Montmorency's future, that was bad enough, Charles thought. But at least he had his life. "That's something, then. It hardly matters, but I keep wondering how he got out of the college. Did he say?"

"He passed as part of a group of foreign tourists visiting your library. He was hatted and cloaked, remember."

"Then that's proof the tutor was in it with him. Montmorency would never have thought of that." Charles sat silently for a moment. "You heard the king tell me that all this is never to be talked about. But what about the Poles? Won't they talk when they return to Poland?"

"The king will probably bribe them to silence and seal it with threats. I imagine their public story will be that the bride suddenly and unfortunately died. Privately, they'll tell their king what happened. The little bridegroom probably won't care what happened, since he's escaped being married off for now. And since the queen is French, I think the king will keep faith with Louis."

"So after all of this, all we know for certain," Charles said bleakly, "is that Lulu killed Bouchel by accident and tried to kill the king. And now she's dead." His voice was rising angrily. "And since Frère Brunet says he's been told that drink can make a liver look as black as poison can, Fleury may simply have slipped and fallen. We think Bouchel killed the gardener, but we'll never know for sure. And none of it gained anyone anything."

La Reynie sighed. "So let that count for justice."

"It will have to."

❦✠ *Chapter 24* ✠❦

THE FEAST OF ST. RODOLPHE, MONDAY, JUNE 23

A soft summer rain was falling in the Cour d'honneur, accompanying Walter Connor's clear tenor and the music of Pierre Beauchamps's violin winding together in a sung *sarabande* for the Spirit of France. The rehearsal was going well enough, with Charles Lennox, recovered from the contagion, once more dancing the Spirit's role. Beauchamps had been complaining all week that the boy's calm gravity made him seem like the Spirit of England, not France. But today Charles found him as soothing to watch as the rain was to hear. At the side of the room, Armand Beauclaire and two other boys were trying on the expressionless masks they would wear as Charles's trio of Fates, hovering on a cloud over the ballet's prologue. Charles wondered why he'd thought that the presence of the Fates would make anyone question the king's lust for war. Now, after all that had happened, their inhuman impassivity seemed only a sadly true comment on life.

The *sarabande* ended and Beauchamps complimented Connor on his singing. Then he called Lennox to him.

"Monsieur Lennox, could your Spirit of France be—

possibly, only just possibly—the slightest morsel less—less—
English?" he said plaintively.

Charles hovered, hoping that Beauchamps was not going to
flay the shy English boy with his tongue. But Lennox seemed
only puzzled.

"But I am French," he said earnestly. "My mother is French.
My father's mother was French. And before them—"

"Never mind before them. It depends on what part of you
is French now." Beauchamps cast his eyes up. "And whatever
part that may be, it is not your feet."

He plunged into his corrections, which Lennox accepted
stolidly, and Charles gave out the wooden swords to the second
troop of French Heroes. They took their places on the marked-
out stage, and Charles helped them work out the confusion
resulting from the redistributing of roles since Montmorency
was gone. And the rector, recovered now and returned from
Gentilly, had withdrawn some of Bertamelli's ballet roles as
discipline for sneaking out of the college. Bertamelli's only
function now in the third Part was to beat a military drum as
the French Heroes entered the stage. But he did it with such
panache that he seemed to have gained rather than lost by the
substitution. That, Charles thought, would always be Bertamelli's way, and it would always help him land on his feet after
setbacks. The rector had written to Signora Bertamelli asking
her to let her son leave Louis le Grand and begin with Beauchamps at the Opera, and Charles was praying fervently that she
would say yes.

Inspired by the drum, the French Heroes were French enough
even for Beauchamps, leaping, thrusting, stamping, feet flickering as they advanced and retreated, swinging their heavy wooden
swords in harmlessly menacing patterns. As they finished, the

enormous lay brother who'd been sent to the scenery *cave* to find a practice cloud for the Fates banged his way into the room from the cellar stairs. Charles recognized the cloud he carried. It was from last summer's ballet *The Labors of Hercules*, brilliantly pink and hardly large enough for three boys. But for now, it would do. The brother's broad feet squashed two of the old hats marking the practice stage as he strode to center stage and put down the cloud. With a slow smiling nod at Charles, he meandered out of the classroom through one of the long windows and went back to helping some recently arrived workmen carry lengths of wood through the warm rain. Something must have fallen down, Charles thought. Because there was certainly no money for building anything. Madame de Montmorency's gift, promised when her son finished his schooling at Louis le Grand, would not be given now. And even though the king had promised a gift, when that might arrive was anyone's guess.

"No, no, *no!*"

Startled, Charles and the ballet cast turned and saw Jouvancy waving both arms at one of his actors.

"Fight like a boy, not like a girl!" Jouvancy thundered.

"But I am playing a girl, *mon père.*"

"You are a boy pretending to be a girl who is pretending to be a boy. So you must fight like a boy!"

"But she's a girl, and girls cannot fight!"

Grinning at each other, Charles and Beauchamps and the dancers went back to work. Charles set the French Heroes to more practicing offstage and got the three masked Fates crowded onto the cloud. Beauchamps played the ending section of the ballet's musical prologue. Then an uncertainly baritone sixteen-year-old delivered the spoken prologue, as the Fates in their expressionless masks mimed spinning, measuring, and cutting the threads of men's lives.

"That is going to work very well, *maître*," Beauchamps said. "Better than I thought." He shrugged a little sheepishly. "It touches the heart, somehow."

Surprised and pleased, Charles thanked him. "So long as the upper stage construction will be able to hold the cloud. It will have to be a good bit bigger than that one is."

"What do you want them to wear, your Fates?"

Charles suddenly remembered Conti dancing in the ballet at Versailles. "There is a color that is somehow all colors. I saw it recently. But I've forgotten its name."

"Ah. *Prince*, I think you mean. Dark, but when it shimmers it shows different colors? Very expensive. But yes, that would be interesting." Beauchamps hesitated, watching the swordplay. "*Maître*," he said quietly, "I have heard that our Montmorency is banished from court. Is that true?"

Charles frowned. "Where did you hear that?"

Beauchamps merely smiled. When Charles said nothing, he lifted a shoulder. "Well. However that may be, Montmorency was the worst dancer I have ever seen. But I am sorry for him. His downfall was inevitable."

"Why inevitable?"

"Because he hasn't the wit to see shadows. He sees only black and white. One who is blind to shadows cannot keep his footing."

The courtyard clock struck the end of rehearsal, Jouvancy offered the closing prayer, and the boys filed out. Except for Bertamelli, who detoured to Charles to ask after his sore shoulder, made a little obeisance to his god Beauchamps, and then ran after the others, executing a perfect full turn in the air on the way. Outside the rain had stopped, and Jouvancy and Beauchamps went into the courtyard to discuss whether red smoke should accompany the Furies of Heresy as they fled back into hell at the end of the ballet. Charles put away the wooden swords and the Fates' masks, lugged the pink cloud out of the way against the wall, shook the two squashed hats back into shape and hung them on their hooks, shut the windows, and picked up his ballet *livret*. He went out to the Cour d'honneur and in again at the always open door to the college chapel. Greeting the lay brother on duty at the street door, he went out into the rue St. Jacques. He lifted a hand to Mme LeClerc, inside the bakery with a customer; crossed the side street that ran from St. Jacques to the lane behind the college; and climbed the deeply worn steps to the little church of St. Étienne des Grès.

Scholastics had been given permission to pray in St. Étienne, and since returning from Marly, Charles had gone there nearly every day. It was an old church, one of the oldest in Paris, and its enfolding darkness welcomed Charles, even though he knew he came there more like an animal homing on its bolt-hole than a Jesuit seeking prayer. He groped his way through the candle-pointed shadows to *Notre Dame de bonne délivrance*. She and her Child were carved from black wood, and were kept from melting into the surrounding gloom only by the painted gold of her hair, the stars on her red gown, her crown, and the golden ball in the Child's hand.

Charles had known other black Madonnas, and their blackness always made them seem to him both more remote and more human. He knelt, feeling pushed to his knees by the weight of grief and anger he'd brought back from Marly and had to keep hidden. He was grieving over Lulu and her desperate choices, and full of guilt for failing to prevent her death. He was also angry—and sad—at her duplicity. He was sad about the murders. He was angry at the king, who had set so much in motion.

And what was he to make, in his heart of hearts, of having

saved the king's life? He'd slapped the cup away simply to prevent a man's murder and would do it again. But he'd saved not only Louis the man, he'd preserved a king he chafed under, a king who sacrificed his own flesh and blood and France itself to feed his lust for *gloire*.

Charles and La Reynie had spent hours with Père Le Picart, explaining what had happened and why. The rector, who had also heard Père La Chaise's account of events, had praised Charles for what he'd done. And was, of course, pleased at the king's gratitude and what it would bring. But when La Reynie was gone, Le Picart had talked gravely to Charles.

"You've been at Louis le Grand not quite a year," he'd said, "and you've been involved with things far beyond the usual scope of a scholastic. There have been good reasons, and I have allowed your involvement. Lieutenant-Général La Reynie is very grateful, to you and to the Society of Jesus, and so is Père La Chaise. But you must remember that the Society does not look kindly on scholastics who call too much attention to themselves. You have not meant to do that, I know. But there are those in the college who disagree."

"Père Donat?" Charles had said.

"I know how much weight to give Père Donat's reports." Le Picart had shaken his head. "Not only him, there are others. I tell you this because I do not want your future marked with questions. The small-minded can make outsized difficulties, and I do not want those for you, Maître du Luc."

Well, Charles thought now, kneeling before *Notre Dame*, he didn't want more difficulties, either, and he was more than willing to be quiet. But he couldn't stop thinking. Especially about the tangle of man and king, justice and grief, desiring and destroying, a tangle no man seemed able to unknot. A tangle even God mostly held his hand from teasing apart, or so it seemed to

Charles. But if there was no unknotting in this world, then how did any temporal good come to mortals? Was the world hopeless? Was he wasting his time trying to be a Jesuit?

In desperation, he leaned his elbows on the rail and his forehead on his clasped hands and prayed for light. For the light of healing on the souls who'd come through these last weeks with him. For the light of mercy on those who'd died. Then his silent praying fell away and he seemed to see a great throng of men and women making their way through shifting light and shadow, as though they walked in a forest whose branches moved in the wind. The dappled light was always changing. The men and women sometimes saw clearly and sometimes groped in near darkness. They helped one another up and stumbled over the fallen. And all the time a deep sighing went with them, whether the sound of the trees in the wind or the sighing of the wanderers, he couldn't tell . . .

"*Maître?*" A hand tapped his shoulder.

Charles came back from wherever he'd been and opened his eyes.

The baker's daughter, Marie-Ange, made a *révérence* to the Madonna. "We saw you go by the bakery, *maître*. The college bell was ringing for your supper and I didn't want you to miss it. *Maman* says you're too thin."

Charles was on his feet now, blinking in the candlelight, which seemed now almost too bright to look at. "Thank you, *ma petite*. That was kind." He hesitated as she knelt in his place. "Are you staying?"

"To pray for *maman*." She looked up at him and her brown eyes were full of fear. "That she'll have a safe delivery when her time comes. So many mothers and babies die." She turned back to *Notre Dame*.

Charles looked down at the little girl's brown curls and

frayed red ribbons, remembering a time when his own mother had nearly lost her life in childbirth. "I'm praying for her, too, Marie-Ange. And I'll tell you a secret. So is the rector."

Marie-Ange looked over her shoulder, her face suddenly bright with hope. "He is? Oh, *Notre Dame* will surely listen to him!"

Treasuring that up to tell Père Le Picart, Charles left her in *Notre Dame*'s care and went back to the college. When he reached the refectory, he halted on the threshold in surprise. Tables had been moved out of the vast room's center and crowded close together around the walls. The workmen were gone, but they had begun building scaffolding in the middle of the room. Remembering his lateness, he hurried onto the dais and stood behind his chair at the far end of the long table. Le Picart said the grace and everyone sat. Charles ate with real appetite for the first time since coming back to Louis le Grand, but as he made short work of the stewed beef and mushrooms, and the lettuce salad, he kept wondering about the scaffolding.

When Père Damiot, sitting beside him, paused in talking to the man on his other side, Charles called his attention.

"Why the scaffolding, *mon père*? Is the ceiling falling down?" The old ceiling painted with gold stars was Charles's favorite thing in the college.

"No, not at all! They're going to repaint our stars."

"Using what for money?"

"Old Père Dainville's niece has given the money. You know Père Dainville's sight is weakening. Well, it seems he told her how much he loves the stars, and she wants him to see them clearly while he still can."

Hardly daring to believe his ears, Charles looked up at the faded little stars. Some had already disappeared, leaving only the faintest of gold smudges.

"That's wonderful news!" he said to Damiot, but Damiot had turned back to arguing points of grammar with the other Jesuit.

Starlight, Charles thought, savoring the word as he looked at the ceiling. He laughed for sheer, sudden happiness. Even a man benighted in a forest could glimpse the stars. Even painted starlight was sometimes enough to steer by.

As I said in the beginning note, this book's Lulu is a fictional member of Louis XIV's family, the Bourbons. I needed a "might have been" place to put her birth, and found it in the only gap in the birth order of the first five children born to Louis and Mme de Montespan. No actual child was born in 1671, so that became the year of Lulu's birth. And because she exists only for the space of this story, loose fictional ends are not left dangling in real history.

Researching Louis XIV's palaces of Versailles and Marly, which were within a few miles of each other southeast of Paris, was a fascinating part of writing *A Plague of Lies*. Versailles was constantly changing, so even if we've seen it as it is now, we haven't seen it as it was then. Tony Spawforth's recent book *Versailles: A Biography of a Palace* was immensely helpful, and is a great read for anyone who wants to know more.

I was so astonished by the Marly Machine that I had to use it. Built on the Seine near the palace of Marly, the Machine had fourteen huge water wheels, each twelve meters in diameter and operated by pistons. It pumped water up a long steep hill to a holding pond and aqueduct, and then to the gardens of Marly and Versailles. It extended far out into the river, like a rectangular peninsula, and was enclosed in a vast wooden casing with many levels and walkways. The Machine operated mostly unchanged until 1817, and then in various updated configurations until 1968.

The seventeenth century was a better time for watering your garden than for getting sick. In 1687, French doctors had been arguing about the medicinal use of antimony for a hundred years. Originally called *stibium*, antimony was a metallic substance that could be used in the making of medicinal cups. These cups were then filled with white wine, which broke down and absorbed some of the metal. When the wine was drunk, it irritated the digestive system and caused vomiting, which was thought to rid the body of illness. The medical faculty at the University of Paris supported its use, but other doctors (notably Guy Patin, who died in 1672) were violently opposed to it, insisting that it killed more patients than it helped.

As for other parts of this book that are real, the flogging the king gave Bouchel's fictional grandmother is real—a woman whose son was killed during Versailles' construction was flogged for confronting and loudly blaming the king on one of his inspection tours. The belief that "demons of the air" caused thunderstorms and were fought off by ringing baptized church bells is also true. In a letter about the baptism of a Paris bell, the king's sister-in-law Liselotte remarked that the bell, garlanded with flowers, looked exactly like a hefty court lady of her acquaintance wearing a new and overdecorated gown. And "the most Christian king" Louis XIV really did covertly support the Moslem Turks in their attack on eastern Europe, because they were keeping his European enemies occupied and out of his hair—or wig, since he was probably bald by that time.

As I wrote this book, I grew very fond of Anne-Marie, daughter of the Prince of Condé and granddaughter of Claire Clemence, the princess of Condé, whose story is partly told in the second Charles book, *The Eloquence of Blood*. Anne-Marie and her three sisters were Bourbons and Princesses of the Blood, but because they were so small—like Claire Clemence—the court called them Dolls of the Blood. Anne-Marie, who never married, died of lung disease at twenty-five. The Duc de Saint-Simon wrote that she had "great wit, kindness, and piety, which sustained her in her very sad life."

READERS GUIDE

*A Plague
of Lies*

DISCUSSION QUESTIONS

1. When the book opens, Charles is dismayed at the thought of being sent to Versailles. Why does Charles dislike King Louis XIV and the Sun King's court so much? Do his attitude and thinking change over the course of the book?

2. What do you think of the way Père La Chaise handles his responsibility as the king's confessor? How does he balance his role's limits with the opportunity to influence the king? Do you think his motivations are ultimately good, self-serving, or both?

3. In what way does the character of the Comte de Fleury, whom we never meet alive, manipulate the novel's development? How do you think things might have ended up differently if he hadn't died?

4. Discuss the different positions of women at court. Is Mme de Maintenon better or worse off, being married to the king but not recognized as queen? How is the Grand Duchess of Tuscany's role different from those of the young girls, Lulu and Anne-Marie? How are the two girls' positions different from each other?

5. Why do you think Lulu was so desperate not to go to Poland? Why does she do what she does at the end? Can you see how she could have made different choices?

6. Do you think the Prince of Conti is indifferent to Lulu's plight? Why or why not?

7. How do the character and personality of Henri de Montmo-rency shape the events of the book? Do you think he has grown or changed by the end?

8. It is often noted that the entire court is obsessed with the idea of poison. Why do you think poison was such a frequently used—or frequently suspected—murder weapon during that era?

9. What struggles does Charles have with Jesuit obedience in this book? How is his attitude toward obedience different from your own? Do you think Charles will decide to continue as a Jesuit, or will he ultimately find the life too constricting?

10. Seventeenth-century Paris was a fascinating period, full of drama and intrigue. Would you have liked to live in Charles's era? Why or why not?

Would you like to have Judith Skype into your book club?
Visit her website at www.judithrock.com for more information!

The Whispering of Bones

A Charles du Luc Novel

BY JUDITH ROCK

When a young man from Charles's soldiering past joins the Paris Jesuit Novitiate, he brings Charles face-to-face with a ten-year-old bloody secret that haunts them both.

But will Charles's attempt to absolve himself of that old sin end in peace . . . or death?

PRAISE FOR THE CHARLES DU LUC NOVELS

"Rock is an exciting new discovery. Her plotting holds your interest, her characters are real, and her attention to details of the time period is extraordinary."

—*Library Journal*

"Rock nails everything about characters, dialogue, setting, historical research, pacing and story development . . . fascinating . . . all of this detail is woven so seamlessly into the story that the reader never falters . . . An excellent historical detective series."

—*Bookgasm*

www.JudithRock.com
www.penguin.com